KILL THE FUHRER
THE VALKYRIE OPERATION

PAULA ASTRIDGE

WOODSLANE

For
Lewis & Penelope

Woodslane Press Pty Ltd
7/5 Vuko Place, Warriewood, NSW 2102
Email: info@woodslane.com.au
Website: www.woodslane.com.au

National Library of Australia Cataloguing-in-Publication entry
Author: Astridge, Paula, 1958-
Title: Kill the Fuhrer : the Valkyrie Operation / Paula Astridge.
Edition: 1st ed.
ISBN: 9781921606519 (pbk.)
Subjects: Hitler, Adolf, 1889-1945--Assassination attempt, 1944
           (July 20)--Fiction.
           World War, 1939-1945--Fiction.
           Operation Valkyrie, 1944--Fiction.
           Conspiracies--Germany--History--20th century--Fiction.
Dewey Number: A823.4

Design and layout by Robyn Latimer
Printed in China

*"The only thing necessary for the triumph of evil
is for good men to do nothing."*
—Edmund Burke

PROLOGUE

The attempt to kill Adolf Hitler had failed.

"The man just won't die! Just . . . won't . . . *die!*"

Count Claus von Stauffenberg slammed his fist down hard on his desk as he said it, knowing that having bungled the assassination meant that his own days . . . *hours* were now numbered.

"It's not your fault," his accomplice, Admiral Wilhelm Canaris replied. "You must remember that to die one must first be human. That's where we made our mistake . . . in assuming that Hitler was. We should have known that the Devil would take care of his own."

He was right. The Fuhrer had fared well under the protection of his unholy Life Insurance Policy—saved from sure death, time and time again, by a series of eleventh-hour reprieves that defied all logic and justice. Between 1938 and 1944 there had been no fewer than sixteen previous assassination attempts made on Adolf Hitler's life by the German Resistance.

The attempt on July 20, 1944, resulted in the arrest and brutal execution of more than 4,800 proclaimed enemies of the Third Reich. Shell-shocked and incensed, Hitler made a clean sweep of his retribution. Every man and woman even vaguely suspected of plotting against him was tortured and executed—the horrific details of their agonizing deaths swept under the carpet to avoid unwanted publicity.

Not that he was concerned about having mowed down his former friends and in-house enemies with such savage efficiency— it was just that he was worried that their mass slaughter might look bad in the press—that his image might suffer if this new-found unpopularity of his were made public. What followed was a media blackout; the newspaper barons given strict instructions not to print the truth. Under no circumstances was anyone to find out just how many people wanted Hitler dead.

So, by means of butcher hook and piano wire (and in between the genocide of the Jewish Race) the bloodbath went ahead unheralded, relegated to the back page of the tabloids. The eye-squinting, 8-point print reading:

"The Reich is successfully ridding the Fatherland of its traitors".

It was a poor piece of investigative journalism that, oddly enough, appeased the people and, for a short time, put a band aid on Hitler's hurt feelings, soothing him just long enough for Heinrich Himmler to race to his Fuhrer's bedside and offer his condolences.

"*This* time . . . " Hitler raged, the very instant the head of the SS rushed into his hospital ward, ". . . the criminals *must* be punished. I want them *dead*. I want their *families* dead. I want everyone who had anything to *do* with it, *dead!*"

Propping himself up unsteadily on his elbow, Hitler took a sip of water to soothe himself. Coughing, he cleared his throat to issue his orders:

"*All* of them, do you understand. Every last one of them hanged at lightning speed. That means no tribunals, no speeches, and *definitely* no military honours. They don't deserve pity *or* protocol. Just string the pigs up on meat hooks. No exceptions. No mercy!"

He wasn't the type to forgive and forget, and he was seeing red, not to mention a kaleidoscope of multi-coloured dots and dashes darting before his eyes. A rather pretty, but most peculiar manifestation of the bomb blast he'd survived by the skin of his teeth the day before.

The horrific explosion in his Map Room at Wolf's Lair had knocked him about, and ever since he had not felt quite himself—either physically *or* emotionally—but could admit to a sense of bitter satisfaction in having disappointed his would-be assassins.

Despite their best efforts he'd escaped and cheated death yet again, which was nothing short of a miracle. Most of the others who had shared his experience had been blown to pieces, lying dead and dismembered around him as he'd quickly pulled himself together; brushed the dust from his shoulders and walked from the bomb site virtually unscathed.

Unscathed, that is, if he could ignore the constant ringing and internal bleeding in his ears, the rather alarming dizzy spells he was suffering and the mind-blowing migraine that just . . . *would* . . . *not* . . . *quit!*

All that aside, it was his heart that hurt most. Not as the result of any stray shrapnel, but with the ache of betrayal. It had shocked him to the core to find out just how many people had put their mutinous, murderous heads together to conspire against him, many of them his nearest and dearest. Trusted civilian and military-based fellow countrymen who apparently had not been satisfied at the prospect of giving him a clean death, but had set their sights on his mutilation. Desiring, it seemed, to see his body and entrails splattered over the walls of his office, leaving no one loyal alive to pick up the pieces.

Now feeling shaken, stirred and forsaken, he was in dire need of Himmler's consolation, and hardly in the mood to have his head henchman decide to add one more wound to those already inflicted.

"You are aware, sir, that this was *not* a one-off, arbitrary incident? That it was a carefully structured, long-term plan, contrived by experts?"

No, he was not! That was the last straw. The sudden, painful truth that brought him undone and made the protruding, purple vein at his temple begin to throb. Throb so hard that it needed the pressure of his shaking hand to steady it. From that day, his once strong left hand would continue to shake, in living evidence of his ordeal—much like the rest of his body, which had started to vibrate violently inside and out at that devastating moment.

He had lost control. No longer wanting or willing to plug his sickening, swirling rage, he allowed it to swallow him up—the whirlpool of red-hot, molten emotions welling in the pit of his stomach, suddenly surging like a volcanic eruption of burning bile up his oesophagus, spewing from his mouth a litany of vile verbal threats. Words that promised reprisals of demonic proportions, foul enough to have shocked the hardiest of men.

But Himmler didn't flinch. Instead, all ears and wonder, he bent over his bed-bound boss with conciliatory concern, listening to the man's plans of revenge and fury-laced flashes of self-pity. Psychopathic mood swings which in themselves would have been pitiable had they not been so horrifying. But the Fuhrer's insane, vengeful mutterings were just the tip of the iceberg—the cold-blooded, lethal prelude to the carnage to come.

"I can't believe that the men who tried to kill me are the very ones who've profited from me most. I dragged them from obscurity. I promoted them, I decorated them . . . I *spoilt* them. And this is their thanks—to put a bullet in my back. That's gratitude for you."

He leant over and dry-retched into a basin, using his sleeve to wipe the remnants of bloodied saliva from his chin.

"*Fools!*" he continued with renewed vigour. "I would have put a pistol to my *own* head to spare them the trouble if I'd known that those I loved best would betray me."

At that poignant moment, Himmler saw an opportunity to gain ground. Taking a sympathetic step forward, he dared to put a comforting hand on Hitler's shoulder. The fear factor in making such prohibited, intimate contact was diminished somewhat by the fact that the man was flat on his back and defenseless before him.

"You can be confident, sir, that *I'm* not one of them . . . that you can trust *me* implicitly."

But Hitler was only listening with half a ringing ear.

"I can no longer allow myself the luxury of trusting *anyone!* I won't make that stupid, sentimental mistake again." With this, he pointedly lifted and removed Himmler's hand from his person, through his delirium and distress making a mental note of its clamminess.

He had never trusted a man who didn't have a firm, dry handshake. But now it seemed he had no choice. All those who had possessed the like had raised those same strong hands against him and left him at the mercy and questionable support of The Nazi Party's "Uriah Heeps".

Never mind . . . he would make good use of them. And to be fair, he knew Himmler had talent. A *great* talent, in fact, for what he had in mind.

"Perhaps it's more appropriate to say that I *rely* on you, Heinrich," he conceded. "I rely on you to take the appropriate measures and get the deed done."

There was no need for Hitler to explain. The machinations of Himmler's mind were far slimier than his slippery palms. "*That*, sir, you may do. You'll be pleased to know that the wheels are in motion. Count von Stauffenberg is already dead. General Fromm had him and three of his friends shot in the courtyard of the *Bendlestrasse* last night . . . after a summary court-martial of course. Good of Fromm to have extended such a military courtesy under the circumstances. I know *I* certainly wouldn't have."

It was that old sentimental instinct of Hitler's that had him look up in genuine surprise. A tell-tale moment of shock and sadness at the mention of Stauffenberg's name which certainly wasn't the man's due, given his leading role in the assassination attempt.

But the truth was that Hitler had had a soft spot for the young Count. Ironic as it now seemed, he'd only recently come down one hundred percent in favour of the handsome war hero with his dashing black eye-patch and charming, debonair manner. When Stauffenberg had been introduced to him not long ago as General Fromm's new Chief of the General Staff, Hitler had sensed an immediate bond between them. And he'd been right, to a degree. They *had* been drawn to each other, but both for very different, dangerous reasons.

The famed wounded warrior had extended his left arm with its mangled, three-fingered hand, and allowed it to be held with love and reverence in the firm, five-fingered grasp of the Fuhrer's. It had been a prolonged moment of warmth between them that had brought tears of pride to Hitler's eyes; assuming as he had, a mutual respect. Never *dreaming* that he was shaking the hand of his assassin. That as he held Stauffenberg's gaze with glassy-eyed gratitude for the brave soldier's battlefield sacrifice, the Count was coming to terms with his murder and sizing up his beloved Fuhrer for his coffin.

If Count von Stauffenberg's complicity in the conspiracy had disappointed and dumbfounded him, it was the news of his dear old friend Canaris' participation that rocked the very foundations of his soul.

"We haven't caught up with Admiral Canaris as yet. But we will . . . we will," Himmler put in, his gaze steady behind his rimless glasses. He was on a roll and well on his way to making sure that Hitler was fit to kill.

"Canar . . . *Canaris!*" Hitler spat out the name in stunned disbelief. "You can't honestly expect me to believe that Admiral Canaris, of *all people,* has been mixed up in this? He's my head of

Military Intelligence for pity's sake!"

There was a certain relish in Himmler's response—a definite desire to draw out the magic of the moment.

"Not only mixed up in it, sir . . . but masterminding it from the very beginning of the War," he elaborated, pausing with a casual disinterest to study his fingernails and admire their manicure. "Seems he didn't approve of your move on Poland back in '39."

"Do you mean to say that he's been making a laughing stock of me behind the scenes with the Allies for *five years?*"

Himmler shrugged his affirmation as Hitler's lips thinned in white rage.

"And to think . . ." he opened those bloodless, cracked lips to say, ". . . that for the same five years that man has sat at my dinner table three times a week knowing that he was doing it; *knowing* that he was actively betraying me and his own country . . . hmmm, pity he didn't choke on a chop bone, the little runt."

Unlike Count von Stauffenberg, Canaris (all 5'3" of him) didn't have the benefit of a handsome face or a tall, impressive body to soften Hitler's heart. Those two sterling physical attributes were apt to find the Fuhrer's favour and give a man at least half a chance of securing his leniency. Without them, Rear Admiral Wilhelm Canaris—Germany's Chief of Military Intelligence and national naval hero, was dead meat.

"You will, won't you Heinrich, see to it that something *special* happens to him?"

"But of course."

Himmler's calm and deadly assurance had Hitler relax back on his pillow, closing his eyes in relief. Given that Himmler was a man of his word when it came to murder, he knew he could rest easy in the knowledge that justice would be done.

Unknown to Hitler, Himmler's justice was a case of killing two birds with one stone. He had no problem whatsoever in keeping Hitler happy by making good on his promise. As far as Canaris was concerned, he had his own agenda and was even keener than Hitler to see the little Admiral removed from the face of the Earth as quickly as possible. Preferably before the man had a chance to squeal about the otherwise well-kept secret that he, Himmler—head of the SS—was desperate to keep under wraps.

Because, *oh* . . . what a secret it was! What hell would have

KILL THE FUHRER ⚡

broken loose had Hitler ever found out that the only reason his dutiful side-kick, Heinrich Himmler, had not involved himself in the assassination plot was because he'd been too busy behind the scenes, *and* his Fuhrer's back, trying to put a different kind of knife in it—attempting to negotiate a personal, secret peace with the Allies.[1]

Hitler had no idea. The problem was . . . Canaris did! As head of the *Abwehr* (German Military Intelligence), the Rear Admiral had spent the last few years compiling a most concise file on Himmler and his nefarious activities, with the express purpose of using it as a safeguard against him. Keeping himself abreast of Himmler's intrigues, Canaris had made it clear that he was prepared to use that information against the head of the SS if need be.

That was, if Himmler and his SS Intelligence Division tried to interfere with Canaris and *his* Military Intelligence Division's conspiracy plans against the Fuhrer. Both of them were actively aware of each other's treason, but feigning ignorance as their protection. The sharing of their respective secrets, despite their long-term loathing of each other, was most effective in ensuring their mutual silence and safety.

But it had been hard on Himmler—this fear-packed obligation to keep his mouth shut—when he had hankered for so long to point an accusing finger directly at Canaris; exposing at last the traitor in their "Nazi Party" midst. For years Canaris had had Hitler's murder on his mind and had been getting away with it. For *years* he'd managed to fool them all. No one more so than Hitler, who, incredibly enough, had always had a particular fondness for the little Admiral.

It had been a farcical charade, frustrating in the extreme for the head of the SS, with his hands tied and Canaris' hold over him implying that he was at the mercy of a more superior intellect and cunning. That was why it had come as such a pleasant surprise when Canaris—that Master of Espionage—had finally shot *himself* in the foot by botching the assassination attempt. That was a blunder of the first order. It had reinstated Himmler's pride and guaranteed his own immunity from prosecution.

Now legally within his rights to slit Canaris' throat and shut him up for good, he knew that the sooner he put the Admiral out of his misery, the sooner he would be out of his.

"Well get on with it then," Hitler said, opening his eyes to watch with a certain disdain as Himmler walked from the ward, the moving maze of psychedelic dots dancing before his eyes not adding any colour to the murky grey persona of the departing man.

Singularly unimpressive, singularly mediocre; it was sad to think that the 'shit-shoveller'[2], as Himmler was not-so-fondly nicknamed in Nazi Party circles, was the only one left he could trust. The only man with the means, methods and mentality to act as head executioner; to put to death the men who had meant so much more to him. The first of whom—Count Claus von Stauffenberg—was already dead, and Canaris soon to follow.

It was the first time that Hitler realized he'd lost his touch— that uncanny, infallible instinct of his to instantly sum up the character and capacity of the men who worked around him. Men whose motives and aspirations he'd always been able to second-guess and fulfill to ensure their loyalty. Somewhere along the line he'd slipped up, and now could not understand how he'd been so wrong about Canaris and Stauffenberg. Could not understand how he'd mistaken them for men of integrity—honourable, superior human beings.

The truth was that he had not got it wrong at all: his embittered, self-pitying summation of his two assassins was perhaps the one thing he'd ever got right. Admiral Wilhelm Canaris and Count Claus von Stauffenberg ranked as perhaps the most honourable and superior men of all time.

This is the story of their lives: a testament to the truth of two brave men who were arguably among the greatest patriots the world has ever known. Unsung heroes, who made the ultimate sacrifice by pitching themselves against evil. They went to their graves for the sake of God and country; knowing and accepting that on their headstones and in the hearts of a nation would be chiseled the word:

"Traitor!"

PART ONE

CHAPTER ONE

It was a sad victory for Wilhelm Canaris. One that filled him with a considerable amount of guilt as he packed his bags in 1905 to set off for Germany's Naval Base on the Baltic Sea.

Having flatly refused to take over the helm of his father's thriving ironworks empire in the industrial Ruhr district, Wilhelm had at long last won the war with regard to his future. But it was a triumph that had come at the expense of his beloved father's life. Midway through their final, furious conflict over flight and fancy versus family obligation, his father had suddenly collapsed with a thud to the floor. Fate stepping in, by way of a massive coronary, to free eighteen-year-old Wilhelm of his father's constraints and open the way for him to sign up with the German Imperial Navy.

Willie was ashamed of himself for taking advantage of such stark family tragedy. And more ashamed still over his secret relief that the premature heart attack had happened only seconds before his father had managed to sign off on the contract that legally named his favourite and extremely clever youngest son—Wilhelm as heir to the Canaris Corporate Kingdom.

But that was an honour and privilege that Willie had never, *ever* wanted. He was so set against it being his career path, in fact, that he was prepared to disobey his dearest father's final wishes to avoid it.

It did not, however, rest easy with him—having let his generous, doting father down at the last. It was just that Willie couldn't help it, when his passion and dreams lay elsewhere. He just *had* to go to sea . . . and his older brother Ernst knew it.

Knew that he was keener for Willie to go and fulfil his ambitions than he, as his devoted brother, was to take up the reins of their father's empire. But Ernst had no choice, it seemed, but to resign himself to the role—his more stable, unadventurous spirit being a better fit for stand-in patriarch, when every fibre of Willie's being rebelled against it.

So at the raw age of twenty-two Ernst, who had been earmarked for a life in the ministry, had to give up his own dreams of pursuing a quiet, religious life. His denied, devout leanings making him capable of self-sacrifice and of accommodating the more demanding aspirations of his younger brother. Destiny had insisted that Ernst turn his back on God to front up to the responsibility of industry and high-finance. A quick exchange of cash for Communion deafened his ears to the sound of hymns and cantatas and filled them instead with the raucous cacophony of money-mongering and machines in perpetual motion.

But for Willie and his family, Ernst would have done *anything*. His lifelong renunciation of private hopes and holy devotion made Willie feel slightly guilty, but forever grateful.

"Well off you go then . . . make us all proud," Ernst said as he helped Willie put his bags on the train—the two of them standing on the platform as the whistle sounded and a cloud of steam surged from the train's engine misting up their stiff, farewell scene.

Willie's alert blue eyes did the same as he shook his brother's hand and got on board the train. A sudden wave of emotion made him jump straight back off it as it chugged into motion, to give Ernst a heartfelt hug.

"I'm so sorry to have dumped this all on your shoulders Ernst. I'll pay you back one day—*I promise*," he said as he reluctantly let go of his brother's embrace and ran down the platform to leap back on board, moments later putting his head out the window to shout:

"And don't worry. If I can't make a go of this sailor thing, I'll be back to drive you mad. You can count on it."

But as his dear, departed father had suspected and dreaded, he *did* make a go of it . . . at top speed. Living up to every expectation he'd ever had of his rather exceptional son.

That included being handpicked by the famous Grand Admiral Alfred von Tirpitz in 1914 to serve on one of Germany's finest battleships. It was a piece of personal flattery that had him stop answering to the name of Willie, not because he had outgrown it as a term of endearment, but because he was now to be addressed as Flag Lieutenant Canaris by his naval subordinates, and as "*Spyglass*" by his peers and superiors. A nickname conferred by his Commander Fritz Emil von Luedecke—Captain of the Light Cruiser, *Dresden*, to which Canaris had been assigned.

Luedecke was a naval leader of Prussian birth whose reputation as a gentle warrior made him an unlikely candidate for the swashbuckling command of such a ship. But he took it on, not only with a sense of honour, but the good sense to capitalize on his new Flag Lieutenant's astonishing skills. Skills which were considerable even at the age of twenty-seven, by which time Canaris had become fluent in five languages and an expert in Latin American affairs. This growth spurt in intellect had long since overshot his stunted 5' 3" height.

From the onset of his naval career, Canaris had engaged in an intense, extra-curricula studying program to cram his head with copious quantities of knowledge, honing his remarkable capacity to not only take in the text but to read between its lines. The lines, that is, of any written or unwritten naval war strategy. His uncanny talent to second-guess the enemy and decipher their secret messages, slotting him into the role of Intelligence officer on board the *Dresden* and quickly earning him his nickname.

Thus it was no surprise when Commander Luedecke nominated him as spokesman to negotiate with the British when their German Fleet lost the Battle of the Falkland Islands. A diplomatic, face-saving manoeuvre that spared Luedecke the indignity of having to personally carry the white flag and hand over his sword. Instead, he kept his pride in tact by taking advantage of Canaris' extraordinary gift of the gab, his perfect grasp of the English language and the aristocratic, witty way in which he delivered it. Luedecke was counting on the fact that Canaris' grace and charm would appeal to their English enemies and give them—the Germans—at least half a chance of securing better terms of surrender.

Because little "live-wire" Wilhelm Canaris could talk the hind leg off a mule; twist any argument to his advantage and come out smelling like a rose; despite the fact that he'd managed to throw in a few well-worded, cleverly disguised insults en route. In short—he had a knack of doing his adversary in the eye in the most congenial of ways.

But English Vice-Admiral Frederick Sturdee was not of a mind to be talked round when his King's mandate had been to wreak revenge on that same German Fleet which, under the command of Admiral Maximilian von Spee, had destroyed *their* British ships together with their naval supremacy, at the battle of Coronel off the Coast of Chile[3] only weeks before.

Fresh from that success, von Spee had lingered only long enough to watch the British ships go down with all hands on deck, before he and his famed East Asiatic Squadron sped towards Port Stanley in the Falkland Islands—eager to strike another fatal blow to the British fleet stationed there. A considerable degree of arrogance, along with a failure to recognize English pique and perseverance, had von Spee request that the Light Cruiser—*Dresden*—join his elite maritime squadron to savour the kill.

But it was a case of *"Strike Two and You're Out!"* December 8, 1914 saw a German massacre on the high seas: mad dogs and Englishmen out in the midday sun fighting a battle of bloodthirsty revenge. Admiral Sturdee—stoic and stubborn and spurred on by a savage sense of justice, cut von Spee's squadron to pieces. With merciless precision, sinking his battleships *Scharnhorst*, *Gneisenau*, *Leipzig* and *Nurnberg* in his determination to see von Spee, his famous squadron *and* his huge Hun's ego settled at the bottom of the sea right along with them. More importantly, his *own* name—Vice-Admiral Frederick Sturdee—etched for history's sake on a commemorative plaque at London's Admiralty House.

"We'll never see our comrades again," Commander Luedecke said to Canaris as they stood on the deck of the *Dresden* with the battle raging around them. The sound of cannon fire and the sickening sight of their sister ships being swallowed up in the flaming inferno was very sobering indeed; not to mention . . . utterly terrifying.

Because there they were—sitting ducks—just waiting for their turn. *Not* sailing past as smug spectators of a pre-empted maritime victory, as von Spee's invitation had promised, but standing on the *Dresden's* deck with their stalwart sea-legs suddenly weak-kneed as they watched the slaughter of their compatriots. Fighting hard, in the demoralizing process, to keep stiff upper lips as their own ship (the only German one still intact and afloat) bobbed brave but beaten in the water—the next ready target to be blown out of it.

Trapped like a fly in a web, the *Dresden* and its crew were out of the ammunition, the will and the wherewithal to win, with nothing to do but resign themselves to their fate, the thick, billowing black smoke from their defeated squadron's wreckage choking them almost as much as their fear.

But for Commander Luedecke, that mind-numbing terror was a call to courage.

"Be prepared Canaris, we can have no illusions about von Spee's end or, for that matter, about our own."

The sombre statement had Canaris look up at his Captain with a calm but resolute expression. Despite what appeared to be the inevitable, he had no intention of resigning himself to such a sad, soggy grave:

"I don't believe, sir, that we should just roll over and die."

It was a note of optimism that Luedecke appreciated under the dire circumstances, but grateful as he was for Canaris' bravado, he knew it was time to face reality and cut their losses. There was nothing now but death on their agenda. It seemed unfair to have to commit such an outstanding young man as Canaris to an early grave, when his future looked so promising.

"It's a matter of honour Lieutenant—you know that. We have no choice but to go down with the ship. We *must* stand and fight, even though the British will out-gun us."

"Yes . . . but not out-*run* us, sir," Canaris said with the conviction and confidence of a man nowhere near ready to die. "Von Spee is dead. What point is there in our staying here to commit suicide? Now more than ever, German Naval Command will be in need of every ship they can get their hands on. Taking honour and practicality into consideration, I think it's our duty to salvage what we can and try our level best to get the *Dresden* back home as quickly as possible. What does it matter if it's not to a hero's welcome? The Fatherland's welfare and ultimate victory is more important."

This pragmatic-plan-cum-pipedream was facilitated, as fortune would have it, by their sister ships' sacrifice. While the British fleet tarried to gloat over their kill—like a flock of grey, metal vultures circling the ships being sucked into the sea, the *Dresden* stoked her boiler fires and simply steamed away.

Slipping silently into the black fog they used the convenient camouflage their squadron's destruction had kindly provided to make good their escape. At their speedy 25 knots, they took full advantage of the *Dresden's* comparatively light complement of only ten empty 4.1" guns, managing to get as far as the Straits of Magellan before they ran out of fuel and their faith in reaching home.

With Admiral Sturdee hot on their scent with his ships—the *Kent* and the *Glasgow*—Commander Luedecke knew that his only chance of survival was to hide the *Dresden* in the numerous inlets along the Chilean Coast. So they played a game of cat and mouse in them, while Canaris sent out a series of encrypted, conflicting reports as to their whereabout, a successful ruse of Morse code mayhem that managed to baffle their English pursuers for weeks.

But it was a delay tactic and nothing more. Luedecke knew that it was only a matter of time before their dogged British trackers sniffed them out. Which they did at long last, cornering the *Dresden* in the narrow channels surrounding Tierra del Fuego, at which point there was no option but surrender. Commander Luedecke sent in his best man—Lieutenant Wilhelm Canaris—to do it for him.

Despite liking the Lieutenant, as Admiral Sturdee instinctively did, he was in no mood to be generous. Not after having had to chase the *Dresden* for three long, time-consuming months across the length and breadth of the Atlantic and Pacific Oceans. All the way having Canaris make a mockery of what they had assumed was their state-of-the-art communications and tracking system.

"We will accept nothing less than your unconditional surrender Lieutenant Canaris. So stop trying to ply me with any more of your alternatives. Just face facts—you've lost the battle. You and your Commander Luedecke *must* accept that."

This was true, and having won a great victory, Sturdee was finding it inexplicable . . . that not only was he having such difficulty in talking this German Lieutenant Canaris down, but that he wasn't deriving any pleasure in doing so. Instead of celebrating his impressive win and taking the opportunity to "put the boot in," he was feeling oddly guilty about disappointing the little Lieutenant standing before him. It was just that there was something most appealing about the young man. Hard to believe, in fact, that he was German, when his charm and engaging, educated manner were so decidedly British.

"That's right Canaris . . . that's right. Do your job . . . keep him talking," Luedecke was mumbling under his breath back on the deck of the *Dresden*.

He was taking full advantage of his Lieutenant's stalling tactics—using the time that Canaris' long-winded truce was giving him to evacuate his crew, open the sea valves and set the charges to scuttle his ship, and allowing himself just a few extra stern-faced, heart-thudding minutes of nostalgia to hoist the German ensign and salute as she went down.

He didn't condemn himself and his crew to a watery grave, but to a land-lubber's jail term for the rest of the war. Every one of the *Dresden* sailors was sentenced to be manacled to the walls of the rancid, rat-infested prison cells of Quiriquina Island, Chile.

It was a sentence four years too long for Canaris. Having served only three weeks of it, he burrowed his way out. With the help of the prison's soft sandstone walls and their obliging susceptibility to hand-made spade and pick-axe, he escaped both its walls and the streets of Chile. Dodging and darting his way through them, managing to secure for himself en route a false Chilean passport under the name of businessman Ricardo Rosas, and a berth on board a boat moored in Conception Bay.

With no money in his pocket, however, he was unable to register as a paying passenger. Aware that his fluent Spanish was laced with a German accent, he was positive that he wouldn't pass as a local merchant seaman. Instead, all blue-eyed, blonde-haired and keeping most uncharacteristically quiet, he slipped stealthily into the boat's bowels as a stowaway, surviving, quite literally, on the smell of an oily rag until the filthy freighter finally docked in Rotterdam, Holland. Spilling from its hold a cargo of fish and the bedraggled, sea-sick remnants of what had once been a German naval officer.

Canaris staggered out on shore, his grey, pin-stripe suit turned black. Its tattered remains, with the help of months of built-up dirt, sweat and stench of raw herring were clinging to his body of skin and bone—both he and his borrowed apparel much worse off for the sea voyage, but holding it together long enough to grope his penniless, starving way home to Germany by the Spring of 1916.

Which still left the enterprising young man enough of the Great War to distinguish himself and be promoted in and up the ranks of the German Intelligence Division. He was charged

KILL THE FUHRER ⚡

with collecting information concerning the movement of ships for the German Naval Attache in their Madrid embassy. This time, however, he opted to travel to Spain in the relative comfort, though confined space, of a submarine,[4] navigating his way over dry land and straight through diplomacy with the help of his false Chilean passport and the sheer force of his personality and charm.

"Well what did you think of her? Wasn't she *sensational!*" his superior officer—Max von Krohn of the embassy—asked.

He and Canaris had just returned from a night out on the town, most of which they had spent in a seedy little café in the back streets of Madrid where he'd introduced Canaris to the delights of the infamous Mata Hari. Her sexually evocative movements on stage had had the smoky room full of salivating spectators dribbling into their paella, while turning Canaris completely off his.

"I think she's laughable—both as a dancer *and* a spy," Canaris replied with a blunt honesty that risked his friendship with von Krohn.

As the gentleman he had been raised to be, which went hand-in-hand with a strong sense of morality and basic good taste, he'd found the woman and her promiscuous antics offensive. Not to mention insulting in the extreme to any man of intelligence who aspired to a career of the like.

"Espionage in the twentieth century . . . ," he continued, ". . . is *surely* going to need some greater technical qualification than swanning around on stage in a sleazy performance of the Seven Veils! Why not just stand on a street corner, for Heaven's sake, and hang a sign around her neck . . . *FREE LOVE FOR FOREIGN SECRETS!*"

Contemptuous as he was of Mata Hari and her ancient, foolproof methods of bringing men and their military secrets undone, it was Canaris' *own* skill as a spy that came into question soon after, when he was arrested in Rome as being one. A sloppy mistake on his part, but one that his quick thinking instantly remedied. Caught out and cornered, he had the cunning to pass himself off as a tubercular patient en route to a Swiss Sanatorium.

It was an alibi which didn't seem so far-fetched to the Italian authorities when they took Canaris' small stature into account and coupled it with the fact that he still had not lost that lean and hungry look he had acquired as a trans-Atlantic stowaway.

But the real deal clincher was his trench coat. That heavy duty cream-coloured item of clothing that had become part of Canaris' daily attire. A coat for all occasions that he sported in every kind of weather. Forever feeling the cold as he did, he chose to wear it even in the blistering heat of an Italian summer.

It was a fashion statement—odd but memorable, that had become part of his trademark on the Mediterranean circuit. His working undercover in a trench coat made him so overtly conspicuous as the archetypal spy that it completely freed him of suspicion. People just refused to believe what was right there under their nose.

"The fellow can't be serious, *surely?*" said the Chief Inspector of Italian Police to his sergeant as they finished up Canaris' interrogation and let him out of his cell. There was no doubt in either of their minds that the small, amiable man was innocent of being a secret agent. *No one* so obvious could possibly have been one!

"Well, there goes what must be the world's worst spy," the Inspector joked at Canaris' expense. Both he and his sergeant watched with amused smiles as their little prisoner walked his trench-coat-clad-self out through the doors of their police station and down the street. When he reached the end of it, Canaris thought to turn and throw them back a wave and a smile of his own before disappearing around the corner.

It would have been a nice gesture, had there not been an unmistakable touch of triumph in it. Enough to say: "*Got ya!*" . . . and to wipe the smug expression off the Inspector's face. A look of bewilderment teetering on self-doubt took its place as he questioned his own good judgment. Could he possibly have just been duped? Was there any chance that he'd underestimated the cunning of this Canaris fellow?

"*No . . . of course not,*" the Inspector reassured himself as he walked back into his office. It *had* to be the truth. He was no fool. There was no question that the fellow was tubercular. He'd seen the blood for himself.

And that he had, but the blood the Inspector had seen—that lavish red splattering mixed with saliva that Canaris had produced on cue, had not come from his lungs, but from his biting down hard on his bottom lip. Mid-interrogation/quasi-coughing spasm (and without ready access to a handkerchief), he'd felt free to spit it up all over the wooden floor of the police station.

A plausible, if not slightly off-putting show, that convinced them all of his chronic tuberculosis and won Canaris his freedom, arousing enough sympathy within the ranks of the Italian Police to let him return, with their blessing, to Spain. Their benevolence and best wishes for his safe journey there mingled with just a tad of bemusement over his choice of transport. Going by submarine seemed such an odd option, considering his infirmity. All of them wondered how on Earth someone with his debilitating, chest constricting sickness could bear its claustrophobic confines.

None of them realized how fond, in fact, Canaris had grown of this particular mode of transport. That, completely content within the cozy comforts of his chosen underwater craft, he was now lying back on his bunk in one of its confined cubicles, enjoying every cramped, cough-free moment of it. Resting, with his hands folded casually behind his head, totally unperturbed by any form of claustrophobia or erroneous blood clot.

With a clear throat and even clearer case of self-appreciation he whistled a catchy little sea shanty, marveling at the fact that he'd never felt better and in more robust health in his life!

CHAPTER TWO

The thing that Canaris had liked about the Great War was its sense of good sportsmanship. Amid the minefields and mustard gas had always hung the over-riding air of honour and fair play: a battle of champions and gut-wrenching courage when a man respected his enemy. With true grit and conviction being able to look his adversary in the eye when putting a bayonet in his chest. Pausing *always* to mentally, if not physically, salute his fallen foe.

They, those men who had fought in 1914-18 had been true soldiers—a breed of men apart, who shared a code of military ethics and nobility that had died along with them in the trenches.

What had risen from their heroic ashes was another breed of men altogether. Many of them—disillusioned, bitter and twisted and *some* . . . Canaris had often suspected this of his new protégé, Reinhard Heydrich . . . not entirely human.

Heydrich was an upstanding member of the Aryan race, an eighteen-year-old naval cadet, seventeen years Canaris' junior and under his direct command. Like other young men of his ilk, circa 1923, he was in training for World War II, working hard to mould himself into a creature who could contend with, but more likely *create*, its upcoming horrors—exceptional horrors that could only be conceived by such an exceptionally sadistic man. But with those abhorrent undertakings of his still in the future, Canaris had no good reason to actively dislike Heydrich when they first met, only to lay claim to a strange sense of unfounded concern over the man's possible capacity to commit them.

Although Canaris was impressed with his underling's astonishing intelligence (one that rivaled his own and promised, in a few years, to outstrip it), it was his more natural instinct to be wary of him despite the fact that young Heydrich extended to him nothing but the utmost courtesy and ingratiating admiration.

Why was it then that the man always made him cringe? It was nothing exactly that Canaris could put his finger on, nothing of real substance with which he could accuse the cadet - more just a sensed thing, an uneasy feeling. The disturbing aura Heydrich's presence exuded whenever he stood to attention before him, made the hairs on the back of Canaris' neck do the same.

Given half a chance he would have excused himself from the role as Heydrich's Naval Training officer. But that was something he couldn't do for three good reasons:

1. The Navy wouldn't allow it. Having captained a U-Boat in the Mediterranean at the end of the Great War, Canaris' peacetime career had advanced him to the position of 1st Lieutenant on the training ship—the *Berlin*. A position of prestige which had its lesser obligations. One of which was the teaching and naval training of hopefuls such as Heydrich.
2. Fear that withdrawal of his tutelage from someone as outstanding as Heydrich might be construed as jealousy—a master belligerent about being outdone by his pupil.
3. Heydrich would not let him go!

From the very first day 6' 3" tall, blonde-haired, blue-eyed Reinhard Heydrich had set foot on board the *Berlin*—one of an eager group of ten officers in training—he had stood out in the crowd. Not only in height and haughty demeanour, but individualizing himself on an intellectual level.

Firstly, by letting his Training officer, Wilhelm Canaris, know that he was equally conversant with international languages and equipped with a complementary gift for guile that earmarked him, as it had Canaris, for a career in Intelligence. The young man's desire to draw an immediate parallel between himself and his tutor well before it was his due to do so had been precocious in the extreme, but it was a fact that Canaris couldn't deny after only a few short weeks of having made the young man's acquaintance.

What worried Canaris was that this parallel Heydrich had drawn between them had quickly flowered into a fixation. Heydrich, forever hovering at his side, with his dark shadow creeping over Canaris' left shoulder, was suffocating.

Although Heydrich was in the habit of walking the appropriate few steps behind his Superior, each day he was taking that one step closer; just waiting for his chance to pick up pace and match his mentor stride for stride. Biding his time and being at Canaris' beck and call while breathing down his neck. Gleaning as much knowledge and know-how as Canaris was prepared, and unwise enough, to offer him.

So keen was this rather exceptional cadet to be taken under Canaris' wing—so keen was he to become his best friend and learn from his tutor's vast experience—that Canaris had quickly lost ground. A mixture of vanity over the student's worship of his ways, together with the physical space closing, quite literally, between them, rendered him incapable of wriggling free of Heydrich's clever, cloying obsession. Each day, Canaris was growing increasingly alarmed by the speed at which the cadet was picking up the tricks of his teacher's trade.

It was a conundrum too close for comfort for which Canaris had no one but himself to blame. Always having had a soft spot for the underdog, he'd made the fatal mistake of feeling sorry, at first, for the awkward eighteen-year-old cadet. Well, it had been hard *not* to when Heydrich's unusually high-pitched voice—still not broken out of its boyish descant—had marked him as a figure of fun and ridicule. Despite his superior intelligence and fine, aquiline features which held such promise of future glory, it had been a cruelty inflicted on him since schooldays which had followed him into the Naval Academy.

That was something Canaris wouldn't tolerate. Perhaps it was a weakness in his own character, but he'd never been able to bear seeing any man made a fool of. A tragedy that by rights should have befallen him, given his own stunted growth, but a torture he'd adroitly avoided by dazzling his peers with his charm and disarming sense of humour.

Heydrich, however, didn't have an ounce of humour about him, nor the good sense to laugh off the jibes. Tall, gangly and introverted, he had managed over the years to alienate everybody. As was the way with all such surly, lonely men, he had closed himself off from the world, shutting his bedroom door and studying as if his life depended on it.

Which, as it turned out, it did, elevating him to a level of scholastic prestige that was to shoot him through the ranks of the military, gaining him fame, fortune and a reputation for infamy well before his time.

But that dubious success in the making wasn't yet his. And in the meantime, unaware of the monster he was helping create, it had been a kind of project of Canaris' to help him move towards it: an act of misplaced charity on his part that he would live to regret.

"You don't seem happy, Heydrich," Canaris had ventured over dinner that fateful first night of his crusade.

Having deserted his seat at the officers' table in the *Berlin's* mess hall, Canaris had made the controversial move of walking over, tin meal-tray in hand, to seat himself instead at the table where Heydrich was eating alone. Canaris had wrongly assumed that Heydrich's isolation was the choice of his fellow cadets. He'd had no idea that it was, in fact, a case of Heydrich thinking his classmates not good enough for *him*, rather than the other way round.

In such a state of elitist separatism, Heydrich was shocked by his Lieutenant's sudden appearance at his table, but more so by the direct and very personal question he had asked, the surprise of which had him stammer out his reply in falsetto.

"The Navy, s-sir . . . w-was not my choice of career?"

"*Why be here then?*" Canaris had asked without uttering a word. The question implied by the shrugging of his shoulders as he'd put down his tray and made himself comfortable on the hard metal bench.

"Money!" Heydrich replied. His answer was short, but not in the least sweet. It had been then, for the first time, that Canaris had noticed the cruel set of Heydrich's lips before they opened once more to elaborate.

"My family was never short of it over the centuries, but the War ruined us financially . . . the *Great* War," he had repeated, snorting the words out with contempt. "There was nothing *great* about it for us. And nothing for my parents to do but cling to their prior glory by passing their penniless son off by whatever means possible. The Navy was their only logical, dignified option."

"I'm sorry," Canaris had said, expressing a sympathy that was quite genuine, given that his own background wasn't so very different.

It wasn't hard for him to relate to Heydrich's dilemma—not

with the arbitrary nature of life. When the toss of the dice could easily have gone against the fortunes his *own* well-to-do clan and laid a like chip on *his* shoulder.

But it had not. . . and this was all too gloomy a subject. Their conversation was shooting off on a tangent that had not been his intention in approaching the young man.

"Well then," Canaris chirped up, as he'd salted his steak and harpooned a mouth-sized, medium-rare piece of it with his fork."Let's just ignore that bit of bad luck shall we, and go back to the beginning. If the choice *were* still yours, what would you have liked to do with your life?"

"Music."

Another short reply straight to the point, but this time said with an unmistakable look of yearning on his face.

"Ohh!" Canaris had been pleasantly surprised. An avid music lover himself, it had been the last thing he'd thought of in connection with Heydrich.

"I would have thought you the more outdoors type," he'd ventured. "Rowing, riding . . . that sort of thing."

"Well yes, I'm that too. I'm very good at sport," Heydrich had confirmed.

It had been a reply that had justified Canaris' talent for drawing quick character assessments, but one which, at the same time, had made him baulk at the man's unabashed conceit.

"But my passion's music. Always has been," Heydrich had continued without missing a beat. "Probably because I was born into it, I suppose. My father was an Opera singer. Founded Halle Conservatory of Music, as a matter of fact."

An interesting piece of information that had Canaris ask for more.

"Really? And your mother?"

"An accomplished pianist."

But that had been where Heydrich's clipped, bitter tribute to his mother stopped.

"And you . . . piano your instrument as well?" Canaris had urged him on, quickly pushing the young man past this obvious stumbling block of his. Chattering on, in his usual charming way, to wipe the slate clean of anything that smacked of controversy. "I can't go beyond it myself. Even though I'm afraid I don't play particularly well. Just for my own amusement, you understand. But I *love* it. Can't say as much for my long suffering neighbours though. Poor devils . . . always having to politely block their ears whenever I get the urge to tickle the ivories."

His attempt to lighten the mood didn't raise the slightest semblance of a smile from Heydrich. For him, the issue of "playing the piano" was very serious stuff.

"No . . . not the piano."

It was only Heydrich's deference to his superior that had forced him to explain.

"It was my first choice, but my mother didn't think I was good enough. I ended up with the violin."

It was an instrument choice that Canaris found a little disappointing—his expression saying as much. He could never understand how anyone could opt for it over the passion and grandeur of the piano. But by the end of his dinner-time talk with Heydrich, he'd got the full picture—learned why a boy of nine had come to see the piano as an instrument of stark terror.

Inconceivable as it seemed, his mother had subjected him to beatings each time he played it. Her disappointment over her own musical career having failed to reach the pinnacle of concert pianist had found an outlet in her son.

She had whipped him each time his tiny fingers pressed a wrong key. Her sadistic teaching methods having her lash him, without mercy, until his blood ran . . . until her terrifying techniques of tuition had scarred him for life. The physical evidence of which could still to be seen on his back and hands, where his flesh still bore the hard, raised welts of her punishment and insanity, to say nothing of his mind and heart that harboured wounds far more frightful. All of them festering with an unprecedented fear and loathing of the human race - in particular the Jewish section of it. These people had a prowess in, and monopoly *of*, the music industry which had become a very sore point with him. Almost as sore as the rumours that had abounded about him sharing their ancestry.

Which, given Heydrich's inherent talent on the violin, was a distinct possibility—obnoxious to him in the extreme. Abhorrent enough for him to dedicate his entire life *and* the lives of many others to disclaim it. Determined to do *anything* to wipe the insinuation and, if need be, the whole Jewish race off the face of the Earth.

A dark desire, still on "simmer", that he wasn't prepared to share just yet with Lieutenant Canaris—that thoroughly decent and all-too-dignified man sitting opposite who was so obviously a gentleman of the highest calibre. An Admiral in the making, whose integrity and embracing of all things noble was in no way equipped to stomach such an outrageous idea.

Having filled that stomach of his instead with his hearty steak and mashed potato meal, Canaris had stood up and taken his leave. He had been pleased with himself for doing his good deed for the day in wining and dining young Heydrich, but at that he'd been happy to leave it, suspecting, quite correctly, that he'd come within a cat's whisker of tapping into the murky depths of his protégé's soul and of making himself a reluctant part of them.

That had been something he had not wished to do, preferring to draw a clean, courteous line under their prospective friendship. This could have been easily achieved with no hurt feelings on either side had Canaris' lovely young wife Erika not thrown a spanner in the works.

Despite the fact that she and Willie had been married for seven happy years and were still very much in love, Frau Canaris had been buoyed by Heydrich's light-hearted flirtation with her at the most recent Naval Academy Ball. She had decided, then and there, to take an instant and immovable shine to him. The flattery of having him sweep her off her feet and whirl her round the room in a series of Strauss waltzes had gone straight to her head, leaving her all in a spin and devoted to him for life.

This indomitable little woman, with her soft, dark hair and pretty, brown eyes, stood 3" shorter than her husband in height, but towered over him in the power she wielded within their household. In command of *it*, him and their two small daughters, Eva and Brigitte, she'd insisted that handsome young Heydrich join her intimate chamber music ensemble. With her beloved viola secured beneath her chin, and with Heydrich and his virtuosity on the violin at her side, it had given her immense pleasure to fiddle her way through Mendelssohn's string quartets.

She played with Heydrich every night, tolerating, if not oblivious to, the presence of the cellist and the plain man plucking the double bass; two insignificant also-rans who had been dragged in to round out the sound of their quartet that performed to small gatherings of guests in the privacy of the Canaris home.

The problem was that Erika's feminine and sublimely naïve response to the strategic attentions Heydrich was paying her added a further social obligation to Canaris' life. Together with those pressing professional ones already in place, she'd managed to turn Heydrich into a 24-hour-a-day proposition for him.

Not wanting to put an end to his wife's pleasure by discouraging Heydrich's constant appearance at his door, Canaris had no choice but to open it to him. Each time he did he was acutely aware that the man had managed to infiltrate every facet of his life.

Had Canaris been a less shrewd man, he might have been jealous. As it was, he felt trapped and ever so slightly alarmed.

He wouldn't have dreamed of insulting his wife by questioning Heydrich's motives, even though it was blatantly obvious to him that the young officer's attentions were merely a means to an end.

It was not, as Heydrich hoped to infer, an obsession with Frau Canaris and her charms, but an active seeking of her company and the intimacy of her home to keep tabs on her husband. Heydrich made himself an integral part of Canaris' every coming and going, Canaris getting the distinct impression that Heydrich would not rest—would not leave him alone—until he had sucked him dry, not only of everything he had to teach him, but of his very privacy and right to live his own life without his every move being monitored.

CHAPTER THREE

Oppressive as that prospect was, it didn't pose a *real* problem until Heydrich was expelled from the Navy eight years later. At the age of twenty-six, while still a Signals officer under Canaris' command, he managed to disgrace himself and the daughter of a shipyard director by seducing, impregnating and refusing to marry her.

Just one in a string of sexual abuses that Heydrich quite literally had under his belt. His fervent pursuit of women and their submission, either by desire or force, had become his favourite hobby. This latest transgression, however, was a serious enough breech of the moral codes in 1930 to have Admiral Erich Raeder himself strip Heydrich of his gold epaulettes and white uniform. The dishonoured officer was railroaded into resigning his commission and finding solace in the arms of his fiancé, Frauleine Lina von Osten.

She was a woman of supposedly good breeding who seemed strangely unperturbed by her man's flagrant emotional and physical duplicity. Rather than being offended and humiliated by it, she chose to stand at his side to protect him from the hurt and slander his sleazy actions had inspired, somehow "turned on" by his sexual betrayal of her. It titillated her enough to turn him on to the Nazi Party, in whose fledgling ranks she was an active member.

Not that it took much persuasion on her part when Heydrich himself, at the age of sixteen, had joined the Freikorps.[5] As a former member of that extreme right wing organization, he knew *exactly* what he was about. For some time he had missed the thrill of indulging in unrestrained, wholesale violence, the pure joy and adrenaline rush that he and others like him had experienced in the brutalizing and bludgeoning to death of any Communist who dared walk the streets of Germany at the end of the Great War.

So from there—that blood-curdling point of evil—it was just

one small step to topple him from frying pan to hell fire. After only a very short time of having ensconced himself within Nazi ranks, he found himself near the top of them; a meteoric series of promotions, posting him as second in command of the SS, that elite organization of black-clad young men, chosen only on the credential of their physical Aryan appeal and their amenability to blanket brutality. Ostensibly a modern-day Praetorian Guard for the Fuhrer, the SS had quickly mutated into something far larger and far, far worse, spreading its powerful, black wings over boundaries of territory and justice to incorporate mass murder.

To successfully lower its standards to that level, there had been a need to put the right men in the right jobs. And to the man at the head of SS operations—Heinrich Himmler—Reinhard Heydrich appeared to be the perfect fit.

"Just fill out this short questionnaire will you Herr Heydrich," the Reichsfuhrer of the SS said as he pushed the pen and piece of military-issue paper across the desk to him.

It was a formality—he had already made up his mind to promote the young man. Himmler was wholly impressed with Heydrich's sheer physical presence and astonishing self-confidence. It was just that he was curious to see how this new recruit of his would handle it.

Grabbing up the pen without a second thought, Heydrich handled it just fine. Without a moment's pause, he filled out points 1 to 10 in regard to the instigation of a new Intelligence division for the SS, and *his* eligibility to take on the role as its head.

"Noting, if you please . . . ," Himmler leant over his desk to instruct him, ". . . your ideas for the purification of the Aryan race. Motives and methods in the respective left and right columns."

He had not expected that within ten minutes Heydrich would have finished the impromptu examination, having not only filled out the prerequisites of the standard form, but having asked for an additional two pages to pin to it so that he might add to them. The clarity and brutal efficiency of his ideas for the improvement of their German State via racial cleansing (points 1-40) came as a source of delight and eyebrow-raising revelation to Himmler when he read through them.

"Do you honestly think that it can be done?" Himmler asked as he eagerly put the rubber stamp of approval on Heydrich's application.

Looking his new superior officer straight in the eye, Heydrich answered, "Yes . . . if you give me a free hand."

Himmler had no problem with that. If Heydrich's hand was as adept with a sword as it was with a pen . . . if he could put into practice what he'd put on paper, there would be no end to what the two of them could achieve. Heydrich had just itemised the horrific ways and means of bringing about the Final Solution.

From that point on, he wouldn't only go down in history as its mastermind, but his hand-written proof of it was carried downstairs to Himmler's office archives, bound in a manila folder and stamped *"Top Secret"*, to be filed under "M" for *madman, mayhem* and *murder.*

Now that he had his job-of-choice in hand, Heydrich was as happy as a pig in mud, taking outrageous advantage of its lurks and perks while working at a frenetic pace under Himmler's wing. It was a full-on occupation that one would have thought would give Heydrich no time for anything or anyone else. His connection and peculiar fascination with Canaris had surely come to an end.

And perhaps that would have been the way of it, had Adolf Hitler not been so impressed by the *"Himmler Adopting Heydrich"* principle, deciding soon after to follow his example by taking Canaris under *his* wing.

By then Canaris had reached the rank of Rear Admiral and recently retired. The formal relinquishing of his maritime duties came soon after he'd been personally introduced to Hitler; a fateful meeting that put an end to Canaris' hopes of living out his life in peace.

The Fuhrer had taken such an instant shine to his Little Admiral that he had ruled his departure from "the scene" incompatible with the nation's and his—*Hitler's*—good, Insisting instead that his new pint-sized pal be dragged out of retirement to head up the *Abwehr*—Germany's *traditional* Military Intelligence Service. It was a career path that, with one major deviation to "The Right", paralleled Heydrich's and fulfilled that same man's prophecy-cum-piece-of-wishful-thinking that he and Canaris would share life's journey.

It was a horrifying prospect that had not crossed Canaris' mind, and it made him all the more astonished at this unexpected turn of events. He not only had to reconcile himself to the fact that

Heydrich's close proximity to himself had now been made official, but he had to come to terms with the rather astounding reality that his *real* life drama was destined to begin *after* his retirement. As if his life and career up until that point had counted for nothing and not been action-packed enough! He was forty-eight, for heaven's sake—in military terms, an old man.

But there you had it. Only a few weeks after the Navy had put him out to pasture they had had to quickly haul him back on deck. Having honoured him with just a fleeting stint as Chief-of-Staff at their North Sea *Swinemunde Naval Base*, they had been ordered by Hitler to call him back to active duty.

It was a compliment—yes; but more an inconvenience for Canaris. On short notice, they were expecting him to psyche himself back out of retirement mode and rethink the impression he'd been under that he'd already done his utmost for the Fatherland.

Not that he was exactly an ancient mariner, but he believed that he had the right to a little rest and recreation after his years of faithful service. After all, he'd dedicated decades to Naval Intelligence; captained U-Boats during the Great War; endured a laborious tour of duty as Training officer on board the battleship *Berlin*; and for five years was in command of the battleship *Schlesien*.

A sterling naval record, after which his appointment to serve behind a mahogany desk, rather than a ship's wheel, was a natural progression. *Swinemunde* was the standard repository for all old salts—the honourable end of the line for sea captains and such.

Going to it meant that Canaris had accepted this, in full knowledge that seating his retired rear in one of its high-backed leather chairs would put an end to his dazzling, daredevil career as he'd known it.

Now, prematurely grey in his late forties, he was actually looking forward to having his portrait painted and hung over the family mantelpiece, right next to that of his adopted ancestor— the naval hero of the Greek War of Independence, Admiral Constantine Kanaris.

That there was no particular connection between this Hellenic Admiral and their Germanic Canaris clan, had been neither here nor there. A "C" or a "K"—what did it matter? Spelt either way, the family had been determined to establish their ancestral connection to the "Great Greek K", and doubly determined to keep quiet about the fact that there had turned out to be none.

When they had stumbled over their far less spectacular Italian roots, it had been their resolve to leave Kanaris' portrait over their mantelpiece with the intention of letting others, less informed, draw their own conclusions. There to hang as a piece of art for the sake of artifice, to provide the Canaris Clan with a claim to fame and glory. One on which, as a child, Willie Canaris had hung his hopes and dreams, while marvelling at the ease with which people were prepared to be taken in.

It had been his first lesson in the art of espionage . . . learning that a lie wasn't really a lie when it was based on subtle inference and assumption . . . when one was careful not to implicate oneself by putting that lie into words. The portrait, coupled with the Canaris' dignified silence on the subject of their heritage, had been enough to fool their friends and influence people. But now that "Wilhelm with a C"'s own naval career had surpassed that of his false forebear, the charade was over. It was a source of pride to Willie that he could provide his family with *two* Admirals "in oils" to gloat over. One of them, at long last, legitimate.

Unlike the Canaris family, however, that wasn't the picture that Adolf Hitler had in mind for him. The Great Man, instead, wanted to write himself into Act Two of Wilhelm Canaris' life story. Deciding to join him on centre stage and give Canaris his cue to play out a leading role in his Third Reich. Neither Hitler nor Canaris had a clue, as the curtain went up on it just prior to World War II, that Fate had cast them as each other's prospective murderers.

But at that point in time, killing Canaris was the last thing on Hitler's mind, because the Little Admiral had become one of his favourites. This was no great revelation . . . not when Canaris was *everybody's* favourite!

Quite aware of the power and persuasion of his personality, Canaris had always used it, unashamedly, to get what he wanted, but still he was surprised that he'd made *such* a dynamic impact on the Fuhrer.

When he'd welcomed Hitler—as the new German Chancellor—on board the *Schelsien* some time before, he had not made a conscious effort to do anything out of the ordinary to impress him. He'd had no idea, when he'd treated the man to tea and scones and the courtesy of listening, for two tedious hours, as Hitler bellowed his theories at him across the table, that he'd won a heart. The soft spot he'd secured in Hitler's that day, effectively deciding his future—a future the Fuhrer was now adamant they share. It was a simple case of opposites attracting; the "bad" in Hitler being drawn to the innate "good" in Canaris. From that day forward, as if by force of nature, it made the Rear Admiral into a magnet for every form of evil on Earth. Starting with Hitler, whose back-slapping approval of him placed him immediately at that evil's hub—a pivotal position of power that laid on Canaris' conscience the heavy onus of having to do something about it.

All in all, it had been an odd outcome of their fateful meeting, when *during* it Canaris had taken the dangerous initiative of punctuating Hitler's histrionics with a series of glib one-liners. Not as an act of audacity, but purely because he couldn't help himself. His wry, ever-on-the-alert mind made it impossible for him to let opportunities for off-the-cuff witticisms pass. Ironically, in having run the terrible risk of offending the new German Chancellor, he'd managed to keep him highly amused all afternoon. Having found both the Fuhrer's favour and funny bone, it was inevitable he would get a reward.

So, as a "thank you" for providing the afternoon's entertainment, and in line with Hitler's peculiar practice of choosing his senior staff at whim, Canaris was earmarked for promotion. A few months later he was made head of the *Abwehr*. Canaris' feelings of ill-ease in regard to taking on such a huge job and associating himself so closely with Hitler were superseded by the enormous ego boost and challenge factor the extraordinary promotion offered him.

But it came as an even bigger thrill and challenge to the now grand and glorious Brigadier-General Reinhard Heydrich.

As head of SS Intelligence he knew that his old mentor, Wilhelm Canaris, was the only man in Germany—if not the world—who was capable of keeping him on his toes. Canaris' appointment to such a complementary position within the Intelligence Network was going to make this whole secret service business much more fun.

Himmler, too, was glad to have Canaris on board. Not through love and respect for the man and his talents, but as payback to his

Abwehr predecessor, Admiral Conrad Patzig, who had recently been relieved of his position as its head, to make room for Canaris.

"And thank God for that!" Himmler said to Heydrich when he heard the happy news.

Patzig had been a thorn in his side for months. Both of them shared a mutual loathing of each other throughout Patzig's short term of office. The Admiral's uninformed, ethics-based interference in Himmler's plans for SS domination of Germany (both on the political and military front) had come close to driving Himmler mad—a state of mind, in Himmler's case, that Patzig had quite openly said was already an accomplished fact.

It was just one of many insults that had been thrown back and forth between them, while Patzig—the brave old warrior—had worked defiantly in direct opposition to every one of Himmler's initiatives.

"The man *never* had what it took to work in Intelligence," Himmler continued, with a considerable amount of smugness now that the physical threat of Patzig's broad-shouldered presence had been removed. "A career naval officer—that's all he ever was. A great pea-brained Neanderthal of a man. Just didn't have it in him to work outside the square."

It was true. Patzig had always been a decent, down-to-earth man, incapable of straying from the straight and narrow. As a member of the legitimate military and an implacable adherent to its code of honour, he had never been able to see eye-to-eye with Himmler on any issue, coming nowhere near understanding the new breed of men who were moving into the Intelligence arena.

He also had a particular aversion to Reinhard Heydrich. The sadistic, devious machinations of the man's mind went beyond Patzig's comprehension and control.

Which had made it all the easier for Heydrich to run rings round him, using his position as head of SS Intelligence as an undisguised threat to topple Patzig from power. Not only with the intention of grinding him and the *Abwehr* into submission, but of incorporating the entire German Military Intelligence Organization under a banner of his own. He, Heydrich, being its intended, supreme leader.

It had constituted a vicious, no holds barred campaign that had been all too much for an old sea-dog like Patzig. And finally, putting his pride on the line, he'd had to admit it.

"I am unable and unwilling to cope any longer with the conniving of Reichsfuhrer Himmler and his side-kick Heydrich," he said, with unmitigated contempt, to Grand Admirals Raeder and Doenitz.

"Rear Admiral Canaris is your man," he continued, counting on the fact that this personal recommendation of his would get straight back to Hitler and meet with his approval.

Patzig and the Fuhrer had just this one thing in common; both of them had the utmost admiration for Canaris. Not only for his astute mind, but for his gentlemanly control of it. These qualities appealed to Patzig because he too was in possession of the like, and to Hitler because they were utterly beyond his reach. To either way of thinking, there was simply no one better equipped than the Little Admiral to take on the two SS tyrants—Himmler and Heydrich.

"Are you absolutely sure that this is the way you want to go?" Admiral Doenitz asked, taking no pleasure in seeing a fellow naval officer admit defeat and humble himself to this degree.

"I haven't the slightest doubt in my mind, Doenitz, that I'm doing the right thing. Canaris will be able to handle Heydrich. I can't. All the back-stabbing and clandestine carry-on . . . it's just not for me. I'm not clever enough to keep up. Nor do I have the vaguest desire to do so. All I want to do is to get back to active service on board my ship where I belong and where I *know* what I'm doing."

"You do realize, Patzig, that this piece of honesty on your part will mean a demotion of sorts for you?" Admiral Raeder put in— unable, in his disappointment over the issue, to look Patzig in the eye as he said it. His sentiments over the man's admission of defeat echoed those of Doenitz.

"Well demote away," Patzig had no qualms in replying. "All I know is that I won't breathe easy until I get the hell out of this Machiavellian nightmare and back on the high seas. At least *there* I'll stand half a chance of survival."

"And you're convinced of Canaris' capacity to take on the job?" Doenitz asked, putting sentimentality aside to get back to business. "I'm not so sure myself. I know Canaris a little and he strikes me as being a man much like yourself."

Raeder heartily agreed with this comment, which was both valid and complimentary to Canaris.

"Perhaps, but Canaris is much shrewder than I," Patzig countered. "Besides, he knows Heydrich well. And Heydrich, *incredibly* enough, likes to think of him as his friend. Can't *imagine* that Canaris would return the compliment, but it's something that will certainly give Canaris an edge in working with him. I know for a fact that Heydrich holds him in the highest regard."

It was just an added bonus that Himmler happened to approach Admirals Doenitz and Raeder the very next day over the same issue. Interrupting the decision-making process, he burst, unannounced, into their office to complain about Patzig's uncooperative attitude and to make his demand that he be replaced immediately.

A happy coincidence that brought them all to an unanimous decision. Himmler, Heydrich, Doenitz, Raeder and Hitler himself were relieved to wave *bon voyage* to Admiral Patzig and to welcome Rear Admiral Wilhelm Canaris to his vacated office.

So began the clash of the Titans. The *Abwehr* and SS Intelligence went at the battle of wits and warfare in earnest, Canaris with the initial handicap of possessing a sense of common decency that he had to train himself out of before he could meet Heydrich on equal terms. Meanwhile, Heydrich had already got a head start in Hitler's good books, and over the last two years had padded them out with his burgeoning list of spectacular achievements.

It had started in a small office with just Heydrich and an old manual typewriter. His tireless determination, his day and night, two-finger tapping on its keys, quickly ballooned his new SS Intelligence Department into a vast and sinister empire of spies and unimaginable sadism. A typewritten account was sent daily to Himmler and Hitler to keep them informed:

INTER-OFFICE MEMO

To: Reichsfuhrer—SS, Heinrich Himmler
From: SS Brigadier General—Reinhard Heydrich
Date: March 4, 1933
c.c. Reich's Chancellor—Adolf Hitler.

Have put in place, as of above date, a small network of informers for the purpose of developing dossiers on all those suspected of being 'unfriendly' to Hitler. It is my intent to conduct a thorough cleansing of the entire Nazi Party organization by means of internal espionage to weed out the troublemakers. It is the most cost and time efficient way to procure information with the minimum of publicity and dissension within the ranks.

Please be aware that I will not stop until the smallest detail on all Nazi Party members and Storm Trooper leaders has been unearthed, analyzed and dealt with appropriately.

INTER-OFFICE MEMO

To: Reichsfuhrer—SS, Heinrich Himmler
From: SS Brigadier General—Reinhard Heydrich
Date: April 18, 1933
c.c.   Reich's Chancellor—Adolf Hitler.

Have set up a new filing system to house the more private details and sexual activities of top Nazis. Will probably need, in the not so distant future, to plant hidden microphones and cameras in their homes and offices to get conclusive proof of finer details.

INTER-OFFICE MEMO

To: Reichsfuhrer—SS, Heinrich Himmler
From: SS Brigadier General—Reinhard Heydrich
Date: May 8, 1933
c.c.   Reich's Chancellor—Adolf Hitler.

I would like to thank you, sir, for your invaluable help in having overseen the mass arrests I organized of Communists, Trade Unionists and all Catholic politicians who were suspected of being in opposition to Hitler.

It must have been hard for you, coming from a happy Catholic home yourself, to have had to organize the arrest and execution of the many Catholic Priests I'd documented as having preached against us. I know that it was the very strength of your religious devotion and your concern for the ultimate welfare of the Fatherland that gave you the courage to do your job without stinting.

I am in debt and in awe of you. And will continue to strive to model myself and my actions on your example.

In the meantime, I have run into a small stumbling block. We have been so zealous in rounding up the Nation's traitors, that we have run out of prison space to hold them before execution.

But please do not trouble yourself with this issue. I have dedicated myself to find its quick solution.

INTER-OFFICE MEMO

To: Reichsfuhrer—SS, Heinrich Himmler
From: SS Brigadier General—Reinhard Heydrich
Date: June 22, 1933
c.c.   Reich's Chancellor—Adolf Hitler.

I have commandeered an old munitions factory at Dachau, near Munich and am in the process of converting it quickly into a concentration camp for political prisoners. On its gates I have taken the liberty of inscribing the words: "WORK SETS YOU FREE". Which I will make sure it does in their case. No man is freer than when he is dead (Ha, Ha!).

To that end, I intend to work them until they drop. All of these enemies of the State to be subjected to the harshest treatment and beatings.

Here follows a list of proposed punishments for your approval:

1. The stealing of a cigarette .... 25 lashes.
2. The stealing of bread or
   other like foodstuffs
   (starvation no excuse) .... Suspension of body from
   .... pole by wrists and/or
   .... incarceration in
   .... standing-room only cell
   .... without windows or
   .... light. We will extend
   .... them the privilege of
   .... making the choice.
3. Answering back to
   German Officer .... Death by hanging or
   .... firing squad.
4. Laying a hand on a German
   soldier of any rank........................ Torture by whichever
   .... means available at time
   .... of crime, followed by
   .... Death by hanging or
   .... firing squad.
5. Reluctance to perform work
   requirements (illness no excuse) The imposing of double
   .... shifts on top of their
   .... original workload. at
   .... half their normal ration
   .... of one slice of bread and
   .... one pint of water per
   .... day. At end of which, if
   .... still alive Death by

```
............................................ hanging or firing squad.
```
6. Any attempt to escape................. Torture by whichever
```
............................................ means available at time
............................................ of crime, followed by
............................................ Death by hanging or
............................................ firing squad.
```
Please let me know if you'd like to add to this list as soon as possible as I am now keen to turn my full attention to the Jews.

It was around about this time that Heydrich earned himself the nickname of "the Blood Beast" in Nazi Party circles. Each and every member of that black-clad clique, with its skull and cross-bone insignia, were scared to death of him. Even those hardened types who had proved themselves, in their own right, to be monsters of the first order knew that there was one amongst them far more terrifying—a sociopath whose dark, dead eyes and icy stare told them that he was without a skerrick of compassion for his fellow man.

It was a case of evil running up against evil, with the promise of a fight to the death, that had their feral senses forever alert to the scent of Heydrich's dangerous, prowling approach. Their bestial instinct for survival at military meetings and even laid-back social affairs at which he was present, warning them to keep their mouths shut; and to watch their "ps and qs" if pressed to open them. Not forgetting, of course, to do a thorough check for bugging devices in their bedrooms each night before settling down to sleep, praying that during its unguarded hours they not mutter anything indiscreet.

This constituted a great ruffling of feathers in the Nazi nest—an angst, particularly among its high-flying five-star Generals, that Himmler found most intriguing. As the power-monger he was, he got an immense amount of pleasure out of suddenly wielding so much of it, of seeing the big boys on the block squirm and shake in their black, knee-high leather boots whenever he or Heydrich chose to join them for even the most innocent "Schnapps" nightcap.

"We know that some Germans get sick at the very sight us," he reported back to Hitler with glee. "The SS uniform alone seems to terrify them. But then," he continued with a nonchalant shrug, "we don't expect to be loved."

Love couldn't even get a foothold during these dark days of Germany's history. Not when a mixture of fanatical patriotism and policies for payback over the unfairness of the Versailles Treaty were rallying its people in the direction of a second World War. Hitler did all in his demonic power to rev them up to fever pitch, while Heydrich's agents scampered like a plague of rats all over Germany, using torture, murder, indiscriminate arrests, extortion and blackmail to crush any opposition to the Third Reich and its plans for world domination.

"Hangman Heydrich", as the general German populace now called him, had provided ample, gruesome proof that speaking out against Hitler meant death. Those who had dared to do so and been foolish enough to stay within his ever-widening reach had been stopped dead in their tracks—their mouths shut for good with a rope around their neck so that others might learn by example.

And these brutalized and butchered citizens were people of Heydrich's own blood: men, women and children of Germany who, like him, were dedicated to its welfare. They were his fellow countrymen whom he was supposed to have loved.

One could only wonder at what he had in mind for the Jews— the people he loathed.

CHAPTER FOUR

It was a plan of demonic proportions that Heydrich put on hold when the rumour started getting round that *he* was of Jewish origin himself.

"You can't *possibly* believe this malicious piece of slander, sir?" he said in his own defence when Himmler confronted him with the accusation. The Reichsfuhrer of the SS, in his fury, hurled the written proof of it across the room at his Deputy.

"When you applied for this job Heydrich, you *swore* that you were of pure Aryan stock. This contemptible discovery that you're not—that you're actually of Jewish descent is not only obscene, but has made a fool of me *and* the Fuhrer. Both he and I are going to have to think hard and fast to find a solution to the problem."

Heydrich was trying frantically to do the same as he waited for the incriminating document to float its way to the floor before he bent, in dread, to pick it up.

"*Well*, do you dare deny it?" Himmler demanded grim-faced.

"Yes . . . I most certainly do," Heydrich replied after having quickly scanned the certificate from the Registry of Births, Deaths and Marriages. "Forgive me for saying this, sir, but I think you've jumped the gun and not thought this accusation of yours through."

"I *beg* your pardon! Do you actually have the effrontery to deny what's there in black and white, staring you in the face? Your grandfather was a Jew . . . a *Jew!* Look . . . *look!*" Himmler strode across the room and jabbed his gnarled index finger, over and over again, at the evidence in print. "There it is . . . your maternal grandmother was married to a Jew . . . *Joachim Cohen!*"

"Yes, that's how it would seem, sir. But please *think* . . . as you can see for yourself in the paperwork here, it was only a second marriage, well after my mother was born. The tragedy and degradation of my grandmother deciding to take on a Jew in her later life, doesn't make *me* one. She was either senile or, more likely, doing it for the money. Old Cohen had plenty of it. But I . . . *I*, thank God, haven't an ounce of Jewish blood in my body.

"This is not the first time that this disgusting accusation has been thrown at me. My rather exceptional musical talent, and, I'm ashamed to say . . . some of my lesser facial features, have had some people question my heritage. But let me assure you that it is *irksome* to me . . . to see the traces of what looks like kike in my own face. So loathsome, in fact, that only the other day, I shot my own reflection in the mirror because it made me want to puke."[6]

"Mmmm . . ." Himmler mumbled, mellowing a touch, but not entirely convinced as he picked up the telephone to put through a call to Hitler's office.

"I shall have to discuss this delicate matter with the Fuhrer. I'll leave it up to him to decide what to do with you."

"Is that entirely necessary, sir? I mean, my situation is quite clear, surely?"

"Are you suggesting that I keep this inflammatory piece of information from the Fuhrer?"

The threat in the coolness of his question made Heydrich back down fast.

"I keep *no* secrets from the Fuhrer, Herr Heydrich. Perhaps you should have extended *me* that same courtesy before putting me in this awkward position."

Their conversation was at an end, but Heydrich, stunned silent, hesitated for a few uncertain moments before he left Himmler's office. He was wondering whether he should linger a little longer to clarify the matter, but the implacable look on Himmler's pale, pinched face told him otherwise. That he wasn't, at this difficult time, in his favour and would be better off making himself scarce.

Before he was able to open the office door to do so, Himmler put his hand over the phone's mouthpiece and called out to him.

"Oh, and Heydrich . . . I wouldn't make any efforts to absent yourself from the scene. You *know* that I'll be able to find you anywhere."

As it happened, it wasn't necessary for Heydrich to make a run for it, or to panic in any way. Not when it turned out that he had Hitler on side. Not when the man himself invited him the very next day to share a meal and a few hours of one-on-one time together.

Apprehensive as Heydrich was about accepting such an unprecedented, personal invitation, he had no choice but to attend. Under the volatile circumstances, he was quite aware that it could well be a last supper before his summary execution.

With that terrifying threat hanging over his head, he went to Hitler's private apartments, uncharacteristically nervous. He strode from them a few hours later, more cocksure than he had ever been—convinced, without a shadow of a doubt, that he had managed to talk the Fuhrer round and win him over for life.

Which was a fair assumption, given that Hitler had shaken his hand and waved him a particularly fond farewell.

A man much more friendly and amenable than anyone knows, Heydrich thought as he got back into his black Mercedes and drove away. With the fear factor of the evening having faded, going that one dangerous step further to think:

Amenable enough, I wonder, to be manipulated?

Something that he didn't realize Hitler had just done to him - forever, as the Fuhrer was, one step ahead of any man and his evil.

For him, the whole nasty issue had become a matter of expediency.

"I want you to drop this whole concern with Heydrich. Cover it up as quickly as possible," was Hitler's order to Himmler over the phone, minutes after Heydrich left his apartment. "I believe that he can be extremely useful to us. I've never, in my life, met such a highly gifted, dangerous man. Rumours or not, our Movement can't afford to lose his special talents. And now that I've let him off the hook, I'll have his eternal gratitude. You can be sure, from here on in, he'll obey me blindly and do anything . . . *anything* I ask."

Himmler however, was unable to cover up this little incident before Canaris got wind of it. The head of the *Abwehr* derived a great sense of satisfaction from the news—not only from Heydrich's near fall from grace, but from the fact that he'd found out about it at all! His being made privy to what should have been a "top secret" affair was proof positive that his two years of hard work at the *Abwehr* was starting to pay off, that his hand-picked, spy network was operating like a well-oiled machine.

An achievement that had come as the direct result of the grueling program of public relations and personnel recruitment he'd inflicted on himself. Twenty-four months of traveling at top gear throughout Germany and whizzing himself around the world at like speed, making stopovers in all cities and countries of consequence to establish high-profile contacts and life-long friendships with as many members of the respective nation's military and civilian hierarchy as possible.

It was an odyssey of enormous importance that had had him wandering the corridors of power—in and out of embassies, negotiating at the headquarters of high finance, wheeling and dealing with the barons of industry, in his official capacity, making sure that he had eyes and ears in all the right places.

With their help, he'd managed to get an inside running on the Heydrich situation. The flash bulletin re the man's possible downfall had marked the start of Canaris' offensive.

Something that for the past two years he'd had to put on stand-by, while he familiarized himself with his new job and the building up of his own extensive espionage framework—that comprehensive nexus between spies on active duty and the loyalties of men in powerful positions who shared his upright, conservative views. Men of honour, who were determined to hold tight to their ideas of truth and justice and to continue to work for the good of God and Country.

All of them who, like Canaris, had initially been great supporters of Hitler and his ground-breaking initiatives, were beginning to get sadly disillusioned by those lesser ones of his which were surfacing with remarkable and ruthless regularity.

In particular, his plans for the annihilation of the Jews, which, as far as they could see, had nothing whatsoever to do with the betterment and welfare of their German Nation, but which were destined, by right of their bloodcurdling detail, to bring about its ultimate destruction.

In the busy process of bringing such altruistic men together, however, Canaris had had to turn a blind eye to the appalling array of atrocities Heydrich had been committing. Now, at last, he believed he was in a powerful enough position to start combating them.

Up until 1937, it had suited his purpose to stay out of the maniac's way while he worked at making himself strong enough to stand in it. In the meantime, he'd chosen to keep a low profile in his game plan, mastering the art of staying out of the limelight so as to keep an eye on those who made targets of themselves because they couldn't live without it.

It was a ploy that had always proved most successful—diverting attention from himself while he pulled more important strings behind the scenes. His *modus operandi* was to extricate himself, quietly and politely, from any complex situation, and in answer to any direct question as to his involvement in it . . . to simply smile enigmatically and pass by on the other side.

But that was the coward's way out and he knew it. Standing by weakly on the sidelines, watching as the three big "H's"—Hitler, Himmler and Heydrich—committed their litany of criminal obscenities was no longer an option—not for any halfway decent man. Now, at last, he was prepared to jump off that fence he had been sitting on and declare himself on one side or the other. It had taken him far too long to stop claiming elitist exemption from the horrors that had been happening around him.

This was something that, to his own shame, he'd done with great aplomb when the SA Reichsminister, Ernst Roehm, had had his throat slit[7] along with dozens of other top SA Leaders back in '34. On that frightful "Night of The Long Knives" all of them had been hunted down and murdered on Hitler's orders.

Heydrich had personally compiled the list of those to be executed, while Himmler and Field Marshal Hermann Goering had helped him plot to bring the massacre about. Goering and Himmler had spread false rumours that Roehm and his four million SA Storm Troopers had intended to seize power of the Reich, their aim being to frighten Hitler into making a pre-emptive strike—to cut Roehm and his Storm Troopers down with one savage, decisive blow before they got the chance.

"To kill a snake, one must act fast and chop off its head," Heydrich had said at the debriefing, unable to resist turning, for a smug, satisfied second, in Canaris' direction to get his nod of approval.

It had been an expectation puzzling in the extreme, given

that many of the murdered men lying splattered with blood in the street had been close friends of Canaris. But even for his beloved mentor's sake, Heydrich had not hesitated to add their names to the list for execution, scribbling them down as fast as he could so as not to forget or leave anyone out, adding as an afterthought the names of a few innocents to pad out the page.

But then nothing, including conscience, ever stopped Heydrich when he was on a roll, and that night he had achieved wonders, effectively rinsing out of the system all evidence of the SA Brownshirts, so that they could be dyed black and sported by members of the Nazi Party.

"I'm sorry to see Roehm go, though," Hitler had replied in a moment of schizophrenic mourning. Looking out his window at the man's body, sprawled bloodied and contorted on the courtyard below, he had experienced a moment of nostalgia. With a sigh, he'd then added, "It was only a week ago that I wrote to him to thank him for his services to our National Socialist Movement and the German people. I wanted to assure him of how very grateful I was to be able to count such a man as he among my friends."

God help his enemies! Canaris had thought, working hard not to change the inscrutable expression on his face as he took an undetectable step back into the shadowed recesses of Hitler's office, thinking that to stand in them might help camouflage the aversion and horror he was suddenly feeling for the man and his Third Reich. Wondering how on Earth, by means other than getting a knife in the back, he was *ever* going to extricate himself from them.

Back then, still finding solace in shadows, he had not had the guts or depth of conviction to make a stand against it, being, as he was, still more concerned for his own skin than that of others.

However, the vile episode of the "Night of the Long Knives" was but *one* of the sideshows in Hitler's Carnival of Carnage. His macabre medley of murders over the subsequent years had managed to stain the hands, hearts and reputations of *all* Germans—not just those of his political friends and enemies.

It was this smear on Germany's once noble status that had finally got the better of Canaris' conscience and forced him to draw a clear distinction between his beloved Fatherland and its leader, Adolf Hitler—realizing at last that the welfare and longevity of the first was reliant on the disposal of the second.

It wasn't such a difficult conclusion to have reached now that Hitler was starting to show his true colours, another example of which was his delight over the resounding success of Heydrich's Dachau Concentration Camp. The graphic, gruesome stories of unspeakable suffering which emerged from it sent shivers down the spine of most, while thrilling Hitler through and through. Enough to have him immediately authorize the construction of many other institutions of the like.

Buchenwald, Sachsenhausen and Lichtenburg were the result. Each of them in turn was an 'improvement', with lessons being learned along the way: using pistols instead of gas for fast, cost-effective kills and the utilization of ovens large enough for human beings, so as to burn all evidence of their genocide. This, progressively, made them more streamlined in their methods of extermination.

Their success at achieving maximum executions with minimum fuss came as a further boost to Heydrich's list of accolades and ego. That supreme self-confidence of his, now having gone into overflow, gave him the impetus to cross the line into new territories of terror. No longer satisfied with testing the boundaries of slaughter and sadism within his own domain, he decided to pop over the border into Russia to see what havoc he could wreak there.

Like a deadly spider, he crawled into every dark corner of that country's internal politics, weaving his web of intrigue to snare its alleged traitors while urging Soviet Leader Stalin to mimic Hitler's moves against Roehm. He prodded the Red Ruler into conducting a purge of his own to rid himself of those top Russian Army generals whom Heydrich had caught in his trap. In 1937, he supplied Stalin with a surplus of evidence in regard to their possible military coup against him.

And Stalin, who above all else was determined *never* to be outdone by Hitler, had obliged as a matter of pride, giving a guarantee in blood that *his* slaughter be bigger and better. The unmatched competitive streak in his nature had him make sure that his Red Square lived up to its name.

But when in November of that same year Hitler and Heydrich worked hand in hand to secure the very public humiliation and enforced suicide of General Baron Werner von Fritsch—one of

Germany's finest soldiers and Commander-in-Chief of its army—
the *status quo* had reached rock bottom. As far as Canaris was
concerned, it had been the last straw.

The false accusation of homosexuality that they had contrived
and leveled at this man of distinction had been unforgivable. They
had discredited, by intent, one of the most revered members of the
military.

Heydrich had employed the services of a convicted male
prostitute to provide evidence against him. With the promise of
granting the criminal release from his prison sentence, Heydrich
had secured from him an abundance of lies—manufactured proof
of lewd, sexual encounters that he vowed, under oath, he'd shared
with Fritsch.

Repulsive accounts of depraved sensuality had ensured the
ruination of this dignified soldier-of-the-old-school. In those days,
particularly within the ranks of the military, homosexuality was
an unspeakable sin, the labeling with which meant disgrace.

In this case, it had laid enough of it on Fritsch's gold-epaulette
shoulders to leave him no alternative but to retrieve his honour in
death—an end achieved soon after he'd suffered the shame and
great travesty of justice they had called his court-martial. Having
accepted its guilty verdict, Fritsch had committed himself to
frontline duty in the Polish campaign of 1939. Taking off his pistol
and holster, he had strolled unarmed onto its battlefield, turning
to his Lieutenant just one last time to say, "Goodbye, my friend.
Please know that I go out strictly as a target."

A prompt peppering with machine gun pellets had mercifully
let him die with some semblance of honour.

CHAPTER FIVE

It was all because Colonel-General Fritsch and Field-Marshal Werner von Blomberg had dared disagree with Hitler. They were the only two men among the host of other military warlords present at the meeting on November 5, 1937, who had thought to question the Fuhrer when he'd announced his long range war plans.

"So what you're saying, sir, is that you wish to achieve living space for Germany at the expense of Austria, Czechoslovakia, Poland and the Ukraine?" Fritsch had said, emphasizing what he had thought to be the sheer stupidity of Hitler's plan by counting the numbers of the countries to be vanquished on his fingers as he spoke. "You do realize that we couldn't even *attempt* to pursue such a grand plan without provoking immediate worldwide retaliation?"

The shock impact of Hitler's strategy for quick-fix-world-domination had overridden Fritsch's sense of discretion, adding a patronizing tone to his voice that had made Hitler bristle with rage.

"Well *of course* there'll be opposition in Europe. Isn't that *exactly* the point! What do you think . . . that I'm a *fool?* France and Britain are the obvious stumbling blocks, but they'll be paralyzed by our Blitzkrieg[8] campaign. By the time they work out what's hit them, it'll be too late to do anything constructive about it."

"It is . . . you're quite right, sir, an admirable, incredibly ambitious plan," Field-Marshal Blomberg had jumped in to say, making a tactful bid to diffuse the tense stalemate. "But might I suggest, perhaps just a little rash? Is it wise, I wonder, to bring all our prospective enemies down on our head all at once?

"Possibly the operation could be paced a little better? A slower, more considered offensive might prove more successful in the long run? There's always the danger of vulnerability if we spread our troops too thin on too many Fronts."

It had been a carefully-worded, polite piece of advice that Blomberg had hoped wouldn't only help his friend Fritsch out of a sticky situation, but would stop Hitler putting the whole country into one.

But Hitler had dismissed his suggestion by calmly ignoring it.

His body language, however, had told a different story as he had started to slap his dog-whip, irritably, against the side of his leather boot—an action, absent-minded at first, that had suddenly picked up pace and punch in line with his smoldering anger.

Blomberg's advice aside, it had not been the first time that General Fritsch had offended him, but it most certainly was going to be the last!

"So, it'll be all of Europe . . . all in one go?" Fritsch had continued with remarkable boldness, not having noticed the tightening of Hitler's jaw and the thinning of his lips. Fritsch's lack of perception and his audacity were justified, in that he had expected the other Generals in the room to back him up in light of the obvious military fiasco Hitler had proposed.

To his dismay they had done nothing but murmur their ineffectual complaints in the background. In their efforts to avoid displeasing Hitler by raising their voices against him, they had managed to displease him even *more*, by failing to raise a rousing cheer for his brilliant military initiative. The Fuhrer realized, as he'd looked around the room at them in contempt, that he'd lost faith in all his Generals' respective capacities to lead Germany's Armed Forces. Then and there he had resolved to take on sole command of them himself.

Before he could, however, he'd had to remove a few impediments. First and foremost—Fritsch and Blomberg, who had had the bare-faced audacity to speak out against him. Fritsch, only a few days before, had added insult to injury by making Hitler very unhappy on his birthday.

"Aren't you going to join in the celebrations?" Himmler had asked Fritsch when the Fuhrer's anniversary festivities were in full swing.

Fritsch had opened his office window to look down on the fun and frivolity going on in the street below, pausing for a moment, with undisguised contempt, to watch as the tickertape parade and brass band passed by. Its bevy of blonde-haired beauties all bounced about in their white shorts and shirts, giving an impressive display of calisthenics as they waved their banners that read:

"Herzlichen Gluckwunsch zum Geburstag unserer Fuhrer"

Which roughly translated as "Happy Birthday Hitler". Their gaudy display of good wishes led Fritsch to say with unconcealed scorn:

"Why on Earth would I want to celebrate that?"

It had been an astonishingly dangerous comment that Himmler had raced to report to Hitler, in the hope that Fritsch had finally done his dash.

But in the spirit of the day, the Birthday Boy had not been in the mood to take umbrage. Instead, he had decided to grant Fritsch a boon by not taking exception to his words, but by refraining from sending him a piece of birthday cake.

It was a magnanimous gesture for which Baron von Fritsch should have been eternally gratefully. But there he was at their military meeting, only a few days later, imposing on Hitler's good nature once more. His abuse of the Fuhrer's favours had pushed the issue too far. In a state of unmasked fury, Hitler had ordered Himmler to report to his office as soon as the meeting had been adjourned and the other Generals dispersed.

The Reichsfuhrer of the SS had promised to do just that, but had taken an inordinately slow thirty minutes to do so. At the end of which he'd rushed back into his Fuhrer's office flushed, flustered and full of excuses.

"Where have you *been?*" Hitler had demanded.

"I'm so sorry, sir, but Reichsprotektor von Neurath had a heart attack as soon as you walked out of the meeting. They say it was over the shock your war initiatives."

"Is he dead?"

"No, the ambulance officer thinks it was only a minor attack, but they've taken him to hospital to keep an eye on him overnight."

"Pity!" Hitler had replied, getting up from his desk. "I was just thinking it was about time we replaced him in our London embassy with someone more effective."

Deep in his own thoughts (not *one* of them concerned about his Foreign Minister's health), he'd started pacing around the room trying to come up with the ideal candidate for his replacement.

"What do you think of von Ribbentrop?" he'd suddenly swung round to ask Himmler, not having taken long to come up with one.

"I don't think much of him at all, to be honest, sir. Perhaps a little weak for such an important position? Besides, you must remember your initial and very valid reasons for keeping von Neurath on in his foreign ministry position. Retaining his services was imperative, you believed, to establish your respectability."

"Yes, yes . . . you're right, but the man *is* now sixty-five. No one will quibble over his retirement. Besides, I don't much like the fact that he had such a negative response to my plans for aggression. Right now I need someone who'll stick by me and not keel over each time I open my lips. At this delicate time in international relations our Foreign Minister must be competent . . . and preferably cardiac-arrest free. Especially because I intend to work him like a dog over the next few years."

"Very well, sir. I'll look into von Ribbentrop's credentials for you. Not that it's necessary," Himmler had quickly qualified, holding his hands up in mock surrender. "I've complete faith in your judgment."

"Yes, thank you Heinrich," Hitler had replied as he'd returned to his desk to continue putting his signature to the reams of documents that were on it. Having made his decision, he hadn't even bothered to look up when he had added, "Oh . . . and while you're at it, I want you to get rid of Fritsch and Blomberg."

An order, out of the blue, that had made Himmler baulk. The retirement of von Neurath didn't pose much of a problem, but to dispense with two men of such high calibre and public acclaim was a task not so easily achieved.

"Will I be able to cite any reason for their dismissals, sir?" he'd dared ask. "I'm afraid the dossiers Heydrich has provided on both men are impeccable. Nothing at all of a subversive nature in them, that I can use to warrant their removal."

"Well then use your imagination and find something that does. I'll back you up on whichever way you decide to go."

The way Himmler and Heydrich decided to go with Fritsch varied only a little from the scheme they had concocted to defame Field-Marshal von Blomberg. Hard to say really, which of the two Generals suffered the most as a result. Fritsch committing suicide over claims of homosexuality or grand old Blomberg resigning his position in complete disgrace at the accusation of lechery.

"Over which it's quite right that he take the blame. After all, Blomberg brought it *all* on himself," Himmler said derisively, when Canaris questioned him over the whole seedy affair.

"Whatever do you mean?" the head of the *Abwehr* asked, making no attempt to disguise his indignation.

"My dear Canaris, what do you expect when a man in such a high-profile position—a man of *sixty*, decides to make a laughing stock of himself *and* the Reich by marrying a girl of twenty?"

"I expect nothing of *the Reich*, but to respect their privacy. Who's business is it anyway?"

"It's the Fuhrer's duty to make such things his business. In his position, he can't afford to be held guilty by association on issues of morality."

"I hardly think that Blomberg's marriage would have put Hitler in a bad light. Age difference between a husband and wife hardly constitutes a case for impropriety—let alone an honourable man's humiliation."

"Her youth, Canaris, wasn't the issue, nor was the fact that the Commander-in-Chief of Germany's Armed Forces degraded himself by insisting on marrying his secretary. The fact that the girl turned out to be a former prostitute *did* come as a slight concern to the Fuhrer, however."

It also did to Canaris, who had had no idea that there had been a seamier side to the girl's career. A glaring gap in his database that was almost more annoying than the fact that Himmler had just won his point.

"However did you find out about it?" he asked, shaken by the discovery but determined not to let Himmler have the last word. "I do wonder sometimes, Heinrich, at your keen knowledge of Berlin's Red Light district. I can only hope that it's a matter of hearsay rather than first-hand experience. Ah, but of course it is. It will have come directly from Heydrich."

Having learned not to take the bait where Canaris' quips were concerned, Himmler simply nodded his abrupt confirmation.

"Heydrich's a good man," he said. "I rely on him implicitly."

Canaris could only reply with a smirk.

"Do you know . . . that's exactly what Blomberg used to say

about him?"

At which point Himmler threw in the towel, leaving Canaris' office without bothering to take exception, making a mental note to add yet another black mark against Canaris' name in that ever-thickening dossier he and Heydrich were compiling on him.

Canaris watched after him with loathing, waiting for the head of the SS to be out of earshot before he turned his attention back to the other man sitting in his office.

"Poor old Blomberg," he said to his deputy of the *Abwehr*, Colonel Hans Oster, who had wisely kept his silence while Canaris and Himmler had been battling it out with their war of words, amused that, as always when pitting himself against Canaris, Himmler had come off second best.

Now that his superior officers' skirmish was at an end, the ball was back in Oster's court.

"Oh please don't remind me of Blomberg. I feel so guilty about the whole wretched affair," he said. The memory of the tasteless part he'd been forced play in it, made Oster shift uncomfortably in his chair.

"Don't be ridiculous Hans . . . it wasn't your fault. You were under orders; and as your *friend*, Blomberg would have understood that. He knew someone had to be the bearer of his bad news."

What Canaris said was true, but it had been a hard call when Himmler had very deliberately and maliciously placed the onus of such an unpleasant duty on Oster's shoulders, insisting that the strikingly handsome ex-Cavalry officer act as courier for Field-Marshal Blomberg's letter of dismissal. Aware of Oster's close friendship with Blomberg and of his new wife's penchant for attractive young men, Himmler had made Oster travel all the way to Capri and interrupt their honeymoon to personally deliver it.

"This is a very delicate and sensitive matter, Colonel Oster," Himmler had said when he'd handed him Hitler's official dispatch. The letter, addressed to Blomberg and full of vile accusations, demanded his immediate resignation.

"I've every confidence that you'll handle the matter with the utmost courtesy and discretion."

And Oster had, but it had been an acutely sad and embarrassing affair. Having to watch his old friend, Blomberg, make a valiant effort to take it on the chin, a pretense at which the General had failed. Instead, he had collapsed into his chair as soon as he'd read it—mortified and in utter despair at its implication. All the while, having to bear the indignity and heartache of watching his blushing new bride flirt outrageously with Oster—the man who had delivered his means of disgrace.

The flirting had been much against Oster's wishes and completely without his provocation. In his keen embarrassment and fear of insulting both the woman and her husband if he dared reject her brazen advances, he'd had to stand by weakly and tolerate them, knowing that her aging, love-sick spouse was being forced to do the same.

"The whole damn thing was a set up in the first place!" Oster suddenly snarled at the sordid recollection.

Unruffled by this emotional outburst, Canaris calmly took a sip of his tea, pausing one moment longer to finish his shortbread biscuit before he responded.

"I know," he confirmed. "Do you honestly think that Field-Marshal Goering would have given the go-ahead for Blomberg's most unorthodox marriage, if he hadn't had his own agenda?"

"I was under the impression he had no choice but to approve it . . . that Blomberg demanded as much."

It was a comment that, in its naivety, had caused Canaris to raise a cynical eyebrow.

"*Nobody* demands anything of Hermann Goering and gets away with it, Hans. Signing his approval to the nuptials was just part of his game plan. There wasn't a hope in hell that Blomberg could push his little bride's secret through the system without causing one honey of a ruckus.

"What *I* can't understand is how a man as shrewd as Blomberg could act like such a simpleton! *Surely* he must have smelled a rat when Hitler himself volunteered to be a witness at *the wedding!* What else could it have been but a ploy to get the hands-on evidence they needed to use against him?"

"Yes, and I was the bunny who got to deliver it."

But Canaris was having no part of this rather self-centred bid for sympathy from Oster.

"You're going to have to toughen up, man," he said as he handed his deputy a cup of tea. A genteel gesture, by way of Royal Worcester fine-bone china, that seemed strangely at odds with the piece of hard line advice he was offering.

"You can't let yourself go soft on issues like this. Not when I'm certain that there are going to be many more of them to come."

The harsh reality of Canaris' prediction didn't come as much comfort, but the fact that they trusted each other enough to talk in such an openly derisive way about Hitler and his Third Reich, did. Over the past two years, he and Canaris had become the closest of confidantes and friends.

Their seeing eye-to-eye on the subject, however, had taken some doing.

Oster, the son of a Protestant pastor and an ardent Monarchist, had been anti-Nazi from the start, while Canaris had had to work his way round to it. Like Oster, he was a right-wing conservative by birth and nature, but it had taken him some time to see beyond Hitler's flattery and friendship. Having had his ego pumped up by the Fuhrer, on a day-to-day basis, had made it most difficult for Canaris to turn against him and to accept the fact that he didn't approve of either the man or his mission.

In a way, it had been easier for Oster, given that his ideals were all black and white, with nothing of the murky grey that clouded Canaris' views on the matter. As a Cavalry officer who had survived the Great War, Oster had come out of it with not only a debonair scar down his left cheek and a chest bedecked with medals, but with a conviction that it *must* remain "the War To End All Wars".

When Hitler, so very soon after, had proved him wrong in his urging of another, Oster had immediately dedicated himself to his downfall, but had to wait for some time for Canaris' chronic fear of Reinhard Heydrich and his disillusionment with Hitler to sink in.

Now, at last, Canaris was drowning in it. The shabby affair of Fritsch and Blomberg had pushed him to point X.

It was the catalyst that had Canaris commit himself to the German Resistance and become one of its leading lights. Both he and Oster placed themselves, at enormous personal risk, at the hub of a small, brave band of men within the *Abwehr*—that very heart of German Military Intelligence and pulse of the nation's warfare that put them in the perfect position to sabotage it. Now they officially considered themselves, albeit in secret, as conspirators against the Third Reich.

CHAPTER SIX

Of course, no one in the army had actually believed the shocking allegations made against Fritsch and Blomberg.

However, given that during their court cases, Hitler had decided to conduct a purge of a further sixteen of his Generals, it had seemed a hell of a lot safer for those left alive to lie low and keep their mouths shut. Using their heads (those not yet on the chopping block), they made sure that they didn't rub the Fuhrer the wrong way, or provide him with any excuse to rub *them* out for good.

This, effectively, rid the army ranks of all opposition to Hitler and cleared the way for him to proclaim himself Commander-in-Chief of the Armed Forces—a crowning achievement that added yet another powerful string to his bow and consolidated the position he already held as their Supreme Commander.

However, still not entirely convinced of the security of his position, Hitler provided himself with backup by promoting one of his best-tamed Generals to Baron von Fritsch's vacated position. Within two days he wiped clean all evidence of the convicted homosexual's existence by giving the Baron's old office a fresh coat of paint and a new plush pile carpet, scraping off Fritsch's good name from its door, to replace it, in gold letters, with the name of a far lesser man.

FIELD MARSHAL WALTHER VON BRAUCHITSCH
COMMANDER-IN-CHIEF OF THE ARMY

"Perhaps Brauchitsch will surprise us and shape up to be a man of substance," said the Chief of Army General Staff, General Ludwig Beck, as he accepted the glass of cognac Canaris was offering him.

"How very optimistic of you, Beck," Canaris replied, deeply depressed at the state of affairs. "You know as well as I do that the man's a fence-sitter. He's borrowed so much money from Hitler that he's now inextricably bound to him. What does it matter whether it's through desire or debt when the result's the same? He professes to be an anti-Nazi, but I don't believe a word of it. He's just like the rest of them. They're all criminals . . . every last one of them hovering round Hitler."

There were few men to whom Canaris could speak so freely. General Beck, as the primary military malcontent in Germany and the recognized head of the Resistance, was one of them. A man of the highest calibre, who Canaris knew would keep his confidence and agree, one hundred percent, with everything he had to say.

This time, however, the head of the *Abwehr's* frankness had worried Beck. He was afraid that his friend, the Little Admiral, might be sailing into dangerous waters.

"Be careful Canaris. You, of all people, should know that loose lips sink ships. It's not like you to be so unguarded. Take your own advice and trust no one . . . not even me. With the best intentions, every *one* of us is capable of betrayal under the pressure of the Gestapo. Perhaps if you feel so badly about what's going on, you should resign and get out while the going's good."

Canaris paused to consider the possibility, then abruptly rejected it.

"Would that I could . . . but I can't. If I step down, Heydrich will be my successor, In which case we can all kiss Germany goodbye."

"Oh hardly!" Beck said casually. "I can handle Heydrich."

This flippant remark had Canaris turn to him in alarm, his piercing, intelligent eyes full of concern at the man's lack of insight.

"With all due respect, Beck, *no one* can handle Heydrich. He's a brutal fanatic with whom not a single man can deal in mutual confidence. Not even Hitler."

"You exaggerate. When all's said and done, Heydrich's just an upstart hanging on Himmler's coat tails."

"But *that's* where you're wrong," Canaris jumped in to say, leveling an accusing finger at his friend. "It's very much the other way round, even though Himmler doesn't know it as yet."

At this interesting juncture, Canaris got up from his armchair and walked over to the fireplace. Turning his back on Beck, he stretched out his hands to warm them over the flames. The talk of Heydrich, as always, had made him go cold all over.

"Do you know," he said, "that Hitler doesn't daunt me in the least, because underneath his madness, there's passion and a warmth of sorts that can be got at. But Heydrich is impregnable. Sometimes I think that he's not a man at all . . . just the living, breathing embodiment of evil. In all the years I've known him, I haven't detected a trace of human frailty in him.

"When you get the chance Beck, just take a good look at Heydrich's face, and a closer one at his eyes. They're peculiar. There's no light in them—not a hint of compassion. And you know, of course, that he's just living for the day I die!"

"Now you're being melodramatic and absolutely absurd, Willie. Everybody knows the man idolizes you. He makes no attempt to hide the fact, and quite frankly, bores the socks off us all by constantly singing your praises."

"Ah, but that's the beauty of it, don't you see. Where I'm concerned, he's got the Uriah Heep routine down pat—obsequious, crawling creature that he is. Just a blood-sucking leech in need of a host," Canaris said with a shudder, having created for himself much too vivid a mental picture.

"The man latched himself on to me years ago with the sole intention of bleeding me dry. Until he does, I know I'm safe. He'll never harm me or let me out of his sight because, for the time being, I'm his life-line. But he'll be finished with me soon. I can sense it. And when he *is*, he'll make short work of disposing of me."

"If you weren't sounding so deadly serious, Willie, I'd find this laughable."

But to Canaris' way of thinking there was nothing funny at all about his nemesis, Reinhard Heydrich.

"I tell you quite honestly Beck, that I can stand in a room with Hitler, listening to his maniacal carry-on; *knowing* what a dangerous and volatile man he is, and yet not bat an eye. But just *one* phone call from Heydrich . . . and I break into a sweat. The man terrifies me."

"But if that's the way you feel, why do you continue to extend him the hospitality you do? Heydrich's in and out of your home the whole time. Everyone presumes that you're the greatest of friends."

"Keeping up appearances, that's all. Let's just say that we tease each other with our so-called friendship *and* hold it over each other's head."

"I don't understand," Beck admitted as took a puff of his cigar and flicked the surplus ash from its tip into his glass ashtray.

"Then perhaps you can understand this. It's got to the stage that I can't make a single move, either in my professional or personal life, without having Heydrich at my heel. He keeps a dossier on me and everyone in the *Abwehr*. I've no doubt that he monitors my every phone call, my every dinner conversation—my every trip to the bathroom.

"You say, he's in and out of my home all the time? Let me assure you that it's no longer by invitation. My family and I have moved house now *three* times trying to put some space between ourselves and the Heydrich clan. And each time, within a matter of a few days, he and his family have moved to the *same* street, the *same* block, within no more than two or three houses walking distance. Even my wife has had her fill of him and grown suspicious about his zealous attentions.

"He's in and out my door on the pretext of a social visit at least five times a week. Coming in these days, I might add, without even bothering to knock."

"*Good God* . . . I had no idea," Beck cut in, genuinely amazed by the deplorable situation and in full sympathy with Canaris for having to suffer it. "With friends like that, who needs enemies? I have to admit, though, that I'm relieved to an extent. I always thought rather less of you for aligning yourself with him. I didn't realize that it wasn't by choice . . . that you were living in a constant state of fear."

"That I am, but I refuse to give Heydrich the satisfaction of knowing it. But it's getting harder and harder to cover up. Like any animal he's got a keen sense of fear—can sniff it out anywhere; and *I know* he's deriving great delight in seeing me sweat. It's become a kind of game between us. One that I've no intention of losing. For my part, I've found it best to tackle it with a sense of humour. If there's one thing Heydrich can't bear, it's to be laughed at."

With an amused, triumphant smile, Canaris walked back to his desk, opened its top drawer and pulled from it a rather tawdry ceramic of the Three Wise Monkeys.

"It's my talisman to ward off evil," he explained as he placed it very deliberately front and centre on his desk.

"See No Evil, Hear No Evil, Speak No Evil," he said as, from left to right, he tapped each china monkey on the head. "I make a point of putting it on show whenever Heydrich walks in my door. I find it keeps everything in proportion and, for the short time he's here . . . our young Heydrich in his place. His reaction to it gives me no end of pleasure . . . and drives *him* crazy."

By the time he'd finished filling Beck in on Heydrich's agenda, Canaris was sure that Beck had got the full picture. The Chief of the Army General Staff left his office fully equipped to paint it over again, in full colour, for the edification of his fellow Resistance workers.

Logic told Beck that it was not only Canaris, but *all* of them who were under the close scrutiny of the SS Intelligence Department (the SD). They had all become a strategic part of the odd little game that *it* and the Gestapo were playing.

Both of these departments of Himmler's were quite aware that there was conspiracy in the wind and had a fair idea from which general direction the stench of treason was blowing.

Yet they were content to let its culprits roam free. With the calm cunning of skilled predators, they didn't bother to pounce on their every quarry, knowing that to allow the small fish to swim free would inevitably lead them to the big fish of the circuit—men who were well worth the reeling in and would make for far better eating.

Being comparatively new to the game of conspiracy to commit treason, Canaris was still in the process of acquainting himself with those other 'Big Fish' in the Resistance, just as Heydrich was, no doubt, analyzing their respective potential and capacity to bring about the downfall of the Third Reich.

Heydrich was putting each of those suspected of high treason under his microscope, to probe for weak spots to use against them, while Canaris, like any good German, was compelled to make a precise account of them in writing—for the record and his future reference, itemizing in his diary every one of his observations about them. Weighing up the pros and cons of their involvement in his schemes, he made sure to cross the "ts" and dot the "is" in regard to their integrity and usefulness.

TUESDAY, JANUARY 6, 1938

<u>**Colonel Hans Oster:**</u> *44 yo. Ex-cavalry. Distinguished service in 14-18. Dismissed from Army in '32. Scandalous affair with wife of fellow officer. Joined Abwehr, under Patzig, straight after the Night of the Long Knives in retribution for the murder of his friend—Major-General Kurt von Bredon.*

First impression—made good one. Tall, slender, handsome, but a little affected in his wearing of the "fashionable" monocle. I liked him, but wasn't sure at first that I could totally trust him. There's no doubt in my mind that he's a man of honour, but I have a concern about his lack of natural guile. Suspect that without it, he's not tailor-made for a career in espionage.

Can't help but admire his courage, but am wary of his rather open temperament and his eagerness to speak his mind. He gets much too much delight in drawing quick, dangerous decisions. But perhaps I can work with him on this.

Any downside to his character, however, has been outweighed by his active participation in saving Baron von Fritsch's life, albeit for the short term. The quick thinking and decisive action Oster took to trip up the Gestapo in their secret plans to murder Fritsch in his home convinced me of Oster's dedication to the Resistance.

His resourcefulness was exemplary, and all the more creditable given that it was done with split second timing. Organizing that impromptu army training exercise on the grounds of Fritsch's Estate to protect him from being murdered was a master stroke—not only scaring off the Gestapo, but putting Hitler right out. Making him have to wait, just that little bit longer, to see Fritsch to his grave.

So the scales tilt in Oster's favour. Rash, but forever optimistic, the man never allows a setback to become a problem. In this, he is a great asset. Such men are needed in this difficult and very depressing duty of ours.

To this end, I have put him in charge of The Abwehr's Central Office—Department Z, with a view to making it the centre of our Resistance operations. I have every confidence in leaving him at the helm whenever I'm obliged to travel overseas in the discharging of my other duties.

TUESDAY, FEBRUARY 23, 1938

<u>Colonel-General Ludwig Beck:</u> *58 yo. Chief of the Army General Staff. Main military player. Recognized head of the Resistance and nominated Head of State at Hitler's overthrow.*

Career officer and brilliant student of military affairs. Distinction lies in work as military historian and instructor, rather than as man of action. Soldier of the old school, liked and trusted by all, but criticized broadly as being an intellectual rather than a strong leader. Personally, I feel that his strategies are brave, but not always well judged.

Right wing. Detests Bolshevism. Noble, thoughtful and hard working, he's thwarted somewhat by a nervous disposition. You can see it in his face—in his bulbous brown eyes and that tic in his left cheek that works like a fury whenever he's put on the spot. Tends to ponder every point and worry about the moral rights and wrongs of any decision he needs to make—his delays often negate their effectiveness.

His authority with friends and business associates rests solely on his undisputed integrity. His chief weapon—reason! Which I fear will be useless when virtually every member of the High Command is subject to Hitler's complete lack of it.

There's one plus . . . Hitler appears to be a little in awe of Beck because he commands such great respect within army ranks.

Huge disagreement between them last week when Hitler demanded that Beck replace his standing defensive plans with his Fuhrer's more updated ones for aggression. Wouldn't be surprised if Beck resigns in protest. Much admire the stand he took against Hitler on this.

If he does resign and make himself free of all War Ministry constraints, he'll be able to work at circumventing the war from outside the High Command. His input could prove invaluable.

TUESDAY, MARCH 2, 1938

Ulrich von Hassell: *57 yo. Another gentlemanly right wing member of the Resistance who doesn't approve of the New Regime and has dedicated his life to its overthrow. Friend of Beck's and married to Grand Admiral Tirpitz's daughter. Good pedigree. Highly cultured and distinguished. Possibly handsome in his younger years, but now a little world-weary and rusty round the edges. Has remarkable capacity to stay calm in all circumstances and to make due allowance for all things and all men. A character trait that I admire immensely and wish played a more prominent part in my own very cynical nature.*

Hassell's a career diplomat and has been German Ambassador in Rome for several years. Soon to be replaced, I suspect, when Ribbentrop is officially appointed as Foreign Minister. He'll be recalled to Berlin, but I don't think offered another embassy, which will come as a blow to his ambitions. I know, for a fact, that he was planning to use his position as Ambassador to modify Hitler's demands in any way he could. But now it looks like he's not going to get the chance. He's not exactly in Hitler's good books. He and his wife have been far too outspoken in their open opposition to him while in Italy.

I suppose it just didn't occur to Hassell that he wasn't permitted to take such liberties any more. That that freedom of speech to which he'd always been entitled, as an Hanoverian aristocrat, was no longer his right. (Just one of the many perks that the Third Reich has ripped from the guts of Germany)

I'm crossing my fingers, though, that he'll retain his diplomatic status and his seat on the Board for the Central European Economic Conference. It'll give him direct access to an enormous amount of confidential information which will prove most beneficial to us.

TUESDAY, MARCH 16, 1938

Dr. Carl Goerdeler: *54 yo. Friend of Beck's and Hassell's. Key player in Resistance. Comes from a distinguished Prussian family. Father—Judge in Prussian government.*

Dr. Carl himself is lawyer and municipal administrator. Has a taste for economics. Is imposing in appearance with his pin-stripe suits and slicked back silver hair, but would make for a better businessman if he practised his poker-face and weren't so obnoxiously passionate about his every cause. His eyes are full of fire, enthusiasm and vulnerability, which is a dead giveaway. I fear he'd fail miserably under interrogation.

Much like myself, not averse to Nazi Party at first. Was Nationalist and disapproved of Versailles Treaty and unstable post-war democracy. Mayor of Leipzig when Hitler was made Chancellor. Actually assisted Regime as economic advisor at the time.

On the bright side, his intransigent nature had him turn quickly and violently against Hitler.

Heated argument with Nazi authorities in Leipzig about the removal of a statue of Felix Mendelssohn from the town square. Being a Jewish composer, the Nazis saw fit to destroy it. In doing so, actively disobeying Goerdeler's orders, as Mayor, to leave it intact for the sake of history and future generations.

Needless to say, it's now a pile of rubble—disgusting! Goerdeler, very commendably, handed in his resignation in protest.

Ever since, has been actively campaigning to overthrow Hitler—none too cautiously I'm afraid. He's no coward and makes no attempt to camouflage his opposition to the Reich. His only cover being the position he holds as a representative for the firm of BOSCH. At least it facilitates his constant— and very necessary—moving in and out of Germany.

Although admirable, the man has a big mouth—is moody and impatient. His plain dealing is often indiscreet. His political ideas—albeit astute at times, are often absurdly theoretical and spilled out to anyone and everyone who'll listen. The Gestapo, I've no doubt, are all ears.

Goerdeler presents a very real danger to both himself and the conspiracy as a whole; but is nonetheless a valuable man whose conviction is true. However, it has come to my attention that other members of Resistance now actively avoid his company because of its ever-present threat to their cover and lives.

TUESDAY, MARCH 30, 1938

Hans Gisevius: *34yo. Comes from family of civil servants. As lawyer, joined the Prussian political police in '33, Was initially assigned to Gestapo, but withdrew himself on discovering the nature of their work. Resigned after Night of Long Knives massacre. Since then has made it his business to know everybody and act as Liaison officer for the Resistance.*

He's close to Goerdeler and Hjalmar Schacht (President of the Reichsbank and Hitler's Minister for Economic Affairs). Good future contact there! Schacht, at the moment, is at serious loggerheads with Hermann Goering and greatly disillusioned with Hitler. There's a chance we might be able to recruit his formidable services later down the track.

I've heard rumours that, like the rest of us, he's done a great deal to facilitate the escape of many Jews from Germany. As I and Oster have done repeatedly, he's provided them with the necessary false passports and currency exchange to make their departure possible.

Must be taking a great deal of courage on Schacht's part to manage it, though, being the political entity he is. Especially when he's got Goering breathing down his neck, just waiting for an excuse to flush him out of Hitler's tight clique.

Gisevius has benefited greatly from their association. Schacht has arranged for a sinecure for him, attached to a factory in Bremen. This has left Gisevius free to conduct liaison on a full time basis and to play general go-between with the various wings of the Resistance.

Well-placed, I think, being the calm, coolheaded man he is. Much the legal type in appearance. Short, stocky build, with wafer-thin blonde hair and rather expressionless green eyes. Terribly near-sighted, which accounts for those black, heavy-rimmed glasses he wears. They make him look as plain as a pikestaff, but oddly enough, lend him an air of distinction.

All in all an effective, highly intelligent man. Shrewd and extremely ambitious, despite what appears to be his rather quiet, unassuming demeanour. As the exact opposite to his friend Goerdeler, I get the itchy feeling that Gisevius hides a great deal, and has mastered the art of keeping his feelings to himself. Which makes him perfect for our needs. I intend to appoint him Abwehr Chief of Special Projects.

Have not as yet got close to him as a friend and suspect that I may never do so. There is an implacable, humourless streak in his nature that appears to be impervious to my charms, such as they are. Oh well . . . can't win 'em all!

TUESDAY, APRIL 6, 1938

<u>*Hans von Dohnanyi:*</u> *36yo. Lawyer. Son of celebrated Austrian composer Ernst von Dohnanyi. Social background good. His family are all members*

of Germany's intellectual elite. This rather remarkable young man was anti Hitler and National Socialism from beginning, but was smart enough to take advantage of both to manoeuvre himself into a position to combat them.

First impression—singularly unimpressed with his scruffy appearance and by what seems to me to be a studied innocuousness. Has a lean and hungry look about him that doesn't quite tally with the world of privilege and over-indulgence from which he hails. His mode of dressing, along with other aspects of his bland persona, work in active defiance of it.

He looks much like the personification of a coat-hanger in his "off-the-rack" suits. Hideous, outdated outfits that hang from his stooped shoulders two sizes too big. His tall, scrawny physique and concave chest go nowhere near padding them out; and give him more the look of a derelict than a renegade from high society.

With his prematurely receding hairline, unprepossessing rimless glasses and protruding (almost duck-like) upper lip, he's not much to look at, but, by God . . . has he got a mind!

Despite his every effort not to stand out in the crowd, this man is really something out of the box! As lawyer, did brief stint in Reich Ministry of Justice (which ironically included the laws governing treason)! Brilliant at his craft. Appointed State Prosecutor in Hamburg at very early age. When Hitler became Chancellor, Dohnanyi returned to Berlin, when only thirty-one, to become assistant to Hitler's Minister of Justice—Franz Guertner.

Used his influence with Guertner to stay in this position of confidence at the Ministry for as long as possible. Gave him access to top secret Nazi files, with their extremely precise accounts (photographs inclusive) of tortures inflicted at their concentration camps. He began immediately to secretly stockpile these files to be used as evidence of war crimes.

Oster is completely bowled over by this man and his dedication to the Cause. Has volunteered to help Dohnanyi with his extremely dangerous work. Dohnanyi has convinced him that the acquiring of written proof of Nazi atrocities is of the utmost importance. Second only to the imperative disposal of Hitler. That in a court of law, the files will be the only means of achieving final justice and of exonerating us all of treason.

Unfortunately, Dohnanyi has just been appointed Judge at the Supreme Court of Leipzig. Much against his will, has decided to accept the position *(at least temporarily). He feels that for one so young to knock back such a marvelous and unprecedented offer might put him under suspicion.*

In this, I trust his judgment, as I suspect I will learn to do in all things. I hope to retain his services on a more full time basis in the Abwehr, early next year. The Resistance will need a strong, legal advisor like Hans von Dohnanyi to help validate the Cause and keep it within legal parameters.

TUESDAY, APRIL 13, 1938

<u>*Pastor Dietrich Bonhoeffer:*</u> *Now here's a turn up for the books! Fascinating man, dedicated to the downfall of Hitler almost as much as he is to God. Which I suppose stands to reason—that as His modern day disciple, he's duty-bound to give both good and evil their due, and commit himself to fight the good fight in God's name.*

32yo. Friend of Dohnanyi's. Dohnanyi's married to his sister, Christina. His father was a pastor from the court of Kaiser Wilhelm 11. Young Dietrich followed in his footsteps and is himself a pastor and Lecturer of Theology at Berlin University. Has already attracted a large following of young, like-minded philosophers.

Which is no surprise, when I, myself, find him the most compelling of men. Gentle, but full of life and energy, he exudes the most amazing aura of "goodness". And manages to do it without even the slightest hint of sanctimony. One feels better for having made his acquaintance and is drawn to him, again and again, in the hope of continuing it.

There is no doubt in my mind that he is a natural leader of men, despite the fact that his mild countenance and charming, convivial manner might initially have one think otherwise.

In a marked departure from most other German Protestant pastors, Bonhoeffer was never enthusiastic about Hitler's ascension to power. Two days after Hitler was made Chancellor, he went so far as to voice his strong opposition on radio. Warning the German people of the danger and pure blasphemy of giving their souls to a man who sought nothing less than their total worship of him.

Needless to say, the German authorities cut off his broadcast, midway through his address. Bonhoeffer thinking to make himself scarce at the sound of screeching police sirens in the street, not long after. Left for England for two years, not exactly a wanted man, but most definitely under a cloud of suspicion.

Became an adherent of Mahatma Gandhi's passive resistance philosophy. Was on his way to India to meet the man, in person, for first-hand tuition in the theory, when his superiors in the German Confessing Church talked him into returning to Berlin to take over a seminary there.

Soon removed from that position because he continued to make use of it to speak out freely against Hitler. Being behind a pulpit gave him no protection from the Gestapo, who'd by then added his name to their "Keep Close Tabs On" list.

With them hot on his heels, he left for the USA. Convinced of Germany's moral decline and concerned that if not imprisoned, he'd face a fate far worse, by being drafted into the Reich Army.

It was only a brief stay though. Didn't think much of himself for running away. His conscience had him return to Germany within weeks. Despite his very deep religious convictions, he's not much of a believer in turning the other cheek. Much prefers to stand and fight.

Hitler made quick work of silencing him by declaring all his writings and public statements illegal, which made all those who'd been keen to read and listen to them, guilty by association. Thereby, urging the general public and even his most avid of devotees to give him a wide berth.

With Bonhoeffer ostensibly ostracized from society, it must have come as a surprise to all Berliners, when I offered him a position with the Abwehr. Dohnanyi organized it on the premise that Bonhoeffer's extensive traveling would give him much insight into the internal politics of Scandinavia, England and the USA.

Which is quite true. I have every intention of sending him to all those countries to warn them of Germany's political situation!

At this point, Canaris yawned and closed the book on his commentary. He was tired and it was time for bed. Tomorrow was going to be a big day.

CHAPTER SEVEN

A big day that he hoped would bring good news. But it didn't.

"You know, sometimes I wonder about the English. I'm convinced they've all got a screw loose," Canaris said with unadulterated contempt, as he handed the morning newspaper to Colonel Erwin Lahousen and pointed, in disbelief, at its headline:

BRITISH PM—
ADOLF HITLER'S
GREATEST FAN!

Its subheading following on with a direct quote from the Rt. Hon. Neville Chamberlain himself:

"I have nothing but the highest regard for Adolf Hitler.
Here is a man, I believe, to be relied upon when he gives his word."

"Famous *last* ones from Chamberlain—*the fool!*" Canaris lashed out in white-faced rage as he flung himself down into his armchair. His fury was wholly justified given all the death-defying efforts he and the German Resistance had made, over the last few months, to warn England and the rest of Europe of Hitler's plans for all out aggression.

He was incensed. Not only had the English chosen to ignore his attempts to help them, but had humiliated him in the process by underestimating his status and clout within Germany. Disregarding entirely his wise, well-informed counsel in regard to Hitler's campaign for world domination.

Every last one of its parliamentarians had chosen, in turn, to consult only briefly with the series of envoys he'd sent to England, before summarily dismissing their advice and pleas that they take a firm stand against Hitler before it was too late.

KILL THE FUHRER ⚡

These included: Sir Robert Vansittart (permanent Under-Secretary of British Foreign Office), Neville Chamberlain (Prime Minister), Lord Halifax (British Foreign Secretary), Sir Neville Henderson (British Ambassador to Berlin) and Winston Churchill who, to his credit, had shown just a tad more concern as to the validity of the information, but still had done nothing constructive about it.

And now they had just capped off the insult by sending that idiot Chamberlain, equipped with his umbrella and total lack of political insight, to share a cup of tea and a cozy chat with the Reich's Chancellor. Emerging from their little tete-a-tete, all bright-eyed and bushy-tailed, to declare to the world what a good ol' boy Hitler was!

As far as Canaris was concerned there was no excuse for such political ineptitude. Their refusal to believe what was right there before their eyes—what they had been *told* point-blank—not only smacked of sheer stupidity, but of a certain patronizing condescension in regard to Germany's capacity to achieve such inconceivable feats.

At this thought . . . the belittling of his own beloved country and the personal slight that they had thrown at him . . . Canaris kicked out hard at the log that had just tumbled from the fireplace, sending its charred, red-hot embers hurtling across his office floor.

"There's no point in taking the Brits' shortsightedness to heart, Willie. You mustn't see it as a personal affront," Lahousen leant forward in his chair to say. "You've got to remember that for all his appalling faults, Hitler is nevertheless the consummate politician. At least that's how outsiders must see him—a veritable powerhouse of positivity and energy. You have to admit that, in the short time he's been in office, he's achieved the most phenomenal things.

"There's no way that anyone, other than those in his intimate circle, would know any better . . . would see through his bluff or even conceive of his *true* self and *true* intentions, as you do. But they will soon enough. Take it from someone who knows."

Having had first-hand experience of Hitler's piranha-like territorial expansion policy, Colonel Erwin Lahousen knew what he was talking about. As a member of Austria's Imperial Army and the head of Austrian Intelligence, he had quite recently not only lost his job, but his entire country's identity. Overnight, the rug had been pulled from under Austria's feet, and whatever had been left of Hitler's charm had been destroyed along with it. Such was the *Anschluss*.[9]

Soon after, Lahousen had been informed that the head of German Intelligence, Rear Admiral Wilhelm Canaris, was en route to Austria to take over his command. On the day he was due to arrive, Lahousen had stood rigidly at attention behind his desk—tight-lipped and determined not to thrust out his hand in salute when this Canaris character deigned to turn up.

It had not occurred to him that this sight-unseen usurper— Wilhelm Canaris—would become one of his closest friends. That as he prepared himself to give the newcomer the cold-shoulder, listening belligerently to the sound of his footsteps coming down the corridor, he would instead end up smiling when Canaris casually popped his head around his office door and said:

"Umm . . . I don't suppose you'd mind if I shared your desk for a while?"

Lahousen learned very quickly what everyone else already knew about Canaris—that it was impossible not to like him! Canaris' charm and tact had made the transition all the easier for him. And now Lahousen felt it was up to him to return the favour and make this most recent of disappointments easier on Canaris.

But his attempts to cheer up his friend had not worked. Unmoved by his words, Canaris was still sitting dispirited and brooding in his chair.

And little wonder when, for him, this past year had been an hour-by-hour, day-by-day, nerve-racking excursion into fear. Risking all—*his* and his fellow conspirators' lives—by sending delegate after delegate to London in the hope of averting a worldwide catastrophe. Canaris himself had flown to Hungary in an effort to stymie Ribbentrop's attempts to get Hungary to hold hands with Hitler while making their mutual claim on Czechoslovakian territory.

And this had been Canaris' reward . . . to fly back to Berlin to find that Prime Minister Chamberlain had just winged his way out of it, having wined, dined and befriended the man who planned to destroy Europe.

"Here, drink this. It'll make you feel better," Lahousen said as he handed Canaris a brandy and offered him a cigarette, the latter of which he declined.

"Thank you, no. I don't smoke," he said – despite his depression, looking up with a mischievous grin to add, "It'll stunt my growth."

Lahousen laughed. This was Canaris at his best - always capable of cutting through the crap with a quick one-liner.

"You *should* you know," he replied, hesitating before he snapped shut his silver cigarette case on the off-chance that Canaris might change his mind. "With the constant political and emotional strain you're under, I think you could allow yourself just that one small transgression. It might help."

Canaris thought it unlikely, now that that constant political and emotional strain was at an all time high. Now that he was beginning to believe that the Resistance was coming unstuck.

At least, that was how it appeared on the surface. His own hands-on plans to save the world had just failed and his fellow conspirators had been running up against much the same sort of bad luck.

General Beck, having resigned as Chief of Army General Staff as predicted, had been making himself useful by canvassing all the other Generals of High Command. As yet, he'd had little to no success in enlisting their support. Which was most disappointing when he'd hoped and half expected to secure their mass resignation in protest against Hitler's "*Operation Green*" —his plan to subdue and divvy up Czechoslovakia to facilitate his claims on the Sudetenland.

It was an issue over which Prime Minister Chamberlain had been most obliging.

"I partially agree with Hitler's claims on the Sudetenland," he'd said. "In fact, I've committed myself to do everything in my power to help Czech President, Eduard Benes, make up his mind to that end. *Starting* with renouncing all Allied support if he refuses to comply with Hitler's wishes."

It was no surprise that Benes felt basely betrayed, even less of a surprise that, as a patriot and a man of honour, he'd refused to give in and simply give up his country.

"No!" he'd said, shocking Chamberlain with his unreasonable attitude.

Just as much of a shock was Hitler, who had turned on the British Prime Minister in an unholy rage for having failed to talk

Benes around.

Chamberlain had never seen a man crack like that before. Snapping, like a dry twig, out of the realms of normality into a bout of uncontrolled schizophrenia. The Fuhrer, with his glassy, blue eyes glazed over in a kind of unearthly detachment had abandoned all sense of restraint and decorum.

"*You*, sir," he'd screeched, "are a walking, talking example of English supreme incompetence! Whatever made me think that I could rely on you to negotiate on my behalf? From here on in, I'll take matters into my own hands. And you can be assured that I'll see to it that Czechoslovakia is *crushed!*"

At which point in the conversation, Chamberlain had picked up his briefcase and umbrella and left the room. He had not cared for Hitler's tone.

"The solution to the Sudeten question," Hitler had yelled after him, never failing to have the final word, "was going to be my *last* territorial demand in Europe."

Not only was Hitler the consummate politician, but he was fast becoming the consummate liar. In a fit of pique over Chamberlain's incompetence, he ordered General Erwin von Witzleben to arrange a military parade through Berlin as a show of strength and threat in regard to those hitherto meagre territorial demands of his. It would let the world know, now that he'd been put out, that those demands might just extend a little bit further. His tanks and troops rumbled through the city streets with three definite objectives in mind.

1. To psyche his people into backing his grand plans for aggression. Displaying his military wherewithal to bolster their courage and confidence in his prospect of success.
2. To make Chamberlain, Britain and the world, as a whole, regret how ineffectual they had been at giving him what he wanted, and to let them know how ineffectual they were going to be at stopping him taking it by force.
3. To frighten the living daylights out of President Benes until he got the hell out of Czechoslovakia and gave it up for grabs.

However, to Hitler's surprise and fury, he failed on all three counts. Instead, he stirred enough pride in Benes to have him dig in more defiantly, and enough indignation among the English to have them straighten their shoulders and stiffen their upper lips. While the anger he aroused among his own people at the suggestion of a second World War had them actually *boo* out loud in the streets; still suffering and struggling, as they were, to overcome the first.

The angriest had been General Witzleben himself. Having organized and led the military parade as he'd been ordered, he had come within an inch of pulling his pistol from its holster and shooting Hitler dead.

As he had marched past the Reich's Chancellery balcony, he'd had to grit his teeth to stop himself from doing it. Instead, and very much against the grain, turning his head mid-Goose-Step, to salute the man with his little black moustache. Wondering how long it was going to take the fanatic to hurtle them back into a second round of global bedlam.

Having lacked the courage to pull the trigger, Witzleben had decided, then and there, to commit himself to the Resistance and to make himself available to stand at the head of the German Military if Canaris and his crew managed to pull off a successful coup.

In such a precarious political climate, the time had been ripe for conspiracy and a certain excitement and expectation of success had swelled the ranks of the Resistance. The prospect of toppling Hitler from power was a very real possibility.

Real, but soon quashed by Hitler's own *bona fide* string of successes.

With the fuse burning on the powder keg that was Europe at that time, it was Benito Mussolini who turned the tide in the Fuhrer's favour. He had suddenly decided to put his finger in the pie by offering to mediate with the Czechs. Doing them in the eye, as had everybody else, by presenting Hitler with the Munich Agreement that had been secretly prepared by Hermann Goering.

"German expansion in central Europe is a normal and natural thing," Chamberlain said, having read the contract's fine print and signed his name to it.

He knew that all that mattered to Britain was to stop Germany's expansion to the West and to sacrifice the Czechs as his means of doing it. Calmly writing off a country that he saw as being too small and remote to warrant England risking war with Germany. His sentiments had echoed those of Hermann Goering, who had put it a little more succinctly in one of his speeches:

*"The Czechs are a miserable pygmy of a race,
and their country—a petty segment of Europe."*

As such, Czechoslovakia was partitioned—Poland and Hungary snapping up their desired portions of its territory, while Benes made his getaway from it. He'd resigned and disappeared into exile just before German troops stormed into the streets of Prague. Bored, as they had quickly become, with the limitations of simply occupying the Sudetenland.

For Chamberlain, this streamlined rezoning program-cum-outrageous piece of militarized theft had meant new hope and a brief renewal of his friendship with the Fuhrer:

"Peace in our time," was his statement to the press. His sentiments were reprinted in newspapers around the world—that very world that was teetering on the brink of Armageddon.

"There's no way that anyone will listen to us now," Canaris said, having sat for some time staring in disillusionment at the flames in the fireplace. "No General in his right mind will knock back the guts and glory of such an outright military success. And Hitler's just handed it to them on a platter, with no fuss and no fighting! Which means that he's done much more than just win Czechoslovakia. He's won over High Command . . . and *that* was the bigger of the two battles for him. Without High Command's support, we haven't a chance of bringing him down."

Leaning forward, Canaris cupped his chin in his hands and let out a heavy sigh of defeat.

"I've failed, Lahousen . . . failed miserably. I just don't know what else I can do. No matter which way we turn, we run up against a brick wall. Every lead we get turns out to be a dead end. Poor old Beck and Hassell have had no joy in talking the Generals around, and now they've lost their opportunity to do so.

"Reichsbank President Schacht has finally pushed his luck too far with Hitler; he's been dismissed and disappeared to India. Our great white hope General Witzleben has been transferred to a command in Kassel, which means that Hitler's either got rid of, or effectively distanced himself from, every major player in the conspiracy - every man who was strong enough to question his authority.

"Without them around, High Command is his for the taking. And he's gone right ahead and taken it, leaving it in the hands of those three dangerous toadies of his—Generals Keitel, Jodl and Warlimont. Heaven help us . . . *and* our poor Germany.

"And as if that isn't bad enough, I've just had word that the Minister of Justice—Judge Roland Freisler—and his side-kick, Dr. Roeder, have now come into the picture. The two sadistic maniacs have set their sights on Dohnanyi and singled him out for Gestapo interrogation. *Damn it all!* I *knew* that he and Oster compiling those files was a dodgy business. All hell's going to break loose if Freisler and Roeder find out what they've been up to. I can only hope that they've both had the sense to store them somewhere safe and to have covered their tracks.[10] My fault . . . I shouldn't have let them do it . . . I *shouldn't* have."

"Willie, you've got to calm down," Lahousen said, suddenly concerned for his friend.

The pressure was starting to tell. Canaris, as always, had taken it upon himself to bear the full brunt of responsibility which, to Lahousen's way of thinking, was much too heavy a burden to place on such small shoulders.

After all, Canaris was a delicate instrument, both in physical stature and character. His personality was one of pure intellect. A man so finely tuned, so *at one* with the ways of the world, that every member of the Resistance had come to rely on him. They depended on his inner strength, intelligence and shrewd intuition to steer their course and help them navigate their way through the myriad of dangerous, death-defying intrigues in which they were involved. The head of SS Intelligence, Reinhard Heydrich, had put it in a nutshell when he'd described Canaris as having "the cunning of a snake with the purity of a dove."

Looking at him now, Lahousen could see that this same clever, complex, highly-strung man was feeling the strain. He was all wrung out and worried sick about the wellbeing of his friends. He couldn't rest until he'd made sure they were safe.

Such a paradox it was that a man standing only 5'3" tall, should be expected to have the courage of Hercules. This gentle intellectual who above all else hated and abominated violence, and therefore hated and abominated Hitler and everything for which he stood. This had made him duty-bound, despite the odds, to make a stand against him.

It was a modern-day David and Goliath scenario with much less chance of success when, in lieu of a slingshot, Canaris was hoping to bring down the mighty Hitler and his legions with the help of only a very small band of brave men. It was a dedication to duty and God that left no doubt in Lahousen's mind that Canaris was, and would ever be, a truly superior human being.

"Take heart Willie," said Lahousen with a smile and a fresh burst of optimism, as he reached out to pat a comforting hand on his friend's knee. "So we've lost round one and General Witzleben. What of it? Hitler's bound to slip up soon and rub another General the wrong way. There's nothing surer. As soon as he does, we'll be there to scoop him up and offer him our alternative.

"All we need is one . . . just *one* field marshal to throw his lot in with us and we're up and running. You know they're all there, playing their cards close to their chest, just waiting to see what deal Hitler has in mind. You know as well as I do that most of them are in full agreement with us. I always find it rather amusing that none of them . . . not *one* of those military men for *all* their medals has the nerve to stand up for the sake of Germany and declare it."

To this Canaris had no answer, other than to nod in reluctant agreement. It was true—the Generals of High Command were acting like a pack of gutless wonders. But then who could blame them under their shaky circumstances . . . under the ever-present threat of Hitler and his violent mood swings? Their chronic fear of him, together with their awe over his astonishingly fast military achievements, had had them completely lose sight of their courage and moral conviction. Especially after Hitler had recently and very publicly humiliated them all with his accusations of their cowardice and defeatism.

But that was just one of the problems. "It's not just their fear of Hitler that stops them from acting—it's that wretched Oath of Loyalty that he made us all take. There's no way that any German officer, or *any* man of honour for that matter, will abuse it," ventured Lahousen.

At this reminder of his moral duty (at least Hitler's version of it), Canaris scowled. He too had been forced to swear his personal oath of allegiance to the Fuhrer. They had been words which had stuck in his throat at the time and had been destined to choke the

Resistance movement as a whole. Their hand-on-heart utterance was proving to be the biggest stumbling block in organizing an effective coup, and even tampering with the idea of assassination.

"I swear by God this sacred oath: I will render unconditional obedience to Adolf Hitler, the Führer of the German Reich and people, Supreme Commander of the Armed Forces, and will be ready as a brave soldier to risk my life at any time for this oath."[11]

With it went the onus of obligation. All those who had made the vow and later signed up with the Resistance had put themselves into an unworkable moral dilemma. Their conscience, honour and deeply-felt religious convictions made them the sort of men who shied away from taking decisive action against the evil they had signed up to combat.

Clinging tight to their noble goals, while holding God up as their standard, made it impossible for them to betray a "holy oath" that they had sworn in His name. Whereas they might, at a pinch, be prepared to abuse it and forsake *Hitler*, they weren't prepared to forsake the Almighty or their souls by entertaining the idea of physically putting a knife in their Fuhrer's back.

"I suppose the best we can do at the moment is bide our time and wait for the right opportunity to strike," Canaris said.

Getting up from his chair, he stretched this way and that to get his blood circulation back into gear. He was paying the price of pins and needles in his legs for having sat feeling sorry for himself for so long.

"I only hope that Dohnanyi and Oster take great care. I've warned them that Roeder and Freisler are on their tail and that Heydrich has been sniffing around my office a little more regularly of late. He's got the scent and it won't take him long to find out what they're up to. God help us when he does!"

"I believe Beck's met with his replacement, General Franz Halder," Lahousen said, suddenly keen to change the subject.

Now that Heydrich had been brought into the equation, Lahousen too had grave concerns for Oster and Dohnanyi's safety. Where Heydrich was concerned, it was just a bottomless pit of fear for all who fell victim to his icy stare and cold-hearted scrutiny.

"Perhaps there's hope there with Halder?" he continued. "He professes to be an ally of ours and surely, as second-in-command to Brauchitsch, he'll prove to be a powerful weapon if we can manage to swing him around."

"Forget Brauchitsch," Canaris was quick to say as he walked over to his desk and began to rifle through his papers. "He was always a slim hope for us, but now that he's re-married, he's a lost cause. The weak sod's got himself totally wrapped up in a woman who's even *more* totally wrapped up in the Nazi Party."

"But I don't think he's become a danger. He's not strong enough to make a stand either way. Only the other day he was discussing a possible coup quite openly with me and said,

'I myself will not do anything,
but I will not stop anyone else from acting.'"

It was a familiar old piece of buck-passing that had Lahousen snort with contempt.

"I've heard that cop-out fifty times over. We can only hope that Halder turns out to be made of sterner stuff."

"Halder's a toss-up," Canaris said. In a moment of contemplation, he tapped the tip of his gold fountain pen on his upper lip. "He's got more guts than Brauchitsch, but is much lighter on moral conscience. He's quite capable of talking back to Hitler. I've heard him do it. But I feel that if he decides to make a stand against him, it'll be on military grounds, rather than ethical."

"Arghh . . . it's all so *damned* frustrating," Lahousen snapped, "You'd think that it'd be easy enough to win just one of the top men over . . . to get him to commit to the Resistance. But I *swear* that Hitler has a sixth sense.

"Every *single* time we get near to closing in on one of his Generals . . . of talking them around to our point of view, Hitler heads us off at the pass. He's got this uncanny instinct about it. Some little antennae he puts out to pick up enemy static in the air.

"Either the General concerned gets suddenly transferred, or put out to pasture, or bought off with a country estate or two. I don't know *how* Hitler does it, but he always knows which one of them's on the turn and how best to neutralize him."

"Well we're going to have to beat him to the punch soon, or get Britain and France to pull up their socks and do the job for us," Canaris said. "Something's got to give . . . *something's* got to stir them into action."

CHAPTER EIGHT

That "something" was Poland. Its invasion and thorough trouncing in three short weeks finally forced the Allies to declare war on Germany. Their decision, a month before, to give Poland their unconditional support had been based, in no small part, on the efforts of Canaris and the German Resistance, every member of which had been pulling out all stops to force Britain's hand. The devastating news of Stalin having signed a non-aggression pact with Germany on August 23 had prompted Dr. Carl Goerdeler and Hjalmar Schacht to declare a state of emergency within the ranks of the Resistance. They were just two of its "notables" who, at that crucial point in the history of the world, had inundated Churchill, Sir Alexander Cardigan, Lord Halifax and Neville Chamberlain with a series of secret memos and clandestine meetings. The general gist of their repeated message was:

"That Hitler intends to invade Poland no matter what the threat."

England and France didn't much like the Fuhrer's inference that their combined opposition was of no significance. It was this prick to their pride that got their wheels grinding into motion, not only inspiring a vigorous debate in the British House of Commons, but a rapid program for Allied re-armament. The dreaded issue of a second World War, at last, had been taken seriously.

So seriously that, in a state of escalating panic, the Brits turned on one of their own. They accused their Ambassador in Berlin, Sir Neville Henderson, of having let Hitler lead him by the nose; of not having kept his fellow countrymen fully apprised of the true situation in Germany and the very real threat it now posed.

Henderson's fair-weather friends back home were not all that sorry when he retired and returned there with a terminal case of cancer of the mouth. All of them saw it as a fitting punishment for not having opened it sooner to tell them the truth about Hitler's list of atrocities and of his personal designs on the world.

Not that it was news to them. How *could* it have been when they had been swamped with information of the like from Canaris & co? It was just that they would have preferred to have heard it from someone they trusted . . . for it to have come from the lips of an Englishman.

But Canaris and his Resistance had not been able to wait that long. Instead, with typical Germanic speed and efficiency, they had worked flat out on two fronts to make up for the time the Brits had lost. Canaris wasn't only trying to whip the West into a fury over the threat of war, but doing the same with his own German Generals; urging them, in every way he could, to stay Hitler's hand.

Canaris even went so far as to stretch the boundaries of his power and diplomatic skills by making direct contact with Mussolini, hoping that a word in his ear might encourage him to do the same.

But it had been too late for that. The fascist leader, who had been in a temporary state of fence-sitting, had already made up his mind to jump to one side of it. Having had his eyes fixed with fascination on the Fuhrer for some time, he'd decided to sign the Pact of Steel between Italy and Germany on May 22, convinced that Hitler's deeds were measuring up to his boasting.

This failure on the Italian front had had Canaris turn his attention to the most famous fence-sitter in Germany—Field Marshal Wilhelm Keitel. The "Nodding Donkey" or "Rubber Lion", as he was not-so-affectionately known in Resistance circles, ranked supreme in the art of taking the middle ground and of holding it at all costs.

"There's no point in talking to me about it. *I* can't do anything to help," Keitel had said, the very instant Canaris had mentioned the controversial "Operation Himmler".

Canaris had hardly needed Keitel to state the obvious, but impotent as the Field Marshal was, he had been his last resort.

Having received Himmler's most recent order that the *Abwehr* provide, *immediately*, two hundred Polish military uniforms, Canaris had had nowhere else to turn. As the Commander-in-Chief of the Armed Forces, Keitel was in the perfect position to provide some sort of clarification on the issue.

"There can no longer be any doubt as to Hitler's plans for Poland," Canaris had said, handing him Himmler's written order. "Hitler is determined to have his wretched war one way or the other. And he's wanting *me* to provide the false evidence that the Poles fired the first shot as his excuse to start it. Isn't the horror of war bad enough, without compounding it with the shame of lies and dishonour!"

"There will be *no* war," Keitel had bounced back with the shaky conviction of a man who was uninformed and had every intention of remaining so.

"Surely I don't need to explain to you what this memo means?" Canaris had come back at him in exasperation.

"Yes . . . I should think you do."

"Think clearly Keitel . . . why would Himmler want me to provide him with *Polish* uniforms? Because . . ." he'd continued, not bothering to wait for an answer that he was sure Keitel would not provide, ". . . he intends to put them on prisoners from the concentration camps, murder them, and scatter their bodies to serve as physical evidence that the Poles launched the offensive on Germany, rather than the other way round."

There had been a moment's pause as Keitel let the information sink in. Canaris, with his body leaning a little in the Field Marshal's direction and his upturned hands gesturing impatiently, had tried to spur on his response.

Slow in coming, he should have *known* what it would be.

"I can't concern myself with Operation Himmler. The Fuhrer has not personally briefed me on it," he'd said, adding to the insult of blithely dismissing Canaris' concerns, by turning his back on the Admiral as he spoke.

From experience, Keitel had found it easier not to look a man in the eye when letting him down.

"If all three of them—Hitler, Himmler *and* Heydrich—have asked you to procure Polish uniforms, then it's your job to do it," he'd continued. "Why do you persist in bringing me these problems? You continue to be a troublemaker, Canaris—a never-ending thorn in my side."

"It was my misguided hope, sir, that I might stir your conscience. This order of Hitler's is a disgrace, for which the world will one day hold not only him, but our long-respected Wehrmacht, responsible . . . because they . . . let . . . it . . . happen!"

Never caring to be reminded of his conscience—that long-lost essence of himself that had gone the way of his courage—Keitel had lashed out on a different tangent.

"It never ceases to amaze me that even in a nation ruled by a dictator, there are people like you who insist on being temperamental when it comes to war. One can only imagine how much more difficult it would be in a democracy! Why do you continue, Canaris, to concern yourself with the Fuhrer's brilliant initiatives? Who are *you* anyway to question them? You would be wiser, I believe, to do as I do and give him your full support. It is your duty, if not your desire."

Having taken what he had believed to be "the high ground', Keitel had felt free to hand out such advice. In having offered it, he'd been greatly put out by the look of disdain that had crossed Canaris' face.

"You think of me as a weak man, I know," he'd continued. "I, on the other hand think of you, Admiral Canaris, as being an astonishingly brave one. Why else would you be so foolish as to risk your life by coming to me with your subversive talk? You should be grateful for that weakness in my nature for which you have such contempt, because it now saves you. *Because* I've always liked you . . . *because* I've always believed you to be a decent man, I'm prepared to forget that we've had this conversation. But be warned . . . I will not tolerate another."

"Are you truly prepared for a second World War Keitel? Because this is what this memo from Himmler means," Canaris had snapped back, undaunted by the man's menacing tone.

Forgetting that he'd intended to round off their conversation by using it, Keitel had been quite ready and willing to continue their debate.

"Nonsense, the British are as weak as water. They'll never intervene. They'll have about as much concern for Poland, when it comes down to it, as they had for Czechoslovakia."

"You're wrong Keitel. You're *wrong*. I've no doubt that if we invade Poland, they'll immediately blockade us and destroy our merchant shipping."

"Well, that'll be of no consequence . . . we'll get our oil and most other provisions we need from Russia."

"Hardly the decisive factor," Canaris had responded sarcastically, before he'd decided to take a fresh approach. "Look Keitel . . . the bottom line is that we'll not be able to withstand a blockade in the long run. The British will fight against us with all the means within their power if it comes to force and bloodshed in Poland and they would have done the same, I might add, had it come to bloodshed in Czechoslovakia.

"This is not a simple case of German military prowess—of how many pretty tanks and troops we can parade at call. It's *economic* warfare with which we should be concerned. *That* will be the deciding factor of a second World War. And despite what Hitler has deluded himself and others into thinking, we have only limited forces with which to fight back, if we actively provoke retaliatory action from the West.

"Do you realize that if war were declared *today*, we could only manage to put ten U-Boats—just *ten* U-Boats—into the Atlantic? Hitler may as well be playing in his bathtub!"

As it turned out, Germany had been given a few weeks grace after this conversation, before that happened. They launched their invasion of Poland on September 1, and England responded with their declaration of War on September 3.

The day Hitler gave the order to march on Poland had brought Canaris close to tears; because three days prior, he and the Resistance had been lulled into a false sense of security, when the Fuhrer cancelled his initial order to invade on August 29.

Canaris had all but leapt with joy at that piece of military mismanagement.

"Well my friends . . . peace in Europe has just been assured for the next fifty years," he'd said to Oster and Hans Gisevius as the three of them had put on their hats and coats and left the offices of High Command. The cloying humidity of the lamp-lit city streets, wet in the wake of a late summer rain, had been unable to dampen their spirits.

"That halt to our offensive has just lost Hitler the respect of his Generals," Canaris had chatted on, as he'd turned up the collar of his trench coat and put his hands in his pockets—forever cold, despite the oppressive heat. "The Fuhrer's finished! He can't *possibly* survive such arbitrary treatment of the High Command."

Not one of the three guessed, at that moment of triumph, that it had been a case of pride coming before a fall. All of them received a terrible shock when Hitler re-issued his orders to march on Poland three days later.

"Perhaps we can arrange another meeting with Brauchitsch and Halder to intervene," Oster suggested, making a feeble attempt to offer his compatriots a glimmer of hope.

But sitting despondently at his desk, Canaris shook his head. With his eyes, stinking at the threat of tears, he reached into his pocket for his handkerchief:

"It's too late now," he said. "This is the end of Germany."

"Has it ever crossed your mind," Hans Gisevius put in, with the cold, calm cynicism of the lawyer he was, "that we're wrong and that Germany just might win?"

Leaning across his desk to speak more confidentially, Canaris replied,

"My dear fellow . . . why do you think I weep? With Hitler as our Leader, Germany's victory will be a greater catastrophe than her defeat."

CHAPTER NINE

"I'm *disgusted* with the events in Poland!"

Dry-eyed and back on the attack, Canaris made his accusation the very instant the War Conference was called to order. Demanding answers directly from Field Marshal Keitel, who as Chief of the Supreme Command of the Armed Forces, had sole control of the meeting and its gavel.

At Canaris' up front interjection, Keitel slammed that gavel down hard on his desk.

"I presume you have something to say, as *always*," he replied, none too pleased that the little Admiral had asserted himself so early in the piece and undermined his authority as the meeting's adjudicator.

And without hesitation, Canaris took him up on his offer:

"Lahousen here," he continued, pointing to his aide, who was standing next to him, "has just got back from an observation tour of occupied territory. He told me that the local SS Chief in Krakow is in a state bordering on hysteria. Neither he nor his men feel capable of carrying out the outrageous orders they've been given for murder and far worse, unless they make themselves drunk in advance."

"Then send them more alcohol," was Keitel's calm response, as he picked up the daily newspaper that was lying on his desk, goading Canaris further by casually perusing its headline.

It took great presence of mind for Canaris to deny the impulse to rip it out of his hands, but, determined to pursue his point, he pressed on—cool and grim-mouthed.

"Are you aware that in Warsaw the Polish intelligentsia, nobility and clergy have been massacred to a man? That the women and children haven't been spared in the process? What are our reasons for such an unholy slaughter? What can Germany possibly gain from such sadistic behaviour? And how on *Earth* will our people *ever* be forgiven for practising it?"

"Forgiven?" Keitel repeated. In a tone, sharp and sinister, he'd suddenly taken enough exception to Canaris' conversation to put down his newspaper and partake in it.

"It's not a question of forgiveness," he said, fixing the head of the *Abwehr* with his icy glare. "The Fuhrer needs to ask forgiveness for *nothing* and from *no one!*"

So that was it, was it? The answer to all the obscenity and insanity of the Third Reich was to give Hitler a free rein and condone his wholesale slaughter of innocents? The realization led Canaris and Lahousen to promptly take their leave of the meeting, depressed and no longer with any doubt as to Keitel's allegiance.

They wouldn't ask for his help again. Obviously he, like most of the other men at High Command, had been well and truly secured under Hitler's thumb—blind to, and terrified of, the evil he was committing.

The problem was that when the world was at war, all power rested with the armed forces. In this case, the closed ranks and clout of men in uniform effectively rendered the civilian branch of the Resistance useless. All hopes, therefore, of it achieving its ends rested solely in finding a military warlord who had the courage and moral conviction to stand up and be counted . . . a man who was prepared to cut loose from the pack and champion their cause.

As yet, no such hero had been found. The ranks that Canaris was scouring for likely candidates had become very thin on the ground.

Thus, it came as some comfort for him to know that Dohnanyi and Oster were making headway on *their* project. Despite the fact that they were exposing themselves to frightful danger in the secret collating of incriminating Nazi documents, Canaris couldn't help but feel glad and very grateful that they were doing it. Notwithstanding the fear-factor of them being under Judge Roland Freisler's and Dr. Manfred Roeder's constant surveillance, he was proud of them for having persisted in their efforts when his own were proving so fruitless.

Short of assassinating Hitler, those documents were the next

KILL THE FUHRER 卐

best way of bringing the Third Reich down. Their detailed, written accounts and photographed proof of inhuman atrocities were the only solid evidence that would stand up in court and make the monsters answerable for their crimes.

To this end, Canaris now dedicated himself, making sure that most of his *Abwehr* staff continued with their normal duties, to cover for the fact that Major Hans Dohnanyi and Colonel Hans Oster were constantly veering off theirs.

The two of them were working "Hans in Hans" (as Oster often joked), exclusively for the Resistance. Their shared, day-by-day danger was making them the closest of friends. Dohnanyi—quick, firm and discreet—was the perfect complement to the reckless, flamboyant Oster; two equal and opposite halves that came together to make a very effective whole.

Effective enough for them to understand why it must be *them* and not Canaris, who had hands-on involvement in the risky business of seeking and securing the top secret documents. They must make sure, in the process, not to leave any trace of a paper trail that might lead the likes of Heydrich back to Canaris' desk.

For all concerned, it was imperative that the head of the *Abwehr* keep a low profile in regard to the activities of the Resistance. Being the master of disguise and deception that Canaris was, no one at that point—not even Himmler or Heydrich—had the slightest suspicion that he was involved, and they would have been thunderstruck had they found out that he was not only a *member* of the Resistance, but one of its leading lights!

As such, it was essential that his positive, pro-Hitler façade stay intact. That the Fuhrer continue to trust him implicitly and make him privy to his home, its hearth and fireside conversations.

In the meantime, Canaris was going out of his way to promote the ambiguity of the *Abwehr*, hiring an abundance of good, level-headed men to replace those National Socialist diehards he had been systematically firing. Padding out its existing network of departments with a surplus of staff and red-tape that went into overflow and demanded the creation of additional and equally unnecessary departments.

This, together with their corresponding subsidiaries and undefined mission statements, made the whole Intelligence Organization into an unwieldy web of incomprehensible paperwork, through which Oster and Dohnanyi could smuggle their own, secreting it, until the War's and Hitler's end, in a small, subterranean safe at German Military Headquarters at Zossen.[12]

The key to this safe Dohnanyi kept quite openly in his office in Berlin—tied to one of his Staff Employment files with a rather conspicuous red ribbon. The very fact that he left it out in the open for everyone to see ensured that nobody bothered to look. No one questioned, or *cared*, for that matter, what it opened, because it was apparently not important enough to conceal.

It was a smart move that was to be followed by one which Canaris thought was even smarter. Having found that all human help had failed to get the results he wanted, he decided to look to God for them . . . or at least, to His next best thing on Earth—the Pope.

Although a Protestant by right of his grandfather having converted from Catholicism in the early 1800s, it was to those ancient Roman Catholic roots of his that Canaris now turned. Not through a maudlin excess of piety, but as an act of sheer expediency. Oster and Dohnanyi had recently suggested that he might like to add *His Holiness, Pope Pius X11*, to his list of contacts.

It was a gift, from out of the blue, that Oster naively believed had come about by pure accident, when he had been interviewing a prospective recruit for the Resistance:

"And you say this friend of yours . . . Dr. Josef Mueller . . . has good relations with top officials at the Vatican?" he'd asked of Dr. Wilhelm Schmidhuber—a Captain in the Army Reserve and a leading businessman from Munich who was keen to offer the *Abwehr* his services.

This was not as an act of humanity, but with the sole purpose of making a substantial financial gain—of raking in a veritable fortune by facilitating the escape of Jews from Germany. To that end, Schmidhuber was keen to provide them with false passports and a fistful and foreign currency in exchange for a hefty 75% commission.

"Why yes," Schmidhuber had replied, settling his portly, pin-stripe-suited self back more comfortably in his chair.

Having feigned an innocence of manner and purpose in his blatant piece of name dropping, he'd decided to draw out the suspense by pausing to take a leisurely puff of his cigar, confident as he was that the mention of Dr Mueller's name, along with those of his many high profile contacts, would ensure that Oster offer him a position with the Resistance.

Schmidhuber had *had* to play this ace card of his, because he'd sensed that he had not entirely won Hans Oster over. Right from the onset of their meeting, it had been obvious that the Colonel had not liked him—that he was extremely suspicious of Schmidhuber's capacity and credentials to become one of them.

"Perhaps I should qualify that comment," Schmidhuber had continued. "My friend Mueller's good relationship with the Vatican is not so much with the Pope himself, but with his principal advisors—Father Robert Leiber and Monsignor Ludwig Kass. I do hope I don't disappoint you by telling you this?"

Hardly!

The look of all-consuming triumph on Oster's face at this revelation had Schmidhuber smother a wry smile. Calmly lifting his chin to exhale a cloud of grey smoke, he waited politely for the Colonel to offer him membership in "The Club". A few further and very strategic moments elapsed before the Colonel thought it "proper" to extend the same offer to his friend, Dr. Josef Mueller.

The good Dr. Mueller didn't hesitate to accept. Being a fearless Catholic opponent of Nazism, he was quick to both sign his name on the dotted line and to dedicate his life and courage to the cause. As a man of God, he felt that it was the very least he could do.

"The Nazis see the Pope as being their implacable enemy. I want you to be fully aware of this and of the extreme danger in which you place yourself before you commit to us."

It was a warning Canaris felt obliged to extend to Mueller, given that he had taken such an instant shine to him. The lawyer from Munich had immediately won Canaris over by introducing himself by his nickname—*Joe, the Mule*—[13]insisting that the head of the *Abwehr* make use of it *and* him in whichever way he saw fit.

"Just think of me as a beast of burden and you'll have got it right," he replied with a laugh.

This comment Canaris found hard to contest when the man sitting opposite him in his office bore such a striking resemblance to the animal in question. Hirsute, plain as a pikestaff, fat as a pig, but with a heart as big as an ox; Mueller's ease of manner and innate confidence made it obvious that he'd not only come to terms with his physical limitations, but gone all out to embrace them. Turning what should have been a negative into an enormous positive.

The man simply exuded "good" from his every unsightly, open pore—his excessive weight, one could easily believe, being the result of him being so jam-packed full of it.

Nonetheless, Canaris got the distinct impression that, despite his merry, sanguine face and open demeanour, Mueller was holding back. Humbling himself to the extent of hiding what was, in fact, a remarkably astute mind, whose knowledge of the world, its woes and their overcoming, was second to none.

Evidently he was afraid of nothing more than the sin of vanity—of pushing himself forward in the seeking of the world's kudos—which was a phenomenon in itself during this era of furious power-mongering. The fact that Mueller had chosen to hide his talent under a bushel instead of taking advantage of it made him a man in a million.

It was little wonder, Canaris realized, that God's representative on Earth—Pope Pius XII —liked to keep him close at hand.

"I feel, rightly or wrongly, that I can put my trust in you," Canaris said, surprising himself with his own candour. It was rare for him to leave himself vulnerable by expressing his true emotions towards another human being.

"What . . . even though I'm a lawyer?" Mueller threw back, enjoying every moment of being so closely scrutinized by the head of the *Abwehr*, a man who, not unlike himself, was obviously as sharp as a tack and equally disposed to good humour.

"No," Canaris clarified with a smirk. "*Despite* the fact that you're a lawyer!"

Polite preliminaries over, Mueller readjusted his enormous self in his chair and said, "Now tell me . . . what can I do for you?"

Canaris responded in kind by not beating round the bush.

"I want you, as soon as possible, to use your contacts at the Vatican to enlist the Pope's help. I would like to request that he act as an intermediary between Germany and England to initiate peace talks. To let both sides know of each other's readiness to participate in them, *without* the presence of Hitler."

*   *   *

"I agree. The German Resistance *must* be heard in Britain," the usually cautious Pope Pius XII stated one week later. Having listened intently to everything Mueller had to say, the pontiff sent him back to Berlin with a personal card that read:

"The bearer of this enjoys the full confidence of His Holiness."

Which ostensibly gave Mueller and his friend Father Lieber in Rome the go-ahead to draft the "X" report, copies of which, written on Vatican letterhead and with the tacit approval of the Pope, were quickly edited by Dohnanyi and sent *post-haste* to London and Berlin. The report outlined the conditions to which the Western Allies would be most likely to agree once Hitler was removed from power.

It was understood in Germany that any peace negotiations with the Allies would depend on Germany ridding itself of the Nazi regime and setting up a responsible government in its stead. While the Allies would be expected to recognize that the Sudetenland should remain a part of Germany, Austria's future would be determined by plebiscite.

In its finished form, the report was presented to General Franz Halder who, in turn, and albeit with justifiable reticence, passed it on to his boss—Field Marshal von Brauchitsch.

"You should *never* have shown me this," said the horrified Brauchitsch, more afraid than furious.

Walking over quickly to shut his office door, his eyes scanned the room for any open window or bugging device through which he might be overheard, making doubly sure that he was *not* by moving closer to Halder and whispering his angry answer through gritted teeth.

"This is pure treason against the State and I will have nothing to do with it. Make sure you let Canaris know that, *once and for all*, he is not . . . *ever* . . . to approach me again. With this sanctimonious, seditious document, he has finally outdone himself and helped me make up my mind to give Hitler my full and unerring support. I would suggest that for everyone's sake, General Halder, you destroy this report immediately!"

Brauchitsch's sentiments were echoed soon after by the Vatican itself. Having made no headway with the help they had offered in the event of a successful *coup d'etat* against Hitler, they requested that all evidence of their prospective participation be destroyed.

In compliance with Brauchitsch's urgent bidding, Halder had thrown the Berlin copy into the fireplace, watching until its papers curled up orange at the edges before burning to black ash.

At the request of negotiators at the Vatican, the London copy was disposed of in a similar manner, but with the added precaution of being shredded beforehand.

The third copy, however, of whose existence only the German Resistance was aware, managed to find its way to a little subterranean safe in Zossen.

Here was written proof that cast a shadow over the Vatican for having weakly backed down at a time when the world was depending on Christianity to see them through—to have the leader of the Roman Catholic Church take an active and very vocal stand against Hitler.

There were many who thought it reprehensible that The Pope did not, that his policy to keep his silence in regard to the Third Reich and its atrocities was in fact his passive-aggressive way of giving it and Hitler his support, at the expense of the millions of Jews who were crying out loudly for his help.

"That's nonsense," Canaris refuted angrily, when the defamatory remarks first reached him. "The man did his best. It was *we* who let him down by not staging a successful coup so that he could follow through on our initiative. The Pope's a diplomat, not a radical preacher. If I'd known he'd come under such unfair criticism, I would never have thought to draw him into this whole, ugly business. I should have realized what the reality was . . . that it *is*, and must *ever* be the Pope's prime concern to maintain the Vatican's neutrality if it is to be a refuge for war victims."

Mueller quietly nodded in agreement, gratified that Canaris had come to such an insightful conclusion.

"You're right," he said. "The man's in an impossible position. He not only has to contend with Hitler but with his partner in crime, Mussolini, who at the moment has sole control of all communication networks in Italy. Without them, how was the Pope meant to get his message out to the people anyway?"

"Perhaps it's better that he doesn't," Canaris said, having rethought the whole issue. "I think that the Pope has had the sense to consider the very real harm it'd do the Jews if he does. If he gets up on his soapbox to lash out at the Nazis and speak against their treatment of the Jews, he'll achieve nothing but the doubling of Nazi efforts to murder and deport them. You do know that this policy of the Vatican's to keep its silence over the whole nasty business is one that's been actively adopted by The Red Cross as well?"

"No, I didn't realize that," Mueller put in, knowing that he'd never heard *anyone* accuse the *Red Cross* of opting out on their responsibility. Somehow it didn't seem fair.

"Yes . . . they've found that they can be far more effective in helping the Jews if they go about doing it, keeping their mouths shut. Their objectivity and silence keeps the Nazis off their back. The Vatican, no doubt, is just following their example. And good luck to them."

"All the same, it's a wretched shame," Mueller tisked, disappointed to have to admit to the good sense of Canaris' argument. "It would have been nice to see the Vatican take a stand."

But Canaris, in one pragmatic sweep of his hand, now dismissed the whole idea of the Vatican being in the picture, of it playing any constructive part in the Resistance. He now realized that the Pope's participation in it would do nothing more than make Hitler see red. Provoking him into lifting his war game to a whole new, unspeakable level.

The ultimate challenge of pitting himself against God's advocate on Earth would give him a new zest for life and the incentive to strip millions of people of theirs. No longer satisfied with the limitations of his blood-stained battlefields in Europe, he would be sorely tempted to strike out at winning the age-old war of Good vs. Evil.

Dramatic, yes, but nonetheless what Canaris believed, deep in his heart, to be the *truth* of Hitler.

"Do you honestly think," he asked, leaning forward to impress his question on Mueller, "knowing who and *what* Hitler is, that he'd give a rat's arse about the Pope's intervention? That he'd be daunted, in any way, by the Church or what it has to say?

"Let me tell you, it wouldn't have the slightest effect on him, other than to further jeopardize the lives of Jews. Particularly those ones who the Pope has managed to hide away safely in his convents and monasteries.[14] Hitler would target them and go out of his way to make an example of them. Butchering them in a way that would undermine *forever*, the power and sanctuary of the Pope's protection.

"It sickens me to think of it . . . the horrendous things of which our Fuhrer (and we, by unfortunate association) are capable. And worse still, that *I've* been the means of implicating the Pope in the horror of it all. I wonder if he'll ever forgive me?"

It was a question to which Mueller had a ready answer.

"That, my dear chap, is a 'given'. He is incapable of doing otherwise."

CHAPTER TEN

While the Pope busied himself behind the scenes saving Jewish lives and his own reputation, Colonel Jacobus Sas—Dutch Military attaché in Berlin—was trying desperately to do the same for himself and his fellow countrymen.

At great risk to his own life and credibility, he was going all out to warn Holland and its people that Hitler's attention had now turned in their direction. But his acts of heroism had hit two snags:

1. Hitler had taken to a policy of postponements in his invasion initiatives. Whether through mistake or sheer military brilliance, he'd called off a series of surprise attacks on the Netherlands—last minute reprieves, that not only delayed the inevitable for the Dutch, but threw the German High Command into a state of confusion. None of its Generals were able to keep up with Hitler's whims and sudden shifts in strategy. None of them knew exactly when and *if* they were coming or going.

2. Sas had done irreparable harm to his own reputation by having already provided Dutch Supreme Command with two prospective dates for a German invasion which had failed to eventuate.

It was a breakdown in the system that had given General Reynders (Commander-in-Chief of the Dutch Armed Forces) the ammunition to bring down and humiliate his old in-house enemy—Colonel Jacobus Sas. Reynders took full advantage of Hitler's mad military maneouvres to relieve Sas of his prestigious government position, citing as his reason "the compromising of their country".

It was an insult and political embarrassment for which Sas

could easily have blamed his friend Hans Oster, the German Colonel who had been responsible for furnishing him with the false information in the first place.

"Your turn is still to come," Oster had first warned in October, 1939. "But before he takes on Holland, Hitler wants to invade Belgium. That's a blessing for you. Make sure you take advantage of it. At least poor little Belgium's fall will give you a few weeks to alert your friends at Dutch Military Command."

It had been a piece of inside information for which Sas had been undyingly grateful. As it turned out, however, he had not had as many friends back home as he had thought. The first time he'd made his death-defying dash from Berlin to the Hague Military Headquarters, his warnings had been met with disbelief and not-so-carefully disguised contempt. In General Reynders case, this had become a flagrant attack on his honour that had brought Sas to the brink of handing in his resignation.

His decision *not* to do so, at that crucial point, had been based purely on love for his country. Despite the incomprehensible blindness of its leaders, he was determined to stick by it, no matter what, sacrificing his dignity to give his beloved homeland half a chance of survival against the coming onslaught of the Third Reich.

"The date has been reset for November 12," Oster had told Sas as soon as he had got back to Berlin. The head of the *Abwehr's* Department Z had requested that Sas join him for lunch to discuss the matter.

It had surprised Sas, when he'd arrived at Oster's house, to find his friend in full dress uniform. Having got used to seeing him in civilian suits and fully aware that Oster had long since abandoned all forms of Third Reich paraphernalia, it seemed strange that he'd suddenly decided to adorn himself in it again— not only resorting to old habits by clambering back into it, but by ordering a military staff car to stand at the ready outside his house, to enhance the image.

"So what's with the uniform?" Sas had asked before putting a fork-load of sauerkraut in his mouth. He had reasoned that to eat was a better option than to speak, if he were to keep the note of alarm out of his voice and not betray the fact that he was a little concerned that Oster may have sold out and swapped sides.

The Colonel had been quick to put his mind at ease. Passing him the pepper and salt, he'd said,

"Just playing my part. While you fly back to Holland to give them this new invasion date, I'm off to the western front to see General Witzleben. To see if he . . . or *anyone* there can do something to stop it."

The fact that Oster was taking such hands-on, immediate action himself had given Sas the impetus to follow suit. Putting his pride on the line, he'd gone straight back to Holland to tackle General Reynders and the Dutch Supreme Command a second time—imploring them to take this updated piece of information seriously.

He had presented it to Ministers de Geer, van Kleffens and Dijxhoorn and had been very much encouraged by the look of genuine concern on their faces. It had appeared, at last, that they were taking him at his word. But Sas had known that he couldn't stop there—he must take it one step further to cover all contingencies.

"It's imperative that this information get to the Queen, and that it gets to her immediately," he'd said. "She *must* be told, well in advance, if she's to make the necessary preparations."

It had been a wholly unreasonable request, to General Reynders' way of thinking, that had him up and out of his chair, striding across his office to confront Sas head on. Taking care to initiate his face-to-face offensive only *after* the three other Ministers had left the room.

"I *forbid* you to pass on this information to Queen Wilhelmina . . . or, for that matter, to any other of our Ministers," he'd said.

Having sat through the meeting, tight-lipped and incensed that Sas had dared tackle them again, Reynders had no intention of taking the matter any further. He most certainly was not about to let Sas go over his head.

"You are nothing but a scaremonger, Sas. And I won't have it, do you hear? If I think it's necessary, it is I and *I alone* who will speak with Her Majesty. Which, at this point, I have no intention of doing."

Bewildered as Sas had been by Reynders' odd behaviour, he had no choice but to obey. It seemed remarkable to him that a man in charge of a country's defences should flatly refuse to give his warnings any credence—to not even *play* with the possibility that they could be correct.

His, however, wasn't to wonder why, but to wait. So he decided to pass off Reynders' negligence as a simple matter of bruised ego—a case of Reynders resenting another man stealing his thunder. If that were the truth of it—if the man were possessed of such a weak character, then Sas had thought it best to stand back for a few days and give him breathing space. Enough, anyway, for the Commander-in-Chief of the Armed Forces to rethink his position, and with any luck talk himself into believing that it had been his *own* initiative to confer with the Queen.

However, a few days down the track not another word had been said about the matter. In growing concern, with the November deadline fast approaching, Sas had decided to bypass Reynders altogether and speak directly to a number of his other contacts in the hope that they could help. They could not, and having now stepped on Reynders' toes meant that the Queen was out of Sas' reach.

Sas had known that to cross Reynders had been a real gamble. His courage to do so had come only from the fact that he could ill-afford not to. If his information had been correct and Holland had come under attack, he would never have forgiven himself for not having forced his point, for not having made sure, in whichever way he could, that he had prepared them for it.

Of course, there had also been the tiny issue of the "I told you so" factor; the delightful prospect of being able to rub Reynders' nose in it if the German guns *had* appeared on their horizon.

But Sas, once again, had been out of luck. For the *second* time, Hitler had changed his mind at the last minute. This would have been a reason to rejoice, had the German Resistance not known that it was merely a matter of delay, rather than cancellation.

"You can't surely expect us to take either yours or your Colonel Oster's information seriously in the future?" Commander Reynders had said, lolling back in his chair to savour his petty victory.

It was a small-minded man's response, which Sas could have tolerated had it not been for the patronizing tone in his voice—the final insult that had Sas turn on him in a white-faced rage.

"Tell me, once and for all, Reynders, whether my word is trusted here?"

"Your word was wrong . . . and for the second time," the Commander had replied, smugly shrugging his shoulders with the undisguised disdain of a man who had won his argument. Of a man who, right or wrong, would never have the class to concede it.

This had been the point at which Reynders had made sure that Sas would never again put him the position of having to do so.

"I'm not a man who listens to idle gossip," he'd said, handing Sas a pen and his formal papers of resignation. "And given that you seem to enjoy nothing more, I am now relieving you of your position. I no longer believe that you are in full control of your wits . . . that you are a fit representative for us in Berlin."

With no one on hand to back him up, Sas had had no choice but to sign his name on the dotted line. Hitler's perplexing progression of military starts and stops had left him without a leg to stand on.

Nor, as it turned out, did Reynders. Within weeks, he was relieved of his own command and replaced by a much better man—General Winkelman. A military leader who, trusting or not in Sas' warnings, had the common sense not to entirely discount them. He certainly refused to hold the fact that they had failed to eventuate against a man of Sas' integrity—a man who had put everything on the line: his reputation, his job and his life—for the sake of his country.

Within days Sas was reinstated to his position. Winkelman let him know (off the record) that he was still prepared to listen to *anything* Sas and Colonel Oster had to say and not to feel, for fear of humiliation, that either of them should hold any information back.

It was advice that Sas took on board when Oster asked him to pass on the date of April 9, 1940 to the Danish Naval attaché (van Kjolsen), and to his Norwegian counterpart (Stang). Kjolsen passed it on immediately to Danish home base, while Stang failed to do as much for his fellow Norwegians, having been paid more by the Germans to keep his mouth shut.

While Sas played *his* part, Dr. Josef Mueller, too, had his work cut out for him. Canaris had let him know that May 10 was the date that Hitler had designated to strike westward.

"Get the information to your friend Father Leiber, will you, and ask him to pass it on to the Belgian envoy at the Vatican. I'm sure he can take it from there."

The Belgian envoy did, unaware, unfortunately, as he sent his lengthy dispatch to Brussels, that it was being intercepted and decoded by the German radio monitoring service. Both Himmler's Security Service and Canaris' *Abwehr* Intelligence organization had been immediately put on the alert to track down the unknown German informant in Rome.

"I'll handle it. Leave it to me. I'll put my whole *Abwehr* network on to it immediately," Canaris quickly volunteered, keen as he was to reassure Himmler that he had the matter in hand.

When Hitler's alarming order to "track down the traitor" had first reached him, Canaris had had to think fast. Doing so, as he walked briskly down the corridor to Himmler's office. Before opening its door, he stopped to mess himself up a bit—tugging his tie askew, ruffling his hair and slapping his cheeks to a burning red to give the effect of a man revved up to fever pitch.

He knew that he had to make a good show of this, if he were to prove to Himmler that he was "on side".

Consummate actor that he was, his performance was first class. Melodramatic enough to convince the head of the SS of his sincerity. Himmler going so far as to be quite touched by what appeared to be Canaris' genuine concern.

It was obvious to him that the Little Admiral wanted nothing more than to take the load off his shoulders in regard to hunting down the traitor. This not only showed Canaris' exemplary devotion to The Reich, but an extraordinary act of friendship for which Himmler was most grateful. Grateful enough to return the courtesy straight away.

"Thank you Willie. Let me offer you Heydrich's service's in lieu of my own. You can be assured *he'll* clear it up, quick smart."

"Oh, I have no doubt of *that*, but no, no, no . . . I wouldn't dream of adding to the man's burdens. We all know what an enormous amount of work Heydrich's got on his hands."

His abrupt rejection of Himmler's kind offer had been a knee-jerk reaction. One based less on good sense than unbridled terror. Canaris knew instantly that he'd made a mistake, that it was possible he'd given himself away.

Himmler was certainly looking at him strangely in response. His eyes, always small and rat-like behind his rimless glasses, were now black pin-pricks, narrowed with suspicion.

"I think I'm beginning to see what's going on here," he said—a cruel, triumphant smile lifting the left corner of his thin mouth.

My God! Canaris was in stark panic. His thoughts were tumbling over themselves to come up with some feasible explanation if, in fact, Himmler had stumbled on the truth of his involvement with the Resistance.

This was all getting too close for comfort. Especially now that the head of the SS had decided to close the gap between them by walking over to put his clammy, conciliatory hand on Canaris' shoulder.

"Willie," he said, looking with amused condescension straight into his eyes. "At some point you're going to have to accept the fact that Heydrich is better than you at his job. Come now . . . you must put aside your jealousy and take pride, instead, in the fact that you trained him to outstrip you."

"You're right," Canaris conceded with a sigh of dejection, letting his shoulders slump in what Himmler construed to be defeat, rather than all-encompassing relief.

"For friendship's sake, and to express my faith in your capabilities, I'm prepared to hand over the entire investigation to you. But take my advice Willie, and never let your ego get in the way of your good sense. It's not like you to do so."

You idiot! Canaris thought as he walked from Himmler's office, having made a show of being suitably contrite and grateful for the insights into his character that Himmler had provided.

As soon as he reached his *own* office, he picked up the phone.

"Long distance to Munich please," he said to the operator. "I'm wanting to speak to Dr. Josef Mueller."

The telephonist obliged soon after with a static connection through which Canaris issued his orders.

"Mule . . . Canaris here. We have a little problem with our Italian connection. Apparently we have a spy wandering around the Vatican who has been passing on top secret information to the Allies. We need a good man on the job to track him down and get rid of him A.S.A.P. I'm going to place the entire investigation in your hands. *Comprendez?*"

"You're coming through loud and clear," Mueller replied, smiling at the apparent seriousness of Canaris' tone. No one but the Little Admiral would have thought to use it to deliver such a laughable order.

And that was that, Canaris assumed after he hung up. Happy to know that Mueller's investigations into the Vatican would go nowhere, he reclined in his chair and folded his arms nonchalantly behind his head. He wanted to dwell for a short moment on the sheer brilliance of his scheme. Laughing quietly at the response he was sure Mueller would be having to it back in Munich. After all, all was fair in love and war. And sometimes—*just sometimes*—there were a few little incidents that fell into place to make it highly amusing.

In such a self-congratulatory state, it never crossed Canaris' mind that there was a glitch in his system. Another member of his *Abwehr* staff—a man not attached to the Resistance and keen to make his mark—had decided to take up the case of the Vatican Spy on his own initiative. Hopping on board a plane to Rome with a first class ticket that read:

Colonel Ernst Rohleder,
Vice-Head, Abwehr Department of Internal Investigations[15]

He returned in his zeal, only a few days later, to report to Canaris that the suspicion of treason by way of the Vatican lay with Dr. Josef Mueller himself.

Raising his eyebrows at the revelation, Canaris stopped short of turning to Colonel Oster to share his genuine surprise. Focussing it instead on Colonel Rohleder who was sitting next to Oster on the other side of his desk.

"Yes, I was surprised too," Rohleder said, having no idea that the other two men's surprise was for an entirely different reason than his own. "Would you like me to pursue the investigation further?"

After what appeared to be a considerable amount of deliberation, Canaris replied:

"No, thank you Colonel. The enormity of your discovery demands that *I* take it from here. You've done quite enough. I don't know where to begin to thank you."

Gratified by having been given such an accolade from a man

KILL THE FUHRER ⚡

of Canaris' renown, Rohleder got to his feet, clicked his heels and threw out a salute.

Canaris stood up quickly to respond in kind, thrusting out his right arm and voicing his "Heil Hitler" with a most convincing gusto, while catching, from the corner of his eye, the amused expression on Oster's face.

But this, Canaris believed, was a time to be serious:

"Colonel Rohleder," he continued. "Please be aware that I take due note of your diligence and insightful actions in regard to this important issue. You, young man, are going to go places."

But not here! were his words left unvoiced, as he escorted the eager-to-please Colonel from his office. Giving him a hearty pat on the back, he sent him on his way. Watching after him with a wave and a smile as Rohleder walked down the corridor. Canaris waiting until the man had turned the corner and taken himself out of sight, before he closed his office door.

"Remind me to fire that young man will you?" he said to Oster as he casually returned to his desk and dumped the Colonel's carefully prepared "*Vatican Dossier*" into his wastepaper bin. "We can't afford to have zestful little Nazis on board . . . particularly not ones with brains!"

But the days of Canaris coming out on top were numbered. Fate allowed him just one more win before everything turned sour.

On May 3, 1940, he and Oster informed Sas for the *third* time that Hitler's invasion of the Netherlands was imminent:

"I'm sorry to burden you again with this information," Oster apologized, knowing the difficult position in which he was putting his friend. "I know what trouble you've had in the Hague. Who knows, it could be a case of 'third time lucky', but if I were you, I'd hang off for a short while before passing this new date on. They'll probably not believe you anyway after all of Hitler's postponements. So let's wait a little longer to see what happens, shall we?"

They waited until May 9, when Canaris and Oster shouted Sas to a last supper at the prestigious Lorenz Adlon.[16]

"Matters have definitely been set in motion," Oster confided over dinner, dabbing the corners of his mouth with his napkin as he spoke, hoping that its starched, white linen fabric might help obscure his words from the prying eyes of the Gestapo. A liberal sprinkling of its members had seated themselves in the same restaurant that evening, many of whom had added the art of lip-reading to their array of savage talents.

"The orders for the western invasion are in force," Oster went on, coughing politely into his napkin.

"Is there a chance of a further delay?" Sas asked in between sipping his soup. "We've been through this three times now."

"Who knows the machinations of the Great Man's mind?" Canaris joined in to say. "I can only suggest that it's to our advantage to be a tad more circumspect this time round. We can't afford to make another mistake. But this much *I do know* . . . The critical hour is 9.30 tonight. If there have been no counter-orders by then, it's final."

The three of them lingered over their meal until 9.05, finishing with a glass of cognac before quickly walking their way through the foggy city streets to Berlin Military Headquarters.

"You'd better wait outside," Oster said to Sas, offering him a cigarette in consolation while he and Canaris made their way into the hub of activity that was High Command.

Sas waited under the misty lamplight, making for a dramatic cliché in his trench coat and grey felt hat. Not only did he smoke his way through the cigarette Oster had given him, but an additional three of his own before Oster rejoined him.

"My dear friend," he said, as he put his hand on Sas' shoulder. "I'm sorry to say that things have already started. The orders have not been countermanded. That swine, Hitler, has already gone to the western front and the invasion has begun. I can only hope that we'll meet again after the war."

Sas dropped his cigarette butt into the gutter and squashed its burning embers with his shoe—pausing before he spoke, as an involuntary shudder ran down his spine. Contrary to Oster's words of optimism, he had an eerie, *awful* feeling, that he would never see his friends again.

Despite the darkness of the smoggy, sultry night, Oster couldn't have failed to see the glistening onset of tears in his eyes. At the stinging threat of them, Sas turned quickly and walked away. He went as far as the street's corner, before he had composed himself enough to turn and say:

"Say goodbye to Canaris for me, will you Hans. And please .

. . both of you . . . take *great* care."

But Oster was by now only a faceless silhouette in the distance. A black, uniformed figure, standing with hands in his pockets, watching him go. His very identity and purpose in life already swallowed up in darkness.

Sas knew, however, that he had to put his depression and fears for his friends' safety aside, quite aware, at that dramatic moment, that his immediate allegiance lay elsewhere. He must get back to the embassy and ring the Hague War Office at all speed.

It was just sheer luck that on his first attempt to get through the phone was picked up by his old friend, Naval Commander Post Uitweer:

Sas said:	"Post, you know my voice don't you? I am here in Berlin. I have only one thing to tell you. Tomorrow at dawn—sit tight! You understand me don't you? Please repeat that."
Uitweer replied:	"Letter 210 received."

On hearing the right response to his code (200 meant an invasion, the last digits were the day of the month), Sas relaxed. He had not realized just how tense he had been, how close to his ears his taut shoulders had been riding.

Nor had he anticipated that, within an hour, they would rise again to that same tense position in response to a follow-up phone call from a Colonel van Plaasche, who, as the Chief of the Foreign News Department, was happy to abandon all caution in his fervour to confirm Sas' story.

"I've had news about your wife's operation," the Colonel said, experimenting with a transparent piece of D.I.Y. code that did nothing to hide his intent. "Have you taken every medical advice?" he asked, infuriating Sas for having compromised him on an open line.

"Why in the *hell* do you bother me in these circumstances," he shouted back over the phone. "I've taken all the medical advice available. The operation's got to take place at dawn. It can't be helped now."

When Sas slammed down the receiver, he was shaking with rage. Or at least that's what he told himself, not wanting to admit that the trembling of his body was, in fact, unadulterated fear. A fear which was to be compounded, a thousand times over, in the days and years to come.

The truth was that he was terrified for himself and his country, and even more so for his friends—Oster and Canaris. He knew that they were skating on very thin ice in their efforts to range themselves against Hitler. There was a time limit to their toying with the Devil—each day spent playing at the life and death game of "Kill or Be Killed" stymied their chance of escape and survival. With the odds and the ever-present SS stacked up against them, they were *bound* to get caught out . . . and soon.

The worst of it was that he suspected that Canaris and Oster knew it. *Knew,* that having dedicated themselves to treason, they would have to see it through to the bitter end. For the sake of God and Country, and at the expense of their own reputations, they were prepared to partake in the crime and had reconciled themselves to paying the ultimate price for committing it.

Desperate to cut and run himself . . . to get as far away as he could from Hitler and his hoards, Sas couldn't help but marvel at his friends' courage in having chosen to stay and fight it out—to actually proceed with that glorious suicide mission of theirs. All the while knowing that if they succeeded in putting an end to Hitler, it would mean their own.

Now, with his new "enemy" status, Sas was no longer in a position to stay and sing their praises. It wasn't until the war's end that he was able to do so, welcoming the long-lost opportunity to speak out on their behalf when his commanding officer addressed him on the matter:

"At the end of the day Sas, you must agree that your friends, Canaris and Oster were nothing, after all, but despicable traitors?"

It was a comment that had Sas lift his shoulders and breathe in deeply before he replied.

"They were two men, sir, who were recklessly courageous in their opposition to Hitler. All the more because they were constantly surrounded by the Gestapo and the threat of their own imminent deaths. I consider that they were the most remarkable men I've ever known and that I was privileged to once call them my friends."

CHAPTER ELEVEN

In the Summer of 1940 those two friends of his were a long way off being referred to in the past tense. At the hub of the action, they were still very much alive and kicking, albeit extremely depressed.

"When is it proper for a German to get married, Uncle Willie?" Canaris' nephew asked of him. "Should I wait until our final victory to make our wedding part of the celebrations? Now that Hitler has Paris, it shouldn't take him long to get England under his belt, which will give him the run of Europe."

"Marry at once and enjoy life while you can," was Canaris' clipped reply. He was unimpressed by his nephew's new-found Aryan arrogance. "Be aware that the future holds nothing but catastrophe for Germany."

His nephew had been shocked by this defeatist response. He was stunned silent and a little ashamed—more so of his Uncle than himself. These last few months had heralded a new and glorious era in German history. One in which Rear Admiral Wilhelm Canaris was poised to play a major part. Why was it then, as one of Hitler's chosen, that his famous uncle wasn't rejoicing—wasn't sharing in the elation over the Third Reich's series of speedy and astonishingly streamlined military victories?

It wasn't like Canaris to be so pessimistic, but having witnessed the fall of France and been present in Belgrade straight after its bombing, it had taken some time to get over the carnage he'd seen there. He had run away to Spain for a couple of weeks of R&R to lick his wounds and wipe from his memory the gaping, gory wounds that he and his kind had inflicted on the Yugoslavian populace.

Being a man who abhorred violence in any shape or form, he'd been unable to come to grips with the sight of the thousands of bleeding, broken bodies in the Belgrade streets. Those, that is, that were still intact.

The hellish, bomb-blasted city landscape had been littered with bits and pieces of human beings. An arm and a leg dangled from the branch of a tree; a severed head rolled down the steps of a burning cathedral. The skeletal remains of once-great buildings loomed eerily over blood-drenched, rubble-ridden roads. It had been the perfect picture of war—a smoke-edged vignette over which hung the lung-choking stench of death, a snapshot of monumental destruction and human suffering in the raw.

Ever since, Canaris had not felt quite himself. His normally resilient nature had been weighed down by a serious bout of guilt and depression that deepened in parallel with every one of Hitler's on-going successes, the devastating string of which had put most of western Europe in the Fuhrer's hands by either alliance or occupation, and thrown the Third Reich into its heyday. The winner take all scenario had effectively rendered the German Resistance redundant.

"Do you honestly think that we'll be able to talk any of the Generals at High Command round to our way of thinking now?" Canaris asked despondently of Dohnanyi and Oster, who were among the group of friends he had invited to dinner. "Can you imagine that *any* of them will be prepared to deny Hitler and forego a share of his triumph? They're saying now that he's a military genius—that he's the reincarnation of Alexander the Great! Have you ever heard such outrageous, sycophantic claptrap?"

"Well then, take heart Canaris," Pastor Dietrich Bonhoeffer put in. "Didn't Alexander die young? By that reckoning, Hitler's already outstayed his welcome. With any luck, he'll follow suit."

Up until this point in the evening, Canaris had taken little notice of Dohnanyi's brother-in-law, but now he was keen to give Bonhoeffer his full attention. He hadn't expected such a razor-sharp remark to come from a man of God. The fact that it had, had doubled its impact and made him want to get to know this rather intriguing young pastor better.

"It'll take a hundred years for the world to realize our luckless state," Canaris said to him as he leant over the arm of his chair to pat his two dogs—that pair of faithful friends of his, with their shaggy fur and distinct lack of pedigree, that he took with him everywhere. He found comfort in their unconditional loyalty and

KILL THE FUHRER ✠

in what he firmly believed to be their superiority over any human being of his acquaintance.

"Should Hitler win his accursed war," he continued, affectionately rubbing each of them behind the ears, "it'll certainly be the end of us and Germany as we know and love it. Should he *lose*, he'll see to it that we and the country as a whole go down with him. There are no two ways about it. No matter which way you look at it, we'll get the raw end of the deal. Traitors win the heart of no man and can look forward to nothing but the scorn of those they've betrayed, and more so, the contempt of those who have benefited from their betrayal."

He didn't know why he'd let down his guard and loosed his disillusionment on Bonhoeffer. Given that he didn't know him as well as the other men in the room—Oster, Hassell, Goerdeler, Gisevius, Mueller and Dohnanyi—it had seemed strange to have done so. Perhaps it had been because those comments of his were a cry for help, in the hope that a man of the Church might be able to offer it.

While waiting for the pastor to drop his pearls of wisdom, Canaris bent over to cup his pups' furry faces in his hands, looking down at them with a guileless adoration that completely belied the tired cynicism of his words.

His open, doting expression gave Bonhoeffer, within seconds, a clear insight into Canaris' soul. Making him realize that this shrewd man of the world—this Admiral of the Empire, was complex in the extreme. A man hard-arsed enough to hold his own against the likes of Hitler, Himmler and Heydrich, but who, in essence, was utterly gentle.

Thus, it made it easier for Bonhoeffer to put their conversation on another plain.

"You forget that we are working for a higher purpose than the world's recognition Canaris. And whether or not we receive it has nothing to do with the moral stand that all of us here have taken. But we *need* you. Don't give up on us now. For your own sake as well as ours, you *have* to go the distance. You know as well as I do that you'd never forgive yourself if you failed to do your duty—not by Hitler, but by God and Country."

"Don't worry," Canaris replied—tired and resigned. "This little Admiral's not about to desert his sinking ship."

On that issue, however, Bonhoeffer was quick to correct him.

"Our ship's not sinking," he said with the conviction of man whose hundred percent faith was in the Almighty. "Just gone adrift for a time, that's all. We'll get back up to speed soon enough."

Suddenly sick of symbolism, Canaris snapped back to the salient point.

"The problem is . . . we've lost our influence. Basically, Hitler's hoodwinked everyone into believing he's invincible. The whole nation's in a state of euphoria over his successes in the west, the Balkans and Russia.

"Why *would* they want to get rid of him? Why on Earth would anyone be interested in our plans to dispose of him? And let's not forget that he's just put the icing on the cake by whipping the nation up into a Jew-murdering frenzy. Who are *we* to compete with the joys of boundless blood-lust?

"As far as the country's concerned Hitler's riding high and can do no wrong. Look how easily he diverted everyone's attention away from Goering's failure to have his Luftwaffe blitz England. And for heaven's sake, the arrogant lunatic didn't even bat an eye when he casually declared war against America the other day."

"Ah but yes . . . that's where he'll come unstuck," Oster interrupted, confident in his prediction as he lit a cigarette. "We all know what 'cometh before a fall'. I think we can count on him taking a little tumble after that madcap ultimatum. But in the meantime, Willie, it does none of us any good to see you so downcast. Why *should* you be after all you've already achieved? You must remember what an enormous success you had in Spain."

That success of Canaris' had been considerable. In fact, it was probably the greatest accomplishment of his life. Single-handedly, he had managed to keep Spain (that beloved second home of his) out of the war. Talking his friend Franco *out* of it, rather than *into* it. This, he had done in dangerous defiance of Hitler's orders, after the Fuhrer had expressly sent him to Spain to pressure them into joining the Axis alliance.

At the mental replay of that honey of a coup he'd pulled off, Canaris' face creased into a smile—his eyes lit up with that old look of merry mischief with which his friends were far more comfortable and familiar.

It had always been Canaris' greatest joy to outsmart the

smartest. And if Hitler didn't rate as being the smartest man of his acquaintance, then he most certainly was the most cunning and brutal. To have got one up on him and come out of the whole deal smelling like a rose had been an achievement indeed.

For not only had Hitler *still* not suspected him of sedition, but he had put his faith in him once more. Soon after Canaris' supposedly failed negotiations with Franco, Hitler had posted him, along with his naval intelligence expertise, to the beautiful bayside city of Algeciras. That strategic southern-most point of Spain made for the perfect vantage point from which Hitler had ordered Canaris to keep tabs on all shipping movements in, around and out of the Mediterranean.

"No need for alarm," Canaris had been quick to report back to German Headquarters. "The buildup of Allied ships in the area is for the relief of Malta and Alexandria."

It had not exactly been a lie on his part, simply a failure to tell the *whole* truth. Canaris had decided to pass on only part of it to his compatriots in Berlin, while keeping quiet about the Allies' more tide-turning plans for Tunisia. Those plans had them dispatch only a ship or two in the direction of Malta and Alexandria, while positioning the bulk of their fleet to invade North Africa from behind Rommel's lines.

Not that Canaris was proud of having given his own country a bum steer. What he'd done, he'd done with every good intention, hoping that it would hasten the Third Reich's downfall, before *it* had a chance to bring about the downfall of the rest of the world and Germany itself.

It was a sort of lose/lose situation—this bad business of working for the Resistance—a career path that promised victories that could be nothing but bitter-sweet.

"Don't dwell on it," Dohnanyi said, topping up Canaris' glass of wine while second guessing his thoughts. "We . . . all of us here, would do better not to over-analyze our actions. Just be satisfied in the knowledge that they are a necessary evil to combat one that's greater. Of course, it goes against the grain to betray one's country, but we know deep down that we do so only to save it. I have no doubt, that when all this horror is over and done with; when our fellow countrymen are finally free of Hitler and his hysterics . . . that they *and* history will see it our way."

"And if not, we'll all be dead and who will care?" Canaris followed through with the smooth cynicism of a man who didn't think so much of himself. "I'm not complaining mind you. Betrayal after all, has its benefits. While I was in Algeciras I found out that I was on the Brits' Hit List . . . that one way or another, they've been planning to capture or assassinate me."

"Well there you go . . . as always, the Master of Escape." said Gisevius, as he raised his glass to toast his fortunate, fugitive friend.

"Oh, I didn't *escape*," Canaris threw back at him with a bitter laugh, gesturing for Gisevius to put that glass of his down.

The Little Admiral knew that he hardly deserved to be saluted for having struck a blow against his own kind. The fact that his act of treachery had saved his skin only made him feel more guilty about it. So he explained.

"Once they realized that I was up to my conspiratorial neck in it, they just decided I wasn't a threat. Leaving me in one piece and in place made me far more valuable to *their* war effort than Germany's."

Of course, there had been one other downside to Canaris' Spanish success—and that was having to do his old friend, Field Marshal Erwin Rommel in the eye. It wasn't something of which he would ever have thought himself capable, had he not been so sadly disillusioned with the man.

He had made a special point of visiting Rommel in North Africa to complain about the inhuman practices that Hitler was inflicting on the Jews. Vile acts of persecution and murder that he had witnessed first-hand in horrifying, blood-curdling technicolour. Unable to simply stand by and let it go on, he had been determined to do something about it, and Rommel, with his national hero status, had seemed his most logical course of action.

Canaris had been absolutely positive that when that noblest of warriors had been made aware of the Reich's atrocities, the Resistance would at last gain the support of the most honourable and arguably most popular field marshal in German history. At last, Hitler would be up against some truly formidable opposition.

He had not expected that Rommel would dismiss his concerns outright, that he would flatly refuse to give them a second thought or to let the chance of their validity twig his conscience.

Much too pre-occupied with his battle plans and personal grab for glory, he'd wished only to get on with the slaying of his *immediate* enemies. Unwilling to accept the fact that back home, sitting behind his desk and without the challenge of sand dunes and self-sacrifice to get in his way, Hitler was outdoing him one hundredfold—wiping his enemies out by the million. Killing more Jews with the stroke of his pen than Rommel, for all his military prowess, was managing to do with his Panzers.

After their chat, Canaris had thought considerably less of Rommel and had had serious doubts as to the strength of their friendship. Quite apart from the fact that the Desert Fox's abrupt dismissal of his concerns had been a personal affront, Canaris believed it had also been a shameful neglect of moral duty on the man's part. Rommel had not even been prepared to lend him a listening ear, let alone his active support.

That, Canaris had decided, was a severing of the bonds between them that could go both ways. From that point on, he believed that Rommel deserved everything he got.

Not that Canaris took any pleasure in exacting revenge or meting out dubious justice. In fact, it disturbed him immeasurably when Keitel kept persisting in putting him in that odious position. Keitel saw him—the head of the *Abwehr*—as being nothing more than the nation's No. 1 hit man:

"We want you to get rid of French General Henri Giraud." Keitel ordered, as Hitler's acting spokesman.

"Get rid of? How?" Canaris replied with a feigned innocence, unable to resist teasing the man even though he was fully aware of the cold-blooded murder the Fuhrer had in mind.

"Don't push me," Keitel came back at him.

Dull-witted and weak as he was, there were times when Keitel got fed-up with being the go-between and the butt of everyone's jokes, particularly those of Canaris, who seemed to derive endless pleasure from making a fool of him.

"You know very well what I mean," he continued. "And that I *mean* that you do it *soon*. The Fuhrer believes that Giraud's become a great concern to us and that he must be . . . removed."

With Keitel so keen to sugar-coat his orders with euphemisms, Canaris thought he would take advantage of it. The word "removal", being such a loose term, left the way wide open for him to act on it in its more literal sense. This he did by swiftly *removing* the French General from danger. Smuggling him out of his precarious position in Vichy, France to the safety of French North Africa.

In secret, and by way of U-Boat, he managed to whisk him out of harm's and Hitler's way, laying the blame for the French General's escape on the Allies. This, under the wartime circumstances, was logical enough. Neither Keitel nor Hitler ever got wise to the fact that it had been he—their own head of German Intelligence—who had arranged it.

Soon after, however, they gave him an even more gruesome assignment. On this second time around, Hitler and Keitel provided themselves with a backup plan by contracting both Canaris *and* his deputy, Major-General Erwin Lahousen, to do the job. Keitel chose his words more carefully, to leave no room for misinterpretation.

"The Fuhrer has ordered the assassination of the Chief of the French General Staff, Field Marshal Maxime Weygand. He fears that the unbeaten part of the French Army in North Africa might look to Weygand to lead their resistance."

That order left Lahousen standing stunned and appalled:

"I have no intention of carrying out that order," he fired back at Keitel, stormy-faced and indignant. "My officers are soldiers, not murderers!"

It was an unchecked moment of honesty and dangerous, hot-blooded confrontation that Canaris was quick to bring to an end. Walking over to his friend, he placed a reassuring hand on his arm.

"Calm down Lahousen," he said. "I'll deal with it."

Words which put his deputy's mind at rest—he had caught Canaris' wink; and Keitel's mind too—because *he* had not.

Hitler's off-sider assumed, as he left the *Abwehr* offices, that Canaris, if not Lahousen, had the wit and wiles to carry out the task.

"It is obvious," Canaris turned to say to his deputy, after having closed the door on both Keitel and their meeting, "that this order will not only *never* be carried out, but it will not even be communicated any further . . . Feel better now?"

"But how can we get away with that? What shall we say when

Keitel asks if it's been done?"

"Nothing much, just keep fudging. Believe me . . . Hitler's mind functions like a machine gun when it comes to murder. In a few days, he'll probably have forgotten all about it and have turned his attention to someone who's more fun to kill. In fact, you can count on it."

CHAPTER TWELVE

It was a pity that Canaris could not count as much on Dr. Wilhelm Schmidhuber. Grateful as he was that Schmidhuber had introduced his friend, Dr. Josef Mueller, to the Resistance, Canaris had always been aware that the charming, ever-so-slightly-unprincipled Schmidhuber was a loose end that he had failed to tie up. One that, on the fringe of the Resistance, had been left dangling and dangerous—poised to bring about its downfall.

How strange it was that the fate of the Resistance should hang on such a slender thread. That having been arrested for the unrelated crime of currency fraud, Schmidhuber had seen fit to secure his release by bombarding the Gestapo with a surplus of information in regard to his unusual dealings with the *Abwehr*.

Well before they had threatened him with torture, he had surprised his SS interrogator by openly naming every top ranking member of the Resistance, providing the Gestapo with that much-sought-after list of military and civilian notables who were actively working against the Third Reich. The name of Admiral Wilhelm Canaris featured among them.

It was a revelation that not only bowled over the Nazi Brass, but put a smug, knowing smile on Reinhard Heydrich's face. For a long time, he had suspected as much. On many an occasion he'd gone to Canaris' office to hint at that suspicion and needle him into "coming clean".

It had been a kind of game the two of them had played, each of them wondering who would be the first to wear the other down. Heydrich was unable to resist the temptation of challenging his mentor, while at the same time feeling a little sad that he might be the means of bringing the man down.

He was nostalgic enough over what their past friendship had meant to him to have begun his interrogations with a subtle warning or two. This evened up the odds by putting Canaris on his guard, while providing a handicap for himself to make the game more exciting.

It had been a battle of wits in which Canaris had managed to stand his ground. That was, until Schmidhuber and his loose lips, had cut it from under him.

"The Gestapo arrested Schmidhuber last night," Dohnanyi and Oster had rushed to Canaris' office to tell him.

Putting aside the documents he'd been reading, Canaris had asked very calmly, "Where are they holding him?"

Obviously much more uneasy than his boss, Oster had been pacing the floor when he answered, "Munich." Stopping suddenly, in a moment of angry self-reproach, to slam his fist down on the desk and say, "I *knew* I shouldn't have trusted that man. Right from the start, I sensed he was trouble."

"On what charge?" Canaris continued, actively ignoring Oster's outburst. He was very practised at keeping his cool.

"Currency fraud."

It had been Dohnanyi who had answered him, taking over from where Oster had left off. "He's been using his position as Acting Consul for Portugal to issue Jewish refugees with illicit passports and to transfer foreign currency on their behalf."

This came as nothing new or even vaguely scandalous to Canaris, given that for some time, he'd been doing precisely the same for many of his own Jewish friends and associates. If *he* had been able to get away with it, he was sure that Schmidhuber would.

"Storm in a teacup. I'm not all that concerned. If nothing else, the man's got the gift of the gab. He'll talk his way round it," he said, offering his compatriots the reassurance of his experience— convinced as he was that Schmidhuber was fluent in speaking with a forked-tongue. At rock bottom, he was a shrewd businessman. Which begged the question, "How on Earth did he manage to get himself caught?"

"It was one of those currency transfers of his," Oster had pulled himself together enough to answer. "One of his couriers was caught carrying a wad of American dollars out of Germany. The one stroke of luck was that Mueller got wind of the authorities being on to him before Schmidhuber did."

"Well . . . I'm sure Mule must have warned him?" Canaris said, assuming the obvious.

"Of course . . . he flew to Zurich to let Schmidhuber know that he was in terrible danger and would be wise not to return to Germany in the immediate future. Shuffled him off to Rome and secured him temporary asylum there. Which, to my way of thinking, was a sterling effort on his part on such short notice.

"But then I suppose he knew it was imperative that he did so. I mean, considering how concerned he must have been about the destructive impact Schmidhuber might have on the Resistance if he were arrested. He knows that for all the man's bravado and big talk, he's basically as weak as water and equally indiscreet. He'll collapse under the pressure of even the mildest interrogation.

"Mind you, Schmidhuber's brought it on himself. He's always liked to big note himself by throwing his money around. It's just that he went overboard with his generosity to the Jews."

"Generosity . . . my foot!" Canaris had scoffed. Master of deception that he was, he had no time for crooks who passed their crimes off as acts of kindness. "The cunning old bastard wasn't doing it for the good of the Jews, but to fill his own pockets. Get that straight! He just got too greedy and sloppy in the process."

Not having an ounce of meanness in his nature, it was unlike Canaris not to give a man his due. It was for this reason that Oster had chosen not to refute his comment, trusting wholeheartedly in Canaris' infallible instinct when it came to human nature. He had always been able to get the true measure of a man. He could sniff out a fraud a mile away.

"Unfortunately, Mueller's contacts in Rome weren't strong enough to protect Schmidhuber," Oster had continued as he'd absentmindedly picked up the small ceramic of the three monkeys that was sitting on Canaris' desk.

"Heydrich been here again?" he asked, interrupting his train of thought re the Schmidhuber saga to express his sympathy, continuing with it once more after Canaris nodded in the affirmative. His straight-mouthed expression let Oster know that he was feeling the strain.

"The German authorities tracked Schmidhuber down and demanded that he return immediately to Munich to face the currency charges. Warning him that if he were entertaining any ideas of skipping town to remember that he was due to be called up for military service and would be charged for desertion if he didn't comply."

"Well, for God's sake, why didn't he just get on a plane and go back? With all that money of his he's so keen to flaunt, he could have just paid off the jury and put an end to the whole inquiry," Canaris had interjected, beginning to sense the growing danger. That that witless, vain peacock Wilhelm Schmidhuber was going to put them *all* under the gun.

"Precisely *my* thoughts!" Dohnanyi had thrown in at that point, lifting his upturned hands in wonderment. "But can you believe it? Probably for the first time in his life, Schmidhuber decided to take a moral stand."

"Go on," Canaris said . . . his jaw tightening in trepidation.

"Apparently he stood up in the middle of the restaurant that he and Mueller were in and said at the top of his voice, for everyone to hear, that he'd only return to Berlin as British High Commissioner, and that since the chances of that were slim, it was now his intention to go to England and offer his services to the Allies."

"Oh the *fool!*"

"Well as you can guess, he was immediately arrested by the Italian police and extradited to Munich. The irony of the whole thing being that the Gestapo had only been interested initially in the currency charges against him, which he could have explained away easily enough. But after his little performance in the Italian restaurant, they'd naturally taken exception and decided to look more closely into his affairs. I suppose that's when he got scared and decided to rat on the Resistance."

This was a turn up for the books. For some time Canaris had been aware that many members of the Resistance had been under Himmler's and Heydrich's close scrutiny, but without having any hard evidence against them, it had been both men's favoured policy to just watch and wait, rather than to actually arrest anyone under suspicion.

The problem was that Canaris had got into the dangerous habit of relying on the SS Chiefs' stalling tactics, not figuring that lower-ranking members of the secret police might decide to interfere with their well-planned timing. In an attempt to fast-track their own personal advancement within the SS ranks, they had begun to make arrests, with or without Himmler's or Heydrich's say-so.

It was a play from left field that Canaris *must* have realized would happen sooner or later. But of all the people for them to have picked on first . . . what a piece of bad luck that it had been Dr. Wilhelm Schmidhuber. The SS had effectively, if not completely by accident, stumbled on the mother-lode.

"Where is he now?" Canaris asked.

"They've transferred him to Tegel Military Prison outside Berlin. Dr. Roeder's taken over the interrogation."

"Roeder . . . Oh my God!"

Now just as tense as Oster, Canaris was up and out of his chair, striding anxiously around his office. The mention of Roeder's infamous name meant that the situation was fast spinning out of his control.

As the legal officer of the Judge Advocate's Department, Roeder had not been given his nickname—*the Blood Judge*—for nothing. Fresh from his judicial inquiry and subsequent victory over the *Rote Kapelle* (the largest Communist Resistance cell in Germany), Roeder had been marked as the most skilled and savage interrogator of the Reich.

It was a title for which he'd had to fight (with his qualifications of evil and unparalleled bloodlust) against a multitude of other likely, bloody-minded candidates. Unsurpassed in his expertise as a sadistic sociopath, he'd soon clawed his way to the top, having recently added to his sterling list of credentials, the horrific executions of Lieutenant Harro Schulz-Boysen and his gentle wife Libertas.

Both of them, on face value, had been guilty of the crime of treason—of passing on German military secrets to Moscow. Their objective of destroying the Third Reich for the ultimate good of their country made them—to Canaris' way of thinking—heroes rather than traitors.

It was just a pity that Roeder had not seen it the same way.

"Schulz-Boysen is implacable . . . nothing but an ill-informed, deluded fanatic," Roeder had had to admit, after having inflicted the most severe of tortures on the Lieutenant, all of which had failed to break the man or to provide Roeder with the information he'd been after. But like that now battered and bloodied prisoner of his, Roeder was never one to give up or give in. Instead, he had decided to pick on someone who was *not* his own size:

"Fortunately his wife proved more forthcoming," he'd reported back proudly to Himmler, who in turn had passed on the good news to Canaris.

The deplorable truth was that the gentle, fairy-faced, twenty-six-year-old Libertas Schulz-Boysen had indeed broken under torture, as she'd warned her compatriots she was bound to do. She'd known that she wouldn't be able to withstand the excruciating pain to which Roeder was eager to submit her.

The result was that both she and her husband, along with one hundred other members of the luckless *Rote Kapelle*, had been executed by whatever gruesome means had taken Roeder's fancy. The man never being quite able to make up his mind as to which gave him the most pleasure—the quick kill with the guillotine, or the slow, savouring of suffering that piano wire around a man's neck could offer him.

Either way, and to the end, Lieutenant Harro Schulz-Boysen had kept his silence. It wasn't until after the war that a poem he wrote was discovered. It had been scribbled on a piece of scrap paper that he'd stuffed into the stone floor of his cell. It read:

> *"If we are to die —*
> *if the executions are to go ahead,*
> *at least we know*
> *that the seeds have been planted;*
> *and one day the human spirit*
> *will triumph over that of the State."*

It was the likes of Schulz-Boysen—men of inconceivable courage and conviction, whom Canaris knew would give the German people something to hold onto after the war.

Because he—Canaris, was sure that *he* would never be capable of such selfless sacrifice and valour. He never dreamed that those two upstanding qualities would, in fact, be the very ones demanded of him further down the track, that he wouldn't only rise to the challenge, but do so without a word of complaint.

That terrifying time had not yet come, and right now, with his troubles only in the *process* of brewing, he was very much in the mood to complain, and was fast whizzing himself into a state of panic. As were his two companions.

"He's already implicated *me*," Dohnanyi said. It was the first opportunity Dohnanyi had had to bring himself into the picture and to alert his friends to his own considerable fear.

"How do you know?" Canaris turned to him to ask.

"Through Mueller. He's already been dragged in for the first round of interrogations at Gestapo headquarters."

"But is he all right?" This time there was genuine concern in Canaris' voice. He was particularly fond of Mule and couldn't bear to think of him suffering.

"Oh don't worry, the Gestapo have been quite civil so far," Dohnanyi reassured, albeit with a note of sarcasm. "Just had him sit in the next room to Schmidhuber so that he could listen to the man squeal. Apparently he mentioned my name repeatedly and made the most incriminating statements about you, Canaris. You'd better watch out."

"Did Schmidhuber know that Mueller was listening in?"

"Not until they took Mueller in to join him, no. At which point the man must have squirmed in his seat. Not over the fact that he'd spilled the beans and implicated his friends, but because he'd done so with a cup of coffee and cigar in his hand. The Gestapo had offered them to him as an option to torture. They're not stupid. With a man like Schmidhuber and his massive ego, they knew that they'd get more out of him that way."

All of this was most alarming for Canaris. Particularly because he was just finding out about it. It was unusual for him not to be the first to know.

"But how do you know all this?" he asked

"Mueller," Oster replied, fully aware of Canaris' concerns and eager to relieve them. "Under the circumstances, Willie, it was damn decent of him to have left you out of the loop. There's no doubt he's being followed. But they've given him a 'get-out-of-jail-free' card for the time being, just so long as he doesn't do a bunk. That he makes himself available for further questioning whenever necessary."

"Trust Mule to swing a deal like that," Canaris replied, smiling as he shook his head in disbelief.

He knew that if anyone could do it, it was Mueller - the man just had a way of making people like and trust him. To have protected his friend, and in the same breath gained the trust of the Gestapo, was a feat indeed.

"All I can say is . . . thank God for Mueller," Dohnanyi now joined in. He had as much respect and liking for the man as did Canaris. "I think that he's managed to put the Gestapo's minds at rest to a degree. By the end of the interviews, I think they were more inclined to believe him than Schmidhuber. Schmidhuber, after all, does come across as being the archetypal stool pigeon."

*　　*　　*

That glaringly obvious piece of character analysis had led Roeder to come down on Mueller's side very early in the investigative proceedings, but had not stopped him from grilling him for ten straight hours.

After he'd brought Mueller into the interrogation room and watched, with wry amusement, as Schmidhuber's face turned a whiter shade of pale, he'd seated the two men together and said, "Schmidhuber here tells us that he gave you 50,000 Slovenian crowns to buy provision stamps."

Mueller had looked his former friend-cum-informer in the eye as he'd replied, "You've forgotten, Schmidhuber . . . it was only 5,000, which was repaid to you in Munich, almost immediately by the *Abwehr*."

At which point, Mueller had turned to address Roeder directly. Speaking calmly, if not a little patronizingly for emphasis.

"I'd been ordered to give these stamps, to which Schmidhuber has referred, to certain contacts in Rome. To people who'd proved themselves very useful to Germany," he'd explained.

Sensing that Mueller had Roeder's ear, Schmidhuber had been quick to jump on the bandwagon.

"Oh that's right. I remember now. It *was* 5000. I'm sorry Mueller, I'd forgotten it was for business and not given to you as a present."

Dr. Roeder had simply smiled and said nothing to this late admission and rather remarkable oversight. Instead, he'd turned to his Gestapo associates to whisper his instructions. Schmidhuber following his example by leaning over quietly to murmur to Mueller, "Should I shoot myself?"

A question to which Mueller slowly shook his head, finding it hard to believe that at such a critical, terrifying time, his capricious, supremely dangerous friend had thought to joke!

CHAPTER THIRTEEN

It had been no laughing matter. Serious or not about the prospect of his own death, Schmidhuber had managed to incriminate pretty much everyone of consequence within the Resistance.

It was just very fortunate that by the end of the preliminary investigation, Roeder had decided to come down 75 percent in favour of Mueller's more plausible explanations. The level-headed lawyer had managed to talk his way around and out of the sticky situation, which by Schmidhuber's account was nothing less than scandalous. Particularly because it had implicated a man of such solid standing as Admiral Canaris.

Of course, there was room for doubt . . . as there always was in any good Gestapo investigator's mind. For the time being, however, although not entirely discounting Schmidhuber's statement, Roeder chose to put thoughts of premature arrests aside. Still not wholly convinced of Canaris' guilt, he decided to give him the benefit of the doubt, along with a little breathing space. He knew from experience that if one offered a guilty man enough rope, he would eventually hang himself with it.

To Roeder's shrewd way of thinking, this was killing two birds with one stone. Firstly, by taking the onus off his shoulders in the hope that Canaris might do his job for him; secondly, by sparing himself the unpleasant duty of having to tell Hitler that his dear old friend, Admiral Canaris, wanted him dead.

From that point on, however, Roeder made sure that Canaris was never able to officially free himself or his agents from the surveillance of Himmler's departments, or to act and travel with the freedom to which he'd become accustomed.

However, wise to Roeder's methods, Canaris wasn't about to pick up that rope and run with it. He resolved instead, *not* to kick against the restraints, but to embrace them. Taking the extra time that having his hands tied offered him to work at cultivating firm, fast—albeit false—friendships with all the men he knew were his deadliest enemies.

The first and foremost of these was Heydrich, who, unfortunately, had grown tired of the game—that peculiar love/hate rivalry of theirs in which he'd at last got the upper hand. In sensing that Canaris' power was on the wane, he wanted nothing more than to slap his mentor's face with it.

But it wasn't the right time for that, and it wouldn't be until the SS had managed to stockpile enough hard evidence against him. Unprepared to go head-to-head with Canaris without it, Heydrich was finding it easier to work behind his back, systematically undermining the entire *Abwehr* organization and Canaris' authority within it. He ran the man and his reputation down while promoting the amalgamation of both the traditional German and SS Intelligence departments, at the head of which, he—Reinhard Heydrich—was to have sole control.

While working to that end, it helped to keep his second in command, Major General Walter Schellenberg, fully apprised of the situation.

"Beware of Canaris," Heydrich warned. "You must not allow him to fool you or lull you to sleep. In his case, it's imperative that you assert yourself more ruthlessly. Because to be frank, Schellenberg, I don't approve of what goes on between the two of you."

It was a comment that had the young, handsome Schellenberg look up in surprise. Heydrich's comment had smacked of jealousy rather than objective advice.

"I'm sorry, sir, but I've no idea what you mean," he replied—his tone clipped and offended. Heydrich's seedy, sexual innuendo had been an affront.

But Heydrich had no intention of retracting it.

"Seeing the two of you together Schellenberg, one could take you for being bosom buddies," he said, unable to take the envious edge off his argument, because he could see that the bond between Canaris and his subordinate was genuine—of a type that all *his* years of close contact and cringing had been unable to secure.

"Let me tell you," he continued, leveling his long, thin index finger at Schellenberg, "you won't get *anywhere* by handling that man with kid gloves. I know what I'm talking about. With Canaris, firmness is the only effective method. And you'll have to be even tougher with his followers—that bunch of talkative highbrows who interpret courtesy as a sign of weakness."

It was the first time that Schellenberg, in fact, detected a sign of weakness in *Heydrich*. For it was there all right: the quavering passion in his voice and that certain fragility in his expression, both of which made Schellenberg realize that he was playing with fire. Heydrich's relationship with Canaris was very personal indeed—a complex web of emotions, in which another's presence was not welcome.

On these grounds Heydrich had every reason to resent him, because what he'd said was true. He and Canaris had become quite close and *did* spend a great deal of time together—traveling, horse-riding, playing tennis and attending the opera—all of which were their shared interests.

On top of which, Schellenberg was keen, as had been Heydrich, to learn a few tricks of the trade from the "Master of Espionage". Canaris, in turn, was happy to pass them on to a young man whom he was inclined to treat like a son.

Which seemed logical, given their twenty-three-year age difference and the fact that Canaris had only two daughters to his name. It made him eager to cultivate that kind of father/son relationship, so as to bequeath his knowledge to someone in his own image, fully aware that Schellenberg was every bit as ambitious as Heydrich, but confident that he lacked the latter's cold, killer instinct and could, to a *degree*, be trusted.

These were feelings that on Schellenberg's part were reciprocated, which made it hard for him to think badly of Canaris, despite what Heydrich had to say.

"I take your advice on board," he replied, to put Heydrich's mind at ease. "But to be honest, I'm going to find it terribly difficult to start disliking Canaris. You're right, we've become great friends and I have to say that he's the best company in the world. We've traveled a lot together and his knowledge never ceases to astound me. It doesn't matter what country we're in, he knows everything about it, from its latest population stats to its finest in food and wine."

At which point Schellenberg stopped to dwell on a memory that made him smile.

KILL THE FUHRER ⚡

"Do you know that when we were in southern Italy recently, Canaris kept insisting that I wear a woolen vest in the blazing heat. You know how much he detests the cold himself. What's more, he kept plying me with every sort of medication to stop me getting a chill. This, I might add, was in one hundred degree heat! I tell you, he nearly *killed* me with kindness."

"Yes, there's always been a little of the *'mother hen'* in him," Heydrich replied with a sarcasm peppered with envy. "The way he chatters on and mollycoddles his favourites. All very sweet, all very endearing. *But*, Schellenberg, you've just proved my point. You must never let yourself forget that Canaris is a skilled professional. What he does . . . he does for a purpose, and usually to trip up his victims. By the sound of it, you've already fallen into his trap."

At this, Schellenberg suddenly grew quiet and introspective— Heydrich had honed into the lesser side of his character—the one that marked him as being the consummate man of expedience. *Had* Canaris been pulling the wool over his eyes? It had never crossed his mind. But one thing was for sure . . . he was no schmuck, and from here on in he intended to be much more careful. The possibility that Canaris had been working his ends by befriending him made him feel sad, a little stupid and extremely bitter.

Bitter, sad and stupid enough to have missed the salient point—that it was in fact *Heydrich* who had just "worked" *him* by planting the seeds of evil in his psyche. Within only a few scathing sentences, Heydrich had managed to put a permanent wedge between the two old friends and guaranteed that his deputy would carry out his Gestapo duties in regard to Canaris with the minimum of conscience and optimum efficiency.

"I'm not telling you that you should *stop* being his friend," Heydrich continued. Having done the damage, he was keen to take advantage of it. "On the contrary . . . you may choose to do as I do—to pursue his friendship fervently in order to spy on him. Over the years, I've compiled a file on Canaris, inches thick, while posing as his pal. My sole purpose has been to bring about his downfall at any given moment. A moment, that is, that suits *me*, and hopefully, provides the greatest pleasure."

Schellenberg was shocked, Until this moment, he'd had no idea as to the depth of Heydrich's cold, calculating intent. He had always been under the impression that Heydrich and Canaris, albeit career competitors, had an understanding of sorts. Which made him curious and just a tad concerned.

"I pity Canaris," he said, knowing that he had every good reason to do so. "Has he any idea?"

"Oh, don't worry about Canaris. He's been compiling an even bigger file on me. And, I have absolutely no doubt . . . one on *you*. You mustn't be hurt or alarmed by this Schellenberg. It just goes with the territory. One cannot afford to be too thin-skinned about it.

"I, for example, couldn't give a rat's arse about what happens to Canaris. Not when he's spent the last years doing everything in his power to advance his *Abwehr* organization at the expense of me and mine. But I believe, at last, that I've got the situation in hand. Bit by bit, I've been working to get rid of both our little Admiral Canaris *and* his entire Intelligence network."

To this, Schellenberg had no objection. Ambitious in the extreme himself, his eyes too had been focused hard on the decline of the *Abwehr*—that huge, top-heavy organization that not only hindered his own advancement in the Reich, but throughout which Canaris seemed to exercise methods far too humane to be of any benefit to it.

It was a scornful thought that crossed his mind, along with one other—the acknowledgement that whenever Heydrich was in the mood to spit his poison, it was he, Walter Schellenberg, who was always there to lap it up. Not only loving to listen to it, but keen to add a few venomous ingredients of his own to spice up its toxicity.

It was the not-so-nice flip-side of his suave, intellectual nature. The better side was the one that had allowed him to grow so fond of Canaris. Or, as Heydrich had put it, to have allowed himself to be taken in by him. Now, thanks to his Superior's advice, he knew better, and was not about to make the mistake again.

"You know, you're right," he said to Heydrich, deciding to stoke the fire. "I sometimes wonder how Canaris has managed to stay at the helm for so long, when he has such an extraordinary disregard for military convention. It's almost impossible to have a serious conversation with him along those lines . . . not when he persists in breaking off in the middle of every formal discussion to talk to his dogs!"

"Ah yes, his dogs . . . they are dearer to him than *any* of us.

One gets the distinct impression that he does it deliberately to tell us as much."

"His implication being, I suppose, that we are no better than dogs, which is outrageous," Schellenberg said with all the vehemence of his new-found contempt.

His gauche observation, however, made Heydrich laugh out loud.

"*That*, my dear Schellenberg, Canaris would see as being an insult to his dogs! I can assure you, he thinks a great deal less of us than that."

Having been provided with all these fresh insights into Canaris' character, Schellenberg couldn't help but wonder at his own naivety—*why* had he allowed himself to be deluded for so long? For all his might and power within SS ranks, it appeared that he'd done nothing but skid over the hard edge of reality, neither stopping, nor daring perhaps, to look it straight in the face.

Now he could see that Heydrich was right. From all points of view, the sooner they got rid of Canaris the better. And any excuse would do.

"The man just hasn't got an ounce of violence in him," Schellenberg said, scratching around for the first of them. "Which, one would assume, was a prerequisite of his job. What's more, his subordinates are aware of this weakness in him and constantly take advantage of it—twisting him around their little fingers the way they do, and getting away with it.

"Do you know that whenever he's actually forced to take strong measures against them, he goes out of his way behind the scenes to make up for his severity? How could a man who's such a soft touch have survived so long in this hard-arsed industry?"

Heydrich's shrewd, dark eyes narrowed in response.

"Don't ever make the mistake of underestimating Canaris. The man has method. Soft touch or not, he's as sharp as a tack; and when push comes to shove, will not *hesitate*—do you understand?—to do *whatever* has to be done. And I might say the same of myself. I am long past being fooled by him and he knows it. He and I have crossed swords just once too often, which has made it a case of kill or be killed."

CHAPTER FOURTEEN

"Heydrich's dead . . . did you know?"[17]

General Beck uttered the magic words as he put his head around Canaris' office door.

Although Canaris had been expecting his friend and fellow conspirator to join him for lunch, he couldn't have guessed that Beck would turn up bearing gifts! This one was big enough to leave Canaris stunned and stumbling over his words.

"What . . . where?" he asked, getting up unsteadily from his chair. The shock news had shaken him to the core.

"In Prague. Two Czech resistance fighters got him. The Brits put them up to it of course. So all I can say is . . . *Bully for the Brits!*"

"*Shhh!*" Canaris warned, quickly putting his finger to his mouth.

He knew that his office was bugged (courtesy of Heydrich's SS). Quietly, he ushered Beck out of it, so that they could talk more freely in the street. There, amid the hustle and bustle of the blissfully ignorant crowds, they both were able to let loose with their elation.

It had been Heydrich's conceit that had finally got the better of him. Unlike most Nazi leaders, he'd always taken great pride in being careless about his personal safety. Much like Hitler, he lived under the assumption that he was impervious to death.

This, given their shared *modus operandi*, wasn't such a far-fetched theory. Evidently the power that guided both men's footsteps had seen fit to dispense with one of them, satisfied, no doubt, that Hitler could "go it alone" and that Reinhard Heydrich had fulfilled his purpose on Earth, having wreaked enough havoc on it to no longer be necessary in the general scheme of things.

Unfortunately, unaware that he'd worn out his welcome, and

was soon to be shuffled off the mortal coil, Heydrich had insisted on traveling to the airport in an open staff car, making himself an easy target. Not as an act of daring, but as one of vanity.

It gave him such an enormous sense of satisfaction to see the fear and respect his presence aroused. He always reveled in the solemn, terrified silence of the crowds as he passed, not realizing that they were waiting for him to do just that, so that they could spit on his shadow.

Heydrich must have been enjoying the impact he was making on the Czechoslovakian masses that day, because he didn't notice his assassins. Two men were lying in wait for him at the street corner with Sten guns and grenades stashed under their trench coats, both of them nervously biding their time until Heydrich's driver slowed down to negotiate the sharp bend in the road.

The moment he did so, they made their move. It had been strategically timed to coincide with the public transport timetable—with the very second that those two tram cars crossed and blocked the busy intersection, cutting off Heydrich's escape hatch.

"Take him out, *now!*" Heydrich must have heard the Czech assassin yell to his compatriot, seconds before the more deadly sound of the killer cocking his Sten gun. But Fate had stepped in, just one last time in Heydrich's favour, to jam its trigger.

However, having planned for such a contingency, the second assassin had hurled his grenade and scored a direct hit. They had watched in relief to see the staff car explode, then, gasped in utter disbelief and horror when the smoke cleared to expose Heydrich still standing in it—alive and well!

It had left his would-be assassins no option but to take to their heels and flee. Heydrich, in what appeared to be robust health, had bounded from his car to take chase. He had drawn his pistol from its holster as he ran after them to get off a few shots in their direction, before he'd suddenly *stopped* . . . his body stock-still but vibrating, before collapsing in a dead heap to the pavement.

"Arghh . . . too easy a death for such a tyrant," Canaris said, as he was filled in on the particulars. He didn't realize that Beck was still only midway through his narration and that Heydrich's story had not yet finished.

"Ah, but he *wasn't* dead," Beck replied, getting as much satisfaction from the idea of Heydrich having to suffer for his crimes as did Canaris. "He was rushed to hospital with massive internal haemorrhaging. It appears that a piece of shrapnel sliced through the base of his spine. The aperture where it'd broken through his flesh was so fine that there hadn't been a drop of blood on his outer body. So you can rest assured that it took him a week of well-deserved agony to die."

Being men of strong moral and religious conviction, it was neither Beck's nor Canaris' practice to take pleasure in another man's suffering, and it didn't rest easy on either of their consciences that they were doing so now. But head of the SS, Deputy Reich Protector of Bohemia and Moravia Reinhard Heydrich was the exception. He was a monster, a murderer, a reaper of death, destruction and despair, and as such, deserved everything he got; *and,* they hoped . . . just a little bit more.

The one thing that *did* disturb Canaris about the man's death, however, was that he, Canaris, had not been informed of it immediately. In blatant disregard of the normal procedure which placed him at the top of the chain, he had been left in the dark to wait for General Beck to pass the news on to him.

It was astonishing, considering that Beck had long since retired from the political and military arena and relegated himself to a civilian position of less consequence, one whose privilege it was only to receive information second-hand. Which made Canaris' receipt of it, third-hand, or worse. It was such a suspicious slip up in the system that it made him feel most alarmed.

The fact that Hitler had wanted to keep Heydrich's assassination *hush-hush* meant nothing. Not when "hush hush" had never applied to the head of the *Abwehr,* and that *as* such, Canaris was always the first to be made privy to top secret information. Given that this time he had not been, it could only mean one thing—that he was beginning to lose power and Hitler's favour.

It was clear that from here on in he would have to watch out.

* * *

Everyone who attended thought it was rather touching that Canaris wept openly at Heydrich's lavish funeral in Berlin. Himmler going so far as to stop, as he walked from the grave, to offer his consolation by patting Canaris companionably on the shoulder.

"I know that you and Heydrich were the closest of friends.

Take comfort in the fact that he returned your feelings."

At which point, Canaris had had to hide his face behind his handkerchief—his tears not being those of mourning, but of pure, unadulterated joy!

"Praise the Lord, he's dead and buried," he said to Beck an hour later, knowing that at last he was free of Heydrich's terrifying presence in his life. The oppressive burden of having the man forever breathing down his neck and sending shivers up his spine was *over*. "This is a real stroke of luck for the Resistance."

"Yes, well that makes two of them," Beck replied, as he casually reached out to take an hors d'oeuvre from the silver tray on the banquet table.

A sumptuous spread had been laid out after the funeral which, like Heydrich himself, was in extremely bad taste, Beck thought, considering the dire wartime conditions. Swallowing down hard on it, he continued.

"Don't forget Stalingrad!"[18]

Well who could? For the Resistance, in particular, these two fortuitous shoot-ups in history had brought renewed hope. At long last they highlighted the first real chinks in Hitler's armour—the impregnable Heydrich's slaughter and the on-going annihilation of the Reich's entire 6th Army in Russia, which was putting a serious dent in Hitler's plans and ego. It drew a line under the fact that he, like Heydrich, was vulnerable.

In the throes of suffering two such blows, Hitler certainly wasn't in the mood to hear any more bad news, and didn't particularly want to entertain the idea that his friend Canaris was involved in a plot against him, but ever since that poison pair—Himmler and Heydrich—had suggested that he was, Hitler had found it impossible to forget, and had grown wary of Canaris. Loathe to accuse him directly of treachery, but no longer responding quite so warmly to his company or conversation.

It was a cooling in communications that came as a great concern to Canaris, who had been quick to pick up the difference in Hitler's manner. His best course of action was, he believed, to bluff it out. To continue to attend the military meetings and dinner parties as if oblivious to all. Hoping that his very audacity in being there, together with his efforts to maintain his usual bright, breezy manner, might go a long way to proving his innocence and averting suspicion.

For some time, it had worked—that was until Stalingrad, when the last of Hitler's good humour deserted him.

Russia wasn't proving to be the "walk over" he had thought it would be, and having been bombarded by his own Generals' advice to retreat and run their way out of it, he'd decided not to listen any more. No longer in a receptive mood, he could only tolerate being told what he wanted to hear, rather than what he needed to know.

In his eagerness to procure just that, he'd ordered Canaris to prepare a status report on the Russian front. He knew that he could always rely on his Little Admiral's honesty.

Which was exactly what he got. Canaris had the effrontery (and, one might say, the inconceivable courage) to present a report packed full of pessimism as to the Russian campaign and the war itself. It was a sad summation of Hitler's hopes and dreams that had the Fuhrer see red and demonstrate for all those present the principle of spontaneous combustion.

Having sat simmering with fury as Canaris advised him on his grim findings, Hitler suddenly exploded into a red-hot rage.

Leaping from his chair, he moved fast across the room in Canaris' direction. Overturning a table en route, before physically grabbing hold of the lapels of Canaris' uniform and shaking him hard with both hands.

"Are you telling me that I'm going to lose the war, little man?" he screamed down at him, taking advantage of both his height and foul temper to make his point.

Calmly waiting for Hitler's spasm of madness to pass, and then for those two extra seconds it took for his Fuhrer to remove his sweaty hands from his person, Canaris simply straightened his collar and answered unperturbed:

"As yet, sir, I've said nothing about us losing the war. I've merely been describing the situation on the Russian front in accordance with the reports that I've received from there. It is *you*, and not I, who is interpreting them with such defeatism."

This statement produced a collective gasp from the other Generals in the room. That same room fell ominously silent as they then held their breath in anticipation of the head of the *Abwehr's* fate.

"My dear little, smooth-talking Canaris," Hitler stepped

back to say—his tone having dropped from falsetto to become dangerously calm and controlled.

With an easy familiarity, he stretched out his hand to brush a few flecks of lint from the Admiral's lapel.

"How glib you are. And how very much I'm going to miss you."

CHAPTER FIFTEEN

Well what else could Canaris assume but the worst—that he was about to be given his marching orders? That's why it surprised him when Hitler didn't dismiss him on the spot. Their past friendship, he supposed, was standing him in good stead.

Short of being fired, he knew he'd lost an enormous amount of ground. That nasty little chat of theirs had turned the tide in their relationship. For Canaris and his fellow conspirators within the *Abwehr*, Hitler's displeasure did not augur well.

Although the Little Admiral was still far from being accused as a conspirator, it was clear that he was no longer on Hitler's "A List". This wouldn't have been such a concern had Canaris not been so acutely aware that that blood hound, Manfred Roeder, was dogging his tracks, sniffing around to pick up the scent of any tiny detail in *Abwehr* operations that didn't smell right.

The bottom line was that it was only a matter time before Roeder hit pay dirt—before he and Hitler went in for the kill.

The trick was to beat them to the punch. If it were soon to come to a shoot-out, the Resistance would have to see to it that they were quicker on the draw; that it was *they* and not Hitler who fired the first angry shot.

For the conspirators, however, pulling the trigger had always been the problem. The bulk of them shied away from using brute force in their bid to set things right in Germany. But it appeared that they no longer had the luxury of being too delicate and high-minded about it. It had taken them much too long to come to terms with murder—to understand that Hitler's assassination wasn't a moral issue, but a must.

The stumbling block, of course, had been that wretched oath that they had all sworn to Hitler in the early days. Their sense of honour and religious conviction had made it impossible for them to betray it.

With none of them wanting to risk eternal damnation, they could only hang their hopes on sourcing a legal loophole that would let them off the hook, a strategic precedent that would free them from guilt and excuse them from the oath's obligation.

At last it appeared that they had found it. Two short sentences (Chapter 6, Subsection 2, Paragraph 5)[19], in the Prussian Code of Military Law proved to be the perfect disclaimer:

> *"Orders of criminal content are not to be obeyed.*
> *The soldier who does obey is liable to be punished."*

Holding tight to that rule, General Ludwig Beck was able, at long last, to speak freely. Confident that his fellow conspirators could now nod in agreement with a clear conscience:

"When I think of the endless train of death in the concentration camps and the armies," he said to them. "Hitler's death and *only* his death can signal the end of this senseless slaughter. It is *his* life against the lives of *millions* of human beings. If ever in history an assassination is justifiable on moral and ethical grounds, this is it.

"I am ordering you not to trouble yourselves any longer over the rights and wrongs of this issue. As a man who's lived by the sword, Hitler can only expect to die by it. Not only for Germany's sake, but for the rest of the world. Because make no mistake . . . if he's not stopped, he'll destroy us all. From this day forward we must go about our business with purpose."

Canaris had not been there to hear Beck's stirring speech. His business at that time had been with Lieutenant Fabian von Schlabrendorff, and his superior, Major-General Henning von Tresckow (Chief of Staff/Central Army/Russian front). All three of them were making a concerted effort to win over Field Marshal Guenther von Kluge to the Resistance.

Kluge's eastern theatre of operations, despite its sub-zero temperatures, was the hot-spot of the war. Its litany of atrocities and unspeakable suffering had inspired the greatest loathing and resentment of Hitler and his Third Reich. Not only from the enemy, but from within the German Army's own ranks.

As the Commander of Army Group Centre eastern front, Kluge had recently become the conspirators' new ray of hope. The Field Marshal, equipped with his modicum of morality, medal-bedecked chest and not-so-clear-sighted Aryan blue eyes, had had a gutful of Hitler and his obscene war. He had seen enough of it to be teetering on the brink of throwing in his lot with the Resistance.

He suffered, however, from the same malignant disease as Keitel, plagued as he was by a serious lack of conviction, night-time sweats and nervous body tremors at the prospect of making a stand against Hitler. All three of which symptoms rendered him incapable of making it. His good intentions, tainted by his chronic fear of the Fuhrer's flair for savage revenge, had had him change his mind at *every* critical moment and challenge Keitel for the title of Champion Fence-Sitter.

This posed an on-going dilemma for his Chief-of-Staff, Major-General von Tresckow. As an aristocrat and one of the leading lights of the Resistance, Tresckow's reputation as a gentleman and a profoundly decent human being made him the only man who seemed to have sway with Kluge. Given that Kluge had done nothing *but* sway back and forward over the issue, it had been Tresckow who had been lumped with the responsibility of having to talk him round on repeated occasions.

Each time he'd walked out of Kluge's office he'd been convinced that he'd won him over—only to find that, in the two minutes it took him to get back to his own office, the fluctuating Field Marshal had changed his mind, putting through an urgent phone call to Tresckow to tell him just that.

For the last few months, Kluge's promise of support had put the conspirators on an emotional rollercoaster. One minute uplifting them with a surge of hope; the next—hurtling them back down into a black pit of despair.

On Monday, he'd boosted Tresckow's and Schlabrendorff's confidence by saying, "Yes, I will go along with the Resistance if that swine has been killed."

But then on Tuesday, he'd invited them both back into his office to share in his joy over the gift that *that swine* had just sent him. There he had sat, gloating over Hitler's handwritten birthday card. Reading it out loud, with a warm smile, to add to his fellow officers' confusion and disappointment:

"For your birthday, my most loyal Field Marshal, I give you this gift of 125,000DM that you may like to use to build on your Estate.

With my warmest wishes and respect, Adolf Hitler."

Schlabrendorff and Tresckow didn't know how to respond, other than to stand and silently marvel at Kluge's shameless duplicity. Watching in complete disbelief as the Field Marshal, with misty-eyed nostalgia, propped up the card on his desk for a keepsake.

This should have been enough to let them know that he was no longer available to front their cause, but Kluge was a man who liked to leave his options open, doing so, by calling out after them, as they left his office in frustration.

"We'll talk later, Tresckow. I need time to think."

The trouble was that time was ticking away and the Resistance was finding it harder and harder to put off taking affirmative action. Before their very eyes, Hitler's brutal genocide of the Jewish race was taking place; not to mention the appalling decimation of his own German troops at Stalingrad.

Canaris, for one, had had enough and wasn't about to sit back and wait any longer. Having helped draft plans for a tentative *coup d'etat* in Berlin, he was in the process of organizing, with Tresckow's and Schlabrendorff's help, a secret meeting to take place at German Headquarters of the Central Army Group in Smolensk. Cover was provided for the covert gathering by organizing a three-day conference for his Intelligence officers on the eastern front. He had then gone that one step further to get the wheels in motion by leading the large delegation to Russia himself.

It went well. The on-going trials on the Russian front bolstered their chances of gaining substantial military support. By the time the meeting was over, Canaris felt that he'd well and truly earned that drink he was sharing with Schlabrendorff. Both men were relaxed and pleased about having successfully pulled it all together.

It was just a pity that Canaris couldn't linger a little longer to revel in the ritual of patting himself on the back. He couldn't afford to—not after he glanced at his watch and realized how late he was running.

"You're not going so soon, surely?" Schlabrendorff said, surprised when Canaris suddenly got up to leave.

"No choice, I'm afraid. I have a meeting in Rastenburg with Himmler. I don't like to keep him waiting."

The Admiral didn't choose to explain himself when Schlabrendorff raised a contemptuous eyebrow at the mention of the SS Reichsfuhrer's name.

"You needn't bother sending *my* regards," was Schlabrendorff's mild reproach as he saw Canaris to the door, extending to the head of the *Abwehr* the courtesy of not questioning him any further as to why he was still so keen to seek Himmler's company.

The truth was that he trusted Canaris implicitly and knew that there must be a good reason for the Admiral promoting their questionable affiliation. This was a view not shared by every member of the Resistance, many of whom constantly accused Canaris of double standards for associating with "that piece of scum".

None of them considered the fact, as Schlabrendorff did, that it was imperative for Canaris to do so. That feigning friendship was his only means of protecting his agents and averting suspicion from himself.

Certainly on Tresckow's part there were no hard feelings. As far as he was concerned, Canaris had already pulled his weight by convening their conference at Smolensk. The progressive get-together had provided the forum to devise their next decisive plan of action.

Tresckow had been nominated to take control of it by organizing a formal meeting between Hitler and Field Marshal Kluge in Smolensk. At which time he'd arranged for Hitler to be shot dead. The scene of his assassination was to be set in the small forest area en route to Kluge's headquarters.

It was an ambitious scheme that had taken a great deal of wheeling and dealing on Tresckow's part, during which Kluge had come up with every excuse under the sun to wriggle his way free of involvement.

"Put your mind at rest, sir. We are not asking for your hands-on participation," Tresckow reassured Kluge for the fiftieth time. "As far as we are concerned, you have nothing to do with the proceedings. You are, by all accounts, just an innocent bystander, quite free of any complicity. It is only our request that you remain so—that you don't actually put a spanner in the works by delaying your meeting with Hitler any longer."

Taking his cue from Kluge's weak nod of assent, Tresckow clicked his heels and saluted. With his heart thudding in his throat from tension and sheer disbelief that he'd finally got the go ahead, Tresckow turned and quickly left Kluge's office to go in search of

Cavalry officer Colonel Baron Georg von Boeselager, the battle-weary warrior who had volunteered to lead the band of soldiers who had sworn to take Hitler out of the equation for good.

It was their plan to surround him in the forest and fire two shots. Guaranteeing a sure kill by aiming the first at his heart and the second at his head.

"Are you set?" Tresckow asked of Boeselager, when he found him in his barracks. The Colonel had been lolling back comfortably on his bunk reading a book.

His relaxed demeanor made Tresckow feel guilty; knowing that it was probably the last time that the man would ever rest in peace—that the burden of the Reichsfuhrer's murder was just about to be laid on his shoulders. Surely it was only fair, Tresckow thought, to give the Colonel one last chance to change his mind.

"Please feel free, Boeselager," he said as he sat down on the bunk opposite, "to tell me *now* if you've had second thoughts. You can be sure that none of us will hold it against you. We are, after all, asking you to take on an enormous responsibility."

Calmly folding down the corner of the page to mark his place, Boeselager closed his book and sat up on the side of his bed.

"There are no second thoughts, sir," he replied, with a serenity and self-assurance that left Tresckow in awe of his composure.

The only way he could thank the Colonel for his courageous commitment to the Cause was to place a companionable hand on Boeselager's knee and to look hard into his eyes. Making sure, without a trace of doubt, that the man fully understood what he was getting himself into—that in putting an end to Hitler's life, he would inevitably be putting an end to his own. It was the sad reality that *no one*, not even one's compatriots, could afford to countenance a traitor.

On an issue of this dimension, however, the concern wasn't over the mercy of mankind, but the forgiveness of God.

"I wouldn't want to think," Tresckow said, "that this order of mine will weigh heavily on your conscience."

"What lies heavily on my conscience, sir," Boeselager replied, with an unflinching gaze, "is not having had the guts to have done something sooner. I have seen, first-hand, the demonic horrors the monster that we call our Fuhrer has created. I've stood by like an impotent coward and watched men, women and children, in their innocent thousands, being slaughtered at his whim. I've seen them stripped of their clothes and dignity before having to line them up for execution. And watched them dig their own graves, in terrified anticipation of it, simply to save our soldiers the trouble.

"Do you know what it's like to have an old woman cling to your leg and beg for mercy? Do you know what it's like to be ordered to push her frail, naked body back into line before being forced to shoot her in the head?

"Do you know what it's like to have Himmler shake your hand and pin a medal to your chest for having played such a sterling part in mass murder? To have to follow in his shadow, like a lily-livered lapdog, as he does an inspection tour of the mass grave site.

"To watch him retch uncontrollably, right in front of you, at the sight and stench of that hell on Earth of his own creation. To see him throw up his hands in dismay at the sheer immensity of it all, and give up on taking an accurate tally of the mountain of bloodied, emaciated bodies piled up to be buried there? And then to listen to the outrageous irony of the sadist declaring himself too delicate to cope with such a scene of unbridled butchery.

"Which, of course, didn't stop him sentencing me to three months solitary confinement for having turned a blind eye to a young boy who'd tried to escape the carnage.

"I'd seen the child—naked . . . all skin and bones, trying to make a break for it in the confusion of one of our massacres. You can't imagine the stark terror on that boy's face when he noticed me watching him. But I'd had enough. I turned and let him go."

"So you saved his life?" Tresckow said, in an effort to put Boeselager's mind at ease, by highlighting that one fragment of good in his nightmare of evil.

"Yes, but not for long," the Colonel confirmed, his lips thinning with resolve. "It was just the boy's luck that Himmler stopped retching long enough to pull his *own* pistol from its holster. The bastard didn't even have the decency to make it a clean kill.

"Do you know that he shot that child *five* times before he fell. Wounding him first in his arms and legs for target practice, before aiming the decisive shot at his chest. So you see, sir, you needn't concern yourself about my finer feelings."

"Good!" Tresckow said, as he got to his feet.

There was no point in dwelling on the gruesome details when

there were so very many of them. The sooner they got down to business, the sooner they could do something constructive about them. Having borne witness to such a litany of crimes against humanity, Boeselager had convinced him that he was the right man for the job.

"We'll need you and your motorbike cavalcade at the airstrip at 9.30, Friday morning. Hitler's plane should land at 9.45. He'll make a fuss about you being there, of course. He's always been adamant about not requiring even a single bodyguard, let alone a motorized contingent of them. Just keep your keys in the ignition and don't give him the option. And, if by any chance your plans to ambush him go awry, don't panic. He's expected to spend the day here. You'll have plenty of time to try again."

A simple plan, one would have thought, for a band of war-hardened soldiers, to surround and gun down just one man.

And it *would* have been, had Hitler not decided, for the first and only time in his life, to bring his own entourage of bodyguards from Berlin, making his visit with Kluge so fleeting that he barely had time to sit down, let alone provide enough of it, for his assassins to fall back on a plan B.

As if pre-empting danger, he'd flown all the way from Berlin to Russia to spend just a half hour with Kluge, insisting that his own, and not Kluge's, motorbike cavalcade escort him to and from the airfield.

He made sure that they drove four-abreast at the rear and front of his car, with an additional two of them on either side of it, for all-round protection. His bevy of Berlin bodyguards spilled from the plane's bowels when it landed. In their long leather jackets, they sat astride their motorbikes to face-off, for a dramatic moment, with Boeselager's contingent of helmeted assassins. The Colonel's complement of twelve men sat on their metal mounts, already in line and ranged against them.

After a serious few seconds of revving engines and weighing up of odds, the latter had had no choice but to put their engines in gear, circle the tarmac and take their leave.

CHAPTER SIXTEEN

The battle of the bodyguards put the ball back in Tresckow's and Schlabrendorff's court, both of whom were quick to pick it up and run with it. Within only half an hour, they managed to put plan B into action.

It had just been a one-off stroke of luck that Hitler had escaped with his life, they reasoned. Neither man had a clue that Hitler having dodged death this day was only the first in a farcical series of near-misses and hapless attempts at his assassination. Fate was determined to have the Fuhrer step clear of every bullet with his name on it—to save him, time and time again, by means surely more than sheer coincidence.

But at this point in the proceedings, without the benefit of foresight, the conspirators felt compelled to continue as planned, urged on by a sense of duty and destiny without the slightest idea that that Destiny had been pre-programmed to work against them.

If they had missed their opportunity to kill Hitler on his way *in* to Russia, they would make damn sure that they got him on his way out. Somehow they would manage to get their bomb on board his plane and set its timer to explode en route back to Rastenburg.

It struck Schlabrendorff and Tresckow as being a safer bet all round, given that it would look more like an accident. Any treacherous, snow-capped mountain range between Russia and Prussia would provide the perfect alibi for a plane crash.

They could only be grateful now to Colonels Oster and Lahousen for having provided Canaris with the bombs he'd brought with him to the conference.

The state-of-the-art explosives were a new-fangled invention that they had recently captured from the British. Given that they

KILL THE FUHRER ᛋ

were not as yet completely *au fait* with their workings, it was going to be a case of hit or miss.

"The beauty of these little babies is that they're completely silent," Canaris had said when he'd taken the new malleable plastic explosives from his briefcase to show Schlabrendorff. "That means no hissing of fuses to give them away."

Handing the device to Schlabrendorff, Canaris had continued his half-baked explanation. Not being a technical whiz himself, he'd hoped that his associate was more that way inclined and would be able to get the gist of it.

"Apparently, you ignite the fuse by breaking open this small capsule of acid. The acid disintegrates the wire that's holding back the striking pin . . . and you know the rest."

Well no . . . Schlabrendorff had not, actually. But he'd been dead keen to find out.

"Astonishing," he'd replied as he turned the object of interest over and over in his hands, holding back from openly commending the Brits on their ingenuity.

"But how do you control its timing?" he'd asked instead, not able to find any facet of its composition that looked likely.

"The thickness of the wire!"

There had been an air of excitement and pride in Canaris' answer that could have labeled him its inventor. Reaching back into his briefcase, he had retrieved another piece of the mechanism and explained further.

"It comes with three different fuses that provide delays of ten, thirty and one-hundred-and-twenty minutes. As far as I can see, there's no fault in its concept or design. I'd be very surprised if it didn't do the trick."

However, with the good sense of the lawyer he was, Schlabrendorff had not been prepared to take Canaris' word for it. Clever as the head of the *Abwehr* was, he was hardly a dab hand at chemistry, or the art of bomb disposal.

"I'll have to run a few tests," Schlabrendorff had said.

He came back to Canaris a day later to inform him that the bombs were indeed silent and extremely powerful, but a bit unreliable as far as their timers were concerned.

"Perhaps temperature is a factor," Canaris had suggested. Knowing how susceptible to the cold he was himself, he had thought it not so far-fetched to theorize over the fuses reacting against the freezing extremities of the Russian climate.

The truth was that they didn't have time to quibble over a few minutes disparity in detonation, one way or the other. No matter *what*, they just had to set it and forget it—and make sure it got on Hitler's plane without arousing suspicion.

* * *

"Colonel Brandt!"[20] Schlabrendorff called out—his voice barely audible above the roar of aeroplane engines.

In the cacophony of noise, it was nothing short of a miracle that Hitler's junior staff officer stopped and turned at the faint, familiar ring of his name echoing through it.

Miracle number two was that Schlabrendorff had managed to get to the airfield just in the nick of time. Having had to stop off on the way to hastily prepare and wrap the bomb, he and his staff car had lagged a few minutes behind the main body of Hitler's cavalcade.

By the time he'd reached his destination, the plane's propellers were already in motion, and he'd had to move fast. He'd jumped quickly out of his car, and run those few extra yards across the tarmac to grab hold of Brandt's arm. The young Colonel was the last of Hitler's entourage to board the Junkers Ju52[21], while its escort of seven Messerschmitt fighter bombers taxied for takeoff.

"I wonder if I could ask you a small favour, sir?" Schlabrendorff said.

He was out of breath as he handed Brandt the small, brown paper package he was carrying. As he did so, he made sure that he pressed down firmly on the fuse of the bomb through its wrapping to set it for detonation.

"General Tresckow asked me to get it to Rastenburg as soon as possible, and I just thought you might be the fastest way of doing it."

Brandt accepted it with a half-smile. Loathe as he was to knock back the request of a fellow officer, he was a little put out by the imposition.

"If it's urgent, it'd be my pleasure," he replied in a tone that fell a long way short of expressing joy over the last minute request. "May I ask what's in it?"

His question had Schlabrendorff lower his voice and lean in a little closer to the Colonel to speak in confidence.

"Just a small, personal gift for General Helmuth Stieff back in Rastenburg. I was hoping that you'd be kind enough to deliver it to him when you get there? Rather important, if you know what I mean," he continued, with a wink. "A couple of bottles of his favourite cognac to soften him up before Tresckow has to meet with him next week over a rather delicate issue."

Brandt nodded in acknowledgement. It was standard practice within the higher echelons of the Military to woo each other in this way.

"I'll see to it as soon as I get there," he said, putting a reassuring hand on Schlabrendorff's shoulder.

It didn't cross anyone's mind to question that small brown paper package that Brandt put casually on the seat beside him. Shaped as it was in compliance with the gift it was professed to be, it never occurred to a soul, on or off the plane, that the second box within it didn't contain a bottle of cognac, but was host instead to the silent British bomb that Schlabrendorff had set to explode an hour and a half into their flight.

Having seen Hitler off with an impressive salute, Schlabrendorff moved directly to Stage Two. He'd been instructed by Tresckow to get in contact with Oster and Dohnanyi in Berlin as soon as the plane had taken off.

"*Operation Flash* is in full swing," was all Schlabrendorff needed to say when Dohnanyi picked up the phone.

Short and to the point, it was the code that signaled the beginning of their *coup d'etat*, and alerted all the conspirators in Berlin to stand ready to take control of the city the very *moment* that Hitler's death was announced.

The problem was that three hours down the track, no such announcement had been made. All the conspirators were still standing at the ready were on tenter hooks because they had heard nothing.

It was alarming in the extreme, considering that Rastenburg was only a two hour flight from Smolensk, and the bomb had been set to explode over Minsk!

But with communications down, one way or the other, Canaris and his colleagues could do nothing but sit and wait in excruciating anticipation. The agony of which had suddenly got the better of Lahousen:

"*Surely* one of the fighter squadron pilots would have radio-ed in by now if he'd seen Hitler's plane go down?" he said.

Fed up with sitting nervously on the edge of his chair, he'd got up out of it, and was now prowling restlessly about the office, his unchecked anxiety doubling that of the other three men in the room.

"*Please* sit down Lahousen. You're making it worse," Canaris said. Unaware until then, that he too had been drumming his fingers on his desk, and that his jaw was set and aching with tension. "There's nothing we can do but wait. We'll hear one way of the other . . . don't worry."

As soon as he'd finished speaking, Canaris jumped in his seat at the shrill ring of the telephone. Its metallic descant cut like a knife through the stressed silence of the room.

It was Tresckow's studied, steady voice on the other end of the line.

"Hitler has landed safely in Rastenburg," he reported to Canaris, before promptly putting down the receiver. The ever-present danger of their telephones being tapped made it sensible to say no more.

"But I don't understand," Oster said in dismay at the news. "Sclabrendorff was *sure* that he'd detonated the device."

"Perhaps he didn't press down hard enough on the fuse?" Dohnanyi suggested. "Who knows . . . the bomb could have been faulty. Perhaps he didn't set it up properly in the first place? He did have to do it in such a terrible hurry."

"Yes perhaps . . ." Canaris replied, his cool cynicism putting an end to the conjecture. "But then again, perhaps it was something else altogether. We'll never know. The end result is that we've failed and will have to try again."

For a moment or two, all four men sat in deep, lip-biting concentration, trying to come to terms with their disappointment and to formulate their next move.

Canaris was the first, apparently, to come up with it. Suddenly, in what appeared to his friends to be a moment of revelation, he picked up the phone and put through an urgent return call to Tresckow. That supposed "revelation" turned out to be sheer panic.

"For God's sake . . . the damn thing might still go off!" he quickly explained to his friends while he waited for Tresckow to pick up.

As soon as Tresckow did, Canaris instructed him to get in contact with Colonel Brandt *immediately* to find out what he'd done with the package.

He was relieved to find out that Tresckow had pre-empted his concerns and already sent Schlabrendorff on his way to Rastenburg to rectify the situation.

* * *

"I can't *tell* you how thankful I am that you haven't already delivered Tresckow's package to General Stieff," Schlabrendorff said, the moment he walked into Colonel Brandt's Rastenburg office. He'd flown there at supersonic speed in his efforts to head off a potential disaster.

"Oh," Brandt replied with what had been his guarded expression, lighting up into one of pleasant surprise. "I thought you'd come to reprimand me for not having been quicker to do so. I was just about to apologise to you."

"No need for that. In this case, I can only be extremely grateful that you've been slow off the mark. You've just saved General Tresckow's skin. He made a *terrible* mistake. He gave me the wrong package to pass on to you. The parcel you've got was earmarked for one of his sergeants as a token wedding gift. A much, *much* lesser quality one than he wished to present to Stieff, as you can imagine. If General Stieff opened that parcel and found the two cheap bottles of plonk inside, he'd have taken great offence. I shudder to think of the consequences."

Colonel Brandt, however, was more inclined to laugh, doing so, to Schlabrendorff's horror, while playfully throwing the package up and down in the air. His impromptu juggling act forced Schlabrendorff to work hard at keeping his calm to share the joke, while his eyes followed the ascent and descent of the parcel, just waiting for it to explode.

"If you give the parcel to me, sir, I'll make the appropriate swap and take care of its delivery myself," he said, making every effort not to arouse the Colonel's suspicion by reaching out to grab it too soon.

Brandt, however, was not content to simply hand it over. Having decided that he liked Schlabrendorff's company, he offered to escort him to the railway station, and to wait with him for the excruciatingly slow forty-five minutes it took for his train to arrive. Not knowing, as did sweat-soaked Schlabrendorff, that each one of those power-packed moments spent standing on the platform might be their last.

"Waste not, want not" had always been Schlabrendorff's motto. Later down the track as he sat alone on the train, he unwrapped the bomb and found that there was nothing wrong with it other than a minor fault in its timer fuse mechanism. That was why he decided to re-use it two weeks later and have another stab at bringing Hitler down.

The venue of Assassination Attempt No. 3 was to be at the Berlin Exhibition of Captured Russian War Equipment, which Hitler was booked to attend.

This time around, it was Baron Rudolf von Gersdorff who volunteered for front line duty. The *Abwehr* attaché to Army Group Centre had offered to model the new winter greatcoat that had been rushed through production for use on the Russian front, the pockets of which were big enough to house and hide the bomb, before he got his chance to literally leap on Hitler and blow the Fuhrer and himself to smithereens.

It was a pretty picture with which Schlabrendorff was finding it hard to come to terms. Particularly because it required expecting another man, rather than himself, to make the gruesome sacrifice.

"You *do* realize, don't you Gersdorff, that this is a suicide mission?" he said for the second time.

He wanted to make absolutely sure that Gersdorff knew what he was about, at the same time running the risk of insulting the Baron's courage and intelligence by questioning his comprehension and offering him a second chance to take the coward's way out.

As the gentleman of noble ancestry he was, however, Gersdorff neither resented nor rebuked him:

"My dear Schlabrendorff," he replied. "Being an aristocrat has provided me with many privileges. Its one downside, however, is that occasionally it is expected that I act like one."

Had Hitler played his part on cue, Gersdorff's gallantry would have gone down in the annals of history. But the Fuhrer denied him that fame in future footnotes by deciding to spend only a couple of minutes at the exhibition. Almost as soon as he arrived, he stormed out of it in a foul temper, his fuse proving shorter than the 30 second one over which Gersdorff's hand was hovering.

CHAPTER SEVENTEEN

That made three acts of stark drama that had gone completely unnoticed by Hitler and his henchmen. Oblivious to the frenetic activity of the Resistance—its bombs, its meetings and heart-stopping attempts on Hitler's life—the Gestapo and the SS were still only concerned with their preliminary investigations in Berlin.

Dr. Manfred Roeder, however, had finally cottoned on to the fact that the Schmidhuber affair was just the tip of the iceberg. With lip-licking anticipation, he was now primed to lift the lid on what was shaping up to be a proverbial Pandora's box of crime and conspiracy. To that end, he'd decided to step up his interrogations a notch.

For the last few weeks, he'd been looking more deeply into the businessman's allegations pertaining to the peculiar operations of the *Abwehr*. He had come to the realization that he'd not just stumbled over one random piece of vermin, but a nest of rats that had been breeding and scurrying their way throughout Europe and the ranks of the enemy, spreading their poison promises of treason.

They had been selling out their own country by offering the Allied forces the hope of a *coup d'etat* against Hitler and his Third Reich, vowing to replace both with a responsible, insanity-free German government in their effort to bring about a quick and peaceful end to the war.

But at what cost to their Aryan pride? Roeder had to wonder, wondering even *more* about the cost such a peace might inflict on his own blossoming career within the New Nazi Order.

Loathe to forfeit it for the sake of morality and mankind, he re-doubled his efforts to complete and present his dossier on the Schmidhuber interrogation to the Reich Military Court. The all-powerful judiciary body took only a few minutes to peruse it before giving him the written authority to call in for questioning Hans von Dohnanyi and his wife Christine; Dr. Josef Mueller and his spouse Maria; and Pastor Dietrich Bonhoeffer, who was to be rounded up by right of familial association. The fact that he was Dohnanyi's brother-in-law was more offensive to Roeder than Bonhoeffer's reputation as an anti-Nazi rabble-rouser.

As it turned out, the latter of these two offences shaped up to be a real boon for the Gestapo. When they had brought Pastor Bonhoeffer in for interrogation, it had been on the grounds of him being just a small-time troublemaker. They had not realized that, by default, they had snared one of the heavyweights of the Resistance.

Another of these was Hans Bernd Gisevius, whose name, too, had popped up quite often in Schmidhuber's testimony. Often enough to have the Gestapo recall him to Berlin for questioning, forcing him, by way of subpoena, to abandon his post as Vice-Consul in Zurich. With little or no notice, they demanded that he wing his way home from Switzerland to testify against his friends.

Although Schmidhuber's words in regard to Gisevius had not been nearly as damning as those he'd used against the others, he'd said all that was necessary to secure the Gestapo's interest. They suspected that the erudite young lawyer was in the know enough to provide them with the information they needed.

Even though they believed him to be relatively innocent, they had decided to make good use of him by submitting him to two torture-packed days of intense cross-examination, in the hope of terrifying him into betraying his friends.

Even beaten black and blue, Gisevius had refused to do it. Instead, he held on by the skin of his teeth, and what was left of it under his lacerated fingernails, until his Gestapo interrogators finally gave up, hampered in their attempts to break the man, because they were under Roeder's strict orders not to kill him. This left them no choice but to let Gisevius go, literally throwing him out the door and leaving him there, on bloodied hands and knees, to pick himself up and stumble his way home through the city streets.

Gisevius, though half dead, still had the presence of mind to stagger in the direction of Canaris' house rather than his own. He was desperate to warn his friend that the Gestapo was closing in.

Although the head of the *Abwehr's* name had not been brought up during *his* cross-examination, it was only a matter of time before they reeled Canaris in—before they found out that *he* was the illusive Big Fish they were after.

Twice now en route, Gisevius had fallen to his knees. Collapsing in a semi-faint from pure physical exhaustion and basic lack of food and water. On both occasions, he'd declined the help of the passers-by who had offered to take him to hospital, but had taken advantage of one of their strong arms to help pull himself back up onto his feet. Apologizing, Gisevius had extended his thanks, but not an explanation for the sorry state he was in.

As a dignified man, he was acutely aware of how deplorable it was—what a sight he must have been in the busy Berlin streets. His business suit torn and dusty, with the collar of what had been his crisp, white shirt turned a filthy yellowish-grey. Now without a button or a tie, it was stained and limp with sweat and blood—the perfect complement to his pale face which dripped with same. What remained of his fingernails now hung loose, jagged and ingrained with red fetid grime.

In normal times, it was a scene that would have stopped people in their tracks. But given their wartime conditions and the fact that they were in close proximity to Gestapo headquarters, it was just par for the course; a common phenomenon which was taken with a grain of salt. Only the brave few bystanders dared to cross the road and come to such a man's aid, while the others put their heads down and scurried past, knowing that the poor soul in dire straits was probably still under Gestapo surveillance and that it was imperative that they didn't risk complicity in his crime by offering him sympathy.

With or without help, Gisevius finally managed to grope his way to Canaris' street. But as he turned the corner into it, he stopped with a jolt at the sight of Dr. Roeder's staff car parked in front of the Admiral's house. Its shiny black, Swastika-stamped presence made his breath catch in his throat, while having him grab fast for the support the large wrought-iron gates that secured the entry to the Canaris estate.

Confused and exhausted, he leant his full weight against them; taking a brief moment to recoup, before quietly creaking them open to lose himself in the grounds. There he hid behind a large oak tree until nightfall when Roeder left. The departure of both day and demon made it safe at last for him to drag himself up the stairs and knock at Canaris' front door. The moment the Admiral opened it, Gisevius collapsed into his friend's arms.

"I'm so sorry I didn't get here in time to warn you," he said, his voice husky and slurred from thirst.

But Canaris didn't answer. Instead, he called out urgently to his butler for help—two men were needed to carry Gisevius into the sitting room and to lie him on the couch.

"Are you all right?" Canaris then asked, having already been filled in on Gisevius' trial by fire, an account of which Roeder had casually brought up during his visit.

The fact that Roeder had tired of Gisevius' torture and decided to take a break from it midway through had left Canaris up in the air as to its outcome. Sure as he had been that Gisevius *must* be dead, he was amazed and mightily relieved to see that his friend was still in one piece—albeit one that was scarred and shaken.

He poured Gisevius a glass of brandy and sat down at his side to support his head as he sipped it. At the same time, telling his butler to bring food and bandages.

"I'm fine," Gisevius replied.

But Canaris was unconvinced. The man looked shocking— within a hair's breadth of death. Yet still, he seemed more concerned for Canaris than for himself.

"I thought you were in danger of being next," he said, with a sudden urgency as he grabbed a fierce hold on Canaris' arm.

"Why? Was my name mentioned?"

"No," Gisevius answered in all honesty, knowing that it had not dropped from *his* lips, but with no doubt in his mind that it had fallen repeatedly from Schmidhuber's. When he'd seen Roeder's car parked outside, he'd logically assumed that Canaris was being arrested.

"I thought Roeder had got to you first."

As had Canaris, those few hours ago, when he'd looked out his window and seen Roeder's car pull up outside. Frozen with terror for one fleeting moment, he'd had to muster his courage to open his door—determined to present himself to Roeder with the utmost calm and courtesy.

But if the sight of the Gestapo agent paying him a visit had startled him, it was Roeder's reason for doing so that had shocked him even more.

"Just thought I'd pop in for some tea and sympathy," Roeder had said brightly, with that savage twist to his mouth that he thought passed for a smile.

Assured of his welcome, he'd stepped inside and shaken Canaris' hand, leaving his host stunned and convinced that he must be playing some sort of sadistic game. Canaris, with his shrewd instincts on edge and as yet, unaware that Dohnanyi, Mueller and Bonhoeffer were under interrogation, had decided to just pace himself—to wait for Roeder to make his move and declare "checkmate".

Roeder had not. Instead, for two long, stress-packed yet strangely convivial hours, the two of them had sat sipping tea and nibbling on scones and sandwiches, while Roeder chatted on about the weather and other subjects equally banal. Obviously he had no other agenda but to revel and relax in Canaris' companionship.

"I couldn't believe it," Canaris said, recounting the story to Gisevius as he handed him some soup and propped him up to eat it. "Those two hours were the most terrifying of my life. Every second I was sweating it out, just waiting for Roeder to pounce— to formally accuse me of conspiracy and put me under arrest.

"But, as you can see, he didn't. And just to cap it all off, the man actually *embraced* me before he went out the door, telling me how nice it was for him to have someone with whom he could confide and feel so comfortable. I'm afraid I couldn't return the compliment. By the time he left, my nerves were red raw."

The shock impact of that odd, impromptu afternoon tea, however, came nowhere near that which Canaris experienced when the Gestapo actually dared to wander into his *Abwehr* domain. Those sacrosanct Intelligence headquarters of his which were off limits to all but its staff . . . and *in particular* to the members to their arch-rivals—the SS. There had always been a firm understanding between the two individual Intelligence organizations, that, in *modus operandi* and office space, n'er the twain should meet.

However, on Monday, March 6, 1943, they had just brazenly strolled in the door and made themselves at home. Roeder, accompanied by his fellow Gestapo agent—Franz Xaver Sonderegger—walked without warning straight into Canaris' office to say, "We have a warrant to search Hans Dohnanyi's office. You are most welcome to accompany us, Canaris, if you like."

He did *not*, neither the idea of catching his associate out, nor the fact that Roeder had done just that to *him*, by bursting into his headquarters unannounced. But if Canaris had been thrown by Roeder's sudden appearance, he'd no intention of showing it.

"What's this all about?" he asked with feigned innocence as he got up from his chair. Extending a smile and gentlemanly handshake, he ushered Roeder and his associate through to Dohnanyi's office, going by way of Oster's and Lahousen's to collect them en route.

With a furtive wink, Canaris silently instructed his two off-siders not to say a word, but to smile their own warm welcome and to follow after their unexpected guests. He was reasonably confident that the three of them, *and* the soon-to-be-pounced-upon Dohnanyi, could carry off being caught on the hop if they managed to keep their wits about them.

After all the warnings they had received about SS/Gestapo lightning raids, Canaris was sure that Dohnanyi had had the sense to remove all incriminating documents from his office.

He had . . . all but one—the one he was reading when they appeared at his door.

"Well, this *is* an unexpected pleasure," he said, casually putting it down as he rose to greet them.

He had cleverly registered no surprise, having quickly taken his silent cue from Canaris to play it cool. His expertise as a renowned barrister stood him and his acting ability in good stead.

"We have a warrant to search your office," Roeder snapped back, not extending him the same courtesy.

Without quibbling, Dohnanyi stepped away from his desk.

"Go right ahead," he replied, holding his hands up in mock surrender. "If you find anything interesting, please let me know. I could do with the diversion, after all the dreary red tape I have to work my way through each day."

Unimpressed with his playacting, Roeder continued:

"If you would please open the drawers of your desk and the door to your safe."

A command that had Dohnanyi hesitate. On the pretense of searching for his keys, he patted his hip and chest pockets to find them. Pulling them out of one of the latter, along with his crumpled, monogrammed handkerchief.

"Sorry about that," he said, unraveling it from the silver keys. "Just a tad unappetizing, I'm afraid."

In no mood to be trifled with, Roeder grabbed them from him. Unlocking the safe, he rifled through Dohnanyi's papers, while his companion Sonderegger stood guard at the door. The tall, scar-faced sentinel watched with his arms folded and his dark eyes intent on the business at hand.

Watching . . . *watching* without emotion until that strategic second when he caught sight of Dohnanyi surreptitiously trying to catch Oster's attention. Having got it, Dohnanyi had furtively steered it in the direction of a particular piece of paper that was lying on top of his desk. The one which was marked with the letter "O" in coloured pencil. Its double-spaced type and rough handwritten corrections outlined suggestions for the political structure of Germany *after* Hitler's removal.

"*Hold up!*" Sonderegger called out, as Oster made his rather clumsy attempt to spirit it away. "What have you got there?"

Snatching it from Oster's hand, Sonderegger scanned it before passing it to Roeder with a satisfied smile. It, along with other materials found in their two hour search, providing the hard evidence to have Dohnanyi, Mueller and their respective spouses arrested. Bonhoeffer knew that he was next in line when he tried to telephone his sister, Christine.

When she didn't answer, he knew something was wrong, a fact that was confirmed when he went to her house to find it empty and vandalized. Every piece of its upturned furniture, every nook and cranny had been stripped, searched and destroyed by the SS. All, that is, except the evidence that they had found to be used against them, most of which directly implicated Bonhoeffer.

He picked up the phone to call his parents:

"And now they will come for me," he said to them very calmly. Hanging up, for the last time on his mother and father, to sit down and quietly enjoy a cup of tea while he waited for the Gestapo to knock at the door.

It was only fortunate that, in spite of Roeder's thoroughness, the Gestapo missed what would have been the most important of all their finds in Dohnanyi's office—the small silver key, tied with a red ribbon to one of his folders, that opened the subterranean safe at Zossen, out of which, if the Nazis ever found it, would tumble the entire and very graphic account of all their atrocities.

But for the time being, it remained a secret. A combination-locked time bomb ticking away underground, that was destined to eventually bring about the deaths of nearly every man who had dared stand against Hitler.

CHAPTER EIGHTEEN

With or without that hard evidence falling into Gestapo hands, however, the walls of the Resistance were starting to crumble. Quite literally, in fact, when the Berlin *Abwehr* headquarters on the *Tirpitz Ufer* were blown apart by an Allied bomb.

It was a most fortuitous piece of airborne destruction, minus any human casualties, which forced Canaris and his entire organization to move shop. Relocating themselves to what had been their secondary headquarters at Zossen. Their shift in situation put them within two floors distance of "the safe", and made it more convenient for them to watch over it.

This shuffle of premises, however, was just the bricks and mortar side of it. Inconceivable as it seemed to Canaris, the *real* destruction of his beloved *Abwehr* was destined to come about, not by the dropping of a bomb, but by the throwing of a tea party.

Frau Hanna Solf's tea party, to be exact. She and her husband—Dr Wilhelm Solf—had long been involved in the anti-Nazi intellectual movement in Berlin. The lady of the house fell foul of the Third Reich by lavishing her hospitality on all those who were against it, and, unfortunately, she made the fatal mistake one day of welcoming a new and rather handsome member to her social clique—a young Swiss doctor named Reckse.

The man, unbeknown to her, was a Gestapo "plant", who had swallowed down her scones and jam, and listened with a curious smirk to the clink of her fine-china teacups and seditious table-talk. Afterward, he'd passed on the gist of it to his Gestapo superiors.

Although the select Solf circle were tipped off and given a chance to flee for their lives, it didn't take long for the Gestapo to round them up for execution. An official from the Foreign Office—Otto Kiep—was one of the unfortunate few to have lost his head, both under interrogation and the blade of the guillotine.

He was the missing link that at last turned Hitler's accusing eyes in Canaris' direction.

It just so happened that Kiep's two best friends were members of the *Abwehr*—Erich Vermehren and his wife, the former Countess Elizabeth von Plettenberg—both of whom Canaris had stationed as his agents in Istanbul.

As a direct result of their close affiliation with Otto Kiep, the Gestapo summoned them to Berlin, but, fearing for their lives, they declined the not-so-kind invitation. Hurriedly grabbing up what possessions were at their disposal, they hightailed it out of Turkey and defected to Britain. It was mistakenly believed back in Berlin that those possessions they had taken with them included all the *Abwehr's* secret codes.

This, despite Hitler's great fondness for Canaris, was the last straw.

"What kind of incompetent *fool* are you to have recruited such defective agents?" was the bellowed, blue-bulbous-eyed accusation he threw at his Little Admiral the moment Canaris walked in his door. "Your Abwehr is falling to pieces!"

In a state of shock—not over Hitler's verbal attack, but over the recent brutal executions of many of his friends and associates— Canaris nodded slowly in agreement.

"You're right," he said. "But then it is hardly surprising, when the same can be said of the Third Reich and its war."

This supremely dangerous statement left Hitler no option but to fire him on the spot.

Those were the last words that ever passed between them. The formal dissolution of the massive *Abwehr* organization itself followed soon after. Its mountains of top secret paperwork and red tape, its labyrinth of corridors and offices, were taken over at lightning speed by the SS. Like a plague of scuttling cockroaches, their black-uniformed squadrons swarmed into the building within seconds of Canaris having vacated it. Himmler was determined not to give the Little Admiral even the slightest opportunity to stash anything of importance under his trench coat on his way out.

It had been a real feather in Himmler's cap—having finally convinced his Fuhrer to place all German Intelligence services under his sole control, with Major-General Walter Schellenberg replacing Heydrich as head of the SS Intelligence Division and

SS General Ernst Kaltenbrunner taking over from Heydrich as head of Reich Security.

Blonde-haired, blue-eyed Kaltenbrunner, with his brutal, pockmarked face, had been hand-picked by Himmler himself. The SS Reichsfuhrer was grooming him in Heydrich's image and issuing him with orders to match those of his predecessor:

(a)   *To keep Canaris in line.*
(b)   *To take over where the Rear Admiral's nemesis, Reinhard Heydrich, had left off.*

By rights, with such wolves at his door, Canaris should have been lost, but it was that tiny little soft spot that Hitler still harboured in his heart for him that saved the day. The fact that Canaris had once secured a small corner of it made it difficult for the Fuhrer to believe the worst of him, or to sign the orders for his arrest. Instead, Hitler found it easier to simply remove his former friend from power by reason of incompetence.

He covered up for Canaris' enforced retirement by giving him the sinecure of Chief of the Economics Warfare Office, while ostensibly putting him under informal house arrest *and* the Gestapo's constant vigilance at his villa at Schlachtensee.

Having spirited his family away to safety, Canaris was forced to live there alone under the constant fear of being found out . . . and far, *far* worse.

His sudden removal from the scene was most disturbing for his fellow conspirators. Canaris had been the heart and soul of their Resistance operations, the motivating force—the brains behind it all. His dynamic presence and astute understanding of the situation had bound them all together and offered them security of sorts. He was the *eminence grise* without whom they not only lost impetus, but access to an enormous amount of invaluable information—not the least of which was Canaris' knowledge of codes and the tapping of telephone lines by the Gestapo.

This practice of had become prolific. The Gestapo's omnipresent telecommunication network was now plugged into almost everyone involved in the Resistance circuit. They were keeping tabs on their every unguarded word, while their every move was being monitored by the all-pervading presence of Gestapo agents in their long, dark coats. Their sinister silhouettes hovered on street corners or in black sedans on twenty-four-hour stakeouts outside their homes.

With Canaris, Dohnanyi, Mueller and Bonhoeffer out of circulation, all was in a state of flux. The latter three were under lock and key in Berlin's Tegel Prison, while Canaris, although still free of prison, was as good as being in one.

Whatever Resistance work was in motion was being done slowly and at great risk to its participants, most of whom, in fear of their lives, had gone to ground.

Having recovered from his episode in the torture chamber, Hans Gisevius had flown quickly back to Switzerland to take refuge there.

Hans Oster had been suspended from duty and, although still free to roam the streets at will, was under close surveillance. Each day, walking to his letterbox, he was fully aware that he was being watched, that the two men sitting in their black Mercedes on the opposite side of the road were keeping close tabs on him.

Haven't they any idea of how ludicrous they look? Oster wondered with a wry smile as he pretended not to see them. It was hard to do considering how ridiculously conspicuous they were, all rigged out in their menacing, mafia-like attire.

Taking his mail from the letterbox, Oster stood with a defiant calm to flick his way through it. There was a delicious satisfaction to be had in teasing his Gestapo onlookers with his relaxed demeanour. It went a long way in taking the edge off their scare tactics.

In fact, had Oster not been so utterly terrified underneath it all, he might have found it vaguely amusing—all this hiding around corners and clandestine, "catch me if you can" business. The trouble was that it wasn't a laughing matter. Not when all his friends' lives were on the line.

That was why he went inside when he recognized Dohnanyi's scrawled handwriting on one of the envelopes. He knew it was something that needed to be read in private:

My dear Hans,

Must scribble this quickly. Am fortunate in Colonel Otto Maas being the Commander here at Tegel. Being in sympathy with me and our cause, he has kindly allowed me to write this note to you.

As far as our inquisition here is concerned, I believe that everything is under control; but please . . . please destroy all documentation at Zossen immediately. Almost every piece of paper in that safe spells out our death sentence, and the Gestapo are closing in on it. All I can say is . . . to hell with history. Our heads are going to roll if they find it!

With all faith in your discretion,

Your friend, Hans

"No way!" was Beck's response when Oster showed him the note. The General drumming home his blank refusal to comply with Dohnanyi's wishes, with the thump of his fist on his desk.

"Under *no* circumstances will I permit the destruction of even one piece of that most strategic documentation," he continued, pulling rank as the recognized head of the Resistance and nominated Head of State in the event of a successful *coup d'etat*.

As such, General Beck had the final say. Although retired from his position as Chief of the Army General Staff, he was still an old warhorse by heart and training, and refused to see beyond the necessity of personal sacrifice to achieve a successful military end.

"To destroy that paperwork would be fatal for us," he explained. "And I must say that I'm astonished that a man of your fine military reputation, Oster, could even *entertain* such a short-sighted idea."

That was exactly what Oster *had* done . . . from the moment he had read his friend's note and noticed the erratic scribbling of its words. The blotched ink and the child-like curvature of its letters had told him that Dohnanyi's hand had been shaking when he had written it. Determined as his courageous friend was not to complain, it was obvious that he was suffering greatly.

Being more prone to sentimentality than Beck, Oster had hoped to save his friends Dohnanyi, Mueller and Bonhoeffer from any more torment. It had been a long shot, he knew, to suggest to Beck that they help out by destroying the vital evidence, but morally he'd felt obliged to try.

"I was just concerned about our associates, that's all."

"And you think I'm *not?*" Beck countered, taking offence. "What do you think, . . . that I have no feelings? How do you imagine that I've got myself in the sorry state I'm in? I've got an ulcer, high blood pressure and thyroid problems. And that's because I spend my every waking hour in a state of chronic tension. You do know, I suppose, that I've just been diagnosed with stomach cancer?"

"No, I didn't," Oster interrupted, his head jerking back in surprise. He was embarrassed that he'd dumped such a problem on Beck when the man had more pressing ones of his own.

It was little wonder, Oster now realized, given that at the age of sixty-five Beck had been keeping up such a frenetic pace in regard to Resistance issues and in his singular, open opposition to Hitler. He was the only man in the Reich from whom the Fuhrer was prepared to accept criticism. For some reason, Hitler had always been a little in awe of the greatly respected, incorruptible General Beck.

"Even in *hospital*," Beck continued, not as a ploy to exact sympathy, but to take advantage of spilling out his hostilities to someone he trusted, "I had Gestapo agents actually stand guard over my operating table! Can you believe it? I was unconscious, for God's sake! What on Earth did they think I could do to endanger the State under anaesthetic?"

"They were hoping, I should think, sir, that you'd speak more freely under the effects of ether," Oster put forward.

And Beck looked up at him, stony-faced:

"They were hoping, my dear Oster, that I would *die* under its effects. Can't you just see the pack of vultures hovering around my bed, waiting for their share of the pickings? But I'm pleased to say that both I and my doctor disappointed them."

"Your doctor?" Oster asked.

"Yes, my surgeon told me that while I was 'under', they suggested to him that he might like to make a small slip with his scalpel. They didn't realize that Dr. Sauerbruch was my oldest and closest friend—that he was a man of the utmost integrity. Nothing . . . and I mean *nothing*, would have forced him to either betray his Hippocratic oath or to lay a harmful hand on me. He knows me better than anyone. He knows that I'm not a hard-liner by nature, Oster. And it is important to me that *you* know that too. That you are aware that I'm as horrified as you are by the thought of our mutual friends' suffering at Tegel. But in war there are imperatives and expendables, both of which are reliant on each other.

"It just so happens that the 'imperative' at the moment is to make sure that those papers stay intact. Particularly the ones in regard to the 1939-40 negotiations. Whether or not we succeed in getting rid of Hitler, it'll be vitally important to us, to be able to prove to the world that we didn't merely start acting against him when everything was lost, but in those early days when the world still believed in our military victories."

"And the expendables?" Oster asked, wondering why he'd bothered to ask when the answer was obvious.

So obvious was it that Beck didn't feel it necessary to reply. It gave him no pleasure to watch as Oster strode from the room, thinking the worst of him, but as far as Dohnanyi, Mueller and Bonhoeffer were concerned, it couldn't be helped. Beck was no longer in a seat of military power, or in the position to order their release.

The only help he could offer them was in sourcing the assistance of other men who still had such power at their fingertips, a thankless job that he'd been doing for the last three years. His pleas to secure the support of just *one* man . . . just *one* field marshal with a moral conscience . . . had constantly fallen on deaf ears and a succession of trembling hearts.

CHAPTER NINETEEN

*"We are going to lose the war. I believe that the wider strategic position
for Germany is hopeless . . . "*

Beck had recently written these words to Field Marshal Erich von
Manstein in the hope that a man of his alleged calibre and courage
might agree to lend his services to the Resistance and make a
stand against Hitler. As Commander of Army Group South, he'd
a reputation for speaking his mind on all issues military, and
wasn't afraid to give back as good as he got from Hitler in regard
to them.

All of this he did, however, while never *ever* questioning the
Fuhrer's final authority as Commander in Chief of the German
Army. Manstein was the consummate strategist, both on and off
the battlefield. As such, Beck believed it might do Manstein, *and*
the Resistance, a great deal of good if he were told a few home
truths.

*". . . I'm not at all sure that you are aware, my dear Manstein," he
continued, "that in your theatre of operations, alone, 250,000 Jews
have been slaughtered. That's enough to stockpile the Olympic Stadium
in Berlin."*

*"No! That's impossible!" Manstein had angrily written back. "I would
have known had a massacre of such catastrophic scale taken place under
my nose. What nonsense is this that you're trying to sell me as fact?
And what sick-minded individual has contrived to circulate such a vile
rumour? I'll have nothing to do with it, do you understand. What I don't
know, in my official capacity, does not concern me."*

This statement gave Manstein the excuse to back away from front
line duty. With the hard-edged vision of the realist he was, he then

covered his tracks of retreat by adding a postscript that reeked of expediency and mock gallantry.

"For all our Fuhrer's failings, I am convinced that his removal will lead to chaos. I firmly believe that Germany will fall to pieces without him. Now is the time to stand with, not against him. Surely I don't need to remind you, General Beck, that a war is lost only when one gives it up as lost!"

Manstein's self-righteous RSVP smartly put Beck back in his place and got Manstein off the hook, relieving the famous Field Marshal of the onerous responsibility of standing up be counted.

Beck scrunched up his letter with disdain and threw it into his wastepaper bin where he believed it belonged. To his way of thinking, Manstein's refusal to follow the dictates of what should have been any decent man's conscience was an act of pure cowardice, just like the many others, from morally deficient field marshals, that had preceded it. All of them, so-called men of action, when put to the test had done nothing but run away from it.

While Beck had tried and failed on many fronts to enlist a military leader's support, his fellow conspirator, Dr. Carl Goerdeler, had also been striking out unsuccessfully with the same game plan, holding talks of late with General Heinz Guderian and Field Marshal von Rundstedt.

Neither, in consideration of Hitler's enormous military bungle at Stalingrad, was averse to a coup *per se*, but they were not willing to play an active part in it. Their sense of honour carried them only so far as to have them not betray the members of the conspiracy, while the more practical side of their nature had them shrink from rubbing Hitler the wrong way. They decided, instead, to accept the Fuhrer's offer of cold, hard cash to ensure their loyalty.

Guderian managing to negotiate for himself a slightly sweeter deal, by adding to Hitler's financial gratuity a two thousand-acre country estate that the Fuhrer signed off to him with his fondest wishes. Hitler had always had an uncanny knack of knowing which of his Generals were on the turn, and precisely when and where to offer them the incentive to jump back to his side of the tracks.[22]

Always being so near and yet so far from securing a military "front man" to lead them to victory was frustrating in the extreme for the Resistance—particularly so for Goerdeler, who had never had the capacity to mark time when an objective was in sight.

Forever a loose cannon with a short fuse, it was beyond him to brook delay. This, when it came to the intricacies of undercover work, was a glaring fault in his nature—one that represented an ever close and present danger to the conspiracy. His constant champing at the bit to take immediate, rash action had, from the beginning, made them all very nervous.

But now that he'd recently received news that his only son had been shot dead on the Russian Front, Goerdeler was at risk of losing it all together; of sailing perilously close to doing something stupid to undermine the already extremely delicate foundations of the Resistance.

"*Someone* has to have the guts to alert Hitler to the fiasco he's made of Germany. *I'm* not scared. If need be, I'll confront him myself." In his wild-eyed passion Goerdeler spat out the words at Canaris.

The man, in his bluster and boldness and *complete* lack of diplomacy, knew no better than to vent his feelings full force at a man who, in mind and method, was his perfect opposite.

It gave Canaris, as the accomplished diplomat, no choice but to sit back and listen to them, knowing that the prospect of Goerdeler ever learning to hold his tongue was bleak, and that the idea of him keeping a secret was less likely still.

Not that anyone ever questioned Goerdeler's integrity or courage, both of which were exemplary, albeit imprudent. It was just that all the other members of the Resistance were afraid that his loose lips and gung-ho antics would eventually bring about their undoing. Most of them, as a result, actively avoided his company for fear of arrest by association, particularly now that the eyes of the Third Reich were so unrelentingly upon them.

Living in seclusion at his villa at Schlachtensee, Canaris now made for the ideal sounding board. That was why Goerdeler had decided to drop in on him unexpectedly, so that he could corner and make a captive audience of the Little Admiral, paying him a not-so-fleeting visit from which Canaris had no escape. For courtesy's sake alone, he'd no choice but to listen to all that Goerdeler had come to say.

"Well, what's Oster doing?" his guest immediately demanded

to know as he poured himself a brandy—too agitated to wait for the offer of one, or to pour a second glass for his host.

"Right now, Oster's not in a position to do conspiracy work," Canaris replied, lifting a scathing eyebrow at Goerdeler's lack of manners. "He's being watched every minute of the day. I've had to warn all other members of the Resistance to keep their distance from him while he's on suspension and under such close Gestapo scrutiny."

"Well then what about Keitel? Have you spoken to *Keitel?*" Goerdeler continued, pummeling Canaris with questions, as if the ex-head of the *Abwehr* were his underling. It was an insult that Canaris wouldn't normally have tolerated, but given the extenuating circumstances of Geordeler's still new and very raw state of mourning for his son, he let the issue pass.

"Yes, I've spoken to Keitel . . . for what it was worth. Which, as usual, was nothing."

Sitting down in his brown leather armchair, Canaris' answer had been calm and controlled, in an effort to counter Goerdeler's anxiety. "I told him that the world would one day hold the Wehrmacht responsible for all the atrocities Hitler has committed, because it allowed them to take place under its nose."

"And did he listen?"

"Yes," Canaris replied simply, as he crossed his legs and folded his hands comfortably in his lap.

"Well . . . what was his response?"

Under the circumstances, Goerdeler was finding the Admiral's composure infuriating.

"He told me to take the matter no further."

Canaris' answer was accompanied by a tight, cynical smile, as he recalled the shaky, sweat-drenched hand that Field Marshal Wilhelm Keitel had extended to him at the end of their fruitless meeting.

The Commander in Chief of Germany's Armed Forces had disintegrated into a worthless and supremely dangerous nervous wreck—too terrified to make a move in any direction for fear of stirring Hitler's wrath, and the very real possibility that his Fuhrer might raise *his* still very steady, sadistic hand against him.

"I know what you all think of me," Keitel had said to Canaris. "That you think I'm a complacent, incompetent yes-man. So I can only wonder why . . . *why* you and all the other Generals, who believe themselves to be so much stronger and morally superior, haven't tried to remove me from Hitler's side. Surely it wouldn't be hard to arrange with *your* finely-honed skills Canaris?"

At which point, Keitel had paused to raise and level his shaking index finger at the Little Admiral. The gesture added a touch of theatrics to his next words.

"But don't tell me . . . let *me* tell *you* why. It's because *none* of you would want to step into my shoes. *None* of you would be prepared to fill my position as Hitler's lackey and wind up as the sorry excuse for a man he's made me."

Canaris had been, at that poignant moment, impressed by Keitel. At the same time he felt a gut-wrenching sympathy for him. He had not realized that Keitel was capable of such honesty . . . that he was so acutely aware of his own weakness and the hopelessness of his disputing any issue with Hitler . . . that he had such a clear picture as to how he'd succumbed, heart and soul, to the inevitable, and given up on even *trying* to be his own man, forming his own opinions.

"Well thank God we've still got Field Marshal Witzleben on side," Goerdeler said, snapping Canaris back to the here and now. "At least that's something."

For a long time it *had* been. At this moment, it was reassurance enough to put Goerdeler's voice and emotions back on an even keel. But his comfort level was short-lived.

"I wouldn't get too excited about that prospect if I were you," Canaris countered.

His unexpected comment made Goerdeler move the brandy glass from his lips to say, "What on Earth do you mean? Witzleben has been true to the Cause right from the start. He's not a man to go back on his word."

"*That* he's not," Canaris confirmed. "But therein lies the problem. It's *because* Hitler knows that Witzleben's a man of his word and impervious to bribery that he's decided to simply remove him from power. Just as he did with me."

Unable to hide his chronic disappointment, Goerdeler's shoulders slumped. Erwin von Witzleben had been their great white hope. As the Commander in Chief of Army Group West, he'd been the only field marshal who had offered his unstinting military support. He had done so on the proviso that one other field marshal join him in the conspiracy initiative; a back-up which he believed was imperative if they were to pull off a successful coup and be in a position to affect a smooth transition in the German government, once Hitler had been removed from it.

"But what excuse did Hitler use to get rid of him?" Goerdeler asked, wondering why he'd bothered, when it was common knowledge that the Fuhrer had never felt himself under obligation to provide one. His violent mood swings and absence of military rationale being reason enough for any arbitrary dismissal that took his fancy.

"Haemorrhoids," Canaris said, plain and to-the-point. The humorous side of the situation made it hard for him not to collapse into a fit of nervous laughter.

"The poor man was in agony and made the mistake of going to hospital for a couple of days to have them cured. Kept it under wraps of course. It's not the sort of war wound one wants to talk about. That's why he was surprised to see the two SS officers waiting for him when he came out of the operating theatre. He was still half *non compos* when they handed him Hitler's orders for his immediate retirement.

"Not to worry, though . . . we haven't lost him altogether. But like me, he's now been relegated to work from the shadows, rather than acting as that front man we so desperately need. So let's notch up yet another win for Hitler, shall we? I have to admit . . . the man's a legend."

Unlike Canaris, Goerdeler had never mastered the art of good sportsmanship and the gentlemanly practice of victim saluting victor.

"That's all we ever seem to do . . . work from the shadows," he lashed out belligerently as he threw back his head and drained his glass. He was in dire need of the burning amber liquid's consolation.

Canaris decided to take advantage of the solace it was offering his associate to brace Goerdeler for the next bit of bad news.

"Right at the moment, perhaps a little shadow play is best. At least I know that's how Ulrich von Hassell is feeling. He wants out of the limelight for the time being. He had a nasty scare the other day."

With an exasperated sigh, Goerdeler slammed down his empty glass on the table.

"What *now*?" he asked, thinking how wrong he'd been to have paid the Admiral a visit. He had come in the hope of being cheered up, but Canaris had done nothing but depress him to his boots. Was there not even *one* positive thing to be said about the state of affairs? Apparently not.

"Hassell dropped in to see his old friend Ernst von Weizsacker when he got back to Berlin the other day."

"Ah, now that *is* good news," Goerdeler interrupted. The backing that the Resistance had received from the Senior Secretary of the German Foreign Ministry had always been most welcome. "At least it's comforting to know that we've still got such friends in high places."

But Canaris cut short Goerdeler's relief with a wry smile.

"Let's put that in the past tense shall we?" he said, determined - as it seemed to Goerdeler - to throw a wet blanket on any hopes of their future success. "I'm afraid Weizsacker has decided to wash his hands of us."

"I don't believe it."

"You'd better. Hassell was shocked by the cold reception he got. Weizsacker made no attempt to disguise how angry and horrified he was when Hassell turned up at his door without warning. Weizsacker checked to see that the coast was clear and then whisked his old friend into his office; refusing to open his lips until all its windows and doors were shut.

"He then told Hassell that he had a very serious matter to discuss with him and proceeded to berate and humiliate him for having been so indiscreet. Telling him that the Gestapo had been watching his every move. That he'd been 'tailed' for the last few months, and in having come to his house, Hassell had effectively lead the Gestapo to *his* door. He told Hassell that it wasn't to happen again—that he must amend his behaviour immediately, and do so without implicating the Weizsacker family and its reputation any further."

"My God!" came Goerdeler's exclamation.

This was all getting far too real—this insidious new custom of good friends turning on each other. A growing, savage culture of "every man for himself", that had even the most refined in society relapsing back to primeval instincts.

None of it augured well.

"Hassell had no idea that he'd been under surveillance," Canaris continued. "He was acutely embarrassed about having inadvertently put Weizsacker's life under threat by pure coincidence of their friendship. *Which*, Weizsacker then advised him, was at an end. He saw Hassell promptly out his front door with the words:

"Now auf Wiedersehen . . . but please, not too soon!"

"But this is dreadful. Is *nothing* ever going to go our way?" Goerdeler said, wondering why he was now feeling compelled to ask his next question—knowing in advance of posing it, that its answer would distress him even further.

"How are the boys at Tegel? Has there been any news about their welfare?"

"Very little, but I believe that Bonhoeffer is coping remarkably well. Has made for the exemplary prisoner apparently. He's already got all the guards on side. All of them a little daunted, I suspect, by his mild manner and higher purpose. I know *I* am. I've never known a man more adept at humbling those around him with the sheer sense of his own humility.

"Unfortunately I've heard nothing of Mueller, which worries me enormously. Dear old Mule, I do hope they're treating him with a little civility. I've no idea how the man's going to cope on a 'bread and water' diet, when he's so used to shoveling down five courses, three times a day. I can only count on his good humour getting him through."

"And what of Dohnanyi?" Goerdeler asked. "With his dicey constitution, he's more of a concern than the others."

"No good news there, I'm afraid. It appears that Roeder has taken a particular dislike to him. For some peculiar reason, he's fixated on seeing Dohnanyi to his grave, even though I've managed to get Keitel to issue orders that he, Mueller and Schmidhuber must not face charges of treason, but merely those of inefficiency in political clearances and currency fraud."

"So what's Roeder's grievance?"

Canaris shrugged.

"I have no idea. Just evil in action. Heaven knows, we've seen enough of it to recognize the signs."

"But what's happened to him? Is he still alive? Is he all right?"

"Oh I'm sure he's still alive. Dohnanyi might be prone to ill health, but he's more tenacious of life than any man I've known. You can be assured that he'll hang on till the bitter end. And while he's doing it I've been pulling out all stops to secure his release.

"But I'm running up against a brick wall. I keep on managing to talk Keitel around to arranging his release, but then he suddenly changes his mind. And he's done so on five separate occasions. Which means that he's got Roeder in his other ear. I'm convinced that Roeder's counteracting my requests behind the scenes. You know what a champion vacillator Keitel is. In the long run, Roeder will win, of course, because Keitel's more frightened of him than he is of me."

"With good reason," Goerdeler confirmed, as he struck a match, cupped his hands around it and lit his cigarette.

"Problem is, we're running against the clock. Dohnanyi's terribly ill. I honestly don't know how much time he's got left. Last thing I heard was that the arteries in his legs had become inflamed and that Roeder denied his family's request that their doctor visit and treat him.

"The bastard's also knocked back the string of Defense Counsels Dohnanyi has commissioned to represent him. All of them have mysteriously disappeared off the scene. One by one, Roeder's obviously blackmailed them, or put the fear of God into them. That's how he works—on the premise that there's a skeleton in every man's closet; and he has absolutely no scruples about rattling it."

"I only wish there was something we could do to help," Goerdeler said, frustrated at having to stand so impotently on the sidelines while his friends were taking the full brunt of the responsibility.

"He *did* get lucky a few weeks back," Canaris replied, to buck Goerdeler up. "His prison cell was blown up by an Allied bomb."

"And you call that lucky?"

"Yes, as it turned out—the highlight of his day. When they dug him out of the rubble, he was in a terrible state, but still in one piece. The beauty of it was that Roeder had no choice but to transfer Dohnanyi to Charite Hospital and put him under Dr. Sauerbruch's care. You know him—he's Beck's great friend and physician."

Goerdeler nodded his confirmation with a sigh.

"At last—a ray of hope," he said.

"Only a short reprieve, I'm afraid. Roeder wasn't about to give up. He kept complaining over and over again to Keitel that Sauerbruch had a dubious agenda in protecting this particular military prisoner and that Dohnanyi must be released for further questioning.

"I can tell you, I've never been more grateful for Keitel's talent for dithering. He kept umming and ahhing; and never actually got around to writing out the order in Roeder's favour."

"So that was that, I presume?" Goerdeler put in hopefully.

But Canaris was already shaking his head with sad resignation.

"Would that I had your optimistic temperament, Goerdeler. You must keep in mind that when a predator has tasted blood, he won't stop until he's made the kill. Roeder simply got round Keitel's ambivalence by approaching another high-ranking military doctor friend of his to examine Dohnanyi when Sauerbruch was out of Berlin. He actually got his physician pal to smuggle Dohnanyi out in an ambulance in the middle of the night and move him to Buch Military Hospital, without Sauerbruch's authority—then demanded that his newly appointed doctor declare Dohnanyi fit for interrogation. It's appalling. The man can barely lift his head off his pillow. He has to be carried into the interrogation rooms on a stretcher!"

"I managed to get another long memo off to Churchill, you know, asking him to hold up on the aerial bombardment of Berlin to help facilitate the coup," Goerdeler said out of the blue, surprising Canaris with his swift change of subject.

But if Goerdeler had hoped to inject some positivity into their conversation, he had failed. Canaris had given up on their British connection.

"That's good," he replied half-heartedly.

He held little hope for Goerdeler's latest dispatch to the UK, when all those he'd sent in the past had been so patronizingly dismissed. There was no chance that the English would *ever* take Goerdeler seriously when he had a reputation for talking out of school, and doing so incessantly.

It wasn't just the Brits' lack-lustre response to Goerdeler that had offended Canaris. Nor was it their slapdash attitude towards the stream of other brave and well-intentioned emissaries who had risked their lives to cross the Channel in an effort to spare England the war.

As yet, Canaris was unaware that Winston Churchill *had* at last taken action of sorts—getting on board a B52 to fly to Quebec and participate in secret talks with Josef Stalin and President Roosevelt.

This, had he known, Canaris would probably have assumed was a good thing, never dreaming, in his naivety, that the three "men of the moment" to whom he'd applied time and time again for help were in the process of bringing him and his nation asunder. They were laying their plans to dismember Germany after their victory. By way of map, lead pencil and eraser, busily divvying it up for east and west post-war occupation.

Had Canaris and the other members of the German Resistance been privy to their discussions, they would have been horrified. Right then and there, they would have thrown in the towel and resigned themselves to Germany's fate. Knowing that, either way, their beloved Homeland was doomed, that both Hitler and the Allied forces were intent on its destruction.

And yet, having been left in the lurch and unenlightened by the Allies, Canaris was still under the false impression that there was a glimmer of hope on the horizon.

"Cheer up Goerdeler," he said, a burst of renewed enthusiasm for their cause having suddenly invigorated him. "I have no intention of lying down and dying. Hitler hasn't beaten us yet. You must remember that no one has ever succeeded in conquering Russia. When the disaster at Stalingrad comes out into the open, it'll set the Generals straight and perhaps the Resistance will get a second wind."

"You think?" Goerdeler said with just a touch of sarcasm. "Well all I can say is that second wind better come sooner than later. You know as well as I do that the ranks of our Resistance are thinning fast. We're all getting too old and cynical for this spy business. If we don't kill Hitler soon, there won't be one of us left alive to pull the trigger."

And *that* was the most intelligent thing Goerdeler had said. Mulling it over, Canaris got up from his chair to pour himself a drink.

Goerdeler was right. Either through corruption, murder or old age, they were losing all the strategic senior members from their ranks. Their steady stream of departures had drained the conspiracy of much of its clout and confidence. Something was needed . . . and needed *soon*, to boost their numbers and inject some fresh energy and guts back into the Resistance.

Deep in thought as to a solution, Canaris uncorked the glass lid of his brandy decanter, pausing before he asked Goerdeler the all-important question:

"How are the youngsters going?"

PART TWO

CHAPTER TWENTY

Having shed his blood, lost an eye, his right hand and seven of his fingers in fighting for the Fatherland, Count Claus von Stauffenberg might well have objected to being referred to in such a patronizing manner.

By the age of thirty-six, he'd been awarded the Iron Cross for bravery, had reached the rank of Colonel and had achieved the status of national hero. Any one of such accolades was reason enough for him to take offence at being categorized as *a youngster*— one of the rookies of the Resistance.

But that was exactly what he was in 1943. It had taken him some years of the war and the severing of several of his body parts to get over his feverish support for the Fuhrer and to come to the conclusion that Hitler must be removed if the Fatherland were to have any chance of survival.

"Now that I've been brave, I can be a soldier and fight in all the wars when I grow up," Claus von Stauffenberg had said when at the age of five he'd come through an anaesthetic-free operation to remove his tonsils, without so much as a whimper. The boy's astonishing fortitude and tolerance of pain at such a tender age had astounded the doctor.

Given that the child had displayed such courage, it was assumed that a life in the military was the career path Claus was destined to follow.

In those early days, his courage had been a case of mind over matter, because Claus' altruistic beliefs and dreams of military glory were tempered by a very frail constitution. His childhood was racked with ill-health, as was that of his two older brothers— Berthold and Alexander.

The three handsome sons of Count Alfred and Countess Caroline von Stauffenberg shared the problem that so often plagued families of the aristocracy. The practice of keeping their bloodline pure had gone further to weaken it, by centuries of inbreeding and social exclusion.

As a result, the boys suffered more than their fair share of life-threatening childhood diseases. Their series of illnesses punctuated their young years with bed-bound months of quarantine and convalescence at their country estate in Lautlingen. Fresh air and good living was believed to be the remedy for the cold, damp, tubercular-inducing surrounds of their family's official residence in the old castle at Stuttgart.

It would have been a sad state of affairs had the children not reveled so much in their regular rural retreats. The country air not only did wonders for their immune systems, but enabled them to side-step the normal rules and regulations that stunted a more pedestrian upbringing.

Syllabus free, the way was left open for them to live and learn "outside of the square"—to read fine literature considered beyond their years, to play and educate themselves to their heart's content, with lots of time left over to romp in the paddocks, ride horses and to pursue the arts, for which all three of them had a passion and a considerable talent. Their unconventional, classical education and appreciation of the sports made the three boys into good "all rounders".

Berthold, Alexander and Claus could go it with the best of them in a game of tennis or cricket; while equipped with their vivid imaginations and wooden swords, they found endless joy in reading and re-enacting the likes of Homer's *Iliad* and the adventures of Alexandre Dumas' *Three Musketeers*.

Although for Claus it wasn't always a case of "*All for one and one for all*". As the youngest, he often found himself left out of the other two boys' fun and intrigues.

Berthold and Alexander were twins and two years older. The combination of their mild sibling jealousy and basic disinterest in the affairs of a younger brother whose legs were too short to keep up often had them exclude Claus from their games and confidence. Their interest in him only piqued when the opportunity arose to tease him.

This was the case on regular occasions, despite their genuine love for him. The twins didn't fully understand the vindictive edge on that gut instinct of theirs to bring Claus down—an envy that was stirred by their suspicion that he was a cut-above themselves and most other men. In looks, talent and purpose, he was in possession of that "something special" which earmarked him for a place in history.

It was a noble but lonely expectation of greatness that condemned Claus to a life-long sense of isolation—one that he'd experienced since birth. Not only had he suffered it by way of the odd piece of neglect from his brothers, but as an inexplicable sensation that he could only describe as being a feeling that part of himself was missing—that he was forever in search of his other half to make himself "whole".

It was a peculiar phenomenon, which was explained away by his mother as she mopped the tears from her eyes. She thought that at the age of seven Claus was old enough to be told:

"Your dear little twin brother, Konrad, died just hours after you were born. You were only five minutes older than he. Each time I look at you, I see *his* face that should have been."

Claus had responded by going out into the garden to make a daisy-chain for her, in the hope that it would cheer her up. It was an act of deep-seated love for his mother that provided Berthold and Alexander with another, ever-so-slightly green-tinged reason to make fun of him.

Their next exercise in spite was thrown at Claus when he was getting over his bout of measles. Their cutting words spurred him on to get out of bed and to run with wobbly legs, and a temperature of 103, down to the local railway station where his mother—the Countess Caroline—was doing her best for the war effort. As the head of the local branch of the Red Cross, she was serving hot tea and soup to the stream of battle-weary WWI soldiers who were on their way back to the western front.

"What on Earth's the matter Claus? What are you doing here?" she asked in dismay at the sight of her seven-year-old son standing on the platform in his dressing gown and slippers with tears cascading down his flushed, red-spotted face.

"Berthold and Alexander said that in nine years they'll be able to join the Army, but that I *won't!*"

His very real distress had her kneel down to give him the hug and guarantee he needed.

"I promise you, my darling Claus, that I shall be heroic when the time comes, and let *all* my boys go."

She had been true to her word, as his mother always was. Gentle and high-minded, it was she who set the standard for his life—never dreaming that it would, inadvertently, bring about his early death. It was to her that he owed the stoic heroism which was to see him through his battlefield days, his series of horrific, life-threatening injuries and the stand he was to make against evil incarnate—the Reichsfuhrer, Adolf Hitler. His mother and the thrills and spills of the Great War lay the exciting and very dramatic foundations for his future. "Captain von Pluskow has been wounded *five* times and *still* wants to go back to the front. He is dauntless!"

Claus had run all the way home to report this piece of news to his parents, doing so with his arms akimbo and his face flushed with excitement. He had just spent hours in the fields with the injured soldier whom the Stauffenbergs had taken in for rest and rehabilitation. In between helping the wounded warrior bale the hay and build up his strength, Claus had listened with wide-eyed fascination to the Captain's many tales of his heroic exploits and grim experiences in the trenches of France.

In those heady days of 1916 there was still a chance that Germany would win the war, and Claus' imagination was running riot with the hope and glory of it all. In his veins stirred a passion and purpose that was never to be surpassed by any other in his life.

It was only to be expected, then, that Germany's subsequent request for an armistice on October 3, 1918, should rouse in him an equally ardent, but entirely different passion—one that brought a surge of hot tears to his eyes. A salty, burning mixture of anger, pride and sentimentality that had him interrupt the banquet his family were sharing with the King and Queen of Wuerttemberg, to spill out his emotions:

"My Germany *cannot* perish. If she goes down now, she will rise again strong and great. After all . . . there is *still* a God!"

His grand, prophetic outburst at the age of eleven left his parents as proud as punch, his brothers—Berthold and Alexander—in a state of shock, and the King, all but ready to stand up and salute him. Which was exactly what every guest seated at the table then did.

Putting down their knives and forks, all twenty of them got

up and raised their glasses to toast the future. Every one of the German aristocrats turned to Claus to salute the brave, new generation which would ensure Germany's resurgence in it.

Proud as Claus had been at that moment, he was still in a profound state of depression. He was not even able to bring himself to blow out the eleven blue candles on his birthday cake. November 15, 1918 was, he believed, the saddest day of his life.

Not only because of Germany's unconditional surrender on the 11th, just a few days before, but because their Monarch—King Wilhelm II of Wuerttemberg—had surrendered his Stuttgart castle and crown without the slightest struggle. He had agreed that his formal abdication should take place on November 30, and had requested that Claus' father—Count Alfred von Stauffenberg—negotiate the settlement of the King and Queen's estate and pensions with the new government of Wuerttemberg.

Despite the fact that every one of the King's men had deserted him in his time of need, the Stauffenbergs had remained loyal to the end. Their family had served the monarchy of Wuerttemberg for centuries, and with their father at that time presiding as the Royal Court's Lord Chamberlain, the Stauffenbergs believed themselves duty-bound—by both honour and nostalgia, to see their King's reign out.

Unfortunately they had to do so without the slightest pomp or ceremony. They were the only aristocrats prepared to drive away from the Wuerttemberg castle with its now deposed King and Queen. The small party took their unheralded leave of both palace and five hundred years of history in the two modest motor vehicles that had been provided.

It had only been his mother's restraining hand on Claus' knee that had stopped him from leaping up to shout out in protest. The totally un-fanfared fall of the centuries-old Royal family of Wuerttemberg had filled him with the most acute indignation. His hot, youthful blood made it impossible for him to understand that, at such a time, it was silence that was called for, that in the solemnity of that poignant, historic moment, such an undignified, albeit patriotic outburst would be in very poor taste.

Such was the power his mother held over Claus. Her enormous influence on him was challenged only by that of Stefan George, the

famous poet who, at the turn of the twentieth century, was considered
to be a prophet of Germany's "conservative revolution".

His sect—"the Secret Germany"—sparked the conscience of
a generation of idealistic young men like the Stauffenberg boys.
His platonic teachings shaped their reality with noble goals, which
lifted them up and beyond the mundane demands of society and
helped mould Claus into the man he was to be, by setting his sights
on God and glory.

"Claus' dreams are filled with the clatter of swords and the
sounds of battle," Alexander said to Stefan George.

Sitting at his teacher's feet, he had been secure in the fact
that they were alone, and had not had the slightest qualm about
sharing such a confidence.

Devoted to his mentor and master as he was, Alexander was
the only one of the three Stauffenberg boys who showed signs of
being a *true* poet, and of following in George's famous footsteps.
That was why he'd been hurt when George had chosen to carry a
poem of *Claus'* in his pocket. The great man was keeping close to
his heart what Alexander was sure was a sub-standard attempt at
verse not worthy of such an honour.

Claus' grasp of rhyme and iambic pentameter came nowhere
near matching his own. As usual, however, Claus' natural charm,
irrespective of his amateur literary efforts, had completely won
George over.

"And that is the way it *should* be. It is *right* that a young man
should dream of his destiny and of his own heroics in it," George
stated, having always thoroughly approved of Claus and his
Achilles-like aspirations.

This was to say nothing of his fixation with the sixteen-year-
old Claus von Stauffenberg's good looks and sharp wit. With his
strong homosexual leanings, George was drawn like a magnet
to the teenager's passionate nature and blooming masculinity;
tantalized by the challenge of Claus' obvious heterosexuality that,
by rights, put him out of reach.

This wasn't the case with Berthold and Alexander, who tended
more towards effeminacy and were much more open to George's
suggestions and love. Nevertheless, tempted as George was by all
three of the Stauffenberg boys, who he considered to be the jewels
in his sect's crown, Berthold and Alexander just didn't stir his

blood as did Claus and his inaccessibility.

"Then you don't see him as being a better poet than I?" Alexander responded, soothed to an extent by George's summation of his brother.

"A poet! Good Lord, no . . . not our Claus. He's as clumsy with his words as are you in hiding your envy."

George's comment came as a sound reprimand that had Alexander lower his head in shame.

"Then why do you choose to keep *his* poems so close to your heart in preference to mine?" he muttered, with his cheeks burning red and his own heart in his throat. Embarrassed in the extreme because he couldn't hide his tears when George gently lifted his chin and smiled down at him.

"Because I admire him," the Master explained. "Because I am *in awe* of him, as any man is of another who is so vastly different from himself. Berthold, you and I, Alexander, are the same. The three of us find fulfillment and solace in our poetry. Our ideals are a world unto themselves which give us peace.

"A peace that Claus, I'm afraid, will never find. He has the restless soul of a soldier and, I suspect, a short, brutal future ahead of him. One that I fear will tear him from us. And that is why I keep him—and the innocence of his verse—so close at hand. It's the nearest he'll ever be to me, and perhaps, some day, *all* that will be left of him for us to remember."[23]

CHAPTER TWENTY-ONE

It was a lucky thing that Claus had not tuned in to that conversation. Had he heard Stefan George's grim prophecy, he may never have joined the army. This he did in 1928 at the age of twenty-one, blissfully ignorant of his mentor's frightening forecast for his future.

Although his health was still not what it should be, his powerful family connections managed to secure him a posting in the 17th Cavalry Regiment and a placement at the Hanover Cavalry School.

There, his already established equestrian skills impressed his Squadron Commander enough to have him overlook the young Count's susceptibility to every passing virus, and to promote him to the rank of 2nd Lieutenant. The Commander went so far as to sit down and pen a memo to Military Headquarters to sing the young soldier's praises.

". . . Here is a man of high intelligence, unblemished character and natural leadership abilities. Apart from his accomplished equestrian skills, he excels at military tactics and weaponry, with the added benefit of being multi-lingual. He speaks English, Russian and Greek fluently and has placed first in the Cavalry Officer Cadets' examination. For his exemplary performance in both theory and practical, he has been awarded the Sword of Honour.

Young Count von Stauffenberg is, I believe, perfect officer material—eminently suitable for a General Staff position. He is extremely popular and admired by his superiors, peers and subordinates, although I have noticed that he is also inclined to arouse their envy, which is a sure sign of him being outstanding in his every field of endeavour.

I write this letter of commendation so that you, at Headquarters, will take note of the Stauffenberg name. I urge you to remember it and keep it on file, because I am convinced that it is destined to become very familiar to us all."

It had already become more than familiar to Claus' fellow officers. All of them, as their Squadron Commander had said, were great fans of "Stauff" (as he'd been nicknamed), but were unable to put their finger on exactly what it was about him that had their admiration forever teetering on the precarious edge of jealousy.

Perhaps it was because there was something of the Greek myth about him. As if, like an Homeric hero, he lived in a world apart and was only on Earth for a short time to grace those lesser mortals around him with his presence. His head-in-the-clouds demeanour, of course, was a product of Stefan George's esoteric philosophies and indoctrination. The elitist nature of his "Secret Germany" had inspired a superiority of mind and ideology that made Stauff appear to be aloof, even though he was determined, at least at face-value, to be one of the boys.

On that score, however, he never quite made the grade—"the boys" were not able to get around the fact that he was *different*. It was a truth that, rather than hold against him, they were happy to accept, given that it was impossible to find any reason to criticize the forever likeable Count Claus von Stauffenberg.

However, not to criticize him was not to say that his behaviour didn't leave them completely perplexed. Stauff was prone, for example, to break off midway through a military debriefing to cite a verse or two of poetry, or to choose to sit and read rather than join them at the pub or a party. It was odd, when at either venue there was no doubt he would be the star turn; assured of capturing every young girl's fluttering heart. The promise of this was of absolutely no interest to him.

Yet despite his somewhat priggish, pretentious carry-on, they had never have dreamed of labeling him a wimp. How could they, when his prowess at sport and all things masculine was so dazzling?

"You know, I can't understand you," his friend—Lieutenant Jurgen Schmidt—said. "There was no one at the Academy who was better at horse and motorcycle riding than you. You were not only good at it, but I don't think I've ever known anyone who enjoyed it more. Yet when I ask you to join me to indulge in either activity just for fun, you prefer to sit in your barracks and play your cello! That's fine, but I just can't get it through my head why someone of your artistic temperament chose to pursue a military career."

There were times when Claus himself couldn't understand it. He certainly found no joy in sharing barracks and six o'clock communal showers with comparative strangers. The group study hours, weapons training and lectures on infantry tactics were a little easier to bear—even though they, too, denied him the privacy with which he'd become accustomed.

He had said as much to his father in a letter he'd scribbled to him one day, smacking of frustration and a kind of patronizing snobbery:

"I knew it'd be hard for me here in the military. It's not easy for our kind to play the common man for any length of time and to renounce the intellectual life. But I know I will be richly rewarded for sacrificing a few years of my youth to serve the Fatherland in even the smallest measure.

I get on perfectly well with my subordinates, but not with people who consider themselves to have the same level of education. I am bored to distraction and have nothing but contempt for their pride in obtuse comment, their pathetic egotism and their puerile sense of tact, which consists of back-slapping familiarity and in deriding what they cannot comprehend."

His flagrant criticism of his friends had his father raise a reproving eyebrow and pray that his youngest son wasn't going to suffer *too* much from that inevitable fall from pride for which he was priming himself. It was a wonder, really, that Claus had any friends *at all*, if this were his obnoxious and supremely arrogant attitude towards them.

What this boy of his needed was a good dose of war and a stint in the rat-ridden, corpse-encrusted trenches that he—his father—had experienced first-hand. It was the only way to learn what friendship and camaraderie was all about.

It was a wish which was fast closing in on becoming a reality, with Hitler and his WWII hovering on the horizon. Both were sure to teach Claus his lesson.

Knowing that his son had always been an excellent student, his father wasn't worried about him learning it—particularly when he was aware that there were two sides to Claus' complicated nature. The second of which far outweighed the slightly less appealing side in question. It was the fact that his youngest son had been blessed with an engaging charm. Claus' larger-than-life persona, infectious laugh and sense of fair play ensured that he would *always* have a battalion of admiring friends and enemies to his credit.

His father just wished that Claus would stop counting Stefan George as being one of those friends. He didn't approve of the aging poet's affectations and his intent to thrust them on his well-meaning, but extremely gullible, entourage of young devotees.

Much as Claus would have leapt to deny it, he just didn't fit the Stefan George mould as did Berthold and Alexander. His father knew, by sad instinct, that his two eldest sons tended in the direction of effeminacy—that their artistic bent and gentle mannerisms came naturally, as they most certainly *did not* to Claus. His youngest son, despite his every effort to make himself one of them, exuded an undeniable masculinity that cast him as the black sheep of George's flock and forever put him on the outer with his siblings.

It was hard for Claus to be left out in the cold, but as far as his father was concerned it was a much more healthy and wholesome place for him to be. The sooner Claus got over his false hero-worship of Stefan George, the better. His third son was a man, in every sense of the word, which made it all the more essential that Claus draw away from the slightly seedy clique before it threatened his sexuality.

When it came to Stefan George, Count von Stauffenberg had been fighting an uphill battle to keep his children on the straight and narrow. He'd had no choice but to accept his three sons' obsession with the poet when, within their household, his wife had always promoted the study and embracing of the Arts. For some time, however, he'd suspected that George had been of a mind and purpose to embrace far more than just the Arts. His eyes were not focused on the talent and beauty of Longfellow and Da Vinci, as much as they were on that of Berthold, Alexander . . . and, in particular, Claus.

He would never have dreamed of suggesting as much to

his sons in a day and age when such talk was taboo, but he was heartily relieved when, off his own bat, Claus began to break free of George's cloying hold over him.

The first stage of this was when Claus joined the army. The second: when he got engaged to Baroness Nina von Lerchenfeld, the pleasantly attractive daughter of the former Bavarian Lord Chamberlain and Imperial Consul General, who had made it his practice to entertain the officers of the No. 17 Cavalry at his home.

Whether through a sense of obligation to the government, or that one more pressing—to his daughter—the Consul General was determined to include their uniformed presence in his social circle, and to make sure that one of them was safely married off to her before her twenty-first birthday.

His gift to Nina was to parade the pick of the German thoroughbreds for her selection, offering, to her shy and socially-correct delight, the chance to participate in the process of elimination—to cull the lesser specimens from the herd, so as to finally pinpoint the most suitable piece of horseflesh for breeding.

It took her no longer than two polite afternoon teas and three stilted waltzes at the Officers' Ball, to settle her pragmatic hopes on the dashing Count Claus von Stauffenberg. He reciprocated in kind by leaving himself open to the marital negotiation. Both were more than familiar with this age-old process of auctioning off aristocrats—the cool-headed bartering of titles in exchange for cash that had little to do with love on either side.

"Why did you choose me?" the rather non-descript Nina had asked when Claus released her from the stiff, passionless embrace that had followed on the heels of his proposal.

He answered, as was always his way . . . with the truth.

"Because I judge you suitable to be the mother of my children."

His explanation had taken a little of the golden glow off their night of moonlight and roses, and a considerable amount of skin off his new mother-in-law's nose when, to *her*, he explained his logic further.

"I consider that to wed is my duty. According to Frederick the Great, an officer's wife is a necessary evil."

It wasn't exactly the fairy tale romance that his father had had in mind for his favourite son, but whether or not Claus' heart was in it, at least it was a step in the right direction.

Nina, with her obliging face and manner, however, proved to be far more than just a respectable partner in life. She not only became the loving mother of their four children—Berthold, Franz, Heimeran and baby daughter, Valerie—but acted as his friend and support for the eleven happy years they shared together. His respect and love for her remained undiminished until death and came as ample compensation for any lack of passion that may have existed between them.

That absence of ardour on Claus' part was never a question of sexuality, but of necessity. Fate demanded that the surplus of passion he had at his disposal was to be deployed to fight for his Germany when WWII began.

CHAPTER TWENTY-TWO

Being twenty years Canaris' junior and attached to a different branch of the Armed Forces, Stauffenberg had to fight his way through many battles (both of cannons and of conscience) before he and the Admiral actually crossed each other's paths. During the course of the second World War, their ways and circumstances were destined to converge, given their mutual determination to put an end to Adolf Hitler.

That resolve, however, was to take Stauffenberg some time to reach, because for the first few years of the war, the Fuhrer kept swinging in and out of his favour. Stauff's failure to make up his mind about him and to settle his allegiance one way or the other had a lot to do with the see-sawing sentiments of the Stauffenberg family as a whole.

The family was very much divided in its opinion of Hitler. Their on-going and very valid arguments over his leadership of their nation made an unanimous agreement between them quite impossible. Half of them were unconvinced as to the worth of the wild-eyed little Austrian Corporal who, by means of brutality and *God knows* what else, had shot up through the ranks to crown himself Head of State.

Despite Hitler's astonishing array of achievements, both on the military and economic front, many family members refused to sing his praises. Claus' Uncle Berthold went to extremes to express his disapproval.

When ordered to replace his Stauffenberg family Arms with the Swastika, he'd promptly walked out into the vast grounds of his country estate and stuck the small red flag, with its twisted black cross, in the middle of his "pig run". The gesture, along with the muddy squelching sound it made, summed up his sentiments about Hitler and his Third Reich.

These sentiments, at that particular time, had echoed those of his nephew. In the beginning, the young Count Claus von Stauffenberg had felt nothing but scorn for the coarse upstart that all German aristocrats thought Hitler to be.

That was why Claus let out a snort of contempt when he was asked to model for a statue of "the Pioneer Soldier", a project meant as a mark of respect for the SA "Brownshirt" Troops that the Fuhrer had commissioned of Claus' close friend—the sculptor Frank Mehnert.

"Stand still, Claus, and keep your head up. Remember, you're meant to be expressing the idea of Hitler's National Resurgence," Mehnert said, well within his rights, he believed, to be fed up with Claus' constant fidgeting and the delight he was deriving from making fun of the whole artistic process.

The latter of which Stauff felt was obligatory, given his disdain for Hitler and the Nazi Party. As for the fidgeting . . . well that was just from pure exhaustion and the tedium of it all. This was the umpteenth time he'd had to strike a stiff pose and stand stock-still for hours on end, his feet fixed to that one spot on the wooden floor of the old Brewery in Bamberg. His friend Frank was taking an age to chisel away at his likeness, to fashion a thing of beauty out of the huge, shapeless lump of marble that the Nazi Party had provided to facilitate the job.

"I haven't quite accepted the fact that I'm to be immortalized in stone," Stauff shot back sarcastically at his friend. "Just make sure that the statue is short on all the Nazi bells and whistles, will you."

"Need you have said that?" Frank replied, stopping with a sudden yelp to suck on the tip of his thumb. The quick slip of his chisel in the wrong direction had just split it open and drawn blood. "Now look what you've made me do. Quick, have you got a handkerchief?"

Stauff brushed aside the plea for help with a dismissive sweep of his hand.

"Ahh, don't worry about it. Just wipe it all over the statue and make it into a faithful representation of Hitler and his Reich. There's a lot to be said for truth in art."

With Stauff in such a contrary, playful mood, it was hard for Mehnert to take his work seriously. It was an outright *miracle* that he managed to finish it in time to meet with Hitler's deadline, if not his wholehearted approval.

"It is *most* un-Nazi-like in its portrayal," had been the Fuhrer's comment.

The disgruntled critique had given Stauff and Mehnert every good reason to celebrate.

"Here's to your appalling lack of artistic interpretation," Stauff said to his friend over a sausage and sauerkraut dinner. Both men raised and clinked their beer steins together to toast their achievement.

Pleased as he was for not having met Hitler's questionable criteria, Stauff was still slightly disconcerted to see himself etched in stone. His serious, handsome image stood seven feet tall and stared down at the medieval Magdeburg township from its vantage point at the eastern end of the Magdeburg Water Bridge. There was an eeriness to its solitary, unearthly grandeur which he found most unsettling; a foreboding that the monolithic marble depiction of himself was a chilling omen of his future.

This it became when, in the dead of night, a band of Nazi vigilantes decided to topple it from its pedestal. Angered as they were by the sacrilege of the statue not living up to the Nazi ideal, they rolled it down the hill into the Elbe river.

When the town officials finally retrieved the colossal, kelp-encrusted work from its watery bed, it was still intact, but minus its right hand and part of its left hand, and sporting a large, unsightly cleft where its left eye had once been.

All damage done in the case of the statue had been easily fixed with a piece of plaster and a splash of glue, but the same clever patch-up job wasn't going to be possible when the genuine article— its model Claus von Stauffenberg—got wounded in *precisely* the same way on the battlefields of Europe later in the war.

It was a prophecy that, much like Moses' Ten Commandments, had been chiseled in stone. The truth of it pointed to Stauffenberg's future obligation and sacrifice to the Fatherland, in much the same way as did the news of the Blomberg and Fritsch affair when it reached Stauff in 1939.

The humiliating accounts of the appalling treatment that had been inflicted on the two Commanders-in-Chief of the German Army, and Baron von Fritsch's subsequent suicide during the

Polish campaign, had Stauffenberg take exception and leap to his feet in the middle of a military conference to say as much. Going that one step further in his verbal outrage, he condemned all the other generals of the Wehrmacht who had failed to act and defend the honour of fellow aristocrats and officers.

"Perhaps *you'd* like to rap the Fuhrer over the knuckles yourself Lieutenant Stauffenberg?" his Commanding officer said, rebuking his subordinate for making the *ad-lib*, impassioned speech that had interrupted his own.

The Commander's sarcastic tone prompted an outburst of laughter from the other officers at the meeting, which had Stauff turn on them in a savage, scarlet-faced rage.

"I'd do more than just *that* if given the chance," he fired back at them.

The hot conviction in his voice quickly silenced his detractors and made them look at Stauff through fresh, slightly suspicious eyes. The more senior, cynical officers among them were most concerned that young Stauffenberg had meant every word he'd said. If he had, he would have to watch each and every one of them from here on in.

Meanwhile, *one* of those shrewd officers present in the conference room—Lieutenant Fabian von Schlabrendorff—was thinking that he might just mention this young Count von Stauffenberg's name to his associate, Admiral Canaris, next time he stopped in to visit him at his *Abwehr* headquarters.

CHAPTER TWENTY-THREE

The prospect of raking Stauffenberg in as a new recruit to the Resistance, however, was a tad premature. At this early point in the war, he was at best only an each-way bet. His attitude towards Hitler blew hot and cold, and did a complete about face when he came home flush with success after having fought in the Polish campaign.

Afterwards, he laughed at his own expense about the bad call he'd made in regard to the Czechoslovakian campaign that had preceded it.

"There's no way it'll come to war," he'd said to reassure his fellow officers at the time. "Hitler's own experience of combat will stop him going there again."

Stauffenberg had made his optimistic and supremely naive statement on the premise that Hitler was like any other man who had fought in the Great War. Hitler must have learned some tolerance and baulked at the reality of revisiting the bitter experience and repeated bouts of shell shock that four years in the trenches had taught him.

Stauff's friend, Lieutenant Kurt Weiss had not been convinced. His gut feeling was that Hitler had been champing at the bit to get the show on the road.

"Well, I can tell you now, that if he *does* decide to attack Czechoslovakia, there'll be a conspiracy to overthrow him here in Germany," he'd fired back at Stauffenberg. "There's nothing surer. *None* of us want another World War. He simply can't afford to overplay his hand."

Not only did Hitler overplay it, but decided to deal an equally good hand to England, France and Italy in urging them to sign his Munich Pact. Each of them agreed to divide up poor little Czechoslovakia and send its President Benes into an humiliating exile.

Which meant that, by default, Stauff had been right about it not coming to war at that point. Physical aggression had *not* proved to be necessary in the annihilation of Czechoslovakia, when the Munich Pact had achieved as much with the stroke of a pen.

That was why the 1st Light Division, to which Stauffenberg had been assigned as Quartermaster General Staff officer, saw little to no action. Stationed merely at the Czech border as a passive occupying force to protect it, they did nothing more than twiddle their thumbs and bemoan the fact that, from a soldier's point of view, the whole campaign had turned out to be a bit of a "fizzer". Their pistols and bayonets had stayed safe in their holsters, with their bullets and blades in pristine condition.

The only thing achieved, they believed (apart from the annexation of Czechoslovakia), was their acquisition of two hundred and fifty spanking new Czech tanks. In having confiscated them straight off the assembly line from their Prague factories, they had managed to swell the size of their own newly named 6th Panzer Division,[24] giving it the greatest firing power of all other German Panzer units.

It marked a huge transition in the art of German warfare. All cavalry units, such as Stauffenberg's, were gradually converted into mechanized armoured formations. Stauff himself was trained, and then put in charge of training, mortar troops, a program of modernization that had him and his 6th Panzer Division fully primed to go into action when they were put on alert to move out to Neuhammer in Silesia. This time, Stauff took the precaution against boredom of packing a suitcase full of books, just in case Poland turned out to be the non-event "walk-over" that Czechoslovakia had been.

In stark contrast, however, he was run off his feet and unable to read a word. From day one of the campaign, he was thrust head first into action, his uphill battle to co-ordinate and supply their much-too-rapidly advancing forces. The amazingly successful German offensive into Poland literally had their troops trip over themselves and out-pace their military equipment and reinforcements.

He was also thrust into controversy, watching in horrified disbelief as one of his fellow officers committed cold-blooded murder, shooting dead two Polish women in the streets of Warsaw, without a second thought or the slightest provocation.

It all happened in an instant—much too fast for Stauffenberg to do anything about it. He had been standing only a few yards from the scene of the crime, but not close enough to intervene and wrest the pistol from the man's hand before the two shots were fired. The sight and sound of it, for one surreal moment, left Stauff standing in a state of shock, before the ear-piercing scream from another terrified bystander, snapped him back into action.

Moving quickly, he snatched the revolver from the officer's hand and, in an impulsive act unheard of within German officer ranks, slapped his fellow officer hard across the face. His open-handed reproof was far more humiliating than his fist.

"Enemy or ally, Lieutenant Bauer, there will be *no* random slaughter in this Division. For a German officer—civilians, women and children are *strictly* off limits."

"I thought you were my friend, Stauffenberg," Bauer threw back at him in surprised contempt.

"So did I, but I've changed my mind. I have no place in my heart for cowards and killers."

"You smug shit . . . you'll pay for this!" Bauer retaliated with his hand nursing his left cheek. Its painful, hot throb didn't sting half as much as his pride, now that Stauffenberg had undermined his authority and dignity in front of his men.

"No, I won't. *You* will," Stauff replied, unperturbed, as he scanned the troops standing nearby to find the soldier he was after.

"Sergeant Krause," he ordered, having spied him and beckoned to the officer to join them. "See to it that Lieutenant Bauer is placed under arrest to await court martial. I will be recommending that he be demoted."

It was a big ask under wartime conditions. But then Stauffenberg—always a stickler for the rules of chivalry and the Geneva Convention—wasn't one to give up easily. Used as he was to getting what he wanted, he wasn't about to rest until Lieutenant Bauer got what he deserved. He would pay the ultimate price for a man in the military, by being stripped of his rank and honour for having murdered two innocent human beings.

Such hard-hearted devotion to duty and justice couldn't

help but gain Stauffenberg a reputation. One that along with his exemplary performance on the battlefields of Poland caught the eye of his superiors, the respect of his peers, and the undying admiration and trust of his subordinates, all of whom came to rely on his ingenuity and dauntless courage, because it never failed to go above and beyond the call of his quartermaster's duty.

This fact was made plain in the written report Stauffenberg submitted at his September, 1939, debriefing.

> *"Transport and supply have been our main problem. Our entire Division could only use one road, sharing it with other divisions and corps troops. Reports on supplies were outdated by the time they reached respective quartermasters because of rapidity of combat. At no time did our Division receive required ammunition rations or fuel. We had to cannibalize components from other vehicles and steal vehicles from other formations. Divisional quartermasters had to draw pistols on each other at army supply depots to secure fuel. The reality is that had we not stolen fuel from the enemy, we would have ground to a halt."*

Stauffenberg, however, had seen to it that *his* 6th Panzer did nothing of the sort—that he kept it mobile at all times, and at any expense. One got the distinct impression that it was *he*, and no other quartermaster on the Polish front, who had taken the bold initiative to draw his pistol on a fellow officer to get what he wanted. The irony was that his bluff had paid off, when he did not, in fact, have it in him to pull the trigger. Had those other quartermasters known what sort of man he was, they may not have been quite so eager to back off and hand Stauff their share of the booty. Stauff's Divisional Commander wrote in his report to headquarters:

> *"We have here, in Count Claus von Stauffenberg, a quartermaster who we hope will never leave us. He is a great organizational talent, untiringly industrious and enterprising,"*

After this, he continued to dictate to his secretary a further two pages that waxed lyrical about the exploits and excellence of this young officer under his command, to whom he was eternally grateful.

He had every reason to be, given that ever since their Division had crossed the Polish border, there had been nothing but confusion, and the dire threat of the whole unwieldy, German military operation getting out of hand.

In the helter-skelter of their untried troops' advance on Warsaw, Stauffenberg had managed to distinguish himself, many times over, by taking the whip hand. His leadership abilities, organizational skills and clear thinking successfully secured a tight line of supply. He not only managed to provision his men, who were among the forces encircling Warsaw, but stretched that line to facilitate the needs and victory of the rest of the 6th Panzer, who were strung out along twenty-five kilometres and fighting on three different fronts against the defenders of the Polish capital.

At the same time, he took on the difficult task of equipping the men engaged in the ongoing guerrilla warfare against the outflanked, but very determined Polish forces, who were trying to breakthrough and join the Warsaw front.

"Sometimes the Poles, fighting with the courage of despair and with superior numbers, have got us into some pretty nasty spots," Stauff had written to Nina in one of those rare moments of peace and quiet he'd managed to grab in between battles.

Its duration had not been long enough for him to scribble his love and kisses, before he had to dodge another bullet and fall flat on his face in the mud. He threw his arms up over his head to protect it from the bomb that had just been dropped, and to spare his ears the wretched ringing sensation of its repercussion.

Standard procedure—this constant close shave with death, for which he had no one else but himself to blame. His insistence on taking part in the front-line forays had nothing to do with his administrative position that only required his presence behind a desk, a long way behind the lines. Yet there was something in Stauffenberg that *needed* to be at the hub of the action—the only place where he could pick up for himself great military acclaim, along with the odd piece of shrapnel.

Most of this, whisking by him, only managed to lift a layer or two of his skin, or to lodge a few non-life-threatening centimetres under it. The bulk of his body and handsome face stayed intact and unscarred for the duration—preserved for his feats of heroism to come.

Many of these were on show during Germany's subsequent invasion of France, where once again he performed to capacity and beyond. Now that their forces were more practised in their war-mongering, they were killing and carving up the spoils like a well-oiled machine. So well, in fact, that there were times when Stauffenberg thought it was just all too easy.

"Our Division has spearheaded many of the attacks here in France, and have already taken twenty thousand prisoners," his note to Nina read.

Because his wife had proved to be an admirable correspondent and the perfect sounding board, he had got into the habit of keeping her informed of his and Hitler's progress in the war. Nina had a way of lending a sympathetic ear, without undermining his courage and initiatives. Giving him an inch, but *never* a mile, whenever his confidence and convictions wavered.

"But, I don't know . . . there just doesn't seem to be much glory to be had in the conquest of a country whose people seem prematurely resigned to defeat. The truth is, I feel no joy in seeing the fall of France. The incipient collapse of such a great Nation—both militarily and psychologically is sad in the extreme.

The French have no inclination to fight and are surrendering in their thousands. I think the Great War must have knocked the stuffing out of them. It's the general consensus that the Poles were better sparring partners—that they fought much harder for their homeland.

The British haven't even turned up as yet. Surely they must begin to give some consideration to defending their bridgehead on the Channel?

In the meantime, I'm getting little sleep, but living well. The wine here is delicious."

On the subject of wine, Stauffenberg was somewhat of a connoisseur. His expertise was largely due to his refined and very social upbringing. Thanks to his aristocratic background, democratic leanings and gregarious nature, he was able to share a glass or two of it with men from every echelon of society. Equally welcome in the rough and ready beer-swilling ranks of his subordinates as he was in those of the military and civilian elite, one of whom had visited and been beguiled by him quite recently.

"Had coffee with von Ribbentrop the other day. He made a tolerable impression, but he's certainly no great lion!"

Stauff had scribbled his comment to Nina on the flip-side of a postcard with a picture of the Eiffel Tower. She'd read it quickly and then promptly thrown it in the bin—annoyed by the smart-arse abruptness of his communiqué that smacked of him showing off. That lesser side of him, she and the war were slowly working at drumming out of his otherwise wholly decent nature.

Unattractive as that youthful arrogance was, it had appealed to Joachim von Ribbentrop. The Ambassador to London, rumoured soon to replace von Neurath as German Foreign Minister, was apparently unaware that he'd failed to impress Stauffenberg. Yet he was so impressed by *him*, that he made a point of putting in a good word for Stauff, both in his personal diary and the Fuhrer's ear.

> *"Young Stauffenberg has an ease of manner and poise which facilitates him turning from one dignitary to the next without missing a beat. He makes no attempt to distinguish between field marshal and private; extending the same liberties and courtesy to both.*
>
> *While in his office, I watched him receive a series of divisional and liaison officers with an unstinting and radiant courtesy; seeing to it personally that they all were offered wine and cigars. In the process of which he continued to make a line of entirely unsystematic enquiries, punctuating them with amusing anecdotes. Suddenly, and just as effortlessly, starting to dictate his orders, with a glass of wine in one hand—the other in his pocket. This young man has brains and panache . . . and most definitely bears watching."*

Perhaps it was a case of them watching him too closely, most certainly one of gross military mismanagement, that had the powers-that-be use Stauffenberg's charisma and heroism on the field as their reason for transferring him off it. Rewarding him for his outstanding performance during the Polish and French campaigns by promoting him to the 2nd Branch of Army General Staff.

It was a back-handed bonus that had Stauff lose all faith in the system . . . and just when he'd come down, *at long last*, on Hitler's side and was thinking it now conceivable that the Fuhrer was steering them in the direction of winning the war.

"If this is my reward, then spare me any punishment!" he said to Nina at this surprise turn of events.

This was said over the phone from the privacy of his cushy new office, with its padded leather chair and safe proximity far, far away from the front. Rather than being flattered, he was thoroughly put out by his new assignment that had him sitting behind a desk, instead of an MP40 machine gun.

"I can't *believe* that I've been forced to take over this Group 11 in their peacetime organizational capacity. How do you think I feel having had to leave my Division in the middle of the war—not to *mention* what must be the most glorious of our military operations. And for what reason? So that I can disappear into a bureaucracy? For heaven's sake . . . *I'm* no pen-pusher. I'm *miserable* here. Why on Earth have they got me wiling away my days in this claustrophobic command structure, when I could be doing so much more . . . something that's actually *constructive*?" he carried on, not allowing his wife to get a word in edgeways. "I *ask* you . . . why would they take a man *out* of action, when he's just been awarded the Iron Cross for his performance *in it*? It just doesn't make any sense."

"Bide your time Claus and make good use of it. The Reich has thought to honour you with this promotion. Make sure you don't throw away the opportunity it provides," was her level-headed advice over the static telephone connection.

Because he'd come to appreciate her friendship and wise counsel, Claus decided to take that advice on board and to throw himself into his new job, rather than resent it. He realized that during his sojourn amid boredom and military bureaucrats he could probably do more for his friends at the front than he could if he were standing shoulder-to-shoulder with them amid the gunfire.

His hands-on experience in the field gave him the wherewithal to fight his way through all the official red-tape and instigate the essential military changes to those outmoded rules and regulations that had so often stymied their efforts at the front. Here now was his opportunity to suggest amendments to the laws of military demand and supply, which he would never have had the power to do when fighting in the field.

They were good, practical suggestions, coming from a soldier who *knew* about soldiers and their most pressing needs on and off the battlefield. Commonsense improvements which would have been put straight through the system, had each and every one of them, in turn, not been arbitrarily vetoed by Hitler himself.

Thus Stauffenberg got his first taste of what it was like to have to adhere to the whims and very questionable wisdom of an "Absolute Fuhrer". So, for the fiftieth time, he changed his mind about Hitler, feeling, as he did, very uneasy at the prospect of serving under such a man's seemingly schizophrenic leadership.

As a military professional himself, it had never occurred to Stauffenberg to think of Hitler as one, and the very real possibility that the Fuhrer was floundering around, without having a clue about what he was doing or the havoc he was causing, concerned Stauffenberg greatly.

Then, however, had come the capitulation of France. Yet another spectacular victory for Adolf Hitler, which meant that Stauffenberg was no longer able to deny that—foibles aside—the Fuhrer had a real flair for military matters.

On June 25, 1940—unable to contain his renewed enthusiasm for Hitler—he spilled out his sentiments once more to his wife:

> *"I have changed my earlier view of Hitler. I now believe that he is a man of vision and dedication; with a particular, almost God-like facility to see the whole military picture. No . . . more than that . . . to actually anticipate it! As if, like Zeus from Mount Olympus, he is moving us like pawns on a chessboard of his own design. How can such a man fail to stir one's courage and creativity? His vigour and insight are second to none, and more stimulating to me than anything else I've ever known. You must forgive the blasphemy of my belief: that with him and through him, all things are possible."*

It was a blasphemy written in blue ink that made Nina cringe. As she read her husband's words, she realized that he, like so many others, had fallen under the Fuhrer's hypnotic spell, something which she hoped was only a temporary state of madness in her husband's case. As far as she was concerned, there was *nothing* in the least God-like about Adolf Hitler. Which wasn't to say that she questioned his great power . . . just its source.

CHAPTER TWENTY-FOUR

Canaris had long since realized from whence it came, having only to wait just a few months longer for the fiasco in Russia to set Stauffenberg straight, and bring *him* round to the conspirators' way of thinking. At which point none of them had to lift a finger to sell Stauff on the idea of treason when the Fuhrer was doing such a dashed good job of promoting their seditious cause all on his own.

The tales of Hitler's atrocities had begun to flow thick and fast. Their gruesome details left Stauffenberg stunned and thoroughly ashamed of himself, not only for having impotently stood back while the man committed his litany of crimes, but for having committed a crime far worse, himself—indulging in the staggering sacrilege of having aligned Adolf Hitler with the Almighty!

Now it was just for the young Catholic Count to wonder why he'd blinded himself to the truth? *Why*, back in June, 1941, had he gone out of his way to side-step it, when the evil had been so evident in the Fuhrer's order for the mass murder of Polish intellectuals, Jews and the mentally ill? It was an outrage which had merely opened the way for Hitler's plethora of more heinous commands to come.

Since then, Hitler's bloodlust had been unquenchable. It was as if, unsatisfied with the wholesale slaughter of the innocents who had been unable or unprepared to defend themselves, he'd decided to add to his killing spree by executing, out of hand, any captured Commissar of the Red Army.[25]

Hitler had ignored outright their "white-flag-waving" bid for clemency by giving the order to shoot them on the spot, without trial or mercy. Over and above the fact that it was an act of cold-blooded murder, it was also a contemptible contravention of the rules of war—that military Code of Honour on which soldiers and gentlemen, on *either* side, depended.

Stauffenberg's only excuse for having neglected his moral duty in not defying Hitler sooner was that he'd been up to his eyeballs in enough blood and guts of his own. Through its murky red haze, he'd been unable—if not, a little unwilling—to see beyond the gore and glory of the battlefields on which he had been fighting at the time.

Bit by bit, however, he was becoming increasingly conversant with the facts—outraged by the reports that were reaching him, one of which had come first-hand from his cousin, Casar von Hofacker, in France.

"It is Hitler's command that for every attack on a German soldier, one hundred French hostages be executed. The regular deporting of Jews is a 'given', of course; as is far, far worse that is inflicted upon them. Atrocities that I find beyond my comprehension and sense of Christianity. So please forgive me if I beg off putting them in writing.

I cannot, however, refrain from making note of our German plundering of this country, which will soon see France's entire agricultural system, along with its lovely Louvre Museum, stripped bare. I can't understand why, in conquest, we should seek to destroy and remove everything that we sought to gain? It is truly an embarrassment to see our fine German troops reduced to a hoard of murdering, marauding Huns. Right at the moment, I'm ashamed to count myself as one of them."

Stauffenberg never thought the day would come when he would share such unpatriotic sentiments—but it *had* . . . and he put down his cousin's letter with a despondent sigh.

What could be done? This *was* war, after all—one of those many mindless periods of global chaos that gave mankind *carte blanche* to rip down and ruin all that was fine. But for a person of integrity and more advanced sensibilities there was no joy to be found in the destruction of the Arts or *anything*, for that matter, of beauty—be it man, mineral or vegetable.

To see the splendour and artistic heritage of France suffer in such a way was soul-destroying, as it must have been, Stauff could now imagine, for Julius Caesar back in B.C., when he'd heard the news that the Library of Alexandria had gone up in flames. How unthinkable it must have been for such a man to take the blame for that moronic act of vandalism, when such wanton destruction of knowledge would have been quite beyond someone of his intellect and wide reading?

Hitler and his Nazi Neanderthals, however, were not quite so sensitive over the issue. Their guilt wasn't only irrefutable, but embraced. None of them sought to deny it, but were proud of their ill-gotten gains and the bone-chilling methods by which they were achieving them. They stated as much by slapping a bright red, white and black "*Goods Confiscated*" Swastika on their crimes against humanity and the devastation they were leaving in their blood-soaked wake.

While Stauff viewed the situation in France as being a shame, he was downright disgusted by what was going on in Russia. In the Ukraine, alone, Hitler's SS squads were running riot.

At least that was what his friend, Second Lieutenant Walter Bussman from the Quartermaster-Generals' War Administration Branch, was in the process of telling him over lunch.

"There are SS mobile killing units conducting mass shootings behind the front. Victims run into the millions!"

Stauffenberg had to swallow down hard on this latest piece of gossip being thrown at him in between entrée and main course. Its slanderous infamy stuck in his throat, along with the mouthful of steak he'd been chewing.

"But how can you be so sure of your facts, Walt?" he said, coughing to clear his windpipe. "Don't you think I'd *know* if such things were true? As a General Staff officer, I'm in constant contact with the eastern front. If things were going awry over there, I'd be one of the first to be filled in."

Stauff's response had been slightly defensive as he put down his knife and fork and took a swig of beer to fortify himself against the even worse news he guessed was to come.

"Then, my dear boy, you must open your eyes *and* your ears," Bussman replied. "Because from what I've heard, it's no secret. It's rather difficult to keep the stench of thousands of rotting corpses under wraps, you know. Apparently the whole of the Ukraine is literally littered with the bloodied unburied. The SS are murdering so many of them, so fast, that they've given up even trying to put them in graves. Well, of course, there's no time for such delicacies with Hitler being such a stickler for keeping to schedule."

"I just can't believe it!" Stauffenberg refuted once more—*this* time, with a marked belligerence.

And why not, when Bussman was talking of the stuff of nightmares? Claus wasn't quite ready to relegate himself and the rest of the Wehrmacht to hell for playing a part in them.

"But you *must*, Stauff," Bussman leant a little forward in his seat to say in confidence, while he fixed his friend with a steady gaze that underlined the truth of his words and conviction. "Because it is merely the tip of the iceberg."

By the time they had finished dessert and paid their bill, Stauffenberg had run up against a big enough chunk of that iceberg to re-sink the Titanic. He was so weighed down with disbelief and guilt that he'd had to rush home to say as much to his wife, hoping that *she*, in her sensible, mild-mannered way, may be able to release the pressure valve on his conscience that was fit to explode.

"Bussman told me that there is a concentration camp called Auschwitz where they are burning Jews in ovens . . . *Children*, Nina, in *ovens!*" he reported back feverishly to her.

He declined the cup of tea she was trying to hand him, because he was too het up to even think of drinking it, or to hold the saucer steady in his hand. Instead, he waved it away and continued.

"Those who don't burn are being gassed, tortured and shot in their thousands. Some of the lucky few Jews are being kept alive to be used as human guinea pigs—subjected to the most obscene medical experiments, without any form of anaesthetic! Can you even *conceive* of that sort of suffering, Nina? Can you *imagine* how we would feel if it were happening to *our* children?

"The SS are actually boasting about the premium productivity of these state of the art death camps of theirs—building some of them now to house 50,000 people at a time, so that they can streamline their 'kill' to 4000 each month. That's German efficiency for you! And the whole murdering-machine is being facilitated by government subsidy and rubber-stamped by Hitler and that sadistic mongrel—Heinrich Himmler. I know that in war, killing is inevitable, but I draw the line at genocide.

"It's incomprehensible to me that all this has been going on under my nose. That I actually have been busting a gut . . . putting my life on the line to champion such an unholy cause. What on Earth am I to do?"

Nina had hoped that her cup of tea would do the trick and calm him down. Now she realized that a little more than a shot of caffeine and two lumps of sugar was going to be needed to settle his nerves, all of which were red-raw and throbbing at full throttle. Her "straight-down-the-line, never-anything-but-noble" husband was distressed to the nth degree, as was she when she saw him break down and put his head in his hands.

She got up from her chair and, kneeling down in front of him, took those hands of his in hers.

"At this point Claus, you have no choice but to continue fighting for your country. We can't undo the fact that Hitler's already implicated us all in his crimes. But that doesn't mean that the Germany we love deserves to be destroyed by them. *Someone* has to fight to set things right, one way or the other. Besides, I'd hazard a guess, that these crimes—ghastly as they sound—have probably been exaggerated. Most likely, just Allied propaganda to weaken our resolve. What else could it be?

"I mean, *really* . . . can you honestly believe that such widespread, medieval atrocities are going on in our times? Can you even vaguely *imagine* Hitler coming up with such an unwieldy idea as obliterating an entire *race* from the face of the Earth! No Claus, put your mind at ease . . . it's preposterous. Better my love, that you get a grip on reality and get back to business."

Stauffenberg's business at that time was to continue playing his part in "*Operation Barbarossa*". For a man of his fighting spirit and ability, it was frustrating that he had to do so only in his capacity as General Staff officer, which meant that he was stationed at East Prussian Headquarters,[26] rather than in the thick of it on the Russian front, where he would have preferred to be. A field command was, he believed, a much better way for the German Army to make use of him and his military skills.

But orders were orders, whether he liked them or not, and if he couldn't help the Fatherland by fighting on the snowfields of Smolensk, then he was determined to do all he could to uphold his country's honour by fighting, in a different kind of way, behind the lines. So before he turned his attention back to the facilitating and supplying of their Moscow-bound troops, he made sure that he'd put the wheels of justice in motion where Hitler and his henchmen were concerned, by doing two strategic things:

1. Asking his friend, Walter Bussman to keep him apprised of any further atrocities being perpetrated by the Third Reich. To not only sit back *waiting* to hear about them, but to make an active effort to seek out and collect every skerrick of information that implicated the SS for his future reference.
2. Going straight to the top to collaborate with Bussman's boss—Adolf Heusinger—the one man who, as head of General Staff Operations Branch, was in a position to validate Stauffenberg's request-cum-demand for an immediate revocation of Hitler's order *"that all Red Army Commissars be shot on capture"*.

These two gigantic steps in the right direction—more easily construed as good deeds, allowed Stauffenberg to turn his attention back to his Staff officer duties with a clearer conscience. He was unaware that his strong, selfless efforts had inadvertently aided and abetted the German Resistance, or that all its members—long on the lookout for a man of Stauffenberg's calibre—had now turned their eyes in his direction with great interest. Because the Count was shaping up to be that man of courage and action they were after to front their cause. A soldier and possible saviour, who was proving to be as good as his word.

CHAPTER TWENTY-FIVE

The problem was that Stauffenberg's words were beginning to trip a little too lightly from his lips. Most of them were unguarded and extremely inflammatory. Confident as he was of his popularity and excellent reputation within military circles, he had no qualms about expressing his views freely.

This was, to a degree, commendable considering that most of his peers didn't have the courage to do the same, but when those expressions of his began to target Hitler's military incompetence, it raised a few eyebrows.

Beginning with those of Stauffenberg's students at the War Academy in Hirschberg, Silesia, who had come to be taught the finer points of German Command Structure. Each and every one of the trainees considered it a great privilege to be schooled, first-hand, by the man who had apparently got them down pat.

"Now let's see . . . where shall we start?" Stauffenberg said as he turned, with chalk in hand, to address the room full of eager young cadets.

None of them, in awe of his handsome, medal-bedecked presence, had reason to believe that the dashing Count von Stauffenberg wasn't taking his tutoring job seriously, which made it all the more astonishing when he launched into his lecture in such a slapdash, sarcastic way.

"Had the most qualified General Staff officers been asked to invent the most absurd command structure possible, they could never have come up with one as absurd as our German Command Structure as it stands today. You must all forgive me, but I've been asked to explain to you something that I don't even understand myself!"

He turned to illustrate his point on the blackboard; drawing on its smooth black surface a rough outline of that command structure in question—first, listing the preponderance of Command headquarters to which soldiers were meant to report in the heat of battle. While gabbling his incomprehensible explanation of them, he let his quick, adept hand, cover the blackboard with a labyrinth-like confusion of yellow-chalked arrows, each of them criss-crossing each other and pointing the way to military chaos.

Calmly stepping back, Stauffenberg surveyed his work before turning to the class once more to ask the question:

"Does even one of you here truly believe that *anyone* could possibly win a war with such an idiotic command structure?"

His students had left the classroom more bewildered than when they had come into it. This, Stauffenberg could safely say, was the state of mind of every German General under Hitler's erratic command.

One of these was General Friedrich Olbricht, who, as head of Reserve Army Supply and Chief of the General Army Office, was destined to become the principal administrator of the July 20, 1944 *coup d'etat*, and to share Stauffenberg's fate. Right at that moment, however, he was only concerned about Germany's fate.

"Our army is a mere puff of wind on the vast Russian steppes," he said to Stauffenberg, in the hope that the Count/General Staff officer would include his words of wisdom in the report he was compiling on eastern operations to take back to Berlin.

Stauffenberg had spent the last few weeks touring the Russian front with an entirely different agenda to the one for which he'd been sent. In between doing his job, he'd been taking advantage of his dangerous tour of duty to sound out the various Generals in command and take note of their litany of grievances as to the frightful mismanagement of the whole campaign.

"We've botched it up, you know," Stauff replied casually, as he scribbled down Olbricht's quote—more for its poetic value than the impact he doubted it would have on the Big Boys back in Berlin.

At this point he lifted his pen from the paper and tapped it thoughtfully on his lower lip, wondering if he could speak freely to this man from whom he'd got the distinct impression of an anti-Nazi nature.

"I can't help but think that we should have just stuck to our original game plan and been content with the quick conquest of the European part of the Soviet Union and the Ukraine that we achieved. But, as is always the way, we got greedy. And for that, I've no doubt, we'll pay. If *Barbarossa* fails, I'm convinced it'll result in the ultimate defeat of Germany."

"Yes, you're right . . ." Olbricht agreed, pleased that Stauffenberg had paid him the compliment of coming down in his favour.

The young General Staff officer had taken a dangerous gamble in confiding in a stranger—Stauff was engaging in a game of hit and miss in the hope that Olbricht might share his sentiments in regard to Hitler. It was an each-way bet on Stauff's part that had paid off and put Olbricht forever on side.

"All it's done," Olbricht continued, now feeling considerably more at ease, "is open up a hornet's nest, making the eastern front into the biggest theatre of war in human history. Already it's seen the most brutal battles and deadliest of atrocities. And that's to say nothing of the unforgivable loss of life on both sides. One doesn't even want to *guess* at the carnage that lies ahead. Our German forces are exhausted.

"As you well know—their supply lines are overstretched and they are completely ill-equipped for winter warfare. Only to be expected that they've ground to a halt in their drive towards Moscow. Trouble is—poor souls—that while they're marking time, they're dropping like flies . . . *frozen* ones in the sub-zero temperatures. I can only be grateful that none of those boys out there are sons of mine."

This brought Stauffenberg's own three sons to mind. He was glad, right now, that they were all still under the age of five and that the hideous prospect of them suffering such a fate wasn't a concern. But having had such a grim possibility take shape in his head, his only comfort was the fact that the war would be long over by the time his little boys reached conscription age.

Well, of course it would be! he silently reassured himself. His eldest—young Berthold, was still thirteen years away from that day, and if Stauff didn't miss his guess . . . this World War II would be over in only a matter of months if Hitler continued to blunder his way through it.

"Hitler's making a huge mistake in redirecting his drive south," Stauff said, letting Olbricht in on his thoughts. "And what on Earth's he thinking in dividing his forces in two for this new "*Operation Blue*" of his?"

"He figures it'll get him what he wants all the sooner, I suppose."

"*Yes* . . . and weaken our whole offensive in the process!"

Olbricht shrugged off his indifference. He had long since resigned himself to the fact that they were going to lose the war, if not on the battlefields, then most certainly in the pages of history, where there was no doubt that their efforts would be written off as a period of heinous insanity of epic proportions. Each and every one of them, either through active participation or by default, was destined to be forever condemned for crimes against humanity.

"You know that our beloved Fuhrer has no capacity to reason things out and bide his time," Olbricht offered up as a contemptuous explanation. "He wants everything . . . and he wants it *now!* Moscow's proved more difficult than he thought, and he's just not prepared to sit around and wait for its downfall.

"He's bored, that's all—impatient to turn his attention elsewhere. Right now, it's firmly fixed on the Soviet oilfields in the Caucasus and he appears to be absolutely *obsessed* suddenly with Stalingrad. Says it's to secure a position on the Volga to guard our Army's left flank."

Stauffenberg promptly swept this much too plausible strategy aside.

"Don't delude yourself. That's all too logical a way of thinking for a man of Hitler's machine-gun tactics. The only reason—and I mean, the *only* reason—he wants Stalingrad is to rub Joseph Stalin's nose in it. Nothing would give Hitler a bigger ego boost than to destroy the Dictator's namesake. And believe me . . . Hitler's just insane enough to sacrifice his entire army to get that kind of sick satisfaction. I just have this itchy feeling that General Paulus and his 6ᵗʰ Army are going to see the worst of it—that their "*Operation Blue*" is just Hitler's code for "*Operation Certain Suicide.*""

"Well, one thing's for sure . . . it's already lost him his Blitzkreig advantage. Our speed and surprise squadrons are now moving like snails."

"Exactly!" Stauffenberg agreed, choosing this pertinent point in their conversation to take a folded letter out of his shirt pocket, saying, as he did so, "Hitler's lost us our 'edge', and given us impassable, thigh-high snow in its place. Just listen to this letter I got from Brigadier Baron von Loeper yesterday."

Leaning forward, Stauff held the army-issue piece of paper under the small table lamp so that he could read it more easily.

". . . It is ironic that 'speed', being our strength, has now become our problem. Our much too quick succession of breakthrough battles has put an enormous strain on the mechanized formation. Our Division has reached exhaustion. There's just no rest. We're lacking ammunition and the men are close to losing heart—without strength, without reserves, without tanks. We have now resorted to fighting in small battalions rather than combat commands; racing from one hectic engagement to the next.

Leadership is inconsistent. Our famed Luftwaffe—supposedly the strongest air power in the world—can't even send up a few dive bombers to help us. And our orders for the 'deep thrust eastward' are farcical when we're having a devil of a job just trying to defend ourselves against an ever growing stronger enemy . . ."

Stauff then had to squint to read the scrawled, hastily written postscript:

P.S.   Dear Stauff. Hitler is well on the way to hounding all our armoured corps to death. Just as Napoleon's General Murat hounded his splendid cavalry in 1812, while the Russians operated with shorter supply lines, which enabled them to reorganize and go into battle refreshed. Help us . . . help us, please, before it's too late. It is imperative that we stop the child before he breaks his new toy."

"You must take this news straight to General Halder, back at headquarters," Olbricht advised, making a point of breezing over Loeper's demeaning reference to Hitler, which he'd noticed that Stauffenberg had read with a particular passion. "There's just a chance that Halder might do something about it. When he took over General Beck's position, there was a gentleman's agreement between them that Halder would continue Beck's good work . . . in *every* way."

However, unlike his predecessor, Halder had failed to fulfill both of Beck's roles, finding himself only capable of one of them. While being well-equipped to sharpen a few pencils and cut a fine figure as the new Chief of Army General Staff, Halder was inclined to shy off the more pressing requests that the Resistance was making of him to stand up and be counted in his opposition to Hitler.

An example of this was the reaction he had to Stauffenberg's news. After listening to everything he had to say, Halder did nothing more but shake his head in commiseration. He handed Stauffenberg a glass of brandy, along with yet another excuse for not stepping in to take control of the situation.

"It seems that our last resources have been expended," he said. "In fact, looking at the situation as a whole, it has become abundantly clear that we underestimated the Russian colossus."

"*Hitler* underestimated it, you mean," Stauff didn't hesitate to reply, annoyed by Halder's mealy-mouthed response and the fact that he was trying to worm his way out of the situation. "It's for the Fuhrer to take the blame, when he went out of his *way* to make sure that any General in his right mind was excluded from the decision-making process. It was a sad day for us all when that *maniac* decided to take sole control of the armed forces."

Sitting down calmly at his desk, Halder dithered with the papers that were on it. It was a stalling tactic that gave him a chance to consider his reply.

"You must watch what you say to me Stauffenberg. *Because* I like you, I must warn you that I'm not entirely to be trusted."

Stauffenberg, in his usual charming, bombastic way, would have none of it:

"That's nonsense! As far as I'm concerned—a man who is capable of admitting as much is a man who can be trusted implicitly. You underestimate yourself and your own courage Halder."

To which the Chief of Army General Staff responded with a short, self-deprecating smile.

"Would that that were true, but I'm a realist, Stauffenberg, and I see myself for exactly what I am: a man full of good intentions, without the courage to see any of them through.

"Which, I might add, was a lesson learned from my friend, Field Marshal von Brauchitsch. Now look what happened to *him* when he stuck to his guns and dared cross Hitler! The poor bastard had a heart attack. And who *wouldn't*, having to face-off with the Fuhrer on a daily basis?

"Do you know that I used to overhear the violent screaming

matches that went on between them several times a week? None of which fazed Hitler one iota, but by the end of it, Brauchitsch's nerves were shot. I sometimes wonder whether that heart attack of his was just his easy way out—the soft alternative to having to see the war through at Hitler's beck and call."

"I suppose we could always look on the bright side," Stauff suggested, as the eternal optimist he was. "Perhaps the Wehrmacht will have a better chance of holding its own against Hitler's *direct* orders, without having to also contend with 'the bumbling Brauchitsch input' factor."

"Wishful thinking Stauffenberg. Let's hope you're right."

He was not. Nothing about Hitler or his war was that simple.

It was just one of the many reasons why Stauffenberg was growing more bitter by the day. The blame for his disquiet rested squarely on the shoulders of the German Commanders at the front. *Not* for their lack of military prowess, but for their shameful lack of moral consistency.

Many of them, in desperation over the suffering that was going on there, had sought his advice as to a solution, the result of which had had each of them in turn make the brave announcement that they would come to General Staff headquarters to set the record straight. It was their intention, *once and for all*, to tell Hitler the plain, hard truth about the way things really were in Russia.

But of course, they never did. All of them pre-empted the Fuhrer's blank refusal to hear anything of the sort, along with his terrifying glassy-eyed glare that threatened their life, both of which proved too much for them. The prospect of Hitler taking exception and ordering their immediate dismissal or execution promptly knocked them off their high horse and cowered them back into submission.

The long and the short of it was that nothing Stauffenberg could say or do was enough to stir them into action and have them stick to it. It was frustrating in the extreme, when it was essential that a man of far more military consequence than himself take such definite, dramatic action. Until such a bold and brilliant field marshal were found, Stauff himself was hamstrung when it came to taking more affirmative action.

That was why he was thrilled to hear that Halder had resigned. Stauff only hoped that the *"position vacant"* ad might attract someone of a more decisive character.

Not that he'd had to hound Halder into making the decision to step down. The abysmal failure of *Operation Blue* had done the trick and made Halder desperate to escape the corridors of power, something he would have done much sooner had Hitler not strictly forbidden *any* of his staff to resign.

"It is bad for German morale," was Hitler's excuse.

The Fuhrer had not quite cottoned on to the fact that the thousands of his men being slaughtered in Stalingrad, at that time, might be testing that German morale just a tad more.

Hitler's obstinance about not letting the Chief of Army General Staff go, however, left Halder no option but to battle it out, headlong, with the Great Man. He had to continue to go one-on-one for the privilege of being handed his pink slip, while praying that Hitler didn't choose, instead, to execute him on the spot for having dared to request it. Halder realized that the only chance he had of getting what he wanted was to take full blame for their monumental losses in the east:

For the record, and for Hitler's peace of mind, he put it in writing:

"I must respectfully request, sir, that you accept my resignation. I was deluded by hopes of greatness for myself and the General Staff. In the process, I abandoned promises made to my associates and followed the course of duty to you, my Fuhrer and the Third Reich, without the loyalty and honour which both deserved. The result of which was the failure of Operation Blue, the defeat of our German troops, and the division and humiliation of the General Staff."

Satisfied that Halder had shouldered the responsibility, Hitler finally nodded his approval, signed his resignation papers and quickly replaced him with General Kurt Zeitzler. He was convinced that this new man—the former Chief of General Staff (*Army Group D*)—might make for sterner stuff than Halder, and get them through this little problem they were having in Stalingrad.

CHAPTER TWENTY-SIX

"My dear General Paulus,
It was so very refreshing to visit you at the front . . ."

Stauffenberg wrote when he got back to headquarters, having completed another two-week circuit of the Eastern War Zone. Three days of this he had spent with General Friedrich Paulus, along with the fear and frostbite of his 6th Army in Stalingrad. When he returned home to write his report, he was all fired up with the enthusiasm of a soldier, but somewhat depressed that his position as a General Staff officer was depriving him of being just that.

In such a state of mind, he continued:

"What a different world yours is, to the one in which I'm forced to function here at headquarters, where so-called leaders do nothing but bicker over prestige and mismanage the far-flung battles they know nothing about. In such an atmosphere, I feel stifled. Ever champing at the bit to get back to the battlefields where I belong and where, daily, life is sacrificed without grumbling. I know that you're in desperate need of every good man you can get. And I can tell you quite honestly that I'd give my right arm to be back in the action again, standing at your side.

Thank you for the hospitality you offered under such dire conditions. I will remember it with gratitude and, I have to admit . . . a certain amount of envy."

The disgruntled tone of Stauffenberg's dispatch soon reflected itself in his attitude at work. Since his return from this most recent trip to Russia, he had made no bones about the fact that he was restless, fed up and uncharacteristically terse. Prone to make the most dangerous, sweeping statements, without the slightest attempt to mask his feelings about being deprived of action *or*, in fact, about his growing aversion to Hitler.

That was why his friend, Lieutenant Julius Trommler, was taken aback when he walked into Stauffenberg's office to see the life-size portrait of Adolf Hitler he'd hung on his wall. Its bright-coloured brushstrokes and gross dimensions, out-dazzled and dwarfed all else in the room *including* Stauffenberg, who was sitting at his desk in front of it.

"My God, you're a man of stark contradiction Claus. What on *Earth* is that abomination you've got hanging up there?"

Without lifting his attention from his work Stauff answered quite simply, "Why it's a likeness of our beloved Fuhrer, Julius. Don't you think that the artist's clever use of light and shade has captured the essence of the man to perfection?"

"Well . . . yes, I suppose," the Lieutenant replied haltingly. He wasn't quite sure whether his friend was making fun of him or whether Stauff had gone completely insane, when for the last few months nothing but the utmost disdain for Hitler had spilled from his lips.

Astonished, and not really ready to accept that Stauff had done such a surprising backflip, the Lieutenant lifted his upturned hands in disbelief and said, "Are you feeling all right?"

His concern had Stauff smile at last, and decide to put his friend out of his misery:

"It's hanging up there, dear boy, so that everyone can *see*, in brilliant technicolour, that the man is mad!"

At this point Lieutenant Trommler relaxed and let out a sigh of relief. This was more like the Stauffenberg he knew - always devil-may-care about his deep-felt beliefs, without it ever crossing his mind to be scared of the consequences.

Such a man was inclined to go to extremes, and Stauff was no exception. Over the next few weeks, he continued to make a series of seditious comments to other members of the military in the only way he knew how—with complete honesty. A hard-edged, no-frills honesty which made them all deeply concerned for his safety . . . not to mention their own. All of them desperately tried to shy away from being implicated in what Stauff had in mind, not quite as willing as he to put their lives and reputations on the line.

This was something that Stauff had done only a few days before when out horse riding with Major Oskar Berg.

⚡ KILL THE FUHRER

"They're shooting Jews in masses. These crimes must not be allowed to continue. Our supremely foolish and criminal Fuhrer *must* be overthrown."

His words had the Major abruptly rein in his horse. Tugging hard on his palomino's bridle, he pulled it up, breaking its gait from full gallop to standstill.

"You speak treason Stauff," Berg said, just as shocked and out of breath as his mount.

And Stauff turned casually in his saddle to say:

"Fluently!"

This was *not*, however, a matter to be laughed off lightly with an well-placed quip.

"But the only way to get rid of such a man is to assassinate him," Berg replied, unamused and stony-faced at the reality of what his friend was suggesting.

Yet Berg's fear-laced instinct was to talk Stauff out of it rather than hold him accountable. He was aware that the intent of such a man as Stauffenberg could never, *ever*, be anything but noble, and that if he *had* spoken out of line, it was only through a misguided sense of loyalty towards the Fatherland.

In such a patronizing mode, he continued.

"And tyrannicide, Stauff, is still murder, no matter which way you look at it. You must remember that a better order can never be brought about by murder."

His sanctimonious-cum-weak-willed reply had Stauff calmly wheel his horse round and head back to the stables—disappointed and insulted by his friend's lack of support.

It was a disenchantment, though, that didn't stop him broaching the sore subject again with Colonel Mueller-Hillebrand, when their dinner conversation turned to Hitler's frequent and much frowned-upon defamation of the officer corps.

"It's about time an officer went over there with a pistol and shot the dirty fink," he said point-blank.

He had assumed, as he very decidedly put down his knife and fork to underscore his startling statement, that it would arouse at least *some* sort of reaction, that the Colonel would either slap him on the back with congratulations, or slap him in jail with a death sentence.

It came as a complete surprise to him when the Colonel chose

216

to do neither; continuing to eat his meal without batting an eye. His unexpected composure gave Stauff more of a shock than the one he'd intended to give the Colonel in having laid it on the line.

This was particularly because Stauff had been privy to the Colonel, and many others like him, spending endless hours mulling over their disgust with Hitler. All of them were trying to come up with some way of talking the Fuhrer into relinquishing his personal command of the army.

At such a strategic moment, it was disconcerting for Stauff to find out that it had all just been words—that none of them . . . not *one* of those high-flying, big-talking members of the military hierarchy, had the least intention of doing anything constructive about it. It had been at this point that Stauff had come close to giving up on the whole idea—seeing that no one appeared to give a damn about their country going to hell.

Yet when fresh reports reached him about the continuing atrocities being committed against the Jews in the Ukraine— accounts of men, women and children having to dig their own graves before being shot and falling into them, Stauff's conviction was renewed with a bloody-minded vigour. He was determined to no longer sit back on the sidelines and be called a coward.

He had reached boiling point during a military briefing in Colonel Mueller-Hillebrand's office. The issue at hand was the ten Air Force Mounted Infantry field divisions which Hitler had specially constituted to reinforce and/or replace his exhausted legions on the eastern front. They were the vital backup on which General Paulus and his 6th Army were relying.

When Stauff had first got wind that something so sensible, at last, was being done about the horrific situation in the east, he'd let out a sigh of relief—nearly choking with dismay soon after, when he heard that Reich Marshal Hermann Goering had decided to redirect these ten divisions for his own use elsewhere and had got the go-ahead to do so from the Fuhrer himself.

This supreme piece of military mismanagement was followed up by Hitler refusing to allow his shattered 6th Army to escape their suicide mission in Stalingrad. To General Paulus, he sent orders instead that they fight to the last man—irrespective of the fact that the battle was lost.

And *that*, for Stauffenberg, was the last straw. The memory of those young boys dying under the most deplorable, sub-zero conditions in Stalingrad was still deeply imbedded in his psyche. He had been with them himself only weeks before. Most of them were still children, barely in their teens, rigged out in German uniform.

Those uniforms had been made for men; two sizes too big and designed to tolerate only temperate climates. In them, those terrified boys had been literally freezing to death by the day. In his mind's eye Stauff could still see their rigid, blue-hued faces, while his ears still rang with the constant replay of their plaintive cries for their mother as they died on the battlefield.

Enough was enough!

"I want to know who was responsible for withholding those urgently needed replacements from our eastern field army?" Mueller-Hillebrand was demanding with the thump of his fist on his desk.

It was a rather convincing display of anger, Stauff thought, considering that Mueller-Hillebrand already *damn well* knew the answer. It didn't surprise Stauff in the least to hear the hypocrite then add to his little piece of play-acting by saying, "Hitler must be told the truth."

Enraged, Stauff couldn't stand the lies any longer. He leapt to his feet and shouted, "*Hitler* already knows the truth. *Hitler* is responsible. You all know that no fundamental change is possible unless he is removed for good. There is only one solution—*kill him!* And I'm ready to do it. I *swear* that it is *he*, and not the Russians, who is the enemy most worthy of my steel."

Calmly, Mueller-Hillebrand urged the other officers in the room to break their stunned silence and continue with their meeting, while he pulled Stauffenberg aside.

"Do you wonder why neither General Halder nor I have ever asked you to accompany us to our briefings with Hitler? You are much too hot-headed and impulsive, and we fear—brave knight—that in your outspoken opposition to our Fuhrer, you run the risk of ruining our best laid plans.

"Please realize that for months, a very dedicated group of us has been discussing the possible methods of removing this monster from power, and to do so without seriously damaging our army's defence of the Fatherland and destroying the whole structure of the State in the process. We are *not*, as you imply, sitting on our hands and doing nothing."

Still hot under the collar, Stauff was not ready to be appeased.

"This endless word-play of yours and others is all taking much too much time. While the lot of you are chattering on, chasing your tail, Germany is sowing worldwide hatred that will be reaped and revenged upon the next generation. It is *scandalous* that millions of soldiers should be risking their lives daily while no one has the courage to put on his helmet and tell the Fuhrer the truth, even though to speak it might mean his life. Fate doesn't honour suffering, but action. It is the *only* thing that will save Germany."

At this point, Hillebrand put a quieting hand on Stauff's arm, feeling, beneath his touch, the violent shaking of the man's every sinew. It was the very reason he chose to leave his hand there until both Stauff and his nerves had stilled.

"I am aware of the passion of your youth Stauffenberg. I'm fully aware of the direction in which you and the younger members of the officer corps tend. You *do* know though, that I'm in mortal danger if I fail to report your dangerous sentiments to Hitler? But I will not, because at heart I share them, and have no desire to put you in the line of fire. But *please*, be smart . . . and take yourself out of it. Assassination is a dirty word, and contrary to what you think, *nothing* good will come out of it."

"I am concerned about our young Count von Stauffenberg," Mueller-Hillebrand said to Generals Halder, Zeitzler and Manstein later that day.

He hoped that sharing his worries with these three other men at the top might help the outstanding General Staff officer in question out of a sticky situation. All four of them were well aware that Stauffenberg was desperate to extricate himself from General Staff duties and to swing a field command. And Mueller-Hillebrand was now thinking that it might be an appropriate time to find that loophole that would let Stauff slip through the General Staff system and do his bit for the Fatherland back on the battlefields, where he had a much better chance of staying alive.

"Yes, I agree," Halder replied, concerned as he'd been that Stauffenberg had paid him a surprise visit the day before. It had been unwise and much too daring, given that since Halder's retirement it had been settled that the people who shared his subversive, Resistance-linked views, were not to keep in touch with him because he was being watched by the Gestapo.

"I am in Berlin to discuss business with my brother," had been Stauffenberg's excuse when he'd turned up unexpectedly at his door. He had come clean with his real reason for being there the very instant that Halder had showed him into his study.

"I can't bear it at Army High Command any more. Since you've left, all efforts to oppose Hitler have ceased and one can no longer speak openly. All that's left to do is idly look on as Germany goes to her destruction. I tell you . . . every last one of those chaps in command have their pants full and their skulls stuffed with straw. They don't even *want* to do anything to fix the situation. They figure it's easier to lick Hitler's boots while he tramples all over the hopes for Germany's future. I'm *desperate* for a field command, because I abhor cowardice and can no longer stand the psychological strain of having to live and work with it."

Field Marshal Erich von Manstein shook his head at Halder's account of his no-holds-barred interview with Stauffenberg. There was now no doubt in his mind that something had to be done about the potentially explosive situation before it was too late.

"Discretion, it appears, is not one of Stauffenberg's better points. But I'm keen to get him out of harm's way because I'm extremely fond of the lad and most impressed by his many other fine qualities," Manstein said, as he lit a cigarette and reached across the table to offer one to Zeitzler.

Zeitzler took a few moments to inhale and exhale a puff of white smoke as he pondered the rather alarming thought that had just hit him.

"I'm worried about Admiral Canaris getting his hands on our young Count. We must make sure that we keep them apart," he said, turning suddenly to Halder in concern to ask:

"They don't know each *already* do they?"

Halder's answer was a snort of amusement.

"Do you honestly think that we wouldn't know about it if they did?"

"Quite right, and exactly my point," Manstein replied as he pointed a finger of confirmation at Halder and then sat himself more upright in his chair to talk seriously:

"I shudder to think what might happen if the two of them ever got together. They'd make for a pretty formidable duo—Canaris with his guile would make short work of a man like Stauff who's *completely* without it. It'd take the Little Admiral precisely two seconds to turn Stauff and his altruistic dreams of glory to his advantage. And I know for a fact that Canaris has been on the lookout for someone of Stauff's ilk for some time.

"Well I, for one, don't intend to serve Stauff up on a platter. Love Hitler or loathe him, gentlemen, I am convinced, as is Hitler, that the German infrastructure will fall to pieces if something happens to him. *Three* times I've approached him personally to ask him to give up trying to be everything from political leader and warlord to field commander and to show some confidence in his Generals. His answer: *'I alone—the Fuhrer, enjoy the confidence of the people and the Army.'*

"And do you want to know something? He's right . . . much as it pains me to admit it. But right at this moment Hitler's forced removal would break what's left of our troops' morale. This is why, for Germany's survival, we must put the issue of 'right' and 'wrong' aside for the time being. It's now a matter of expediency. We simply can't *afford* to make Hitler a casualty of friendly fire."

Having made his speech and gone a long way to winning his point, Manstein stubbed out his cigarette and got up to leave. He paused as he put on his peaked cap to turn to his fellow officers and say:

"You'll see to it, won't you Zeitzler? Stauffenberg's under your command and I hear that the Africa Korps is short on good officers at the moment. Let's get the young Count over there right away. See if he can't expend some of that pent up passion of his on sand and Panzer tanks for a change. Believe me . . . it'll be safer for us *all* that way. And with Stauffenberg's flair for fighting on the front . . . a damn sight more detrimental to the enemy."

CHAPTER TWENTY-SEVEN

"I've gotten myself into some tight corners and must retreat to the front,"
Claus wrote to Nina.

In a state of excitement over his new orders for North Africa, he thought to stop and scribble three kisses and hugs at the end of his letter to his wife.

It was an extraordinary display of emotion on his part to which she was most unaccustomed; between them, "'love" had never really figured. The fact that they had managed to produce four children had not been the natural result of shared passion, but merely a manifestation of Claus' conscience—aware as he was that for a man in his aristocratic position it was his duty to perpetuate the Stauffenberg line.

So with the formalities of fond wishes having been expressed to his spouse, Stauff was on his way to where his *true* passion lay. In February, 1943, he took the quickest route to Tunisia to give Field Marshal Erwin Rommel a helping hand.

It was really just a forestalling of his fate. Manstein's intervention in his military career was to only delay, rather than prevent, Stauff's date with destiny and his preordained collaboration with Rear Admiral Canaris and the other members of the Resistance. Most of them, by now, were intent on seeing Hitler dead and were just waiting for the right man to pull the trigger.

However, it wasn't until Stauff himself had been shot, bombed and punctured with a liberal sprinkling of shrapnel that he was in a position to offer his services. His horrific wounds, suffered as a result of his "gung-ho" heroics on the battlefields of Tunisia, excused him from combat and confined him to a hospital bed, from which disinfectant-drenched point he was just an operation, or *twenty*, away from getting back on the road that was to lead him to a more dubious glory.

The detour from this road, by courtesy of Generals Manstein and Zeitzler, had lost him his right hand, two fingers from his left hand and his left eye. Stauff's only compensation was that their loss had given him a much keener perspective. The irony of it all made him laugh out loud. Who would have thought that with one eye he would be able to see more clearly than with two?

The way he was looking at it now, there could be no more beating round the bush. Hitler had fast-tracked the Fatherland for destruction, which meant that he had to go. One way or the other, Stauffenberg was determined and quite prepared to take the responsibility of putting both the Fuhrer and the Fatherland out of their misery.

He had come to that conclusion when lying with his face buried, inches deep, in the foul-smelling, blood-soaked mud of the Chabita-Khetati Pass in Tunisia. As he lay semi-conscious, waiting for the stretcher bearer to reach him, he'd been aware of only the excruciating pain that swamped him, while wondering *why* . . . when he had leapt from his jeep and covered his head with both arms to protect himself from the bomb blast, he could now only feel that protection over his left ear. His right, which should have been shielded by its corresponding hand, for some reason, was wide open to the sounds of swooping spitfires, rapid machine-gun fire and the gut-wrenching screams of the battlefield.

There had been so much blood splattered in every direction around him that it had been inconceivable to think that it was just his own. Just as inconceivable had been the prospect of looking up to see that elusive right hand of his, that now detached from his body, was hanging like a gruesome piece of entrail-encrusted foliage from the burnt tree stump ten yards from where he lay. And that was not even to contemplate what had happened to the two fingers from his left hand which had just disappeared into oblivion—been blown away to God knows where.

Every minute that the field ambulance delayed he was losing blood by the bucketful, drifting in and out of consciousness and oddly enough through the pain and delirium, dreaming of the most beautiful, inconsequential things. The most prevalent of these had suddenly been the memory of his statue. Its significance made him roll over and moan in distress—not as a result of his pulsating, blood-pumping wounds, or the fact that he was teetering on the brink of an agonizing death; but because he was cursing himself for not having recognized it as the omen it had been.

Gone was his right hand and a proportion of his left. Just as it had been prophesied by the damage done to his stone image after it had taken a dip in the Elbe river. And its chipped eye . . . *his eye!*

It had only been then that the awful realization had hit him. Only *then*, that he'd tentatively reached up with his three-fingered left hand, to touch on the empty, bloodied socket where his left eye had been only minutes before.

The temptation to shed tears with the one that was left had seemed pointless, however, when Stauff supposed that he was nigh on dead anyway. It was a reality that he had believed to be very near, when he'd lapsed for the last time into unconsciousness.

It was the last time, only because he awoke to find himself safely ensconced between two fresh white sheets at a field hospital. The doctor's prognosis was that he was "on the mend", but strictly on the proviso that Stauff was prepared to accept that his return to full health would be an on-going, painstaking process. He would be provided with a glass eye to wear on formal occasions and a few other prosthetic appendages to replace those of real flesh and bone that had gone missing.

The surgeon warned Stauff that his stitch in time had not saved nine, but had been just one in a series of many more to come. The first had secured his life by suturing the wounds; the last had been the initial step in reconstructing what remained of his body.

Yet Stauff had no regrets. *That* luxury wasn't the privilege of any soldier once he wandered onto the battlefield, and especially not a soldier like himself, who had wanted nothing more than to throw himself into the hub of action.

It was a dream that had come true from the very minute he had reported for duty as Senior Staff officer for the 10th Panzer in Tunisia. He had arrived to find its Commander—General Friedrich von Broich, and his entire Division in the midst of a ferocious foray against the British 8th Army. The Brits, along with Eisenhower's American troops, were hell-bent on cutting off the German supply line through Tunis that provisioned the German-Italian Africa Korps.

They called it *"Operation Spring Breeze"*, which Stauff had thought was highly inappropriate when he'd first arrived on the scene. The bombs and bodies flying in every direction around him had given him more the impression of a wild winter apocalypse.

Never one to be afraid of thunder or lightning, he'd gone straight out into it. Not waiting for orders, he'd grabbed a gun from the hand of a dead compatriot and raced to take cover at the side of another who was still alive and under siege. An unknown soldier who, in his dusty, bullet-dented helmet, had been in dire need of help. For some time he had been sheltering, almost out of ammunition, behind the inadequate protection of a few split sandbags and surrounded on all sides by enemy forces.

When Stauff had flung himself down beside him and begun firing at the foe, the besieged trooper had taken a two second time-out to turn in his direction. His tired, bloodshot eyes had been swimming with tears of relief. He'd had no idea who this stranger was who had just stopped off to save his life, but he was eternally grateful that he had.

It was a feeling that, by the end of the battle, was shared by every soldier who had come in contact with Stauff. The general consensus was that he was a man in a million and a soldier extraordinaire, who had fanned that "Spring Breeze" considerably and, in the short time he'd fought at their side, gone a long way to turn the winds of war to their advantage.

"Our new Senior Staff officer Stauffenberg is terrific!" was Second Lieutenant Klaus Burk's sentiment.

Ignoring protocol, he had walked boldly into Brigadier von Broich's office to express it. His audacity in approaching and speaking to his Commander with such easy familiarity was understandable, given Broich's immense respect and gratitude for Stauffenberg's selfless courage during the battle.

The Commander himself had not only agreed, but soon embellished on Lieutenant Burk's praise in a letter he'd sent to his friend, Field Marshal von Manstein.

"In the very short time he's been with us, your Count von Stauffenberg has proved himself beyond measure. The impression of him being a newcomer has faded faster than the African sun has been able to bleach his fresh uniform. He has won his comrades' respect and affection with his competence, courage and reliability.

What's more, he's his own person, which in the Army these days is a phenomenon in itself. He's not afraid to speak his mind, albeit with respect, to his superior officers. Thwarting them to a degree, because he's usually right in his advice. He discusses military tactics as astutely as he does history, literature and philosophy. At the latter of which, he seems quite the master.

A man of unquestioned honour, in that he considers his religious principles to be part of his business practice. Thank you for putting this very capable, decidedly anti-Nazi General Staff officer in my way. I now not only have the privilege of him fighting at my side, but of calling him my friend."

As friends, Broich and Stauff had often sat over a late evening bottle of wine, talking about Hitler's removal. Stauffenberg had never made any bones about his feelings towards the Fuhrer.

"Someone ought to kill that chap," was one of the first things he'd said at their initial military briefing. He had not baulked at throwing the highly contentious comment at Broich and the other six officers who had been in the room.

Stauff had scanned their stunned faces with a roguish grin before offering an explanation that had them smile broadly in return.

"As you can probably now understand, gentlemen . . . I got myself into hot water at General headquarters and am so very, very glad to be so very, very far away in Africa. I do hope you're not going to mind having me around?"

They did not . . . not in the least. In fact, in the grueling weeks that followed, they didn't know what they would have done without him.

From February 14, when their 10th Panzer tanks had rolled into action and driven forward through Faid to Sidi Bou Zid, until the day they came under the brutal combined attack at the crossroads of Biar Zelloudja on April 6, there had not been a day without a bloody encounter. Rommel with his aggressive, brilliant agenda had clashed violently with the Allies and *theirs*, which had left Broich and his Division under constant fire and threat of annihilation.

By April 5, both Broich and Stauffenberg had been calling urgently for a withdrawal of their crippled Division, but the German Afrika Command had delayed the order until April

6—*much* too late for them to make an orderly disengagement.

Under the extenuating conditions of the men's fear and loathing, it had been largely up to Stauffenberg to hold it all together. He drew on the trust and respect they all felt for him, to keep them under control and calm until they got the go-ahead to "*move 'em out*". It was only then that Stauff was given half a chance to salvage the ragged remains of their tanks and troops.

It had been on that very busy day that Lieutenant Friedrich Zipfel had reported to Stauffenberg with his new posting to the 10th Panzer. It had been just in the nick of time, seeing that Stauff and his command post were under heavy bombardment.

Zipfel had burst through the door covered in dirt and dust from the bomb that had just exploded only a few feet from his face. His appearance, however, had been of no consequence, given that it complemented that of his new superior officer's. Unshaven and disheveled, Stauffenberg was rigged out in a bloodied, sweat-soaked Africa Korps shirt and a pair of pilfered American trousers. Under the dire circumstances it had been obvious that he was in no mood for polite introductions.

Stauff had done only a quick double-take at his new, shell-shocked Lieutenant, before he'd got back to the business of battle. He had been too pre-occupied to ask whether Zipfel was all right, or, in fact, to even bother inquiring as to his name. Skipping all preliminaries, he had gone straight into issuing orders.

"When that shelling begins again," he'd said, shaking the map he was studying free of the glass from the shattered western window, "you take the foxhole on the right. I'll take the one on the left."

Before Zipfel even had a chance to brush the dust from his hat and coat, Stauff had thrust a machine gun into his hand and positioned him at the western wall. The two of them waited for that strategic break in the bombing before they opened up with a barrage of rapid gunfire at their respective targets.

All the while, through the terrifying cacophony of cannons and battle cries, Zipfel had been aware of the phone that kept ringing and *ringing* in the background, and the fact that, amid the chaos and carnage, Stauffenberg still had the presence of mind to calmly take the series of calls from his frantic Command officers and to lull them into a false sense of security. It had been his only recourse when he'd been ordered to deny them the reinforcements and permission to retreat for which they had been begging.

Finally, at 5.00am on April 7, Brigadier von Broich had sent Stauff and his troops on their way. Ordering his General Staff officer to direct the Division's retreat from his Horch jeep, he'd instructed Stauff to drive on to the new Command Post near Mezzouna. Unable to shrug off the uneasy feeling that when he'd saluted his young friend goodbye, it was for the last time.

"Look out for fighter-bombers Stauff. I'll be following after you in about an hour when the last battalion passes."

It had hardly been a deliberate defiance of Broich's orders that got Stauff caught up in an inferno of fighter-bomber attacks when he reached the narrow terrain of the Chabita-Khetati Pass. The slow progress of his debilitated tanks had made them into sitting ducks for the enemy planes which had kept up their relentless attacks without a break. Each one of the Allied Airforce Aces was making a sort of sport out of shooting into burning, swastika-stamped vehicles, because they had made for such easy targets.

Unfortunately, this meant that the German wounded inside them were unable to escape and were incinerated on the spot. The bonus of having their booty of ammunition explode was merciful to the extent that it hastened the process of their excruciating death.

Meanwhile, the luckier, burn-free soldiers of the Armoured Artillery Regiments had had to leap out of their traction engines and run for cover. If they couldn't find it in time, they had had to wait until the fighter pilots had committed to an approach and couldn't change their aim, and then fling themselves aside. In between sorties, they jumped into any usable vehicle that could get them the hell out of the burning bloodbath.

Throughout the horror, heat and hysterics of the massacre, Stauff had been driving back and forward between the various units to direct them. With no thought of his own safety, he'd been standing in his jeep when it came under fire.

When he'd seen the grenade being hurled in his direction, he had thrown himself out of his jeep onto the ground—lying flat to it with his face in the mud and his arms flung over his head for protection. The irony was that in his bid to escape the explosion he'd made himself into its "bull's eye". The hand-flung bomb intended for his jeep fell a few feet short of it, to make a direct hit on *him*.

CHAPTER TWENTY-EIGHT

Will you be wanting your eye today, sir?" Asked Stauffenberg's batman, Private Scherer.

It was part of the morning grooming routine for him to offer his Commanding officer the option of sporting the glass replica of what had once been Stauffenberg's left, blue eye.

"No, put it away, private," Stauff replied, agitated at the sight of it *and* the fact that he was having trouble doing up the button on his shirt collar with only the three fingers he had left at his disposal.

He had never quite got used to the rather macabre ritual of taking out part of his anatomy and putting it on his bedside table each night. That was why he usually chose to wear just a plain black patch over his dead eye socket instead. Somehow it seemed a little less ghoulish.

"I'm sorry to say, sir," Scherer continued, now sounding a touch more flustered than before. "But I've looked *everywhere* and I've been unable to find your ring with the Stauffenberg Family crest on it."

"Oh, I shouldn't worry about that Scherer. They threw it away in Africa, you know . . . along with my right hand."

Red-faced with embarrassment over the Colonel's straight-faced quip, private Scherer wasn't sure whether to laugh or commiserate. He chose instead to kneel down and help Stauffenberg buckle up his boots.

It was an act of kindness to which Stauff took offence. It had become a matter of pride that he do all such things himself. From the very day he'd got himself out of his hospital bed, he had been determined to train himself to perform such menial tasks.

That had been difficult indeed for a man who had lost what had been his rather remarkable four-limbed facility. Sad for a person of his former outstanding physical prowess to have to come to terms with the fact that he was now less adept than a baby at simply doing up his shoe.

Today, however, it was important that he made a good job of it, because he was going to be introduced to Admiral Wilhelm Canaris and his associates.

The *Abwehr's* elite clique of conspirators formed just one of the three concentric circles of the Resistance which were in operation at that point. Each of them operated under their own steam and under different banners, which effectively rendered all three of them useless.

Wheels within wheels, working *with*, but more often *without*, each other, stymied what should have been a somewhat smoother process. Their contrary objectives and wrangling over methods had had them lose sight of the fact that they all ultimately wanted to achieve the same end—Hitler's!

What they needed was a cohesive force to bind them. A type of "common cause glue" that would have them stick together and act as one decisive force—and Stauffenberg believed that he was made of the stuff to do it.

Of course, it wasn't as simple as it sounded. First, he had to acquaint himself with, and be accepted *by*, the leading lights in each of the conspiracy cells— a process that was a project in itself.

Not entirely convinced that he had managed to commit all the main players' names to memory, he'd scribbled a list of them down on a piece of paper and put it in his pocket as backup.

For the last few hours, he'd been prepping himself as if for an exam, running over and over in his head all the necessary names of those involved in their respective Resistance circles. Learning them by rote, so as not to forget exactly who was linked to whom, or to run the risk of appearing uninformed when he met them face-to-face.

It was only when he was leaving his Berlin apartment, reciting the list for the fiftieth time, that he realized that one of the more strategic names had slipped his mind.

He stopped, put down his briefcase, and pulled the scrap of paper from his pocket. Scanning it, he quickly filled in the mental gap with the name—*Pastor Dietrich Bonhoeffer*—and rebuked himself for having forgotten it. It was the reason why he decided to read the list out loud, just one last time, to forever lodge it in his memory:

The Abwehr Circle of Resistance:

<u>Admiral Wilhelm Canaris:</u> *Ex-Chief of Military Intelligence attached to High Command.*

<u>Hans von Dohnanyi:</u> *Abwehr's head Administrator and Legal Advisor. At present, under Dr. Manfred Roeder's interrogation. In very poor health and in custody at Buch Military Hospital.*

<u>Major-General Hans Oster:</u> *Abwehr Chief of Staff. Currently on suspension from duty and under Gestapo surveillance.*

<u>Major-General Erwin Lahousen:</u> *Former Chief of Austrian Intelligence and member of Austrian Imperial Army. Committed member of Abwehr and Resistance.*

<u>Pastor Dietrich Bonhoeffer:</u> *Connected only to Abwehr through his brother-in-law—Hans von Dohnanyi. Scholar and teacher. Attempted to make contact with British on behalf of Resistance. At present, under Roeder's interrogation at Tegel Prison.*

<u>Josef Mueller:</u> *Lawyer and leading Catholic agent of the conspiracy. Major link to the Vatican. At present, imprisoned and under Roeder's interrogation at Tegel Prison.*

<u>Hans Bernd Gisevius:</u> *Civilian lawyer attached to Abwehr. Has just been freed after interrogation by Roeder. At present in Switzerland.*

<u>Carl Goerdeler:</u> *Former Mayor of Leipzig and Price Control Commissioner in Hitler's government. One of the old boys of the conspiracy circuit and principal advocate of Resistance. Apparently a bit of a loose cannon.*

<u>Ulrich von Hassell:</u> *Another old boy and former German Ambassador to Rome. Acts predominantly as political go-between.*

<u>Baron Rudolf von Gersdorff:</u> *Abwehr attaché to Army Group Centre. Recently volunteered as suicide bomber to kill Hitler at Russian Captured Arms Exhibition. Assassination attempt aborted.*

<u>Hjalmar Schacht:</u> *Former Minister of Economic Affairs and President of the Reichsbank. In close contact with Resistance but keeps low profile.*

"Right!" Stauffenberg said, closing his eyes to commit the men's names to memory. Opening them once more, to follow through with the major conspirators from the military. They were a little easier to remember, given that he was already acquainted with most of them:

The Military Circle of Resistance:

General Ludwig Beck: *Former Chief of the Army General Staff now in retirement, but fully active in Resistance. Its nominated Head of State at Hitler's fall.*

General Franz Halder: *Beck's successor, now also in retirement. Slowly, I fear, withdrawing himself from the Resistance.*

Field Marshal Erwin von Witzleben: *Retired from active service. Nominated as Commander in Chief of the German Army after coup d'etat.*

Field Marshal Guenther von Kluge: (After which Stauff had put a red-penciled question mark). *The man's involvement with the Resistance extremely precarious. Has just been made Army Group Commander in France subsequent to his eastern front command. By no means a sure thing. Just a ray of hope.*

General Friedrich Olbricht: *Head of Supply section of Reserve Army. Up and coming mover and shaker of Resistance. One of the younger bloods.*

Major-General Henning von Tresckow: *Chief-of-Staff Central Army Group on eastern front. Young blood. Is working on Valkyrie Plan to facilitate takeover of Berlin as we speak.*

Lieutenant Fabian von Schlabrendorff: *Lawyer. Tresckow's Staff officer on eastern front. General Resistance liaison with Berlin.*

General Heinrich von Stuelpnagel: *Military Governor in France. Principal co-ordinator of coup d'etat in France.*

Major-General Helmuth Stieff: *Chief of the Army High Command. Supplies and stores British silent bombs for Resistance use. Committed, but a little gun-shy.*

"That's two down, one to go," Stauff mumbled to himself, feeling a little exhausted by this sudden influx of information that was rolling around in his head.

Thank God there was only a little bit more of it to digest—the couple of aristocratic elite who belonged to the Kreisau Circle. This was the intellectual section of the Resistance, with whom his brothers Berthold and Alexander chose to link themselves, doing so because in the early days of the conspiracy, it had been the members of this circle who had been the strongest advocates of non-violence.

The Kreisau Circle:

<u>Count Helmut von Moltke:</u> *Leader. Circle itself is named after his vast estates. A young blood, with a reputation for his superior intellect. Has quite a distinguished following.*

<u>Adam von Trott du Solz:</u> *Attached to the Foreign Office and close friend of Moltke's.*

There were many, many more notables involved in the conspiracy whom Stauff had not jotted down, but this brief synopsis would, he believed, suffice to get the ball rolling. Every one of them on the list had at last decided to put aside their own agendas and to meet at Canaris' house in the hope of dove-tailing their efforts. All in the dead of night of course, and with every guest taking great pains to make sure that he wasn't followed en route.

All this made for a cloak and dagger gathering of the first order. Each of the men present was in possession of enough clout and intelligence to know what was what, and to watch their respective "ps" and "qs". There was the very real possibility that one among them might just be clever enough to be a Gestapo spy.

It was a bit of an ordeal for Stauffenberg—a kind of grueling initiation ceremony, where his ethics and intentions were being put under the microscope. For the first time in his life, he was without that natural physical and intellectual edge that he was used to having over his peers. On this occasion, he had to live up to the very demanding standards of a room *full* of men whose intelligence, conviction and courage rivaled his own. So it was entirely up to him to win each and every one of them over and to convince them of his sincerity.

With Canaris, however, the strain was all but non-existent, which surprised Stauff. Given the man's reputation as Germany's master spy, he'd expected Canaris to be the hardest nut to crack, but from the moment they had shaken hands, theirs was an instant affinity. The only friction between them was that they vied for the title of "the One Most Charming". Canaris quickly and most graciously conceded that title to Stauff's 10" advantage in height and the fact that the dashing young Count had been better blessed with beauty.

"Mussolini's fallen," Canaris said, launching straight into their discussions, without the slightest doubt in his mind that he could trust Stauffenberg completely and that they would become the closest of friends.

Canaris' eagerness to embrace their budding relationship was in no small part due to the fact that he knew how imperative it was to win Stauffenberg over. As a national hero and well-respected war veteran, the handsome young Count was the perfect front man to launch their offensive.

"Well, that's a good start. One tyrant down . . . one more to go," Stauff replied, taking his lead from Canaris' candour and accepting the little Admiral's friendship as easily as he'd accepted the glass of brandy Canaris had handed him. "All we have to do now is put a bomb under Hitler and we'll be pretty much despot-free."

How nice it was at long last, Stauff was thinking, to be able to speak so freely with men who shared his dedication. To not have to explain himself any longer, and to *know* that all those around him understood his intentions and were themselves motivated by the same religious convictions and resolute patriotism.

"I believe that you and General Tresckow have already put your heads together on the *Valkyrie Plan*?"[27] Canaris asked him, nodding his polite acknowledgement of the General he'd just mentioned, who was sitting at the other end of the conference table.

It wasn't Tresckow, however, who then decided to join their conversation.

"*Valkyrie?*" Count von Moltke chimed in with a certain sarcasm from his seat, three chairs away. "What a pretty, poetic code name for something so prosaic as Military Mobilization Orders. That should throw the Nazis off the scent."

"Yes, we're in the middle of a revision of the original draft," Stauffenberg replied.

Canaris noticed that he did so while deliberately ignoring Moltke's patronizing interjection. Obviously Stauffenberg was a

KILL THE FUHRER ✠

man who liked to be taken seriously. There was definitely a limit to his sense of humour when he suspected that *he* was the butt of the joke.

"It's the first step only," Stauff continued. "But I firmly believe that until we streamline the Emergency Home Army Rapid Mobilization Orders, we'll be in no position to pull off a successful *coup d'etat*. If Hitler's assassination is actually achieved, there'll be one hell of a hole in the system back in Berlin for a few days that'll need to be plugged up pronto to stop any political power play. This Valkyrie Plan that Hitler has Tresckow and me working on at the moment is the perfect stop-gap. If we can just manage, behind Hitler's back, to adapt it to suit the requirements of a *coup d'etat*, I think we'll be home and hosed.

"For example, we can arrange that six hours after our code word is issued, *our* version of Valkyrie—*not* Hitler's—will go into effect. Military units in and around Berlin will be ready for deployment with a mandate to secure all prime objectives like telephone exchanges, power plants and bridges.

"It's all important at the same time, however, that we have ready and waiting in the wings a new structured, competent government to step in and take control at the moment of his death. If both components come together, I think we might just be able to pull it off."

*　　*　　*

"I'm so glad that at last someone is getting a real grip on the organization of the conspiracy," Major-General Henning von Tresckow said to Canaris.

He, along with his Staff officer Lieutenant Schlabrendorff, had specifically returned to Berlin from the eastern front to attend the meeting, doing so on the pretext of it being their well-earned R&R from frontline duty.

"Yes, so am I," Canaris agreed as he lowered himself with a sigh into his armchair. He was relieved that the bulk of his guests had gone and that the difficult meeting was all over. Which left him, Tresckow and Schlabrendorff alone to enjoy a relaxing fire-side debriefing.

"So what do you think of him?" Schlabrendorff asked, knowing that between the three friends there was no point mincing words.

Everyone at the meeting had known that it had been Stauffenberg who had been on trial this night and they all wanted to know the verdict. Shrewd, smooth-tongued Canaris' was the most important.

"I think the young Count came out of it with flying colours," was Canaris' encouraging answer as he patted his thigh, signaling to his small dog to leap up onto his lap.

"He seemed to go down well with everyone," Treschow now felt free to agree.

"With a few exceptions, of course," Canaris put in, unfazed. Experience had taught him that there was no such thing as a clean sweep when it came to a man being liked or loathed.

"Stauffenberg got Goerdeler off side with his unequivocal stand on assassinating Hitler. Goerdeler just doesn't get the fact that it *must* happen if we're to get rid of the evil. He's as weak as water on the matter. Mind you, it didn't help Stauff's case when he *said* as much to man's face."

"No, but then a confrontation of the like between them was no surprise. I actually overheard Goerdeler calling Stauff a '*precocious puppy*' at one point. Can you believe it?" Schlabrendorff said, crossing his legs and relaxing back in his chair.

It was just lucky, he believed, that it was only Goerdeler's response to Stauff that was in question, rather than the other way round. They couldn't afford to have a petty insult turn Stauff away from their cause when they needed him so badly. Whereas, in the broader scheme of things, Goerdeler's finer feelings were of little consequence. Well liked as he was by the bulk of conspirators, they had all got so sick and tired of his dangerous carry-on.

"But then you know Goerdeler," he went on to explain. "Lovely chap, but super sensitive on certain issues. I think we've all learned to take his pet hates and passions with a grain of salt."

"Ah, but did you pick up on Moltke?" Canaris asked with a degree of glee. As always, he derived great pleasure from seeing what others did not.

"No! What do you mean?" Tresckow now cut in, surprised that Canaris had picked up a problem that had completed slipped past *him*.

"A bit of tension there, I suspect," Canaris carried on. "Fair few pithy remarks flying between the two of them all evening.

Odd really, when Moltke is usually so subtle, but it was a little like a fencing match. I can't tell you how tempted I was to hand them a couple of swords so that they could get on with it in earnest."

The thought of this had Canaris smile in wry amusement. The glamorous, erudite Moltke would have been mortified to know that he'd allowed himself to succumb to such a base instinct as jealousy, when he'd always sold himself on being above such things.

It had been, however, quite obvious to Canaris that the two Counts, Moltke and Stauffenberg, had had it in for each other from word "go". This was logical enough, he reasoned, when they were a matching pair—two handsome, imposing men, equal in intellect and panache, who were compelled to lock horns.

Still, if Canaris didn't miss his guess, Stauffenberg would be the one who would come off second best in their sparring relationship, because there was something of the schmaltz artist in him. His, was a romantic "White Knight" vulnerability that would be no match for Moltke's sharp tongue and deep-seated scepticism.

CHAPTER TWENTY-NINE

*"Many a man will have the courage to die gallantly, but will not
have the courage to say, or even to think, that the cause for
which he is asked to die is an unworthy one."*

Stauffenberg had not been able to resist throwing this favourite
quote of his into the conversation. He did so during the most
recent gathering of Count von Moltke's Kreisau Circle.

As a devotee of the poet/philosopher, Stefan George, Stauff
had got a reputation for twisting iambic pentameter and the like
to his advantage. In fact, it had become a sort of party trick of his.
In this instance, it helped him trick *himself* into believing that he
wasn't feeling grossly uncomfortable as a guest in Moltke's house.
Their complicity in the conspiracy had made Moltke's invitation
obligatory, and Stauff's RSVP (*"Yes . . . I'd be happy to attend"*) into
a downright lie.

Putting himself centre stage, however, came as a red rag to
Moltke.

"Oh spare us, Stauffenberg," he said as his stubbed out his
cigarette and wandered over to casually rest his arm on the
mantelpiece. "We've all had our fill of that old fag's verse."

"I beg your pardon!" Stauff came back at him, almost as if he
welcomed the opportunity to attack. "Stefan George was one of
the greatest minds of our time."

"Well yes. In fact, one might say that he 'queened' it over us."

Moltke's pun roused a round of laughter in the room and
stiffened Stauffenberg's jaw. The inference of his mentor's
homosexuality had been in extremely bad taste . . . and, quite
frankly, none of anyone's business.

"George's sexual preferences were none of my concern," he
said.

"Of *that*, I'm convinced, Stauffenberg, but I'd wager that they were his. Surely you must have thought it odd, that not *one* of his young poet prodigies was plain, plump or pimply? In fact, I was quite offended that he never picked up on *my* talent with the pen to include me among them."

"What you say, Moltke, is reprehensible. Especially when the man is no longer alive to defend himself. I find it most offensive."

"Oh wake up and smell the roses, Stauffenberg. The man was a raving queer, abusing the Arts so that he could abuse his pupils. To be honest, *I* can't understand why a man of your insight and quite *obvious* masculinity was ever drawn in by him."

For Stauff, this obnoxious bit of banter had gone too far.

"That's enough Moltke! You've made your point. Now if you'll excuse me, I'll make *mine* by taking leave of you," he said, already up out of his chair and striding towards the door. There, he stopped to say, "Oh, and by the way—it wasn't Stefan George, but Bertrand Russell I was quoting. Given that you seem blessed with the wisdom of the ages, I'm surprised you didn't know."

* * *

"Come on, we're getting out of here. I can't *bear* that man," Stauff said, as he grabbed hold of his cousin—Annabel Siemens—by the arm, and told her to get her hat and coat so that the two of them could leave Moltke's house immediately.

This, to the other women sitting with Annabel in the kitchen, seemed extraordinary—Stauffenberg suddenly bursting through the door to tear his twenty-six-year-old cousin away from the party, without warning or the least concern about social etiquette. More astonishing *still* to them was that the beautiful Annabel followed his lead without complaint, like a good, compliant wife.

But that was just it. She *wasn't* his wife . . . just his housekeeper.

Since he'd received his permanent posting as General Army office Chief-of-Staff,[28] Stauff had been living at his Berlin apartment, finding it far more convenient than having to continually trot back and forward from his family estate in Lautlingen.[29]

It was a view that was shared by his brother, Berthold, who was working at Naval Command headquarters in Bernau, and in equal need of a place to stay that was at the centre of the action.

Both men had decided to share the apartment as a place to snatch a few hours sleep in between their profusion of military meetings.

It had been the brothers' older cousin, Count Peter Yorck von Wartenburg, who had suggested that *his* niece, Annabel, might be prepared to help them out with their housework. Men, at the best of times, were not such dab hands at it, and there was also the consideration that Stauff was no longer in possession of a pair of hands to even try. Therefore, it was assumed that a feminine touch was in order.

Given that Annabel was only in the apartment on alternate days to tidy up, and that the two men were in and out of it at random times, it was rare for any of the three to run into each other.

That was, until that Sunday night when Berlin came under a particularly heavy Allied bombardment. Having sat alone and afraid in the "blacked out" apartment, Annabel had chosen to stay there for the night after the first wave of aerial attacks was over. Presuming that there would be a second, she had not wanted to risk spending hours in a freezing cold air raid shelter if she got caught up in it on her way home. So she'd curled up on the couch, closed her eyes and soon fallen asleep.

It had been Claus who had woken her in the middle of the night. Sensing someone's presence in the room, she'd opened her eyes to find him standing silently over her, which had left her wondering, with some degree of embarrassment, just how long he had been there, steadily regarding her.

"Are you all right?" he'd asked, as she sat up and straightened her skirt. Running her hands quickly over her long dark hair, she'd made a self-conscious attempt to tidy it.

"Yes, perfectly," she'd replied, abandoning her attempt to readjust the clip that had been holding her hair in place, and letting it fall softly around her shoulders.

It had not been intended as an act of seduction, and it had surprised her, as much as it had Claus, when he'd responded to it; smiling and feeling oddly shy when she'd lifted her dark blue eyes to look up at him.

"I hope you don't mind me staying over?" she'd asked, in a bid to cut through the tension. "I was a little nervous about getting home with the raid going on."

At that point he'd pulled himself abruptly back into line and put her mind at ease.

"No . . . not at all. You did the right thing. I'm only sorry I woke you up."

Following his lead, she'd forced herself to remember exactly what her role was within this particular household.

"You must be tired. Would you like a cup of coffee?" she'd asked, making moves to get up so that she could put on the kettle.

"Yes . . . yes, I would, but don't let me disturb you. I'll make it."

His reply had been a polite gesture of the domestic kind that was most unusual for a man of his vintage and breeding, to whom such menial jobs were women's work.

It had been the reason why she'd wanted to insist that *she*, and not he, did it. Still, her better instinct at that time had told her not to offer. It had become a point of principle for Claus to do as much as possible for himself without anybody's help.

She had been impressed that he'd got through the task with such speed and style. He presented her with not one, but a series of cups of coffee that they shared, along with a meaningful chat, throughout what remained of the night.

Annabel, even though she was quite familiar with Claus' charm, had been pleasantly surprised and flattered by his keenness to open up to her and share his innermost feelings. He was also a bit puzzled by his desire to do so.

It was just that they felt so comfortable in each other's company. The two of them talked one-to-one, while sitting casually on the rug in front of the fire—he, with his back resting up against the paisley-design armchair, and she . . . an appropriate few feet away, sitting with her legs curled up gracefully at her side.

Did he know that she was in love with him, she'd wondered. Was it *wrong* of her to be in love with her cousin? Frankly, Annabel no longer cared, not since she'd realized that her feelings for Claus had gone beyond familial obligation and was reasonably sure that he returned them.

It was an impossible situation, of course, with two insurmountable stumbling blocks standing in the way of their happiness.

1. They were related.
2. He was a happily married man and a father of four children.

She could only blame herself for having fallen for him, but how was she to have known how she would react to this second cousin of hers—Claus von Stauffenberg—when they had never met before? Had she known that there would be an instant attraction between them, she would never have agreed to keep house for him and Berthold. Yet that in itself was a lie, when she now thought she might die without him—without seeing his face . . . without being a day-to-day part of his life.

"Come in Anna," he'd said, when he'd opened the door to her on the day they had first met.

Without the slightest hesitation, he'd scooped her up and given her a hug. His easy familiarity had been most engaging. She'd quickly learned that with Claus it was the rule, rather than the exception. His charm and warmth were so ingrained in his nature that he just couldn't help himself.

Since then, however, he'd stopped touching her in that easy, open way. The two of them felt awkward and strangely shy whenever they were together, finding that even the slightest, accidental contact between them made them flinch. The innocent touch of a hand, or the unexpected bumping into each other in the hallway, made them very smartly back away from each other to make sure that the appropriate space forever remained between them.

Such was the way of love, or at least physical attraction, Annabel assumed, but having never truly experienced it before, she was hardly wise in its ways. She only knew that when Claus looked at her in that particular way, or when she heard him say her name, her entire body warmed at the thrill of it. The guilt and concern over the fact that it *had*, always following soon after, much as it had on that fateful Sunday night with them sitting so close in such tempting, intimate circumstances.

"What happened between you and Moltke the other night?" she'd asked in a deliberate attempt to draw him out. It was a question she'd wanted to put to him many times before, but had never had the courage. "You normally get on so well with everyone . . . as does Count Moltke. It seems strange to me that two men as similar as you both are, should clash. Why don't you like him?"

"Because the man's the consummate egotist—always *me-deep* in conversation," he threw back at her, before pausing to take a sip of his coffee. Looking up at her then, with a sheepish grin, he qualified his comment. "And I've no doubt that he'd return the compliment. It's obvious that he loathes me."

But on this issue Stauff was quite wrong.

Turned off as he was by Moltke's haughty, I'm-better-than-you manner, he didn't realize that the man was incredibly impressed by *him*. For some time, Moltke had been on his friend, *Berthold* von Stauffenberg's back, to involve his brilliant younger brother in the conspiracy. Moltke was convinced that Claus' dynamic presence and drive would produce results.

All the rather predictable head-butting business that had been going on between them since was simply nature in action—the result of two fine male specimens staking their territory.

It was a struggle for supremacy which had been blatantly obvious to Annabel.

"Oh I wouldn't worry about what other people think of you. It's just that you're more intelligent than most, and that's inclined to make everyone a little nervous," she'd said very calmly, surprising him with her candour and insight, both of which led Stauff to suspect that *her* intelligence might very well outstrip his own.

At that point, Annabel had known that she'd got his full attention. She'd gone beyond just being a pretty face to him, and he had decided to take her seriously. That was why she'd pressed her luck by tackling the taboo subject head on.

"Are you involved with the Resistance Claus?"

Her unexpected, power-packed question had stunned him. Annabel had not known whether his tight-lipped silence, or the way he was looking at her so coldly in response, was anger, or his on-the-spot attempt to sum up her capacity to handle his honest answer.

It had been unfair of her to have hurled such a scandalous accusation at him without warning. He had not been ready for it and had been thrown off his guard.

She'd put him in an almost impossible position. How was he to speak with complete honesty, given the very real danger of admitting as much to someone who had not, as yet, made their own feelings clear on the matter?

So she'd helped him along by saying:

"You can trust me. I can safely say that I share your sentiments."

"Yes, I am involved," he'd then admitted, plain and to the point.

"And my uncle Peter? And your brother Berthold? Are they involved too?"

That, however, had been where Claus had drawn the line. It was one thing for him to confess his own treason, but quite another to implicate someone else in it. Instead he'd said, "The less you know the better, Anna. But now that we're on the subject, please let me ask *you* a question . . . Do you think it is right for a man to sacrifice the salvation of his soul to save the lives of thousands?"

Without hesitation and with her eyes alight with passion, she'd answered, "Yes! And I would make the sacrifice with you if you'd let me."

So the barriers between them had broken down. In that intense moment, Stauff had had to fight harder than he'd ever fought on any battlefield to kill the urge to commit himself to her for life.

It had been the ultimate overcoming of temptation when the firelight had been casting such a warm, rosy glow over her porcelain-perfect face. It turned her dark hair a deep amber and the dancing reflection of its yellow flames in her navy blue eyes, transformed them to turquoise. Their exquisite colour and wanton expression beckoned him to make that one definitive move in her direction.

In those urgent few seconds of suppressed desire, it had taken enormous restraint on both their parts to stop straying from the straight and narrow. Their brave decision to behave themselves was based on their shared and very strict sense of morality, an ethical guideline that saved them from what threatened to be an explosion of passion between them. Both of them believed that adultery was the ultimate act of self-indulgence, one that would lead to a lifetime of unhappiness for all concerned.

That was why they promptly put their conversation and relationship back on an even keel by changing the subject to the issues of State, talk of Hitler and his assassination being eminently less dangerous than the alternative at hand.

"You understand, don't you Anna, that I'm speaking of committing murder, for which I'll earn for myself eternal damnation?"

His carefree-cum-sarcastic manner had not fooled her in the

least. How could it when she knew what a deeply religious man he was, and how terrified he must have been, underneath it all, by the prospect of breaking one of the Ten Commandments? *"Thou Shalt Not Kill"* was the most serious among them—the most heinous of crimes to commit against God.

"But why must this responsibility fall on *your* shoulders?" she'd asked. "Why should it be *you* who makes such an enormous sacrifice?"

"Because Anna, I'm one of the few men who has regular access to Hitler. That, and the fact that no one else is prepared to do it! Which is fair enough, I suppose. As a soldier, I've sworn to protect my country and its people and now I'm being called upon to do so. None of us in the Resistance can stand by any longer, just weakly allowing Hitler's reign of terror to continue. If someone doesn't do something about it soon, it'll destroy us all.

"It's too late to save Germany as an independent power, unfortunately. But I still have to believe that it's *worth* showing the world that there was opposition inside Germany to the unadulterated evil of Hitler's regime.

"Please understand that I'm not doing this for myself, but for my children. It is *we* who made the grievous mistake of backing Hitler's cause, a sacrilege for which we must hold ourselves wholly responsible. Therefore it is up to us to make amends by doing everything humanly possible to save Germany's future generations from guilt and culpability."

"And you must do this dreadful thing all by yourself?" she'd asked, allowing herself the one-off intimacy of leaning forward to stroke her hand compassionately down his cheek.

"Yes," he'd confirmed as he took that hand of hers in his. For one warm, tempting moment he let it linger there, before he placed it gently back on her lap and relinquished its hold. ". . . with a little help from my friends."

From this, Annabel had taken her queue and relegated herself, then and there, to the ranks of friend rather than lover. From that point on, the two of them were inseparable, but strictly on a "working for the Resistance" basis.

CHAPTER THIRTY

Canaris guessed that that was why Claus and Berthold brought her with them to the next meeting. He had to guess again during the course of it, when he noticed just how close Claus was sitting to the lovely Annabel and how often their gaze seemed to drift in each other's direction.

The obvious, however, had apparently escaped big brother Berthold's attention, which was remarkable, Canaris thought, considering that the three of them lived under the same roof and it was *right there* for anyone who had the eyes to see.

But then Canaris had a flair for such things. Many people, both friends and enemies, were able to attest to the fact that he'd eyes in the back of his head. *Nothing* escaped his attention—least of all the personal and business affairs of those he had in his sights, and right now they were focused on Count Claus von Stauffenberg playing centre stage.

"I do hope that we still have your undivided attention Claus," he thought it wise to ask when he had a chance to speak to Stauff alone.

"But of course . . . why would you think otherwise? You must surely know by now that I'm dedicated, one hundred percent, to our cause."

The conviction behind Stauff's words made Canaris smile a little indulgently at the passionate young man standing in front of him. It was clear that Stauff had no clue of the danger he was in. Not in regard to him assassinating Hitler, but to the more dire threat of him committing adultery.

"My dear Claus. Please forgive me, but I couldn't help but notice that you and your beautiful young cousin are a little smitten."

It shocked Stauff to know that he'd failed to mask his emotions. Given that he'd been striving to keep them under wraps, he was nonplussed that they had been so transparent. The straightening of his mouth and firm set of his jaw told Canaris as much.

"You have every right to take offence at my interference, Claus. It is, of course, none of my business. I wouldn't have even dreamed of mentioning it if I hadn't been concerned about it putting a glitch in our plans."

"*That,* it most certainly won't do," Stauff snapped back, more out of acute embarrassment than anger. "Annabel is my cousin and therefore off limits."

"And a *second* cousin Claus, which would make it doubly dangerous—I mean, genetically speaking."

Now it had got a little too personal for Stauff's liking. Canaris' blatant attempt to sabotage his personal life wasn't appreciated, nor necessary. He knew that the little Admiral had a vested interest in keeping his would-be assassin on track, and if that meant blackballing Annabel so that Stauff's blinkers stayed in place and channeled his vision in the direction of Germany's liberation from evil, well then so be it.

"You needn't worry Canaris. I have my priorities straight. I love and respect my wife and would never dishonour her *or* my family name by indulging in inappropriate behaviour. But I won't insult your intelligence by pretending that what you've picked up between Annabel and me is not the truth. Unfortunately, Fate has decreed it to be only wishful thinking—a case of 'look and love, but don't touch'! The reality is that I care for Anna too much to let her mourn my loss. And we both know—you and I—that it's very unlikely I'll survive the coup."

This brought them back to the salient point—Hitler's assassination and the strategic part Stauff was being primed to play in it. Farcical as it was, that as the only man in Germany prepared to do it, he was also the one man least physically capable of it.

To think that they had all hung their hopes—not to mention their lives—on him seeing it through. Every last one of those other hale and hearty conspirators were letting *their* four workable limbs go to water at the thought of taking on such a massive responsibility. Instead, they had chosen to put their trust in the questionable dexterity of a man with only one eye, one arm and half a hand to pull off the coup of the century.

Stauff's three, left-hand fingers were all that they were

relying on to fiddle with the intricate workings of the bomb to be detonated at Hitler's Eastern Front military headquarters—*Wolf's Lair*,[30] doing as much under the sweat-drenching pressure of split second timing and chronic fear.

No one needed to tell them that their chance of pulling off an assassination attempt was slim, at best. The chance of Stauff coming out of it alive . . . was infinitesimal.

It was going to be no mean feat for a man who had been born right-handed to set that bomb with his left. He would have to reconnoitre his way through its state-of-the-art, untried technology, and then position it for a direct hit on Hitler, before making his not-so-fleet-footed escape.

Yet there was method in the conspirators' madness. The fact that Stauffenberg was such an unlikely candidate for such a death-defying mission made him perfect for it.

Right at the moment he was the flavour of the month. A national war hero, who was the apple of Hitler's eye—Stauff having lost one of his *own*, along with a few other parts of his person, fighting for Fuhrer and Fatherland. It was a sacrifice that had gone way over and above the call of duty.

So as far as Hitler was concerned, Count Claus could do no wrong. In such a loving frame of mind, it wouldn't have occurred to the Fuhrer that this wonderful, wounded warrior of his was, in fact, his most dangerous and most dedicated enemy.

"But then, Hitler's always had a soft spot for men in uniform," Colonel Oster had jibed, throwing a wink in Canaris' direction. "For various reasons of his own."

In response to the quip, Canaris returned a warning wince, knowing that Stauff was standing only a few feet away from them at the meeting and wouldn't take too kindly to the inference, despite it being intended as a joke. Just now, Canaris wasn't of a mind to rub their "White Knight" the wrong way. Especially not after Stauff—minus the protection of any armour and the promise that he would survive his suicide mission—had kindly volunteered to be their hit man.

Not that there had been much choice. The conspiracy's options had been seriously depleted after Major-General Helmuth Stieff—the man they had been counting on to pull the trigger—had let them down. His last minute dash for cover had left his fellow conspirators all out on a limb and at their wits' end.

"He's pulled out. He's not going to do it!" General Beck had said in disbelief.

The other men in the room had been just as stunned when he'd told them the bad news. Stieff had passed on the unexpected change to their plans, in a fast and fearful conversation over the phone.

"It's not safe for me any longer. I refuse to act alone," he'd said to Beck over the phone.

In the throes of a last minute panic attack, he'd rattled off his excuses.

"Over the last few days, Hitler's made it abundantly clear that he's suspicious of me. He's actually taken to calling me 'his Poisonous Little Dwarf'! Now why . . . why would he do such a strange, insulting thing, unless he'd something to hold over my head . . . unless he knew of my complicity in the conspiracy?"

The fact that Hitler was a little contemptuous of Stieff came as no surprise to the other conspirators, when Stieff had always been so free with his criticism of Hitler and his Third Reich. The Fuhrer's reason for not having bothered to react against it sooner was that he'd never taken the neurotic, pint-sized Stieff all that seriously.

But *Stauffenberg* had, when some months before Stieff had ranted and raved about Hitler's appalling leadership abilities when he'd come to pay Stauff a friendly visit in hospital. Stieff's criticism had been so bold, brave and outrageously vindictive, that the Lieutenant who had accompanied him there had chosen to excuse himself from the hospital ward for fear of guilt by association.

It was an escape hatch that had not been available to Stauff at the time. Lying flat on his back, with a network of intravenous tubes shackling him to his bed and life-support system, he'd been Stieff's captive audience.

Why Stieff had waited until that strategic eleventh hour to chicken out was incomprehensible. He had *known* that they were all sitting on tenter hooks with their nerves in tatters, just waiting for the "green light" to go . . . go . . . *go!*

The last thing they had expected was for that light to suddenly turn red so late in the piece—pulling them and their plans up to a reverberating, heart-thudding halt.

It had been unforgivable . . . that irresponsible, last minute passing of the buck—a damn nuisance that had made Stauff want to spit chips. He was fed up. Stieff's cop-out had been just the most recent in a series of false starts and stops—of bungled assassination attempts that had not amounted to a hill of beans. Boeselager, Tresckow, Schlanbrendorff and Gersdorff had all failed, through bad timing, bad luck—or Hitler's supernatural monopoly on the reverse, to fire the last angry shot and get rid of him for good.

Not to forget the exemplary courage of Captain Axel Baron von dem Bussche, who had approached Stauff in November, 1943, to offer his services. He had been shot in the chest on three separate occasions in various eastern front battles. In between this, he'd witnessed the SS massacre of three thousand Jews in the Ukraine. He, like Stauff, had come to the conclusion that an end must be put to Hitler as quickly as possible.

"Does your faith deter you from taking decisive action?" Stauff had quizzed him.

He had felt on safe ground to do so, because Bussche's aversion to Hitler and his horrors had been obvious. At that point it had been merely a matter of protocol to hear the man confirm his conviction out loud. And so Stauff had continued to grill him.

"Are you prepared to no longer tolerate criminals and liars running and ruining our nation? Do you believe as I do, that we must act now under the dictates of our conscience?"

This, however, had all been a little bit too high-minded for the likes of Bussche who had dallied with death and destruction much too long to concern himself with such delicacies.

"I set little store in philosophical argument," he'd replied, straight to the point. "I've long since transcended any such considerations after what I've seen and experienced."

"What are your feelings then on our Soldier's Oath?" Stauff had felt obliged to ask, because it had been the stumbling block for most of his fellow conspirators.

"The oath was founded on mutual loyalty. It has been broken by Hitler and is therefore null and void."

"In that case, Bussche, you must go and see Stieff," Stauff had said, wholly satisfied that he'd found his man. "He has access to Hitler and can arrange for your access too."

"Well then, why doesn't *Stieff* do the deed?" Bussche had

asked, greatly puzzled.

"Stieff is as nervous as a racing jockey, and about the same size. He's not up to it. But what he *can* do is provide you with one of the new silent British bombs to get the job done."

"No, I don't want that!" Bussche had been adamant. "It's German explosives or nothing. I don't want any implication of the enemy having supplied the materials. If a hissing fuse is the problem, I can always conjure up a sudden coughing fit to cover the noise."

And that had been fine. Bussche had got what he'd wanted in exchange for accepting the suicide mission of blowing himself and Hitler up at the forthcoming Exhibition of New War Materials. Only to be told by Stieff a few days later that the exhibition had been cancelled. *Not* because Hitler had decided not to turn up, but because an Allied aerial bombing mission had blown up the train that had been transporting all the items to be displayed.

It made for an unforeseen cancellation over which both Bussche and Stauff had been mightily frustrated, while Stieff had seemed enormously relieved.

Bussche had no option then but to return to the front and take over his battalion of the no. 9 Potsdam Regiment.[31] Stauff still had great hopes that the man would return to his assassination duties on request.

Bussche would have happily done so. . . had he not had his left leg shot away from under him in a heavy mortar attack—January 44.

For the conspirators, it had been just one stroke of misfortune after another. Hitler escaped sure death in whichever way the Devil could contrive it.

Stauff, however, had been determined not to give up.

"Obviously, if you want a job done properly, you have to do it yourself," he'd said in a fit of frustration to his associates. "I'm sick to *death* of all this endless procrastination. The time for tea parties and small talk is over. I'm going to kill Hitler myself. And *nothing* in God's name—*or* the Devil's—is going to stop me."

"But that's impossible!" Canaris had jumped in to say straight away. "You can't be in two places at once, Claus. We're going to need you in Berlin. Someone else has to handle the Wolf's Lair end of it. I thought that had been decided."

"Who?" Stauff had asked point blank. Neither Canaris nor anyone else had the answer.

In a state of extreme agitation Canaris had started pacing about the room. He had never been one to cope well with loosing the reins of control, and that day had been no exception, when he'd realized that the situation had got out of hand. And so he had continued, somewhat frantically, to put it back on track:

"It's *imperative* that you stay in Berlin, Claus, and be on hand immediately after the assassination. We're relying on you to oversee *Valkyrie* and quash any unforeseen military opposition. That's been the plan all along. You're one of Its masterminds, for heaven's sake. We simply can't *afford* to lose sight of you in the middle of it. Nothing . . . *nothing* will work without you being on deck in the capital at the time of the coup."

"Don't worry . . . if all goes well, I'll get back to Berlin in time."

However, Stauff's attempt at reassurance had not worked. Canaris had turned away from him with a frustrated sigh, knowing that he may as well resign himself to the plot's failure. Once Stauff had made up his stubborn, splendid mind, there had been no way to change it. Nor had there been any chance at that point for Canaris, as a man of honour, to extricate himself from an assassination plot that he now believed was doomed to failure.

Because there had been just one small problem with Stauff's idea that Canaris had not had the heart to say to the man's face. That if brave young Count Claus *did* manage to get the bomb to go off at Wolf's Lair, he would either be blown to pieces along with Hitler, or be unable to make his escape through the series of checkpoints that were manned by Hitler's personal bodyguards. There wouldn't be a hope in hell that they would let *anyone*—even the revered Count von Stauffenberg, pass in the wake of such an unexpected, horrendous explosion.

So it wasn't a question of Stauff getting back in time. More so, it was a *fait accompli* that he wouldn't get back to Berlin at all.

CHAPTER THIRTY-ONE

The prospect of his imminent death, however, had not fazed Stauff as much as the patronizing reprimand he'd received from Dr. Carl Goerdeler.

With the conspirators' plans for the *coup d'etat* supposedly in place, the date of December 25 had been tentatively nominated for Hitler's assassination. It was intended to be the conspirators' Christmas gift to the world—their welcoming in of the New Year, 1944, with a Hitler-clean slate.

"Please alert all political delegates to be at the ready for a takeover," Stauff had advised Goerdeler, assuming that it was the right thing to do.

Goerdeler, however, had not been so sure, and was rather surly about passing on the Count's orders. He was annoyed that he was being instructed by a man twenty years his junior, and was still smarting over Stauff's opposition to *his* logical candidacy for head of Cabinet in the new transitional German government. He, Dr. Carl Goerdeler, believed himself to be eminently suitable for such a prestigious post, given his political credentials and the respect he was due as one of the instigators—one of the *main* movers and shakers—of the Resistance.

That was why he'd been secretly pleased when those initial plans for the coup fell through. He was *anything* but reticent about passing on his sentiments to Stauffenberg in regard to his mismanagement of the affair.

"Don't *ever* do that again!" he'd said, shaking a reproving finger at Stauffenberg mid-reprimand. "Your unthinking, impulsive actions have put hundreds of people's lives in jeopardy."

Which had been true, but hardly Stauff's fault or intent. It *had*, however, represented the perfect opportunity for Goerdeler to put the "precocious puppy" (as he was fond of calling Stauff) in his place.

However, the indignant Stauffenberg had responded in kind with a few well pointed words of his own.

"You're quite right Goerdeler. You can rest assured that I'll *never* give you advance warning again!"

Inevitable really, that such a clash of personalities should creep in to undermine their best-laid plans. The antagonism between Goerdeler and Stauff was just one of the many "kinks" that existed within the highly-strung, loose-spun web of conspirators.

Another was Commander in Chief of the Reserve Army— General Friedrich Fromm—who, with his weak chin and equally weak will, had posed an on-going dilemma for the conspirators. Much like that other champion vacillator in their midst—Field Marshal Guenther von Kluge—Fromm's see-sawing loyalties were forever hanging in the balance. Swaying one day from his adamant standpoint that:

"Yes, I'm with you . . . we must get rid of Hitler"

to the next day's doubly fervent conviction:

"Leave me out of it. I see nothing, I hear nothing. I will do nothing!"

One way or the other, however, he was involved up to his eyeballs. Having initially worked under General Beck and been recruited to the Resistance by same, he'd found it hard to back out . . . but not for want of trying.

When he'd been promoted to Commander in Chief of the Reserve Army, Fromm had seen it as his chance to make good his escape from his prior commitment to treason, but had found himself working at even closer quarters with a man fifty times more dogged than Beck. General Friedrich Olbricht—Chief of Supply (Reserve Army)—had made it his mission in life to bar Fromm's backdoor exit.

As the new Principal Administrator of the coup, Olbricht was dedicated to the Resistance and to making sure that his superior officer, Friedrich Fromm, remained an active member of it. He knew that Fromm was that crucial lynch pin they needed to pull it all together.

Olbricht was so convincing in his argument re what should be a good soldier's duty to God and country, that Fromm had been guilt-tripped into sitting meekly on the sidelines, while his underling in the next office, ran the show. Olbricht had the courtesy, every so often, to pop his head round Fromm's door with a wink and a smile, and *always* with an ulterior motive. Usually this involved getting Fromm's stamp of approval on one issue or another, or to have him agree to look the other way whenever the cohorts of conspirators traipsed in and out of his Berlin offices.

Contrary to Olbricht's low opinion of him, Fromm was no schmuck. Yes, he was weak and unreliable, but he was blessed with the finely-honed shrewdness of a man whose priority was self-preservation, armed with enough evasive weaponry to keep himself safe, and Olbricht forever on his toes.

This, Fromm had done only a few weeks before—answering with a simple "Thank you", when Olbiricht had risked life and limb by daring to fill him in on their most recent plans for "an intervention against the Reich's leadership."

Such were the loopholes that Fromm had at his disposal, the likes of which he knew would excuse him from any complicity in their crime if worst came to worst. Still, that had been before Count Claus von Stauffenberg had signed up as his new Chief of Staff in June, 1944, and deprived him of his safety net.

Even though he'd been so badly wounded the year before, Stauff was still greatly sought after for a General Staff position. Aware of the famed soldier's anti-Nazi sentiments, Olbricht had been quick to scoop him up the minute he'd left hospital.

He had offered Stauff the position as his *own* Chief of Staff, which was an enormous compliment when Stauff at that time had only been a Lieutenant-Colonel. Tradition dictated that such a prestigious position be earmarked for nothing less than a Colonel being fast-tracked to the rank of Brigadier.

As far as the Resistance was concerned, speeding up procedures had become a priority. News had reached the conspirators that after the Vermehrens'[32] widely publicized defection to London, Hitler had sacked Canaris from his position as head of the *Abwehr* and had dismantled the whole German Intelligence Organization in favour of Himmler's complementary SS Intelligence Division. It was a move that, in one fell swoop, had done away with the very heart of Resistance operations.

Soon after this, Count Helmuth von Moltke had been arrested.

He, joining the many other top names of the Resistance, had been recently put in jail and under interrogation. The torturing of those who were behind bars had scared off those conspirators who were still lucky enough to be on the other side of them. This, effectively, had taken them *all* out of circulation . . . at least until the heat died down.

It was a breath-holding hiatus in their plans that had threatened to be their undoing. Indeed it might have been, had Stauff not decided to take up the reins. He was one of the few leading lights of the Resistance who was still roaming free and nowhere near the point of coming under suspicion.

Time was ticking away, just as fast as their freedom and opportunities. That was why Stauff's short stint in Olbricht's employ had been contrived so that he could quickly familiarize himself with all the ins and outs of Berlin's streets, and the strengths and deployments of its home troops. That added up to 300,000 men who had to be manouevred by way of the *Valkyrie Plan* into a defensive position once Hitler was dead, directly after which a plan had to be in place for an immediate, conservative-based occupation of Berlin.

It was a massive task, towards which Major-General Tresckow had wanted to contribute, lending a helping hand by first procuring for Stauff the services of a few good men.[33] They were: Major Hans-Ulrich von Oertzen as his aide, the very charming and eager-to-please Lieutenant Werner von Haeften as his Special Missions officer, and Colonel Albrecht Mertz von Quirnheim, who had succeeded Stauff as Olbricht's Chief of Staff. Both Quirnheim and Haeften were destined to fight at Stauff's side until the bitter end.

Second was Tresckow's offer of his wife Eta's services. There was a definite need for someone who could type up the successive drafts for their plans with all ten, key-tapping fingers, so, as the 100wpm stenographer she was, she set to it. Her husband's explicit instructions were that she implement the strictest top secret measures:

1. To *always* wear gloves when typing
2. To *always* use a borrowed typewriter
3. To *always* take typed drafts to air raid shelters
4. To *always* burn any obsolete drafts

5. To *always* type them at home.

This meant that she had to be escorted there from the office each day. Concerned for his wife's safety, Tresckow always made sure that he and Stauffenberg had that privilege. To keep up a casual appearance, the three of them often stopped off at a local café to have afternoon tea en route. Their quasi-carefree routine succeeded, for some time, in evading SS attention.

That was until that terrifying day, when they thought they had been caught out by them.

As usual, they had been walking three abreast down the street. Eta, with the drafts tucked comfortably under her arm, engaged in a lively conversation with Claus. The problem was, that having got away with their little game for so long, they had begun to get a little sloppy, allowing themselves to be lulled into a false sense of security that changed in a flash to stark terror when that truck-load of SS soldiers came hurtling around the street corner. With sirens blaring and machines gun at the ready, the swastika-stamped vehicle was heading straight in their direction—its driver slamming on its wheel-skidding brakes right in front of them.

Both Stauff's and Tresckow's faces had blanched out in horror. They had been caught out . . . or so it had seemed.

When the black-shirted, pistol-wielding Lieutenant had leapt from the truck with purpose and moved quickly towards them, Stauff had taken that one brave step forward. Firstly, to shield Eta Tresckow from danger, and secondly, because it was his soldier's instinct to take the offensive—all the while, his three-fingered, left hand hovering over his pistol holster.

Prepared for death, he had not expected the Lieutenant to thrust out a friendly hand instead of a gun.

"I just wanted to shake your hand, sir," the SS Lieutenant had said. "You are, without *doubt*, our Third Reich's finest possession!"

Stunned silent, Stauff had only been able to respond by shaking the man's hand and allowing himself to be saluted. The smiling Lieutenant had no idea, as he jumped back into his truck to get happily on his way to his next Jewish slaughter, that the Great Stauffenberg's silence had *not* been due to gentlemanly restraint, but to the fact that Stauff was shocked out of his skin and shaking in his boots.

After that alarming little episode, Stauff had not been all that sorry to take his leave of Olbricht's Department. It had been intended from the start that his stay there be only transitory.

Once he'd finished his research for the post-coup occupation of Berlin, it had been planned that Olbricht would do a quick re-shuffle of his and Fromm's senior staff to suit the conspirators' more pressing needs. To that end, he moved Stauff on to become *Fromm's* Chief of Staff, rather than his own; knowing that where *he* had failed to talk Fromm round, the charismatic Stauff was sure to succeed.

As the hero of the day, the one-eyed, one-handed Count was adored and admired by all. No one was prepared to question his nobility or call to duty when he was there confronting them—so bold, so beautiful . . . so utterly upright in stance and morality. One just couldn't look beyond his handsome face with its dashing black eye-patch, or his uniform weighed down so heavily with medals—a weight that was balanced, to a degree, by its right sleeve having only to accommodate an arm without a hand.

Olbricht was counting on the fact that Stauff would make mileage out of his handicaps—he would play those physical mutilations of his up to best advantage by throwing them unmercifully in Fromm's face. Olbricht hoped that the sight of such selfless sacrifice might trigger Fromm's conscience and spur him into action. At least, that had been Stauff's mandate.

"We want you to *invigorate* Fromm," had been Olbricht's orders when he'd sent Stauff on his way.

It was precisely what Stauff had done when he'd reported for duty. The very second he'd walked in Fromm's door, he'd made no bones about why he was there.

"I am working to overthrow the Fuhrer," he'd said, instead of extending the more traditional "Good Morning". "You know, of course, that the war is lost. These new rockets Hitler's skiting about will have no tactical significance. There's no prospect of a separate peace with the West. The enemy alliance, which is demanding Germany's unconditional surrender, cannot be divided.

"The field marshals all understand the peril, but are indecisive about doing away with Hitler. But it must be done, because the man is evil personified. It has therefore been left up to the younger generation—men like myself—to assume the responsibility. When this appalling war is all over, none of us will be able to look the relatives of the fallen in the face unless everything in our power has been done to end this unholy perversion of our soldier's commitment. Hitler has betrayed his military forces and his nation. Therefore, it is only right that he be removed from both."

Having listened without uttering a word or registering the slightest shock in response to Stauff's impassioned speech, Fromm had simply picked up his pen and proceeded with his work.

This he had done, Stauff had assumed, in either shameful indifference or dangerous disdain. The latter of which would have at least made Stauff think a little more of him as a man. Yet it was obvious that Fromm was still the two-faced coward Stauff had always known him to be.

So that was that, Stauff had supposed. There had been nothing left for him to do but salute and walk out the door. He had not expected, as he opened it, to hear those magic words he'd been after.

"Supposing you *do* go through with your coup," Fromm had said, very casually, not even bothering to look up from his work as he spoke. "Be good enough not to forget that chap Wilhelm Keitel."

So it was a case of personal vendetta was it? Stauff had thought. Fromm was taking advantage of another man's courage to do his dirty work.

What of it? Taking Keitel out of the equation along with Hitler could only be a plus, just one more criminal down—an added bonus for mankind.

That had been D-Day on two fronts. June 6, 1944, had seen the Allied invasion of Normandy and Stauff's way clear to proceed, at long last, with his assassination plans. Now that Fromm had ostensibly given him the go-ahead and provided him with that essential ready access to Hitler he needed, Stauff was up and running—well on his way to blowing the bastard off the face of the Earth!

CHAPTER THIRTY-TWO

Given the great affection Hitler harboured for Stauffenberg, he would have been *more* blown away by the young Count's sentiments towards him than any bomb thrown at his feet. He had no idea as to the depth of the young Count's animosity towards him, because Stauffenberg was his most cherished warlord—the archetypal German soldier on whom Hitler wanted to model all others.

In fact, the Fuhrer had so much faith in Stauff that he had instructed his right-hand man—Armaments Minister, Albert Speer—to collaborate in every way possible with Stauffenberg and Fromm.

It was an order that had made the astute Speer baulk and raise a cynical eyebrow, because he'd known for some time what the men of the Resistance were up to. He had been approached by the conspirators in a bid to have him join them. The Resistance had even gone so far as to scribble his name on their list in anticipation of his involvement.

This wish list was soon to double as a roll call for those same men's executions when their assassination attempt failed. Involved or not, Speer's penciled-in name with a question mark beside it had put him in the line of fire, along with all the other conspirators who were running for their lives—as fast and as far away as possible from Hitler's unrelenting, blood-curdling revenge.

But that horrendous episode was still in the future, and right then, it was just easier for Speer to play dumb and obey Hitler's orders. Therefore, on June 7, when Fromm and Stauffenberg arrived at Hitler's headquarters at Berchtesgaden,[34] Speer was the first to greet them at the door. At the sight of the briefcase Stauff was carrying in his three-fingered hand, however, he wished he had not!

"Oh dear," he said, in a lowered voice, as he put a friendly hand on Stauff's shoulder, in lieu of the man having a right hand to shake. "I do hope that I'm not in the right place at the wrong time?"

His implication was obvious as his eyes flicked quickly in the direction of the briefcase.

"Your very presence here, sir, means that you're not," Stauff replied, thinking to illustrate his point by promptly dropping that heavy briefcase of his.

Unable to resist throwing a teasing smile at Speer when it landed with a bomb-free thud on the floor. *It*, along with the room and its occupants, remained completely intact.

After he'd got over the shock . . . after the beat of his heart had slowed from gallop to trot . . . Speer laughed and once again put that companionable hand of his on Stauff's shoulder. Over and above the man's rather brutal attempt at humour, he had recognized Stauff's words for the compliment he'd intended them to be.

Stauff, on his part, was grateful that he'd been given this opportunity to extend it. It had been his chance to let Speer know that he held him in the highest regard; that he valued his friendship and future prospects of taking over the leadership of a Fuhrer-less Fatherland. Stauff, like most of the Wehrmacht's hierarchy, had absolute faith in Speer—and *Speer alone*—to put Germany back on the right, insanity-free track once the coast was clear.

Besides, it had never been Stauff's intention to set off the bomb that day. It being his first, official military meeting with Hitler, he was more concerned with familiarizing himself with the territory and easing Hitler into a false sense of security in his presence.

Both of which he did to perfection, taking his leave of headquarters, with not only the flattery of the Fuhrer's warm, misty-eyed handshake, but having to bear the awkwardness of his intimate, fatherly hug. So overcome was Hitler with emotion for this young man who had given his *all* for his country.

Having had this very human element injected into their relationship made it all the harder for Stauff to stick to the plan with a clear conscience. For him, being false to *any* man—even Hitler—went against the grain.

On his way back to Berlin, he was feeling restless and uneasy—tense enough to tell his driver to stop off at his friend Werner von Haeften's house en route. He was hoping that to grab a quick lunch and a few words of encouragement from a Resistance co-worker might cheer him up and renew his conviction.

It did, but not in the way he'd expected.

"I'm still very concerned about Fromm's loyalty. Are you absolutely *sure* that he can be trusted?" Haeften said, as he passed Stauff the salt and pepper.

And sprinkling a liberal helping of both over his steak and mashed potato, Stauff felt sure enough to reply all too flippantly:

"Don't worry about Fromm. Just don't tell him about our plans to abolish the existing military structure and *his* position in it, and you can speak to him quite openly about anything."

Haeften, however, was not fooled by Stauff's bravado. It went nowhere near hiding the fact that his nerves were red raw. Although still handsome, his face was showing the strain. This last year had aged him ten, with its series of failed strategies, intense stress and on-going battles of conscience. He was exhausted—completely wrung out, both physically and emotionally. It was little wonder, considering what he had on his plate.

As it turned out, what he had on his plate was to be the deciding factor.

The dilemma of how Count von Stauffenberg was meant to cut up his steak with only his three-fingered left hand became the subject of hot debate between the von Haeften's head cook and his housekeeper.

Both, as die-hard Nazis, were bowled over by the fact that the famous Stauffenberg was actually sitting at their table. They were so besotted by his person and presence that they were both vying shamelessly for his attention—going hammer and tongs to take him under their motherly wing.

Their bickering over which of them should be allowed to lavish their attention on him quickly picked up momentum and ferocity. What had begun as light-hearted banter between two dignified women soon spiraled into a jealous, vicious-mouthed frenzy. Their crude, Nazi *"give-me-that-it's-mine"* habits had them actually resort to shoving each other out of the way, in a full-on brawl over which one of them should cut up Stauffenberg's steak.

The man in question, quite able to do the deed himself, chose instead to sit back and watch the show. Marvelling at the swift transformation of so-called civilized human beings into primeval hissing harpies. The two women revved up to such a fever pitch that they were quite ready to rip out each other's eyes to gain his favour.

Neither of them, in their savage eagerness to degrade themselves, had a clue that they were actually fighting to put food in the mouth of the man who was just about to deprive *them* of their life-blood. These handmaidens of Hitler, Stauffenberg realized, were the perfect example of Germany's Godless deterioration—products of the Nazi War Machine and just two of the defective millions being spat off its assembly line.

Their live, passionate performance of *"Our Country's Gone To Hell"*, left no doubt in Stauffenberg's mind that it was time to flick the switch and turn Hitler off for good.

Despite his brave conviction and determination to "go it alone", however, he was very glad when Canaris turned up unexpectedly at his door on the eve of the assassination attempt. The hours of July 19, 1944, had hung very heavily, and been fraught with tension. When he opened the door, it came as a great reassurance to find the little Admiral standing there offering his support.

"I do hope you don't mind me dropping in uninvited like this?" Canaris said, working hard at lightening what was quite obviously Stauff's very dark mood. "But I thought you just might fancy a bit of company with your last supper."

And *that*, Stauff did.

Not that he felt much like eating, but he was craving a good cigar and a little bit of table talk—*anything* to divert his attention and get him through the long, difficult night.

It was exactly what Canaris had supposed, when on the spur of the moment, he had doubled back on his tracks to go elsewhere, and decided to spend the time with Stauff instead. A combination of guilt and compassion for the man on whom they had all dumped the bulk of the dreadful responsibility compelled him to at least *share* some of its nail-biting last hours.[35]

"Oh . . . I'd half expected that Berthold and Annabel would be here," Canaris said as he hung up his trench coat and hat. A brief scan of the apartment's dimly-lit empty rooms told him that he and the Count were in fact alone.

"I sent them away. It all got a bit too much," Stauff admitted as he wandered over despondently to pour Canaris a brandy.

He was depressed, among others things, because he had not been given the opportunity to say goodbye to his wife and children. After all the years of the conspirators' procrastination—after all their endless fussing and fumbling around, they had suddenly issued him with a last minute, extremely urgent directive:

ALL STATIONS GO! TOMORROW—JULY 20, IS THE DAY!

That had given him just twenty-four hours notice and left him only enough time to contact his loved ones by phone, but half an hour before, when he'd picked up the receiver to do just that, his ear had met with nothing but dead air space—the telephone lines had just gone down in an Allied aerial attack. This unforeseen contingency effectively rendered him and his family *incommunicado*. Stauff supposed, in his fatalistic state of mind, that it would serve as a useful practice run for them in light of his imminent death.

It wasn't hard for Canaris to pick up on Stauff's morose mood. The gloomy vibes he was exuding were strong enough to make Canaris wonder whether he'd made a tactless mistake in coming.

"You must be honest with me Claus if you feel that I'm intruding," he said. "Would you prefer that I made myself scarce?"

"No . . . no, please don't misunderstand me," Stauff snapped back to his more normal optimistic self to say. "I can't tell you how grateful I am that you're here. Thank you for coming. I don't know . . . it's hard to explain, but somehow it's different with family. Much too much emotion involved. But with you . . . forgive me for saying . . . well, the very distance between us, gives me comfort."

This had been Canaris' hope—that they could just sit as casual friends for a few hours, passing the time and tension in each other's company. At the onset of their night of good conversation, cognac and cigars, Canaris became curious to know:

"Did they take it well? Berthold and Annabel, I mean, when you sent them away?"

"My brother understood," Stauff replied.

But Annabel had *not*, Canaris surmised when Stauff then fell silent, making it clear that he had no intention of answering the other half of the question. The look of pained resolve on his face said far more than words.

The truth was that Stauff couldn't bring himself to talk about it. The memory of the inconsolable expression on Annabel's face when they had said goodbye made him incapable of opening his lips to speak.

That look had not been one of love, but of despair—tears of misunderstanding and unimaginable hurt welling in her eyes. A hurt that he'd inflicted on her quite deliberately:

"We have no need of you any longer," he'd said, straight to her face the day before.

It had been an unforgivable thing for him to say and he knew it, but it was something that *had* to be said when he knew that *nothing* . . . not even the threat of death would make her leave his side if she were aware of the impending danger he was in.

Her leaving his side was a must now that their conspiracy plans had become reality and he'd been given the definite date for Hitler's assassination. The truth was that the odds of his own survival were nigh on non-existent.

"But what do you mean?" she'd answered in stunned disbelief. His use of the royal plural—"we"—had done a pretty poor job of covering the fact that he was speaking for himself and himself alone. "I thought . . ."

That was where he'd stopped her by putting his finger gently to her lips. Because she had not needed to say it, when he'd known *exactly* what she thought . . . that they loved each other and that she would follow him to the ends of the Earth if he asked her to.

It was a fact which had left him no option but to be utterly brutal in order to save her life.

"I *mean* . . . that I am finished with you. Do you understand?"

What was there *not* to understand in those cruel words? They had broken her heart, but only half as much as it had broken *his* to watch her go. Claus having to suffer the final blow of having her turn her tear-stained face to him just one last time, before she closed the door. Her deep blue, searching eyes begging for a response . . . for an explanation in his.

It had taken every bit of his courage to keep his expression cold and emotionless at that poignant moment before she'd shut the door and walked out of his life. His only hope was that after his death she would understand his reasons and the depth of love on his part that had driven him to do it.

For the time being, however, his feelings had to remain a mystery, both to Annabel and to Canaris, whose acute understanding of human frailties had stopped him pressing Stauff for an answer on the Annabel situation.

Besides, it was more important that they talk business. Essential that they spend the upcoming hours running over and over their plans for the next day until they had them down pat, making sure that they had accounted for all Stauff's movements towards, in and away from Wolf's Lair—that every second . . . every possible contingency had been covered.

At the crack of dawn on July 20, Canaris wound up the conversation with one last little piece of advice.

"And make sure you wear something warm," he said.

The furrowing of his brow in concern over Stauff catching a cold, when he was more likely to catch a bullet in the back, made Stauff laugh out loud. Canaris' comment was just the tonic he needed to settle his stomach.

"Good God man . . . it's the middle of summer—*forty degrees* outside! What do you want to do . . . kill me?"

"No . . . just make sure that you stay in good health to kill Hitler."

This, Stauff was now de-sensitized enough to do.

"Come on . . . I'll drive you home," he said, as he got up and handed Canaris his coat.

It never ceased to amaze him, as it did everyone else, that the little Admiral insisted on wearing it, no matter what the season.

"I can walk. It's not necessary to give me a lift."

"Yes, but it's necessary for *me*. I have to make a stop on the way."

Stauff made that stop directly in front of St Hedwig's Catholic Cathedral.

"You don't mind if I pop in for a few minutes do you?" he said as he pulled on his Mercedes' handbrake and twisted it into "lock".

"No, not at all."

"Perhaps you'd like to come with me?" Stauff suggested.

"*Yes, perhaps I would,*" Canaris thought, given that the time was ripe for him, too, to find peace of mind.

Even though it had been a long time between church visits for him, he was every bit as devout a Christian as Stauff. Devout enough to take only two steps into the Cathedral before he decided to back out of it—his cynicism and mission in life somehow still at odds with his concept of God and His forgiveness.

Although he'd taken on that mission of his in God's name, he still wasn't entirely convinced that his years of conniving against evil and the methods he'd employed to combat it were not an offence against Him.

So he let Stauff go in alone; choosing to wait for him outside in the musty, bible-bedecked vestibule. There Canaris stood and watched patiently through the glass-paneled doors as the young man, with such an enormous load on his shoulders, knelt in front of the altar.

The grand and glorious Stauffenberg, at this terrifying time, was in dire need of his God's condonation and strength, and unlike the ever-questioning Canaris, was blessed with his blind faith in God's power to provide.

CHAPTER THIRTY-THREE

As arranged, Stauffenberg arrived at Rangsdorf Airfield at 7.00am to find his Special Missions officer—von Haeften—waiting for him. So far, so good. Their timing was of the essence.

Haeften, however, was on edge. As soon as Stauff's car circled to a stop on the tarmac, he rushed over to open its door. The urgent look in his clear green eyes instantly telling Stauff that there was something wrong.

"Our plane hasn't turned up," he said.

"What's the problem?"

"Fog . . . it's the damn fog. It's delayed all flights," Haeften answered—his words picking up pace in panic.

Stauff put a steadying hand on his Lieutenant's arm as he quickly scanned the airfield to see what other planes might be made available to them at a pinch. But the paltry display of four battered, bullet-ridden Messerschmitts midway through repair, didn't give him much hope of falling back on a plan B.

Still, it wasn't time, as yet, to give up on plan A.

"Don't worry. The fog will lift. The plane will get here. Keep your cool."

It was easier said than done, when Stauff himself was fighting hard to keep his own fears at bay. Being the superstitious man he was, this *strike one* against them so early in the piece didn't augur well—but it was too late to turn back now.

Fortunately, it wasn't necessary to do so. Their courier plane arrived ten minutes later to wing them off to Rastenburg—arrival time: 10.15 am.

It had amounted to just a half hour delay in their schedule that could be easily swallowed up along with their morning tea—that cup of coffee with cake that Stauff and Haeften had been booked in to share with the headquarters' Commandant's Staff.

The mess hall in which it was served was situated in the outer ring of Hitler's *Wolf's Lair* compound—commonly known as Perimeter 2. This was a military base in itself with its collection of well-regimented barracks, sandbag barricades and air raid shelters that stood as a preliminary checkpoint for all those who wished to enter the higher security Perimeter 1—Hitler's more heavily fortified inner sanctum.

Perimeter 2 was intended as a shakedown station for those visitors who came uninvited. Its proliferation of uniformed guards with their impressive array of "frisking" facilities was enough to deter the hardiest of souls from entering the unholy hub of Nazi operations.

Stauffenberg had been permitted entry to that core of military control only once before, which had given him all the opportunity he needed to study its surrounds. To take note of the innocuous looking hut that housed Hitler and his henchmen; to be impressed by its ground-hugging, wood and cement structure that cleverly belied its strategic importance as Hitler's stronghold; and to look with satisfaction at its thick concrete ceiling and steel-shuttered windows, both of which would be a real plus when his bomb went off. The closely-confined, sealed quarters were a guarantee of optimum impact—of a sure kill.

At this point, getting *in* to the maximum security complex wasn't Stauff's concern. It was getting *out* that posed the problem. The whole forbidding, tightly-knit compound was fenced off with row upon row of barbed wire barriers—studded, at very regular intervals, with savage, salivating contingents of fang-bearing dogs and SS guards. Both men and mongrels, to Stauff's way of thinking, were one and the same. No point in laying bets on which of the two feral species was the more ferocious.

Whereas he had a *Pass to Enter* that would ensure their phalanx-like formations parting to let him through like Moses and his Red Sea, he knew they wouldn't be so eager to stand aside and let him leave after the Big Bang.

The way it was, however, Stauff had no choice but to go ahead as planned and play it by ear. With any luck, he would be long gone and on his way back to Berlin before the bomb exploded and the SS got wise to the fact that it was he who had set it off.

It was at 11.30am that the show got under way. Stauff, with

his bomb-bearing briefcase, set out on his way to the preliminary meeting which was to be chaired by Keitel, until Hitler turned up at 12.30 to host the main event. It was going to be a pressure-packed two hours, at the onset of which von Haeften's tension was palpable as he walked stiffly at Stauff's side.

"Settle down! You're as nervous as a cat," Stauff whispered urgently to his Lieutenant, doing so from the corner of his mouth so that no one could detect that his lips had even moved.

That was until he made a *point* of moving them into a broad, handsome smile, throwing *it*, along with a rather flamboyant salute, to the two SS sentries stationed at Perimeter 1's gates. Both of them, in response, were quick to open the wooden barriers in welcome.

"See, that wasn't so hard," he muttered to Haeften after they had cleared both gates and guards. "Bluff it out man . . . take the offensive. Soldiers are less suspicious of it you know."

They were sensible words of advice that had Haeften lift his game—booting his confidence up a level by taking a deep breath and lengthening his stride, not realizing that he was cruelling his pitch by holding so tight to the brown paper package Stauff had asked him to carry. He was clinging on to the hessian string that was binding it together as if his life depended on it.

To an enormous degree, it did . . . even though it contained nothing more controversial than a fresh change of shirt—a starched cotton item that Stauff had insisted he needed for the meeting.

This wasn't for reasons of vanity, but because it gave him the perfect excuse to absent himself from it, so that he could set the fuse on the bomb. His need to change his shirt was a ploy that would justify privacy and call for Haeften's assistance.

Everyone would naturally assume that the crippled Stauffenberg would need his Lieutenant's fully-functional, ten-fingered hands to help him dress. None of them would suspect that those ten fingers, with the help of Stauff's remaining three, would be frantically fiddling with fuses rather than doing up shirt buttons.

Before this plan of theirs went into effect, however, there were to be two stumbling blocks in their way—one apiece for Haeften and Stauff.

Stauff tripped over his first when he was greeted by Keitel's

Adjutant, Major John von Freyend.

As one of *War Hero Stauffenberg's* greatest fans, the Major was intent on bending over backwards to accommodate him. He couldn't understand why a man of the Count's calibre . . . of his courage and fine reputation (not to mention the handicap of only having half a hand and three fingers), should be expected to carry his own luggage.

"Please, sir," he raced over to say. "Let me carry your briefcase for you."

Freyend's unforeseen act of courtesy kick-started Stauff's heart into full gallop. It was only his quick thinking that overrode panic mode and countered his impulse to pull the case abruptly out of von Freyend's reach. Stauff's astonishing presence of mind, had him pass it instead, quite casually, to the Major with his thanks and audible sigh of relief. It was an award-winning performance that, for the time being, allayed all suspicion.

He had to struggle, however, to keep that fake calm demeanor of his in place for the tense ten minutes it took Freyend to carry the briefcase proudly into the meeting room. The cocksure bounce in the Major's step made the case swing from side to side, and that galloping heart of Stauff's catch in his throat, but he managed to carry off the dramatic little incident without breaking a sweat.

Haeften wasn't so lucky. *His* forehead was sprinkled with beads of it, twenty minutes later, when Keitel's meeting was in full swing.

Of course, as a junior officer, he had not been invited into it, but Stauff had asked him to remain close at hand in the corridor outside. Haeften had been doing so, refraining from checking his watch every minute, for fear of giving himself and his acute anxiety away, while at the same time not being aware that his fingers, tapping anxiously on the brown paper parcel at his side, were doing just that—their rhythmic drumming becoming fast and furious enough to attract Sergeant Hans Vogel's attention. This particularly hard-arsed member of Keitel's staff had grown very suspicious of the Lieutenant sitting alone and very much on edge in the corridor.

"Is that yours?" he walked over to ask Haeften, pointing at the parcel—his question more accusation than query.

Too shocked to take advantage of his senior rank—to take

offence, as a Lieutenant, to the Sergeant's dictatorial tone—
Haeften made the mistake of faltering in his reply. The stutter that
had not afflicted him since childhood came back with a vengeance
to haunt him now.

"It's Colonel C. . . Count von Stauffenberg's. He'll be ne . . .
needing it for his presentation to Hit . . . Hi . . . *Hitler* when he
arrives."

The explanation, albeit stammered, should have sufficed,
but Haeften sensed that the NCO was not satisfied, even though
he turned with what seemed to be a placated smile to stroll back
to his desk. Haeften's better instinct, however, warned him that
Vogel's blue-collar, bully-boy hackles had been raised. He was on
the alert and dangerous.

There was no time to ponder the problem when soon after
came Haeften's call to action. Stauff walked out of the Briefing
Room and signaled for his Special Missions officer to follow him.

"Where can I freshen up and change my shirt?" Stauff asked
directly of Sergeant Vogel, who was still hovering, sly-eyed, in the
vicinity.

Vogel, responding as he *should* to Stauff's voice of authority,
had instantly obliged by showing both him and Haeften to a
vacant sitting room, a few doors further down the corridor.

Finally they were alone.

Stauff closed the door while Haeften quickly snapped open the
metal clasps on the briefcase, taking out of it the two 975g lumps
of German plastic explosives, along with the two British primer
charges that they had put in each of them. In one lump, both
primer charges had thirty-minute fuses; in the other, only one.

It was important that *both* lumps of explosives were used to
do the job if it were to be decisive. Their objective was to kill
everyone in the Briefing Room. Not because they relished the idea
of wholesale slaughter, but because they couldn't be sure of Hitler's
precise positioning at the time of the bomb's detonation.

The only way to ensure his death was to make a clean sweep
of the entire area. Stauff had to close his eyes and conscience to
those few men in the room who he knew didn't deserve to die.
His reassurance being that theirs would be a sacrifice to match
his own for the good of the Fatherland.

Haeften looked at his watch: 12.28.

"Hitler will be in the Briefing Room in couple of minutes."

It was a reminder that Stauff didn't need as he frantically fiddled to attach the right red, green and black wires with a pair of pliers. The handle had been bent to accommodate his three fingers, but, accommodated or not, they were not moving fast enough to suit his purpose.

"Here, let me do it," Haeften said anxiously, reaching out to take over. Stauff wouldn't have a bar of it.

"*I* am the assassin . . . ," he insisted. "From this responsibility, I *order* you to distance yourself."

And so Stauff continued with his hand shaking and sweat dripping down the side of his cheek, knowing that he had to remove the fuses from the primer charges and squeeze the copper casings to break the glass vials inside, so that the acid could seep into the cotton enveloping the retaining wires. A false angle of pressure or too *much* pressure might break the wire instead of it being slowly corroded to produce a calculated delay.

After this he had to determine, through a tiny inspection hole, that the spring with the striker-pin was still compressed; remove a safety bolt and then re-insert the fuses into the primer charges.

All the while he kept telling himself that he could do it . . . *he could do it* . . . and do it fast enough to keep them smack on schedule.

Perhaps he could have done, had his fellow conspirator not stuffed it up for him at the crucial moment.

Stauff had not counted on the fact that General Erich Fellgiebel's anticipated phone call from Perimeter 2 would throw their plans into chaos. Not when that very phone call had been strategically intended to streamline them.

Fellgiebel, as Chief of the Army Signal Corps, had worked closely with Stauff on their plans to cut off all forms of communication from Wolf's Lair, to coincide with the bomb's explosion. It was an isolation tactic that would help delay any hostile reactions to Hitler's death back in Berlin.

Fellgiebel's pre-planned telephone call was to be Stauff's mid-conference excuse to leave Hitler's Briefing Room after he had placed the bomb. No one would question the fact that Stauff was duty-bound to return the General's call.

The problem was that Fellgiebel's initial telephone call had come just a couple of minutes too early . . .

"I'm afraid Colonel Stauffenberg is not available," Major von Freyend informed Fellgiebel, having answered the phone in Keitel's office.

Hanging up, he called out his order to Sergeant Vogel.

"Quick as you can Vogel . . . get down the corridor and let Stauffenberg know that General Fellgiebel has phoned and wants him to return his call a.s.a.p. And while you're at it . . . for *God's sake*, tell Stauffenberg and Haeften to hurry up! Hitler's already here and he's waiting for him."

* * *

"Who is it?" Stauffenberg demanded when Vogel knocked at the door—his tone more agitated than he'd intended.

It was agitated enough for Vogel to smell a rat—to choose not to answer, but to open the door instead. But he was frustrated in his hope of catching the two men out at whatever they were up to, when the movement of the door was impeded by Stauffenberg's back.

"It's Sergeant Vogel, sir," he was forced to answer, given that his entry to the room had been blocked.

"What do you want?" Stauffenberg asked—his words brusque and coming through that now semi-opened door, which only afforded Vogel a cropped picture of what was going on inside.

Enough for him to see that both Stauffenberg and Haeften were preoccupied with an object the Colonel was holding in his hand. As far as Vogel could make out . . . an object that looked nothing like a shirt button!

Who was he to question the great Count von Stauffenberg? When the time was right, he could do as much directly to General Keitel.

"Major von Freyend asked me to tell you that General Fellgiebel called and wants you to call him back. And also, if you'll forgive me, sir . . . to hurry up . . . that the Fuhrer is waiting for you."

Which meant that Stauff and Haeften had run out of time.

"That's it! We'll have to go with what we've got," Stauff said, carefully placing that one lump of primed plastic explosive back into his briefcase. He took an extra second to make sure that all was in order before he clicked shut the case's metal clasps.

"But will one lump of explosive be enough?" Haeften asked uneasily.

"We've got no choice . . . it'll have to be. *Damn* Fellgiebel's lousy timing . . . *damn* Vogel for interrupting. You'd better get on your way Haeften and make certain that my car's out there ready for us to make a quick getaway to the airfield."

It was an order to which Haeften dutifully responded by turning quickly to go, but as his hand reached out to open the door, he stopped dead in his tracks. In all the panic and commotion, the reality had suddenly hit him that he may never see his friend Stauff again.

"Will you be all right?" he asked, not knowing what else to say at this poignant moment, when it would have been far more appropriate to say so much more. Meaningful, heartfelt things like:

> *Take care of yourself dear friend.*
> *I admire you above any other*
> *man I know . . . God go with you.*

But the slightly shy-cum-roguish smile on Stauff's face told him that it wasn't necessary . . . that he understood:

"Your guess is as good as mine. But don't worry about me . . . you should know by now that I'm indestructible!"

*   *   *

That was certainly the impression he gave the other officers in the Briefing Room when he entered it.

The dauntless Count Claus von Stauffenberg—the classical image of a warrior, with his dashing black eye-patch and empty uniform sleeve, standing tall and straight and looking directly— *unflinchingly* at Hitler.

"Ah . . . my dear Count Claus . . . how good to see you," Hitler stopped mid-speech to say. Immediately, he directed General Heusinger, who was standing next to him at the map table, to relinquish his place so that his new-found favourite—Stauffenberg, could take it.

Which made it all the easier, Stauff thought, as he accepted Hitler's kind invitation to stand so close. It gave him the perfect opportunity to place his briefcase on the floor as flush up to the

Fuhrer as possible. Unfortunately he was unable to manouevre it beyond the massive table support that stood between the case and Hitler's leather-booted legs.

Near enough was surely good enough, Stauff told himself now that the countdown had begun. Ten minutes down . . . with only twenty left to go before the bomb exploded. Stauff sat in on the meeting for a further five of them, so as not to arouse suspicion. After which he beckoned to Major von Freyend.

"Be kind enough to get General Fellgiebel on the line for me will you Major," he said.

He had chosen the perfect moment to excuse himself from the room—Hitler's attention having finally turned from him, back to the Reich's military strategies. The Fuhrer was so engrossed in the ways of his war that, as he leant over the map table to explain them, his body was lying almost flush to its surface. It was a happy coincidence that would provide him with a shield against the upcoming bomb blast.

It was an awkward position that only facilitated him patting Stauff briefly on the arm in acknowledgement of his excuse for leaving. Stauff had to indulge in the intimacy of bending over, with his hand resting on Hitler's shoulder, to whisper that excuse in his ear.

When he reached the outer office, Major von Freyend handed him the phone.

"General Fellgiebel on the line for you, sir," he said, before immediately returning to the Briefing Room.

Stauff waited for him to close the door and get out of sight before he promptly put the receiver back down without saying a word into it, knowing full well that Fellgiebel was no longer listening on the other end of the line. He and Haeften were, in fact, waiting for him outside, distancing themselves from the bomb's repercussion and getting in position for a quick getaway after its explosion.

Stauff took a moment before he joined them to remove his peaked cap and leather belt—throwing both items of military apparel on the floor of the Briefing Room's outer office. A small decoy, that in the frenzied aftermath of the bomb would divert suspicion from himself . . . at least for a while.

Logic would tell the SS squads in their preliminary analysis of the bomb site that *he too* was dead, an assumption which would give him and Haeften enough time to get clear of Wolf's Lair and get on the plane back to Berlin, as he'd promised Canaris he would do.

It was twelve minutes later that the bomb exploded. Stauff, Haeften and Fellgiebel were unable to avoid the kneejerk reaction they had to it. Although standing in the compound, bracing themselves for the blast—the sound and impact of it, when it actually *did* happen, nearly knocked them off their feet—its aftershock *slammed* their teeth and jaws into "lock" and reverberated through their bodies' every fibre.

Amid the surprise and confusion, the sirens and screaming, they knew they had to linger long enough to make sure that their deed had been done. In the meantime, they feigned concern and involvement in the chaos at hand, while keeping a keen eye on the medics and ambulance staff who were running to and from the scene of carnage.

With bated breath, they waited until, at last, they saw those two stretcher-bearers emerge from the smoke and flames. Both medics' mouths were covered with makeshift masks to stop from choking on the dust and debris, and the blood-soaked stretcher they had in hand bore the burnt remains of a man's body.

The reverence with which they carried it and the fact that it was covered with Hitler's own coat told the assassins that they could rest easy—that they had done their job.

"He's dead!" Fellgiebel said to Stauffenberg—his teeth gritted in pale-faced triumph, sick as he had been for six long years from the stench of death and Hitler's reign of terror. "You and Haeften must go *right now*. Take advantage of the confusion and go quickly. You can rest assured that I've seen to it that communications are down between here and Berlin for the next few hours."

"It feels wrong to leave you here alone. Are you sure you won't come with us?" Stauff said as he got into his Staff car and held open the door in the hope that Fellgiebel might change his mind, get in, and leave with them.

It was out of the question—each of them had a job to do.

"Don't concern yourselves. I'm in no danger. You must remember that they'll be needing me to restore communications. I'll be extremely sought after and busy for hours and hours trying to get them up and running again. You can count on that. So *go*

. . . and go like the wind!"

What *Fellgiebel* had not counted on, however, was to see Hitler walk alive and well out of the burning ruins.

Just two minutes after Staufftenberg and Haeften had sped off in their car to carry the news of his death to Berlin, Fellgielbel had reached for a cigarette, but stopped midway through lighting it to look up in dismay. He couldn't believe his eyes when he saw the Fuhrer emerge from the smoke and ashes like the proverbial phoenix. Not stumbling or gasping for breath, but striding from the bomb-induced bloodbath with nothing but a shaking left hand and shattered eardrum for having had the experience.

The Devil incarnate was still in possession of all his limbs and faculties, whereas at that mind-numbing moment, Fellgielbel had all but lost his. In shock and stark terror, he was unable to speak or to feel his own legs beneath him. Realizing that with communications down, he was unable to let Stauffenberg know. The Count was blithely on his way to initiate a *coup d'etat* in Berlin that was destined to fail before it started. Worse still . . . it was *they*—the conspirators—whose heads were going to roll instead of Hitler's.

In blissful, albeit anxiety-packed ignorance, Stauffenberg and Haeften were making good their escape. Their staff car passing through checkpoints one, two . . . and three, without the slightest hitch.

In the confusion, none of the guards thought to bar their way, when it was logical that all Nazis of note were making themselves scarce on the Fuhrer's or Keitel's orders. The Third Reich simply couldn't afford the loss of any more high ranking officers when Wolf's Lair was under what they assumed to be a full scale Allied attack.

Stauff and Haeften's only moment of alarm was when one of those SS Guards—panic-stricken and disoriented in the midst of the danger—stopped their car and hammered on its windscreen. With his eyes wide in demented disbelief, he screamed out the question:

"Is he dead . . . is he dead . . . Is our Fuhrer *dead?*"

And calmly winding down his window, Stauffenberg said:

"Yes . . . Long Live Germany!"

CHAPTER THIRTY-FOUR

He answered the same to all who asked when he got back to Berlin at 4.30pm, the most sceptical of whom was General Fromm.

"Are you sure?" Fromm asked, having heard rumours to the contrary not long before. The speculation over whether Hitler was alive or dead had had him take the precaution of closing his office door to speak more privately to Stauffenberg and Haeften.

"*Of course* I'm sure! I saw Hitler's body myself," Stauffenberg snapped back at him.

He was angry. After all he'd been through, it was wrong that they should question his word. Because they all *had*, he sensed that something was askew. Ever since he'd arrived at the *Bendlerstrasse*,[36] there had been a strange atmosphere hanging over the whole Military Headquarters. The building's normally up-tempo environment was ominously quiet. The eerie silence pervading its long, empty corridors was most unsettling.

Not that Stauff had exactly expected a fanfare on his return from his successful mission, but he'd thought there might be just a *whiff* of support from his fellow conspirators. Instead, the mood was dark and menacing—menacing enough to put him on the alert and to make the hairs on the back of his neck stand to attention. His hardy, soldier's instinct having him counter his fear with an outburst of anger.

"So where in the *hell* was Corporal Schweizer when we needed him? It was arranged that he meet us at Rangdorf Airfield, but he didn't even bother to show up. He just left Haeften and me high and dry—stranded in the middle of nowhere. We actually had to borrow someone *else's* staff car for the privilege of getting back here to set the coup in motion. Just a tad slapdash at such a pivotal point in time, don't you think? So much for the *Grand Plan!*"

Fromm, however, chose not to challenge Stauff's attack;

merely shrugging his shoulders in response.

"Perhaps your driver—Schweizer—got wind of the same rumours that reached me? Perhaps he's running scared? Perhaps we *all* should be."

"But this is ridiculous! Haeften, Fellgiebel and I . . . we *all* saw Hitler's body. There's absolutely no doubt he's dead."

* * *

Back at Wolf's Lair, however, there was absolutely no doubt he was *alive*. General Fellgiebel had been summoned to the Telephone Exchange Bunker to be issued with his new orders.

"You are to close off all communication and prevent any information about the bomb and the Fuhrer's welfare from getting out without authorization," Keitel instructed him.

Fellgiebel saluted, taking heart from the fact that these new orders of his happily coincided with his old. That the two-to-three hour communication black-out he'd been ordered to impose had the mutual consent of both bomb survivors and conspirators.

"Does that apply to us all, sir?" he thought it prudent to ask.

"Don't be absurd man. Of course it doesn't," Keitel shot back at him. "It goes without saying and you and I *must* have an open line to Berlin at all times."

This was just fine by Fellgiebel, who now had the clearance to put through a desperate phone call to his associates waiting on tenterhooks at Berlin's *Bendlerstrasse*.

"Something terrible has happened," he whispered urgently to General Olbricht over the line. "The Fuhrer is alive!"

But the static over the wire was breaking up his words, its crackling staccato making every second one of them incomprehensible. Olbricht was only able to piece together those which seemed the most salient:

"*. . . terrible . . . is alive!*"

This had not been quite enough to go on, but certainly sufficient to instill the fear of God in them. Because for all their months of finely-tuned planning, the conspirators had made no provision for the assassination going wrong. Given the catastrophic scale of its failure, it was little wonder that its participants had begun to run helter-skelter to distance themselves from the plot and its consequences.

Every one of them knew that it was too late to turn back the clock when, two hours before, Colonel Mertz von Quirnheim, at General Olbricht's order, had implemented phase one of *Valkyrie* in all military districts of Berlin and its surrounds.

This meant that the formal announcement of Hitler's death had already been made and that the military forces had taken over all executive powers to maintain order. Further negotiations were already underway to incorporate the Waffen-SS into the army, while Field Marshal von Witzleben was en route to Berlin to take over as the new Wehrmacht Supreme Commander. In line with this, General Beck had formally assumed leadership of the State. So with their backs pressed hard up against the wall, the conspirators had no alternative but to proceed as planned on the very slim chance that they may still pull off their *putsch*. That is, if they had the guts to stick together—to be strong and brave enough to stand their ground and bully their way through to its successful conclusion.

In reality, though, there was little to no hope of that happening when they had never, at *any* point, been a firmly bonded band of brothers. Each of the three sects of the Resistance had always been too strong in itself and its own agenda to meld compliantly with the others.

Now that the proverbial had hit the fan, however, they were all in it together. Each and every one of them was tarred with the same brush and running for their lives. Very few of the conspirators were prepared to stand and fight . . . to even *try* to bluff it out. Not when they had seen Adolf Hitler in action and could make an educated guess at the vile methods of revenge to which he would subject them.

There were a brave few, however, who stood steady when in a tight spot. One was Colonel Mertz von Quirnheim, who was a great believer in taking the offensive as his best line of defence.

"I really *do* think it's imperative that we be bold and order the second phase of *Valkyrie*," he said for the third time to his superior officer, General Olbricht. "We have no choice, sir. Whether we like it or not, there's no looking back for us."

Olbricht, in a blind state of panic, was trying to do just that, not having heard a word his Chief of Staff had said.

"Do you think that it's too late for us to still deny any knowledge of the whole affair?" he turned, instead, to ask of his co-conspirator.

Mertz von Quirnheim could only respond with a resigned smile.

"Yes Olbricht, I do. Besides, do you honestly think that you could live with yourself knowing that you'd betrayed your friends when they needed you? With that in mind, sir, I must ask you to reconsider . . . will you *please* give me the go-ahead to implement phase 2."

Olbricht had not answered him. Stark terror had led the General to relinquish all power and complicity. His impotence left Mertz von Quirnheim no option but to implement phase 2 *without* his superior officer's sanction.

He did so at 4.30 when he heard that Stauffenberg and Haeften had made it back safely to Berlin. Their escape from Wolf's Lair and their unscathed presence back in the capital had given the conspirators renewed hope that Hitler *was indeed* dead, and that the rumours of his survival had been nothing but propaganda.

It was a ray of hope that had Olbricht make a remarkable recovery—snapping back to his senses to wholeheartedly agree with the initiative Mertz von Quirnheim had taken. In such a positive frame of mind, he went with Quirnheim, Stauffenberg and Haeften to confront General Fromm. The four delegates were intent on either requesting or demanding Fromm's official ratification of coup proceedings.

"No! I will *not* give my approval to go any further with the coup," Fromm said, surprising them all with his uncharacteristic decisiveness. None of them had ever heard Fromm being so emphatic or so sure of himself.

"But why ever not?" Stauffenberg asked. "Hitler's dead. And I'm living proof of it—right *here* in Berlin to testify to it. I saw them carry out the burnt remains of his body on a stretcher. *Don't* back out on us now Fromm . . . not when the coup is on track."

"*Is* it indeed?" Fromm replied, looking much like the cat who had swallowed the canary, as he lolled back nonchalantly in his chair. "Do you know who I was speaking to on the phone when the four of you burst into my office?"

Supposing it to be a rhetorical question, none of them opened their lips to speak. They assumed, quite correctly, that Fromm would provide the answer.

"It was General Keitel, letting me know that, although slightly wounded, Hitler is *most definitely* alive."

Stauffenberg instantly brushed the statement aside.

"Keitel is lying as usual," he threw back at Fromm with contempt.

"And we all *know* that Stauffenberg doesn't," Olbricht put in, now very much back in form. "That's exactly why we activated *Valkyrie* when he heard he'd returned to Berlin. Do you honestly think that if Stauffenberg had failed in his mission to kill Hitler, he himself would still be alive?"

At this point, there was no talking Fromm round. Having sat on the fence for so long, he'd finally chosen sides, falling in favour of the Fuhrer at the eleventh hour, in the hope of dissociating himself from the Resistance and what he suspected was to be its members' horrific punishment. It was just for dramatic effect that he slammed his fist down hard on his desk—a physical gesture that rammed home his betrayal of his friends:

"This is high treason and carries the death penalty!" he stated. "I want to know *exactly* who it was who issued the orders for *Valkyrie*."

Without hesitation, Mertz von Quirnheim stepped forward to take full responsibility—effectively lifting the burden from Olbricht's shoulders.

"It was I, sir," he admitted, for a fleeting second shaming both Fromm and Olbricht with his courage.

Fromm was quick to wave away that show of courage, along with his own disgrace.

"Not that it matters which of you is *physically* responsible, when each of you is equally guilty. I am therefore placing you *all* under arrest."

Fromm had at last laid his cards on the table and demanded that they now play their hand. Knowing that he'd been dealt a raw deal, Stauffenberg had no choice but to bluff it out.

"On the contrary Fromm . . . ," he said, stepping forward to take the lead. "It is *you* who are under arrest."

It was an affront to which Fromm could only scoff.

"You are delusional Stauffenberg. The assassination attempt

has failed and you must shoot yourself."

Fromm presented the option, along with his handgun, to streamline the process, but neither the option nor the means of taking it up were in the least bit appealing to Stauffenberg.

"If you don't mind, I think I shall decline your kind invitation," he replied, quite unperturbed.

This infuriated Fromm beyond words. Knocking over his chair as he leapt up from it, he strode towards Stauffenberg with his fists raised. At which friction-fraught point, Haeften made *his* play in defence of his friend, by barring Fromm's way and holding his *own* loaded pistol to the General's stomach.

"I think that we should all just calm down," he said, with an authority most commendable coming from a Lieutenant to a General. The clout and commonsense of his words had Fromm stand at ease, while giving Stauffenberg the cue to issue his ultimatum.

"We will give you five minutes, General, to decide whether you are with us or against us . . . whether or not you'll join the uprising."

At this all four officers left Fromm alone to consider his verdict. Olbricht returned those five minutes later to find that the General had placed his gun and holster, as a token of surrender, on his desk.

"I regard myself as relieved of my command authority," Fromm said, as he voluntarily submitted himself and his Special Missions officer, Captain Heinz-Ludwig Bartram, to be placed under guard in the adjoining office.

CHAPTER THIRTY-FIVE

In the meantime, General Beck had arrived at the *Bendlerstrasse*. The grim expression on his face told Stauffenberg that the game was up.

He sat down opposite Stauff at his desk, loosened his tie and looked up with a tisk of contempt at the life-size portrait of Hitler looming over them. Was he or was he not imagining the gloating expression on the Fuhrer's painted face? What appeared to be a triumphant smirk under his tiny black moustache, quickly bringing Beck back to his point.

"I've just received a telephone call from General Stieff," he said. "He informed me, in no uncertain terms, that Hitler is *definitely* still alive and that *he*, Stieff, will be forthwith withdrawing his membership from the Resistance and denying all knowledge and support of us. Apparently, he has no qualms about betraying his associates. But I'm sure his cowardice won't get him far. Hitler is very thorough in his methods and I doubt very much that he'll let his little *'poisonous dwarf'* off the hook."

Stieff's welfare was of no concern to Stauffenberg, who had long since lost all trust in the man's courage and integrity. What was uppermost in his mind, in light of what Beck had just said, was that he himself had failed to save friends and Fatherland. What he had seen as being his God-given mission on Earth—his life's crusade—had amounted to *nothing* and been easily sabotaged by the forces of evil. The strength of this force had undermined his faith—that promise of God's power and protection on which he'd always relied.

"So the monster isn't dead after all," Stauff replied. "But the machine is still running. One can't yet say how it will go, given that Home Army Command has already proclaimed a Military Government here in Berlin."

This comment made Beck suddenly sit up erect in his chair, wide-eyed and astonished.

"Your communications have slipped up, Stauffenberg," he said. "You don't *know* that Major Remer's been the fly in the ointment and put an end to all hopes of our *Valkyrie Plan* being successful?"

"Major Remer! What in the hell has *he* got to do with it? He's just some low-life, Nazi Party prick . . . *hardly* a man of consequence."

"Well no, he wasn't . . . not until Goebbels *made* him into one, half an hour ago."

"What do you mean?"

"I *mean* that Remer is now a Colonel . . . and a very effective one. I *mean* that we made a terrible mistake in not arresting Goebbels and seizing his propaganda Ministry when we had the chance. Lord knows, it would have been easy enough, considering he's the only senior Minister on deck in Berlin at the moment. But as it happens, we weren't that clever and he's singlehandedly managed to turn the tables on us."

"Why? What's he done . . . and what's it got to do with Remer?"

"Everything! When Goebbels saw the units of the Reserve Army carrying out our *Valkyrie* orders down in the streets, he went straight out into them and pulled Major Remer aside. You have to hand it to Goebbels—he's got guts and he knows how to get action . . . and how to get it *fast!* Apparently he recognized Remer as one of his Nazi loyalists, and dragged him off duty and into his Ministry offices, so that the Major could speak directly to Hitler over the phone. It was one sure-fire way of putting an end to all the conjecture about whether or not Hitler was still alive and kicking."

"But how do you know all this?"

"From Stieff of course. He was in Rastenburg with Hitler when he was speaking on the phone to Remer. He reported their conversation to me verbatim."

Beck repeated it now for Stauffenberg's benefit.

"Do you recognize my voice?" Hitler asked Remer.

According to Stieff, Remer responded by throwing a salute and shouting an exuberant *Heil Hitler* into the mouthpiece. He was ecstatic, no doubt, to know that the Fuhrer was alive and that he had the privilege of speaking to him one-on-one.

That was a pretty big honour for a no-name grunt like Remer. Especially when Goebbels decided to add to the Major's joy by promoting him, *on the spot*, to the rank of Colonel!

The shrewd bastard shot the Major up the rungs of the military ladder to ensure his loyalty and to give Remer the authority to see to it that our *Valkyrie* orders were reversed and that the Home Army troops returned immediately to barracks. Remer reassured them all on their way back that their beloved Fuhrer was still at the helm—fit as a fiddle and breathing fire.

"Well that's that then," Stauff said getting up from his chair. He had no other recourse now but to be gracious in defeat.

"So it seems," Beck conceded. "We stuffed up big time in failing to take control of all broadcasting facilities. They were the key, and Goebbels knew it. He was smart enough to realize, before *we* did, that our plan really all hinged on getting through to the German people and bringing them on side. If we were to have any chance of success, we needed to get them all out into the streets to start a revolution. Power in numbers—that was the name of the game.

"Which is funny really, when you think about it. All our endless struggling with conscience and morality . . . all our high-minded preoccupation with upholding our honour and religious conviction, when it really all just hung on rounding up a lynching mob and scrounging up the support of the supremely fickle masses. Frankly, I don't think we should have bothered."

"We *had* to bother, and you know it . . . with or without the benefit of such hindsight," Stauffenberg replied, doing up the top button of his uniform jacket and putting on his peaked cap to ready himself for what was to come. If nothing else, he was determined to go out with dignity.

However, before he and Beck left the office to face their fate, Stauffenberg doubled back to make one quick, final phone call.

"Wait one moment will you Beck. I'll have to let Canaris know."

It was an afterthought that was quite unnecessary when Canaris was already fully apprised of the disastrous situation. As was Field Marshal Witzleben, who chose that precise moment to come storming into Stauffenberg's office.

"A fine mess this!" he said. In a red-faced rage, he was directing the full force of his criticism at Stauffenberg. "Whether Hitler is dead or not, the fact remains that neither the Capital nor the radio installations are in our hands. And that means that we're all dead meat!"

That was all that Witzleben had to say before he took his leave. In his wake, down the corridors of the *Bendlerstrasse,* was fast filtering the news that Hitler was alive. The validity and fear factor of the flash bulletin bolstered the courage of the many ambivalent staff officers on duty who had been lying low in their respective offices.

All of those officers were now suddenly determined to make a renewed show of their steadfast loyalty to the Fuhrer—to cast aside all semblance of integrity and gather together in a concentrated counter offensive within the Military Headquarters' walls.

Meanwhile, still under lock and key, Captain Bartram was making every effort to stir Fromm out of his lethargy—to urge him to rally his staff to Hitler's cause. A few offices further down, *Olbricht's* staff were similarly occupied. Having turned against their superior officer, they had grabbed up every submachine gun, pistol and grenade they could get their hands on, so as to confront Olbricht and demand Fromm's release.

It was when they were en route to free him that the gunfight began—the narrow hall that led to Fromm's makeshift cell, providing the venue for the conspirator's Last Stand. Its confined space—that only minutes before had been a silent, empty cavity within the *Bendlerstrasse's* walls—exploded into a full-on, kill-or-*be*-killed corridor of war.

So began an intense, marble-floored battlefield of hand-to-hand combat. Brother fighting against brother amid bullets, bayonets and blood-splattered walls. One of the shots fired at random ricocheted down the hall to hit hard, and go clean-through, Stauffenberg's left shoulder. Its high-velocity penetration spurted rivers of red down his uniform jacket and rendered the last of his trigger fingers useless.

This final war wound of his had Stauff reel and retreat into Fromm's office. General Beck, Olbricht, Mertz von Quirnheim and Haeften all backed into the same room to take refuge with him.

"They've all left us in the lurch," Stauff said, as he sat down heavily on the edge of Fromm's desk. His loss of blood, but more so his loss of faith in his fellow conspirators, had sucked the life out of him and left him on the brink of blacking out.

"Are you all right?" Haeften asked urgently as he saw his friend teeter. Rushing over, he used the full weight of his own body to stop Stauff from collapsing to the floor.

"Does it matter?" was Stauffenberg's fatalistic reply, as he looked up to see Fromm and his contingent of armed guards walk into the room.

"I am now going to do to you what you did to me," Fromm announced, with the conviction and courage of a man who no longer had to fight his own battles. "The five of you have been caught in the act of committing High Treason. You are under arrest. Please hand over your weapons."

This was something General Beck refused to do. In a passing moment of supreme courage he said, "Fromm . . . I would ask that you let me keep mine so that I can shoot myself."

Fromm saw no reason not to oblige the old General—sorely regretting his act of mercy soon after, when Beck's efforts to put an end to himself back-fired. *Three* times, Beck's shaking hand was on the verge, but failed to pull the trigger, which finally made the old General realize that he didn't have the guts to do it.

It was then that a spasm of intense nervous strain had him collapse to the floor—his convulsing body in the throes of an uncontrollable anxiety attack. It was premier performance of a man in acute distress to which Fromm paid no attention, turning it instead to his other four prisoners.

"Does anyone *else* have a final request?"

General Olbricht responded, as the only one willing to take Fromm up on his offer. He requested that he be given permission to write his final statement. A laborious project that lasted for an excruciatingly long and demoralizing half hour.

Throughout all this, Stauffenberg stood in angry, blood-soaked silence. The poignant sight of the once brave General Beck writhing on the floor, along with the sickening sound of his resigned whimpering, was rubbing salt into Stauffenberg's seeping wound. His pride wasn't allowing that wound or his *own* stark terror to weaken his resolve *or* his legs, which were threatening to give way under him.

All was lost, and he knew it, but he was determined to

stand his ground to the end. He had no intention of denying his crime, but rather sought to embrace that guilt, together with the loyalty to God and country which had obliged him to commit it. In the tense standoff, he decided at last to open his lips and speak in the vain hope that he might save his *friends'* lives.

"For all our actions, I assume complete responsibility. These other men have merely acted as soldiers under my command," he said to Fromm, who had been impatiently pacing the floor waiting for Olbricht to sign off on his own monumental, time-stalling eulogy.

Fromm didn't respond to Stauffenberg's eleventh-hour act of heroism—mainly because his own agenda was to free himself, as quickly as possible, from all connection with the conspiracy, and to rid himself of the threat of these few good men who could bear witness to it.

Their time was up, and having reached the end of his tether he walked over and ripped the pen out of Olbricht's hand.

"You are now finished!" he decreed, ordering Olbricht to get to his feet. He then opened the office door and stood aside, giving his silent order that the four men go through it and then proceed out into the *Bendlerstrasse* courtyard to be executed. Saying, as they walked past him, "As a matter of fact, you are *all* finished."

The words were cruel and unnecessary when all four men were fully aware that their lives were over. Stauffenberg and his compatriots—Olbricht, Mertz von Quirnheim and Haeften—calmly walked over to stand in front of the courtyard wall to be shot.

Fromm's order, "*Ready . . . aim . . . fire!*" was interrupted by the sound of Stauffenberg's voice as he shouted out:

"Long live our Holy Germany!"

PART THREE

CHAPTER THIRTY-SIX

The news of Stauffenberg's death brought Canaris to the brink of tears.

"He was only thirty-seven," he said when General Oster told him the awful news.

The all-too-vivid mental picture of the brave and brilliant Stauffenberg lying dead out in the cold was near impossible to bear. It made Canaris sick to his stomach and thoroughly ashamed of himself to know that those four young men had sacrificed their lives in his stead.

He need not have worried. Stauffenberg's, Olbricht's, Mertz von Quirnheim's and Haeften's summary court-martial and execution wasn't just that one isolated sacrifice on behalf of the conspirators, but merely the first in a series of horrific murders to come. An experience that Canaris was destined to share. No one . . . not even *he*, with his renown as the *Master of Espionage and Escape-Artist Extraordinaire*, had a chance of side-stepping Hitler's hell-bent retribution.

"But what about Beck?" he asked Oster, still not having completely pulled himself together—the slight tremor in his hands mimicking the nervous affliction that had troubled General Beck in the last few months.

It was just one of the reasons why Canaris was concerned for his old friend's frailty. For some time he'd known that Beck's nerves were shot. That the immense mental and physical strain of heading up the Resistance for years and being at constant loggerheads with Hitler on a one-to-one basis had taken its toll on the much-venerated military warlord. As it had on every man of decency who had had the misfortune to come within the Fuhrer's reach.

"I don't suppose Fromm let him off the hook?" he continued, in a masterful piece of wishful thinking.

He received Oster's ice-cold expression in answer.

"Let's just say that Fromm put him out of his misery. As soon as Stauffenberg and the others were dead, he sent one of his Staff officers back into the building to finish the job Beck hadn't been able to do for himself. He then ordered that all five bodies be bundled into a truck and buried at a cemetery in Schoenberg. Told his men not to stand on ceremony, but to throw the bodies—complete with their uniforms and medals, into the grave as quickly as possible."[37]

"Well at least that's something to be said for Fromm's decency," Canaris sighed—the mourning process having temporarily dulled his wits.

"Don't delude yourself! Fromm's only concern was, as ever, to take care of himself. It's not right to credit him for something that's not his due."

Having expressed his flagrant contempt for Fromm, it surprised Oster when Canaris countered it with sympathy for same.

"Poor old Fromm," the Little Admiral said, shaking his head. "He's sacrificed everything to save himself and probably thinks that he's home and hosed now that he's got rid of Stauffenberg. Obviously he has no idea that the truth about him is already out there . . . that Himmler has known, for some time, about his tentative complicity in the coup. As he's known about the involvement of each and every one of us. It's just suited his purpose to keep quiet about it and give us a bit of rope. But now . . . he's set to hang us all with it."

*   *   *

"You've been in a damned hurry to get your witnesses underground," Himmler said to Fromm as they completed their inspection tour of the *Bendlerstrasse* courtyard—the two of them hovering, for a ghoulish moment, to study the fresh bloodstains that coloured its cobblestones.

"But I thought, sir, that that would be what Hitler wanted," Fromm replied anxiously. He had not missed the SS Reichsfuhrer's implication, nor the fact that Himmler seemed well enough informed about his complicity to throw it at him.

"Well you were wrong! Now kindly take me to the cemetery where they're buried, and I'll show you *precisely* what the Fuhrer would want."

This was to have the men's bodies exhumed; to strip them of

their uniforms and medals, and then burn their naked corpses to a cinder, scattering their ashes at random in the open fields so that nothing remained of them to be remembered or revered.

Himmler didn't realize, however, that in his efforts to obliterate the Stauffenberg legacy he'd in fact perpetuated it. The essence of the great soldier was now spread and taking root in the rich earth of his beloved Germany—an end for which Count Claus von Stauffenberg would have wished.

Stauffenberg had got lucky twice over. His quick, soldier's death had been a mercy, when the others who were to follow in his footsteps were destined for far, far worse.

The first was his older brother, Berthold, who by right of bearing the Stauffenberg name was doomed. Hitler had decreed that that family name, with all its ancient, noble roots, must be removed from the face of the Earth. None of its guilty members were to even rate a trial or the slightest trace of compassion.

That was why, only days after Claus' execution, Berthold was put to death by means unmentionable. All those of the Stauffenberg clan who survived Hitler's cull were forever unable to speak of him or the deplorable suffering he endured.

For the other conspirators there came months of imprisonment under Gestapo interrogation and torture. The horror of which, for these proud men of prior distinction, was interspersed by being paraded through the People's Court. All were denied their dignity and had to suffer the humiliation of being herded like cattle to the slaughter—branded traitors to their country.

Emaciated and stripped down to the bare essentials, they were deprived of their right to speak up in their own defence, and even of the more basic privilege of having a belt to hold up their trousers. Each of them were forced to file in and out of the witness box and stand for hours on end under rigorous cross-examination.

As part of the demeaning process, they had to clutch their pants in place and bow their heads as Judge Roland Friesler hurled his vile accusations at them. His trademark, high-pitched scream made them the focal point of his frenzied Nazi fanaticism. None of the defendants were allowed to get a word in edgewise when it was the foregone conclusion that they would be found guilty.

The only flexibility in the verdict was in the choice of deaths— whichever sadistic means of execution that took the Judge's fancy on the day. Freisler's distinct leaning was towards hanging them all with butcher-hook and piano wire, with the occasional guillotine thrown in for the sake of variety and the relief of tedium.

On Tuesday, July 28, 1944,[38] the People's Court called Ulrich von Hassell to the witness stand. For three weeks Friesler ranted and raved—slandering and haranguing the former German Ambassador to Rome, before he slammed down his gavel:

Guilty! Death by hanging!

Hassell had then stumbled his way to the scaffold—his half-starved body was hunched over and three sizes too small for his threadbare clothing. His withered skin was tattooed from top to bottom with the red-raw, weeping welts of torture.

His early execution, however, was a mercy. The noose that was tied around his neck to snap it was made of rope rather than piano wire—the latter a more ingenious form of execution earmarked for his fellow conspirators. The use of a thinner, metal medium to slowly sever a man's throat while choking him to death promised better entertainment value in its more exquisite, lingering pain.

As far as Hassell was concerned, there had been no compassion intended. The only reason he had been, quite *literally*, let off "the hook" was because his trial and punishment had preceded Gestapo agent—Franz Xaver Sonderegger's staggering discovery of the conspirators' safe at Zossen.

His monumental find spilled out the names of all traitors and their targets, in alphabetized, easy-to-read black and white. The incriminating evidence fell from manilla folders in such abundance that it was undeniable. It provided the SS with all the justification they needed to step up the barbarity and frequency of their executions; making sure that their punishments outstripped the horror of the conspirators' crimes.

This gave them *carte blanche*—opening up their fertile imaginations to every conceivable perversion of justice and abuse of human decency.

On Tuesday, September 8, 1944,[39] the People's Court called to the witness stand Dr. Carl Goerdeler. This time, Friesler took only a few days to reach his verdict:

Guilty—Death by hanging!

The condemned Goerdeler was then shoved savagely from the courtroom. His order to *"Move fast"* was given the added incentive of having an SS rifle-butt slammed full force into his face. Its impact shattered his cheekbone and sent him hurtling to the hard, marble floor. His struggle to get back to his feet made for the perfect, poignant moment for Friesler to scream out the final insult to make his humiliation complete.

"Dr. Goerdeler . . . while you await execution, I want to urge you to continue writing those interminable memoranda of yours that you've been so fond of sending to Winston Churchill. I do hope that you keep up the good work; but this time, for the enlightenment of the SS."

It seemed only fair when the SS believed that Goerdeler owed them, in a big way, for services rendered. The process of having to track him down had expended an excess of SS energy and resources for which they were determined he pay. Despite chasing him for months across the length and breadth of Germany, they had not caught up with him until he was betrayed by a woman who recognized him and turned him in for the huge financial reward.

So he'd finally been arrested and put under interrogation at Prinz Albrechtstrasse[40] Prison; keeping company with the many other conspirators who were already in residence there. Most of whom refused to speak to him for fear that he might repeat their words to the Gestapo.

Goerdeler had taken Friesler at his word—hoping to twist it to his advantage by providing the Gestapo with the mother lode of hand-written information about the failed coup and its complex network of conspirators. What appeared to be his flagrant betrayal, however, wasn't done to save himself, as his fellow prisoners assumed, but to stall proceedings in the hope of saving them *all* from execution.

His plan was to inundate the Gestapo with so much inside information that their investigations into it would keep them busy—busy and happy enough to ensure that the conspirators stayed alive for as long as possible . . . for as long as it took the Allies to win the war and rescue them.

It was a thankless task that had his compatriots keep their distance and eye him with contempt. All of them were unaware that Goerdeler's hand-written confessions—either true or untrue—concerned only people who were already dead and out of harm's way.

Their names, albeit betrayed posthumously, generated enough SS interest to give Geordeler's confessions validity. So excited were the Gestapo about his gripping exposés that they considered Goerdeler far too valuable to be executed, going to the extreme of leaving his cell door open at all times, so as not to run the risk of him committing suicide, or to deprive themselves of such a sensational stool pigeon.

It was unfair and most unfortunate for Goerdeler that his shrewd gameplay was misread by his friends and associates—sad, but quite understandable, given that the Gestapo enjoyed making mileage out of it; deliberately blackballing him with his fellow prisoners:

"With friends like *him*, who needs enemies?" SS General Ernst Kaltenbrunner made a point of saying to Hjalmar Schacht, during one of his rushed inspection tours of the *Albrechtstrasse* prison facility.

The SS head of Reich Security had been strutting down Cell Block 5's cold, concrete corridor, when he'd come to an abrupt stop. Locked up in prison cell 512 he'd recognized the former Minister for Economic Affairs and President of the Reichsbank. The famed, erudite Schacht was no longer sitting in a pinstripe suit behind a mahogany desk, but was lying, emaciated, on a prison bunk sporting filthy convict overalls.

As Heydrich's successor in both mind and method, it had been quite beyond Kaltenbrunner to resist the temptation of getting a bit of payback, when for so many years the grand and glorious Schacht had looked down his nose at him. He wasn't about to pass up his chance to return the compliment.

"I must say, Schacht . . . we're most impressed by your Dr. Goerdeler's comprehensive statements. He's made for the ideal witness, from whose information, you and your friends have *everything* to fear."

Had Schacht been a lesser man, he may well have taken exception to Goerdeler's "freedom of information" policy. That is, if, on his arrival at the prison two months before, he had not been so stunned by Goerdeler's shocking appearance.

It had been painful for him to see the marked deterioration in his old friend. Goerdeler had always been a man so alert and full of confidence, but he'd been beaten down into a complete state of collapse. His gaunt face, with its grey complexion, expressed his inner disillusion and utter despair.

He was a man grown prematurely old, shackled hand and foot, wearing the same light summer clothes in which he'd been arrested months before—his shirt, shabby and collarless . . . his trousers tied around his painfully thin waist with a piece of frayed rope. But it was those once bright grey eyes of his that said it all. In their fire and passion, they had always been the most impressive part of him—the way they had flashed with intelligence and astute interest in everything around him.

But when Schacht had come face-to-face with him in the prison yard, he could see that the light had quite gone out of them. Goerdeler's now dark-circled, deep-socketed eyes were those of a blind man—still quite able to see, but staring straight ahead into nothingness; glazed and distraught in their desperate search for a realm beyond reality.

Into this realm the Gestapo dispatched him on February 2, 1945. Having used him for all he was worth and given him the false hope that he and his friends *may* just avoid the gallows, the executioner was suddenly in a hurry to see Goerdeler on his way. Without warning, one day, he turned up at his cell door to say with brisk efficiency:

"Come on, come on . . . your turn today!"

For Pastor Dietrich Bonhoeffer, the gavel came down on April 9, 1945:

Guilty! Death by hanging!

Bonhoeffer had been incarcerated at Tegel Prison for eighteen months. There he was fed on water and bread crusts which were thrown, twice a day, on the floor of his cell. The sub-zero temperature wasn't relieved by the blankets which were all too putrid to use. However, his refusal to complain and his gracious acceptance of his guards' brutal treatment slowly but surely won over their respect and had them relax their grueling regimen just a little.

It was a leniency that wasn't encouraged by Dr. Manfred Roeder. As the man in charge of the *Abwehr* investigations, he saw no reason to extend any form of compassion.

Bonhoeffer, being so obviously a gentle man of God, rated no special treatment. Conversely, his innate goodness drove Roeder to step up the intensity of his torture—intrigued as he was to know how much strength a man could derive from the *One On High*. From a completely clinical-cum-demonic point of view, Roeder had wondered just how far such a man could be pushed before breaking.

He started by denying Bonhoeffer's father the right to visit his critically ill son in prison.

To: *Dr. Karl. Bonhoeffer*

In the action against your son, Dietrich Bonhoeffer, you are informed, in reply to your letter of April 17, 1943, that your application for permission to visit is refused.

By order of: *Dr. Manfred Roeder, Army Inspector of Justice; Judge Advocate of the War Court.41*

In response to this, Bonhoeffer had to smuggle out (via a now amenable guard) a carefully worded letter to put his enraged father's and desperate mother's minds at ease. His scribbled note of reassurance was the only time in his life that he found it necessary and wholly justified to lie.

Dearest Father and Mama,

Please do not distress yourselves on my account. You know that I'm not alone. I have no doubt that you are imagining my life to be difficult, but it's not. Life in prison is much like everywhere else. I spend my time reading, meditating, writing, and pacing up and down my cell, without rubbing myself sore on the walls like a polar bear!

I've found that the important thing is to make the best use of one's possessions and capabilities. Believe it or not, there are still plenty left. The trick is to accept the limits of my situation, and to not give way to feelings of resentment and discontent. It's a trick I'm fortunate enough to have mastered.

That's why I beg of you not to fret over my welfare. I am still fit and full of the faith that sustains me. So, no matter which way it goes, my future looks bright."

Throughout his imprisonment—the venues for which spanned the delights of Tegel and Prinz Albrechtstrasse prisons, followed by the horrors of *Buchenwald* and finally *Flossenburg* concentration camps,[42] Bonhoeffer remained serene and full of hope—a constant inspiration to all with whom he came in contact.

On the day of his execution, he knelt in his cell to pray. When he got up from his knees, he was completely composed, calm and forgiving enough to leave his well-worn Bible and treasured volume of Goethe on the prison Warden's desk.

Afterwards, he walked out into the execution yard, stopping only once, en route to the scaffold, to reassure his friend Schlabrendorff, who was standing with tears in his eyes watching him go.

"Please don't let this upset you," he said, taking hold of Schlabrendorff's hand. "I'm not afraid. This is not the end, but for me it is just the beginning of life."

April 9 was also Judgment Day for Hans von Dohnanyi who had been imprisoned for as long as Bonhoeffer, but under far more stringent interrogation. For some peculiar reason, Dr. Roeder had taken a violent dislike to him and dedicated himself to perpetuating the young lawyer's suffering.

During the process of this, he gave no consideration to Dohnanyi's extremely poor state of health. Delicate as Dohnanyi's constitution had always been, prison life and his daily dose of torture had made his prognosis dire. The fact that his legs, arms and face were paralysed, and that he was suffering unspeakably from the effects of diphtheria, didn't seem to impact on Roeder, and came nowhere near having him soften his approach.

"Come now, Dohnanyi . . . you can no longer deny your involvement in the conspiracy now that the Zossen papers have come to light. Most of them are written in your own handwriting!"

Roeder was right. The Zossen papers were solid proof of his complicity that he could not dispute. Nor did he intend to confess. No matter what the intensity of pain being inflicted, Dohnanyi simply closed his eyes in a feigned faint—a ploy that took the edge off Roeder's fun and rendered his state of the art implements of torture useless.

In frustration, Roeder finally threw in the towel. He'd had his fill of Dohnanyi's stubborn refusal to break under torture. Never being one to give up entirely, however, Roeder transferred his prisoner to *Sachsenhansen* concentration camp and requested that the very adept Franz Sonderegger have a go at bringing Dohnanyi undone.

Sonderegger failed too, because it was very hard to draw a man out with the threat of breaking his legs when Dohnanyi's had long since been out of commission. His withered limbs doubled the degree of difficulty for Sonderegger because they were compensated for by Dohnanyi's strength of will—a will and courage which proved to be unbreakable. Dohnanyi was shrewd enough to use his chronic illness as a most formidable weapon.

"Well, what am I meant to do?" Sonderegger demanded of Roeder over the phone—his voice high-pitched and irritated. "I've tried every possible means of extracting information from the man, but he just won't crack."

"Try harder!" was Roeder's response over the line.

"But what's the point? He's too ill to be of any constructive help to us. Besides, whenever I get him to 'screaming point', he simply faints or falls asleep . . . *anything* rather than talk. Problem is . . . the man just isn't afraid of dying."

Which made Sonderegger wrong on two counts.

Firstly, because sick as he was, Dohnanyi had never *really* fainted in his life. He used it merely as a ploy to escape whenever his interrogation/torture got "too hot" to handle.

Secondly, like most men, he was *very much* afraid of dying, but had long since reconciled himself to the fact that he was destined to do just that, and to do it very soon, if not from natural causes, then at the hands of the SS.

He had no illusions whatsoever. From the day of his arrest, he had known that Roeder would eventually have him executed. On his way out, however, he was determined to make life as difficult and frustrating as he could for Hitler and his henchmen.

When the time came for his sentence to be handed down, Dohnanyi had to be carried on a stretcher into the courtroom. He was only capable of lifting his head a few inches from his pillow to mumble his defence through semi-paralysed lips. His words, of course, were unintelligible. What did it matter when they fell on deaf ears?

Guilty! Death by hanging!

His execution took place in secrecy. *So* secret that his family didn't even know that he was dead. When his wife, Christine, came to visit him in prison the next day, it was Sonderegger himself who insisted that she open her handbag so that he could check it for contraband.

"I can assure you that there's nothing in it of interest to you, Herr Sonderegger," she said, as she clicked open its gold clasp and stretched it wide for his inspection.

All that he saw inside it was the cheap, new comb and small block of chocolate that she'd brought to cheer up her husband.

"He won't be needing those," Sonderegger said. Not bothering to explain any further, he simply handed her a brown paper parcel in which were her husband's neatly folded clothes.

On Tuesday, April 16, 1945,[43] the People's Court called to the witness box Count Helmuth von Moltke. The once handsome man in his mid thirties now looked sixty. Only half his normal weight, with his dark, ungroomed hair prematurely greyed at the temple.

Much to Friesler's annoyance, months of excruciating torture had failed to strip him of either his pride, his arrogance or his supreme debating ability. Moltke was still in good enough form to give Judge Freisler a run for his money.

Holding tight to the witness box rail to steady himself, Moltke endured thirty minutes of Friesler's neurotic tirade—listening as his vile, falsetto accusations reverberated around the courtroom. The last had Moltke's lips suddenly tighten with rage.

"You'll die like the piece of scum you are," Friesler yelled at him. "Like that pig-dog of an assassin, Stauffenberg, who betrayed Germany and its people."

It was at this point that Moltke drew himself up. Straightening his shoulders, he looked directly at Friesler and shouted out his command.

"*Be silent* Herr Friesler, for today it is *my* head that is at stake. But in a year, it'll be yours!"

The courtroom fell into a deadly hush. For the first time in his life, Judge Friesler was lost for words. His open-mouthed shock marked a brief hiatus in proceedings that gave Moltke just a tiny window of opportunity to say his piece, all of which he dedicated to the man he had come to admire most.

"Just to set the record straight, Herr Friesler . . . I've no intention of denying my guilt, but to be proud of it. In fact, I uncommonly regret that I could not take the place of Count Claus von Stauffenberg, who was prevented by his disabilities sustained in combat from completing the deed.

"It was ever Stauffenberg's criticism of me that I was all words and no action, and he was right. His courage has become my shame, and it is with the utmost humility that I now dare call him my friend. So go right ahead and kill me . . . but make it sooner than later, because I am looking so forward to seeing him again."

CHAPTER THIRTY-SEVEN

There were a fortunate few who didn't make it to the witness stand. A fine line between stark terror and supreme courage had them quickly take their own lives, rather than face the horrors Hitler had in store for them.

One of these few was the ever-vacillating Field Marshal Guenther von Kluge, who had beaten a hasty retreat from his command on the eastern front to take over where Field Marshal von Rundstedt had left off as Army Group Commander in France.

Those in the know assumed that Kluge's willingness to "go west" had had more to do with wanting to be free of General Tresckow's pressure to join the Resistance, than the flattery of Hitler having chosen him to head up his French operations.

But it had been a case of leaping from frying pan to fire. Kluge's new second-in-command in France—General Heinrich von Stuelpnagel was every bit as intent as Tresckow to involve Kluge up to his neck in the conspiracy.

As Military Governor, Stuelpnagel had also been the principal instigator of the correlated *coup d'etat* in France. It had been under his direction that all SS and Gestapo personnel in Paris had been put under arrest when it was first thought that Stauffenberg's assassination attempt had been successful.

By the time Stuelpnagel had found out otherwise, it was too late. The wheels of the doomed coup had already been put in motion, which meant that he had a lot of explaining to do to his boss—Kluge—who, true to form, was keeping his distance from responsibility. On the evening of July 20, 1944, he'd been doing a sterling job of fending off General Beck's last minute pleas over the phone that he back their cause.

"Stauffenberg is absolutely *sure* that the Fuhrer is dead, Kluge," Beck had hastened to reassure him. "All we ask is that you stand fast and be prepared to take up the reins if we call on you."

But Stauffenberg's word had not been enough for him to put his neck on the line. Kluge had thought it more prudent not to volunteer for front line duty, when there was more advantage to be had in taking cover until he knew exactly which way the wind was blowing.

"I'm telling you for the last time, Beck, that I shall not commit myself to the coup until I'm *convinced* that Hitler is dead."

"Would I lie to you?" Beck had pressed on, pulling out all stops to embarrass Kluge into gathering his courage and conviction.

Because of the respect Kluge had always had for Beck, it was an end almost achieved. Beck had at last detected a ray of hope in the wavering tone of Kluge's voice. Its suddenly softer, faltering pitch implied that he was reconsidering.

It was only a pity that, at that strategic moment, Kluge was handed the typewritten transcript of Goebbels' latest broadcast—its bold banner headline reading:

HITLER SURVIVES BOMB BLAST!

In response to which, Kluge's hand tightened into a fierce, white-knuckled grip on the telephone receiver:

"*The bloody thing's misfired!*" he screamed down the phone at Beck. "You can *damn well* leave me out of it."

At this he slammed down the receiver, making the naïve assumption that his words and action had exempted him from all complicity in the coup.

This may very well have been the case had Stuelpnagel not put a spanner in the works. It was impossible to fathom the fear factor that must have been Stuelpnagel's when he had to tell Kluge the bad news.

"I regret to inform you, sir, that in anticipation of Stauffenberg's success, I've *already* ordered the arrest of all SS and Gestapo personnel in Paris. I did so because it was my designated role in the coup."

Kluge was appalled. His face drained white with shock, he took an unsteady step backwards:

"You *idiot!*" he threw back at Stuelpnagel—too stunned for any form of military or gentlemanly civility. "What in God's name possessed you to do such a *stupid,* dangerous thing?"

"To that, sir, I've no appropriate answer, other than to request that you refrain from calling me an idiot when I was only acting under orders, and in what I believed to be the best interests of Germany."

"Well then, in the best interests of Germany, I suggest that you immediately free all your prisoners and get on bended knee to Hitler. And remember . . . the onus is yours and not *mine*. It is up to you . . . and to you *alone* to explain your hideous mistake to the Fuhrer."

So, like the good soldier he was, Stueplnagel did as he was told—bar that of getting on his knees to beg forgiveness from Hitler. Instead, he freed his prisoners and then attempted to take his own life—an attempt at which he failed.

It wasn't through lack of courage—he didn't baulk at pulling the trigger—it was just that he missed! The bullet that ripped through his skull was a little left of centre; only grazing his brain to leave him alive, but blind. In hale and hearty enough condition to be arrested and nursed back to some semblance of health, so that he could be tried and hanged for treason.

His arrest meant that for a short time, Kluge was home free, which left the Field Marshal in a temporary fool's paradise, letting him linger there longer enough to believe that he actually had some sway over Hitler, and that there was a chance that he might be able to talk some sense into him.

"Normandy has been a disaster, sir. You must withdraw our western troops to hold the Rhine," he'd advised.

"I must do nothing of the kind! I've no intention of yielding even an *inch* of territory," Hitler had fired back in an unholy fury.

In response to this, Kluge had stormed from the meeting in a white-hot rage of his own. The suspicion with which Hitler eyed him, as he left, was wholly justified in that he suspected that Kluge was on the brink of betrayal; that he was within a hair's breadth of surrendering to the Allies and negotiating an armistice behind his Fuhrer's back. Hitler's fears had been confirmed by Kluge's conspicuous absence from Military Headquarters the very next day.

"This is the worst day of my life!" the Fuhrer had said, with his fingers pressed hard at his temple to still its throbbing vein. "I want you to make sure, Himmler, that it is also the worst day of

Kluge's."

Kluge had beaten the SS Reichsfuhrer to the punch by promptly swallowing a cyanide capsule. The news of his suicide had not augured well for those other members of the Military who were under suspicion.

General Fromm was one of them, even though he'd convinced himself that his head was no longer on the chopping block.

It had been a reasonable assumption, given his expedient betrayal of his friends and the fact that he'd taken such immediate, drastic action to dispose of them. Brushing the dirt from his hands as he'd walked from their grave to provide ample evidence of his loyalty to the Third Reich—this, he had believed, was proof enough of his fidelity towards the Fuhrer to keep same on side.

He had been wrong.

"Fromm's going to lose his bonnet soon, too!" the Minister of Justice—Otto Thierack—had said to Albert Speer.

His casual-cum-devastating comment over the dinner table, had made the Armaments Minister lose his appetite and push his meal aside. The prospect of eating the extremely bloodied, rare steak he'd been served had not been in the least appealing when many of his closest friends were at that very moment being hung out to dry on the same meathooks which had probably hosted the cow's carcass.

He had been physically ill at the thought of it. *Sick* over the fact that he'd been unable to save any of them. Yet at that moment, with Hitler sitting companionably at his side, he had seen it as his perfect opportunity to take a stab at appealing *directly* to Hitler for Fromm's life.

"Sir, haven't we already gone far enough to prove our point? I know for a fact that General Fromm has always been *entirely* loyal to you," Speer had said.

He was lying through his teeth, of course. He was as fully aware of Fromm's duplicity as he was of almost the entire Wehrmacht being guilty of the same crime. The bulk of the German military hierarchy had lost all faith in Hitler now that his maniacal brutality had hit so close to home. His madness and methods no longer concentrated on the enemy, but on his own Generals and members of the German aristocracy.

But, Speer had reasoned . . . if he could manage to catch Hitler in a vaguely amenable mood, he may just be able to talk him round to putting an end to the atrocious massacre of good men that had been going on for months.

Speer had been heartened by the fact that Hitler had said nothing in reply. Instead, he had taken his time to calmly cut up the soft brown-skinned pear that was on his plate. Unlike his dinner guests, Hitler had refused being served meat because he abhorred the sight of blood in any shape or form. Which, under the gruesome circumstances of his own making, had seemed most peculiar.

So too had been his unusually composed demeanour. Speer had taken advantage of it to go one step further, not realizing that it would be that one step too far.

"I'm not ashamed to admit that Fromm is my friend," he had dared say. "And if you will grant me permission, sir, I would like to testify on his behalf at his trial.

"I make this request because I want to impress on you that he is, and has always been, *your* friend too, sir . . . as am I. As such, I can only hope that *my* support of Fromm will have you realize *yours* for him."

All that it had made Hitler realize was that his favourite, Albert Speer, had dared cross him, and that it was time to pull up on the free rein he'd given his young architect/Armaments Minister for so many years.

Down went the Fuhrer's knife and fork *hard* to the table, and with them, what remained of his calm facade.

"It is *unprecedented* for a Reich's Minister to act as a witness in the People's Court. I will therefore not permit your testimony. But rest assured, my dear Albert, that I've taken note of it."

There had been no mistaking his meaning. Speer had read into it his own fall from favour and the fact that he'd lost a considerable amount of ground. Hitler had rammed home the fact that Speer's *own* trial might very well be on the agenda.

Fromm was executed on March 12, 1945. His death followed soon after that of General Henning von Tresckow, who had chosen to spare Hitler the trouble of doing away with him by committing suicide.

He did so by following in old General Baron von Fritsch's footsteps—walking unarmed onto no-man's land on the Russian front. The Allied soldier who shot him down wasn't aware that he had just felled one of the noblest of men.

It was a fact of which his off-sider, Lieutenant Fabian von Schlarbrendorff was most humbly and acutely aware. Having worked and fought at Tresckow's side for so many years, he'd come to think of him as his closest friend, which was precisely why the Gestapo chose to use that dead friend of his to extract a confession from Schlabrendorff.

They took him to *Sachsenhansen* concentration camp and made him stand at Tresckow's graveside while they exhumed his body. Their hope was that the macabre sight of it might bring Schlabrendorff undone.

Instead, the Lieutenant simply saluted his comrade. Defying all sense of revulsion at the sight and smell of his friend's decaying body, he knelt down beside it and placed his hand gently over Tresckow's—ignoring the feel of the cold, rotting flesh to say a prayer and goodbye.

From that point on, Schlabrendorff knew that he was on his own—now it was time for his *own* trial to start.

"The People's Court calls Lieutenant Fabian von Schlabrendorff to the witness stand".

It had come down to a matter endurance. Schlabrendorff knew that all he had to do was put up with Friesler's screamed accusations for as long as it took him to come to his most predictable verdict:

Guilty! Death by Hanging!

With such a foregone conclusion in sight, there was no point in speaking up or protesting. Numbed by the brutal executions of his friends and associates, Schlabrendorff had quite lost faith in the Cause, himself and God.

Indeed it appeared that God, under whose standard they had fought, had forsaken them all. The fact that He had chosen to desert men far more brave and brilliant than himself, made Schlabrendorff all the more surprised when the Almighty suddenly saw fit to save him!

This, ironically, He did by way of Friesler.

At the very moment when the judge grabbed up Schlabrendorff's file—case no. 622(a)—the air raid siren sounded. Its crescendo-ing wail had Freisler rise from his chair, adjourn the Court and, with Schlabrendorff's file tucked under his arm, proceed with all in attendance down to the air raid shelter.

It was a strange set of circumstances, with archenemies—judge, prosecutor, defendant and witnesses all huddled together in such a confined space. For one short, claustrophobic moment in time, the sentence of death was hanging over *all* their heads.

That sentence was pronounced on Friesler *alone* when a bomb shook the very foundations of their bunker and dislodged a twelve-inch-thick rafter from its ceiling. The block of roughly hewn hardwood fell with a decisive thump on the judge's head.

It killed him outright. The SS guards had to fight their way through the dust and debris to find the judge's body and prise Schalbrendorff's file from his hand. That stone-cold, right hand of Friesler's was all that was visible—clenched and protruding from under a pile of smoking rubble.

Considering the unusual circumstances of such a man's death, the German Judicial System had no choice but to mark down Schalbrendorff's case as a mistrial and put his execution on hold.

CHAPTER THIRTY-EIGHT

Being saved by the bell spared Schlabrendorff the scaffold, but not prison. He, along with a few lucky others, had to sit out its horrors until Germany declared its unconditional surrender and the more heartening news that the Russians were coming.

The Reds arrived to release them in the nick of time, which meant that Schalbrendorff, Hjalmar Schacht, Dr. Josef Mueller, Hans Gisevius and Major-General Erwin Lahousen all miraculously survived Hitler's purge. The five of them stayed alive long enough to bear witness to the fact that Admiral Wilhelm Canaris and Major-General Hans Oster did not.

In a manner of speaking, both men had committed suicide— not in its literal sense, but in their mutual decision to stand their ground and not run.

It was an act of supreme courage, when their options had been so wide open. Both of them knew that a private plane and U-Boat were standing at the ready to make good their escape from Germany. Their strategic exit from hell was the strong recommendation of each and every one of their powerful foreign contacts, all of whom wished to welcome them with open arms and to fill their pockets with enough foreign currency to make their lives away from home extremely comfortable.

Instead, Oster had chosen to sit quietly in his Berlin apartment. With cognac and cigar in hand, he'd waited patiently for the Gestapo to knock at his door, which they had done on July 21, 1944; putting him under arrest to await trial and execution at a later date.

Two days later, it had been Canaris' turn to answer *his* door.

Bracing himself for what was to come, he'd forced a smile and flung it wide open, not entirely surprised to see his old friend— Walter Schellenberg—standing in full dress uniform to greet him.

The head of Kaltenbrunner's SS Intelligence Division was holding himself stiffly at attention to perform the formalities of the arrest, but with the look of the most sincere, sad apology on his face.

"I'm so sorry Willie, but Kaltenbrunner insisted that it was I who come," Schellenberg had said.

"Don't concern yourself Walter. It was only predictable that those pigs would send you to do their dirty work. Who better to deliver bad news than a dear friend? So come on in and make yourself at home while I pack my bag."

"Making himself at home" had hardly been something Schellenberg could do under the circumstances. His acute discomfort had made him incapable of even accepting Canaris' kind offer of a drink—even though it would have gone down well, when his mouth had been parched dry with tension. He'd marveled at the Little Admiral's composure and the courtesy he was extending to a visitor who had come calling as the Devil's advocate.

"It's too bad that we have to say goodbye in this way," Canaris had said as he'd held up his own glass of brandy in salute, before swilling down the fortifying shot of amber liquid. "But never mind . . . we'll get over this."

His injection of positivity had gone straight over Schellenberg's head when there had been something far more pressing he'd wanted to ask.

"At the end of the day Willie, was all this really necessary? A man with your mind power must have *known* how it would turn out—that you didn't stand a chance of pulling it off, with the odds stacked sky-high against you."

Schellenberg was right. Canaris had known from the start that he was fighting a losing battle. Ever since it had become one of conscience, however, he'd had no choice but to play it out.

"The world is a dangerous place, Walter," he'd replied. "Not because of those who *do* evil, but because of those who look on and do nothing. I made a promise to myself that I wouldn't be one of them."

That said, their conversation was over. Canaris had made his point and left Schellenberg suitably contrite for not having seen it sooner.

In frustration, Schellenberg had begun pacing Canaris' sitting room—that cozy nook, with its familiar old Persian carpet, to which he'd been invited on so many happy occasions. *That* day, however, had not been one of them. Schellenberg knew that if there were anything to be done to help Canaris, it had to be done right then and there.

It was a decision that had had him stop, turn and speak with frank formality to the Rear Admiral.

"If the Herr Admiral wishes to make other arrangements, then I beg him to consider me at his disposal. I shall wait in this room for an hour and during that time you may do what you wish. My report will say that you went to your bedroom to change."

Schellenberg's sudden "get out of jail free" offer had made Canaris' throat clench with emotion. Putting down his glass, he'd walked over and given his young friend a warm farewell embrace.

"No dear Schellenberg. Flight is out of the question for me. And I won't give Hitler the satisfaction of killing myself either. I must see this thing through to its end."

Canaris had then excused himself to go and say goodbye to his wife and two daughters. He urged his three girls to be brave and confident of the fact that they would see him again soon. It was a flagrant lie which had given his children reason to hope . . . and his wife, reason to cry. Love, age and experience had blessed her with the wisdom to read the truth in her husband's eyes.

For that husband's sake, she'd pulled herself together quickly. Drying her tears, she'd helped him put on his grey, tweed overcoat, making sure that she turned up its collar to keep out the cold.

Her poignant parting gesture had made it impossible for Canaris to respond. His throat was clenched so tight with emotion that he'd been incapable of even opening his lips to speak. Only able to do so, twenty minutes later, when he and Schellenberg were in the car en route to Prinz Albrecthstrasse Prison. Canaris had at last collected himself enough to lay his cards on the table.

"I would like to ask you one last favour, if I may Walter? Will you promise me *faithfully* that in the next three days you'll secure me a private interview with Himmler? I have a strong case that'll stand me in good stead, once he and I iron out a few of its wrinkles. As for the others . . . Kaltenbrunner and his crew . . . keep them as far away from me as possible. They're just a pack of filthy butchers out for my blood."

That was going to be hard to arrange, Schellenberg thought as he nodded his assent and looked out the car window to watch the night shadows flash by—taking note of the prophetic darkening of the sky around them.

When all was said and done, however, it was only a very small favour to extend to a friend who had extended so many to him in the past. Surely it was little enough to give Canaris as a parting gift.

The very thought of that finality—of him being the means of Canaris' demise—had had Schellenberg start fidgeting nervously with his gold fountain pen—twisting and turning it in his hand and drumming its 18-carat stem so hard against his leg that it had begun to hurt. His self-inflicted pain was finally relieved when Canaris stretched out his calming hand to still it.

"Don't let it distress you," he'd said.

"But it *does* distress me Willie, because there's something that you don't understand about me," Schellenberg owned up. "There was a time, you see, when I turned against you—when I was weak enough to allow Heydrich to win me over to your detriment. It was behaviour on my part over which I am now profoundly ashamed."

"Water under the bridge, my boy . . . water under the bridge. We all, at some point in our lives, falter in our judgment. And you're quite wrong, you know. I was very much aware of your duplicity. As much as I was certain that you'd eventually see the light and work your way free of it. Because, unlike Heydrich, you are at base a good man. That's why I have faith in the promise you've given me. I'm only sorry that you've been dragged into this whole nasty business.

"I think I should warn you, though, to be on your guard. I've been around the traps long enough to know that they'll be after you too. Not yet perhaps, but soon. So give me my chance to speak to Himmler and I'll see to it that he gives you his protection."

"Why should he?" Schellenberg had asked.

"Because he owes me one."

Himmler did indeed. There had existed, for some time between them, a sort of gentleman's agreement. Canaris keeping quiet about Himmler's secret peace negotiations with Sweden behind Hitler's back,[44] while the SS Reichsfuhrer kept his mouth

KILL THE FUHRER ⚡

shut about Canaris and his coup.

Now that that coup had failed, with all its dirty washing hanging out in the open, Himmler no longer had a bargaining chip to keep Canaris quiet. The Little Admiral now thought that it just might be expedient to offer him another. Over the issue of the knife Himmler was planning to put in Hitler's back, Canaris would promise to keep his silence, in return for Himmler keeping *him* clear of the hangman's noose.

For a while it was a fair exchange, Himmler sparing Canaris the scaffold, but nothing else. The distinguished Rear Admiral/ex-head of German Intelligence was subjected to the most inhumane treatment, the worst of which, for Canaris, was the deplorable cold!

He had never handled it well, but solitary confinement in the dark, dank prison brought him close to breaking point. The chill factor of his incarceration not only permeated every crevice of his stone-walled cell, but spread its icy tendrils into every cell in his emaciated body. Seeping from his toes, up through his entire torso to permanently freeze his jaw rigid and set his teeth chattering. His drastic weight loss from a diet of bread and water, left him barely enough flesh to warm his bones.

The fact that he was nigh on frozen to death didn't stop Canaris lending his precious overcoat to his fellow prisoner, Lieutenant Schlabrendorff. What had always been Canaris' deep-seated kindness and genuine concern for his friends had him forever watching out for their welfare.

Being behind bars didn't mean that Canaris wasn't on the job. Until the day he died, his wits and wiles never failed to operate at peak performance. In Schlabrendorff's case, they had facilitated Canaris getting wind of the fact that the Gestapo was desperate to wring a confession out of the young Lieutenant.

Schlabrendorff's refusal to break under torture had had them resort to medieval methods, by taking Schlabrendorff on a gruesome trip to view his friend Tresckow's dead body. They hoped that the worm-ridden sight of it might just be enough to swing the tide in their favour.

Anticipating what was to be Schlabrendorff's anguish, Canaris managed to slip a small note into the coat's pocket that read:

> *"Keep your chin up. All we need to do is hang on until*
> *the Allied troops arrive."*

That, however, was easier said than done, when the Gestapo decided to pick up the intensity of Canaris' torture. Having tired of the traditional means of making him suffer, they had opted to put him in chains, locking them so tight around his ankles and wrists that his skin was rubbed red raw—large chunks of it hung loose and bleeding under the metal restraints.

To this was added the slow torment of having his cell light left on night and day so that he couldn't sleep effectively depriving Canaris of his only form of escape. His eyes, with their keen 20/20 vision, forever open, burning and focused on the cold, grey reality of his living hell.

Despite the severity of his treatment, it was a challenge that Canaris was up to. His talent for using mind over matter to overcome all odds served him well and frustrated his guards into dropping back his food ration to *one third* of that of the other prisoners. The chronic weight loss which resulted wasn't enough to tempt the guards to offer him an extra crumb, but pushed them even further to fine-tune their cruelty. They relentlessly searched for the one thing that would break him, finally finding it when they stumbled over his dignity.

It had taken them some time to realize that, where Canaris was concerned, tackling the physical wasn't the answer. His Achilles Heel was his pride and self-respect - those two tangibles were oh, so very easy to undermine.

They started by subjecting him to a daily routine of having to get on all fours to scrub the prison floors, adding to the former Rear Admiral's ultimate humiliation. They stood by in jeering groups to watch him do it, swilling down beer and sharing jokes at his expense as he crawled with bucket and brush across the floor.

"Well, well, well, Little Sailor," one of them jibed. "How the mighty have fallen. I bet *you* never thought you'd have to swab the decks!"

Throughout, Canaris held on, *knowing* that it was only a matter of a very short time before the Allied troops reached Berlin. Just a few more weeks of gritted teeth and determination, before their so-called enemies arrived to set them free.

Up until then, all he had to do was stall for time. He did so by using Goerdeler's tactics—inundating the Gestapo interrogators with a surplus of irrelevant, convoluted information to keep them busy and off his back.

It was a ploy that had kept Goerdeler alive and had stretched out his "use-by" date for months. The fact that he'd suddenly been dragged from his cell without warning to be executed had not deterred Canaris from pursuing his program, not when he believed himself to be smarter . . . no, not smarter . . . just more wily than his friend.

Unlike Goerdeler, he had managed to baffle the Gestapo with one ruse after another. His skill at acting a part, his cunning at affecting a naïve stupidity (which inevitably emerged into the most subtle reasoning) had completely disarmed them.

At the same time, he practised a similar ploy on the more simple-minded guards who harangued him. He gained information about the outside world by throwing at them what appeared to be a casual series of uneducated comments, which they couldn't resist correcting.

"I suppose by now, our German troops are pushing back over the Vistula?" he said one day, emptying the grimy soap and water from his bucket.

"Rubbish!" his guard replied with blustering contempt. "The Russians are approaching the Oder!"[45]

It was just one of the many SS reproofs that sufficed as newspaper headlines for Canaris. Now that he no longer had access to the daily broadsheets, they were his and his compatriots only way of keeping up-to-date with the news.

He would then relay what he'd learned to his fellow inmates by tapping out messages on his cell wall. Employing a form of "Jailhouse Morse code", which worked on the simple basis of breaking the alphabet down into groups of five letters . . . of tapping out the number of the group and then the letter.[46] Canaris' in-house memos regularly echoed down the prison corridors to keep his fellow inmates informed. Every so often he would tap out just a little something extra to keep them amused.

His flash bulletins and humour went a long way to keep up their spirits. Canaris kept up his *own* by trying to maintain some semblance of dignity in his physical appearance.

By courtesy of Himmler, he'd been allowed to wear his civilian clothes—at least, the one and only suit in which he'd been arrested. Nine months down the track, it was in a pretty sorry state—hanging on him two sizes too big, with its cuffs and collar yellowed and frayed. It had nevertheless become a point of principle. Canaris insisted that each day he put in on, along with his coat and tie, to set an example.

This gave his guards yet another reason to make fun of him. One of them, in passing, had yelled out:

"What are you doing . . . trying to impress us?"

"You've gone out of your way to make that impossible," Canaris had replied, with a tight smile. "But surely you can allow an old man just this one last conceit."

For a brief, brutal-minded moment, the SS soldier had been tempted to deprive Canaris of even that, but the fact that his fellow guards were not present to share in the joke, had him err on the side of kindness.

"Go on . . . get on your way Little Sailor. Your fine rig-out wouldn't fit anyone else anyway."

For Canaris, keeping up appearances on the outside was much easier to do than keeping on top of his inner emotions, all of which, despite his calm facade, were in a state of turmoil.

"Do you think Canaris is coping?" Schlabrendorff asked of Hjalmar Schacht.

Both men were deeply concerned when they caught sight of the Little Admiral standing alone and looking very frail in his overcoat, at the far end of the prison yard.

"No, I don't think so," Schacht replied. "But it's not the torture that's tearing him apart. It's because Canaris has always been, at base, a great patriot. For him to die labeled as a traitor is a sin for which Germany should never be forgiven. In a strange sort of way, I feel more sorry for him than all the rest of us put together. You must be able to see it in his face—the necessity of his divided outlook has convulsed his whole inner nature and shattered his balance."

"You speak of him as if he were already dead, when it's been *he* who's kept us all alive with the promise of our liberation."

Schacht turned slowly to Schlabrendorff to set the record straight.

"And thanks to Canaris, there is still a very slim chance of it for us . . . but not for him. No matter what happens to us, Hitler has ordered that *he* die."

Schlalbrendorff was stunned. Given that Canaris could talk his way out of any situation, he'd just assumed that he would eventually wrangle his way out of this one. It seemed only fair, when for the last few dreadful, dire months they had all drawn strength from Canaris' fighting spirit and endless optimism. *Why,* Schlabrendorff wondered, had he bothered to fight so hard for a future in which he wasn't destined to play a part?

"But does Canaris know?" he asked, trying hard to keep the tremor out of his voice.

Schacht's answer was firm and simple.

"Yes."

* * *

It was 6.00am when Schlabrendorff, Schacht and Mueller woke with a start. The abrasive, metallic sound of the SS guards running their batons down the length of the prison cell bars had them sit up in their bunks to listen, in breath-stopping terror, for the number of their own cell to be called.

It had become an amusing ritual for the SS to operate their daily execution routine like a kind of macabre, life and death lottery. Each day they picked random numbers out of a hat, to nominate the unlucky group of men who were to be sent to their deaths.

"Seems like they've forgotten you this time," one of the guards said with a sardonic smile, as he wandered past Mueller's cell.

But Mueller wasn't listening. He was straining his ears instead, to hear the faint sound of Canaris' voice that was coming from further down the corridor. He couldn't exactly make out what he was saying, but guessed that it must have been an objection to the SS guards demand that he and Oster strip naked to walk to their execution.

It was the final humiliation for two brave men of distinction, that had Mueller lower his eyes as they were paraded past his cell.

Beyond caring, Canaris had stopped in front of it to say:

"If you survive Joe . . . please let my wife know that everything I did, I did for Germany."

No one ever found out exactly how Canaris and Oster died. All Mueller knew was that it took thirty minutes. Afterwards, he had seen the grey smoke of their funeral pyre through his little cell window, its murky, hot remnants spitting out little fragments of unburned skin into the air—the smell and sight of which should have made him sick, but instead made him proud. Proud, and very, very grateful that he had been given the privilege of this last physical contact with his friends.

Picking up his pencil, he sat down to enter the date of their execution in his diary:

Monday, April 9, 1945.[47]

He only had to turn the page to Tuesday, April 10 to make his final entry:

"The Russians have come . . . we have been liberated!"[48]

* * *

The only guide to a man is his conscience; the only shield to his memory is the sincerity of his actions. We are so often mocked by the failure of our hopes, and the upsetting of our calculations. But with this shield—however the Fates may play, we march always in the ranks of honour.

—*Sir Winston Churchill*

AUTHOR'S NOTE

This has been a work of fiction. I have made a point, however, of incorporating as many historical facts as possible about Admiral Wilhelm Canaris, Count Claus von Stauffenberg, and their fellow conspirators to add to the book's authenticity. Theirs was a story of exemplary courage for which they were condemned. Not only by the Third Reich, but by a post war court of law, whose findings ruled that the People's Court had acted and judged in perfect accordance with the law of its day. It was a judgment that effectively found the conspirators guilty of treason for a second time—the Court kept to the letter of the law, resulting in a gross miscarriage of justice. It is my hope that this book sets the record straight and goes a little way to show that these men were not criminals, but heroes of the first order. That what was construed as their failure, was in fact a great triumph of the human spirit and its sense of morality. Their supreme sacrifice left a legacy of truth, honour and unerring compassion for all mankind.

ACKNOWLEDGEMENTS

My thanks to Roger Manvell, Heinrich Fraenkel and Peter Hoffman, whose extensive research, fine writing and fascinating insights made this book possible.

BIBLIOGRAPHY AND HISTORICAL

POINTS OF INTEREST

MAIN REFERENCES:
Roger Manvell and Heinrich Fraenkel
"The Canaris Conspiracy"
Published by: David McKay Company, Inc., New York, 1969

Peter Hoffmann
Stauffenberg—A Family History 1905-1944"
Published by: Cambridge University Press, New York, 1995

NOTES

1   Himmler's lawyer, Carl Langbehn (the friend of Dr Johann Popitz—in 1933 made Prussian Minister of Finance) had been acting in Switzerland with Himmler's knowledge, making veiled inquiries concerning terms of peace. By grave mischance a message from an Allied source implicating Langbehn as an agent of Himmler sent to investigate the possibilities for a negotiated peace was intercepted by German monitors and decoded. Langbehn was arrested. The Himmler connection, however, remained a secret: Roger Manvell and Heinrich Fraenkel. (Source: *The Canaris Conspiracy*, p 171)

2   Heinrich Himmler began his career with a diploma in Agriculture and worked as a salesman for a Fertilizer Manufacturer.

3   The November 1, 1914 naval battle of Coronel off the coast of central Chile galvanized the British Admiralty into action once news of the complete destruction of Admiral Sir Christopher Cradock's Squadron by German Admiral von Spee had filtered through. Spee's German East-Asiatic commerce-raiding squadron of five vessels led by the armoured *Scharnhorst* and *Gneisenau* with three light cruisers had been operating in the Pacific. Cradock was unable to escape the superior firing force of Spee's squadron. Both the *Good Hope* (Cradock's flag ship) and the *Monmoth* were sunk with no survivors—Cradock went down with his ship. On news of the British defeat along with its humiliation, British Admiralty assembled a huge naval force under Admiral Sir Frederick Sturdee, dispatching them to destroy Spee's fleet which they did at the Battle of the Falkland Islands. (Source: *www. firstworldwar.com/Battles/The Battle of Coronel 1914*)

4   By 1914, the German Navy had the "U-19" class, which were impressive vessels with heavy armament, diesel power for surface running, electric power for underwater running and a range of 8,000 kilometers (5,000 miles). These U-boats were fully capable of conducting blue-water naval operations.

5   Freikorps—In German means "Free Corps". Originally applied to voluntary armies. After 1918 the term was used for the far-right paramilitary

organizations that sprang up around Germany as soldiers returned in defeat from World War I. It was one of the many Weimar paramilitary groups active during that time. Many German veterans felt profoundly disconnected from civilian life and joined a Freikorps in search of stability within a military structure. Others, angry at their sudden, apparently inexplicable defeat, joined up in an effort to put down Communist uprisings or exact some form of revenge. They received considerable support from Gustav Noske, the German Defence Minister, who used them to crush the Spartakist League with enormous violence, including the murders of Karl Liebknecht and Rosa Luxemburg on January 15, 1919. They were also used to put down the Bavarian Soviet Republic in 1919. Officially disbanded in 1920, although former members later backed the Kapp Putsch in March 1920. Some became leaders in the Nazi Party, including Ernst Roehm and Reinhard Heydrich. (Source: *Wikipedia*)

6 Heydrich did actually shoot at his own reflection; as cited by Roger Manvell and Heinrich Fraenkel in *The Canaris Conspiracy.*

7 Ernst Roehm was actually shot in prison after having refused to commit suicide.

8 Literally in German—*Lightning War*

9 The general German term *Anschluss* (literally connection, attachment) is part of the specific political incident *Anschluss Osterreichs*, referring to the inclusion of Austria in a "Greater Germany" in 1938. This is opposed to the earlier historic *Ausschluss*, meaning the exclusion of Austria from Germany at the creation of Imperial Germany in 1871.

10 Dohnanyi/Oster's files came to be known as the Zossen Files. Stored in a sub-level safe at Zossen Military Headquarters, thirty miles South of Berlin. Dohnanyi kept the key to the safe at Abwehr headquarters. For reasons of camouflage he kept this key tied to a folder which contained various strips of paper indicating harmless routine files, as well as various codes for secret official documents. Among these was a coded list of contents of the safe at Zossen. (Source: *The Canaris Conspiracy*, p 150)

11 Hitler's oath as cited in *www.historyplace.com*: World War II in Europe (Hitler becomes Fuhrer)

12 Small town, thirty miles south of Berlin. Abwehr offices were transferred there on April 19, 1943 as part of German Military Headquarters.

13 Dr. Josef Mueller's nickname was actually Joe, the Ox.

14 Contrary to popular belief, Pope Pius XII managed to secure the safety of more than 860,000 Jews during the course of WWII while maintaining an open policy of "keeping his silence".

15 Colonel Rohleder's correct Christian name not known. This was not his actual position with the Abwehr.

16 Founded by Lorenz Adlon in 1907, the *Hotel Adlon Kempinski Berlin* was the most beautiful and luxurious hotel in the world. Its gourmet restaurant was named after its founder.

17 Assassination of Reinhard Heydrich—May 27, 1942. Died in hospital one week later.

18 The Battle of Stalingrad: August 21, 1942 to February 2, 1943.

19 This is not the actual placement of this regulation in the Prussian Army Code.

20 Colonel Heinz Brandt, ironically, was the same man who both unknowingly carried the bomb onto Hitler's plane and also inadvertently kicked Stauffenberg's bomb aside in the later assassination attempt at Wolf's Lair (July 20, 1944). He wasn't killed in that initial explosion, but died several days later.

21 The Junkers Ju 52 served as a versatile workhorse the German Transport fleet. For a period, Adolf Hitler used the Ju 52 as his private transport. They delivered the attacking forces and their supplies during the German invasion of Norway, Denmark, France and the Low Countries in 1940. (Source: *www. wpafb.af.mil/museum/outdoor/od16.htm*)

22 It was actually Count Claus von Stauffenberg and not Goerdeler who approached Field Marshal Runstedt in regard to his participation in the coup d'etat.

23 After the assassination attempt of July 20, 1944, Hitler ordered that all records of Count Claus von Stauffenberg be destroyed. Very little documentation on his life survived. Two of his poems that Stefan George had kept close to him were left in tact. Both yellowed and with deep crease marks that suggest they were kept safe in George's pocket for many years.

24 Renamed the 6th Panzer Division after the Polish Campaign.

25 The Commissar Order (German: *Kommissarbefehl*) was an order given by Adolf Hitler on June 6, 1941, prior to Operation Barbarossa, that any captured Soviet political officer be immediately shot. Field Marshal von Manstein in his memoirs, while acknowledging that he gave his written assent to the order, states that he, along with some other field commanders, instructed the units under his command not to follow it, despite the prevailing opinion among the German officer corps that the commissars were a species of war criminal. On May 6 1942 Hitler cancelled the Commissar Order (Jacobsen, p. 184). The Commissar Order has been of interest for historians of the Holocaust, as many believe that the order was gradually interpreted more and more broadly and eventually provided justification for the extermination of all Jews. (Source: *Wikipedia*)

26 On June 23, 1941 German General Staff moved to new headquarters at Camp Fritz near Angerburn in East Prussia.

27 Valkyrie: From Norse Mythology, meaning maidens who served Odin as choosers of slain warriors who were taken to reside in Valhalla. In this case, it was the code name for the conspirators' Emergency Home Army Mobilisation Plans, which, in the advent of Hitler's death, enabled the Berlin police force to join the Guard Battalion and seize government buildings and communications centers. The *SS* and *Gestapo* would be subjugated, and a new government would be formed and a cease-fire would be negotiated with the western Allies. The revision on "Valkyrie" provided that military district commanders in Berlin could trigger "Valkyrie" measures for their districts independently if the need arose (Kaiser, diary 29 July 1943; Schwerin 319;

"Walkure" 31 Aug. 1943, BA-MA, WK XVII/91; as cited in *Stauffenberg—A Family History 1905-1944*, p187).

28 Stauffenberg's new permanent posting came into effect on November 1, 1943.

29 Lautlingen is a populated place in Baden-Württemberg, Germany. The Lautlingen Manor was just one of the Stauffenberg Estates—the home of Count Claus von Stauffenberg, his wife Nina and their four children.

30 Wolf's Lair (*Wolfsschanze*) was the codename used for Hitler's major Eastern Front military headquarters during World War II. The remains of the complex are located in Poland at the village of Gierloz near Rastenburg, although at the time of operation this area was part of the German province of East Prussia. It consisted of a group of bunkers and fortified buildings in a thickly wooded area, surrounded by several rings of barbed wire and defensive positions. The complex was served by a nearby airfield. It was built for the 1941 Wehrmacht offensive against the Soviet Union and was abandoned in 1944 as Soviet troops approached East Prussia. Hitler first arrived on the night of June 21, 1941 and departed for the last time on November 20, 1944. (Source: *Wikipedia*)

31 The 9th Regiment of the Potsdam-based 23rd Infantry Division had the peculiar distinction of suffering more officers executed by the Nazi regime than any other unit of the German Army. Twenty six of its officers were involved with the conspiracy to overthrow Hitler.

32 Erich Vermehren and his wife, the former Countess Elizabeth Plettenberg, were associates of Canaris stationed in Turkey. When they were called back to Berlin for questioning after Count Helmuth von Moltke's arrest, they defected to London instead. This led to Canaris being removed from his position as Head of the Abwehr and the Abwehr itself being dissolved as an organization.

33 Not included in this list are Brigadier Hans Guenther von Rost and his Special Missions Officer, Lieutenant Heinz-Guenther Albrecht, who played a major role in this procedure.

184 The area of *Obersalzberg* was appropriated by the Nazis for their senior leaders to enjoy in the 1920s. Hitler's mountain residence, the *Berghof*, was located here. Berchtesgaden and its environs were fitted to serve as an outpost of the German Imperial Chancellery, which sealed the area's fate as a strategic objective for Allied forces in World War II. A number of relics of the Nazi era can still be found in the area, although only few of them are still well preserved. There is the *Kehlsteinhaus* (Eagle's Nest), which was built as a present for Hitler's 50th birthday in 1939 and owes its continued existence only to lucky circumstances that saved it from demolition. The remnants of homes of former Nazi leaders such as Adolf Hitler, Hermann Göring, Albert Speer, and Martin Bormann were all demolished. (Source: *Wikipedia*)

35 Stauffenberg in fact spent this night of July 19, 1944 alone with his brother Berthold, who drove him to Rangsdorf airfield first thing in the morning. (Source: *Stauffenberg—A Family History 1905-1944*, p 263)

36 Home Army Command and General Army Office in Berlin.

[37] The five bodies were initially buried at *Matthaikirche Cemetery* in Schoneberg.

[38] This is not the exact date of his trial.

[39] This is not the exact date of his trial.

[40] Former Gestapo Headquarters and Prison in Berlin.

[41] Source: *Lettters and Papers from Prison*, by Dietrich Bonhoeffer. Bonhoeffer was actually executed on the same day—April 9, 1945—as Wilhelm Canaris, Hans Oster and Dr.Karl Sack (Judge Advocate General of German Army).

[42] Established 3 March 1938, the Flossenburg concentration camp in Germany was consistently in operation until liberated by American troops on 23 April 1945. On 20 April, 1945, 13,000 inmates were marched away. Those who could not keep up the march were killed by the wayside. About 2,000 were left in the camp when U.S. troops arrived.

[43] This is not the actual date of his trial.

[44] Himmler came to the realization that if the Nazi regime was to have any chance of survival, it would need to seek peace with Britain and the United States. Toward this end, he contacted Count Folke Bernadotte of Sweden at Lübeck, near the Danish border, and began negotiations to surrender in the West. Himmler hoped the British and Americans would fight their Soviet allies with the remains of the Wehrmacht. When Hitler discovered this, Himmler was declared a traitor and stripped of all his titles and ranks the day before Hitler committed suicide. At the time of Himmler's denunciation, he held the positions of Reich Leader-SS, Chief of the German Police, Reich Commissioner of German Nationhood, Reich Minister of the Interior, Supreme Commander of the *Volkssturm*, and Supreme Commander of the Home Army. (Source: *Wikipedia*). Classifed British intelligence documents realsed by London indicated Himmler sought to win asylum for himself and 200 leading Nazis in the final days of the War by offering cash and the freedom of 3,500 Jews held in concentration camps. According to the documents the concentration camp inmates were to be sent to Switzerland in two trainloads. (*Source: Wistrich, Robert S. Who's Who in Nazi Germany; Routledge 1997;* as cited by: *www.jewishvirtuallibrary.org/jsource/Holocaust/himmler.html*)

[45] The Oder (Odra) is a river in Central Europe. It begins in the Czech Republic and flows through western Poland, later forming the northern 187 km of the border between Poland and Germany, part of the Oder-Neisse line. The river ultimately flows into the Szczecin Lagoon north of Szczecin and then into three branches (Dziwna, Swina and Peene) that empty into the Baltic Sea. (*Source: Wikipedia*).

[46] To break down the alphabet into groups of five, the letter 'j' was omitted. (Source: *The Canaris Conspiracy*)

[47] On April 9, 1945 Admiral Wilhlem Canaris, Major-General Hans Oster, Dr. Karl Sack (Judge Advocate General of German Army) and Pastor Dietrich Bonhoeffer were executed at Flossenburg Concentration Camp.

[48] Flossenburg Concentration Camp was actually liberated on April 23, 1945.